ALSO BY MARK JOSEPH

To Kill the Potemkin

Mark Joseph

SIMON & SCHUSTER   NEW YORK   LONDON

TORONTO   SYDNEY   TOKYO   SINGAPORE

SIMON & SCHUSTER
Simon & Schuster Building
Rockefeller Center
1230 Avenue of the Americas
New York, New York 10020

Copyright © 1991 by Mark Joseph
All rights reserved
including the right of reproduction
in whole or in part in any form.
SIMON & SCHUSTER and colophon are registered trademarks
of Simon & Schuster Inc.

DESIGNED BY CAROLINE CUNNINGHAM

MAP BY RAFAEL PALACIOS

Manufactured in the United States of America

10 9 8 7 6 5 4 3 2 1

Library of Congress Cataloging-in-Publication Data
Joseph, Mark.
  Typhoon/Mark Joseph.
    p.   cm.
  I. Title.
PS3560.0776T95   1991
813'.54—dc20   91-31931
                                             CIP

ISBN: 0-671-70865-1

FOR JESSE, MY SON

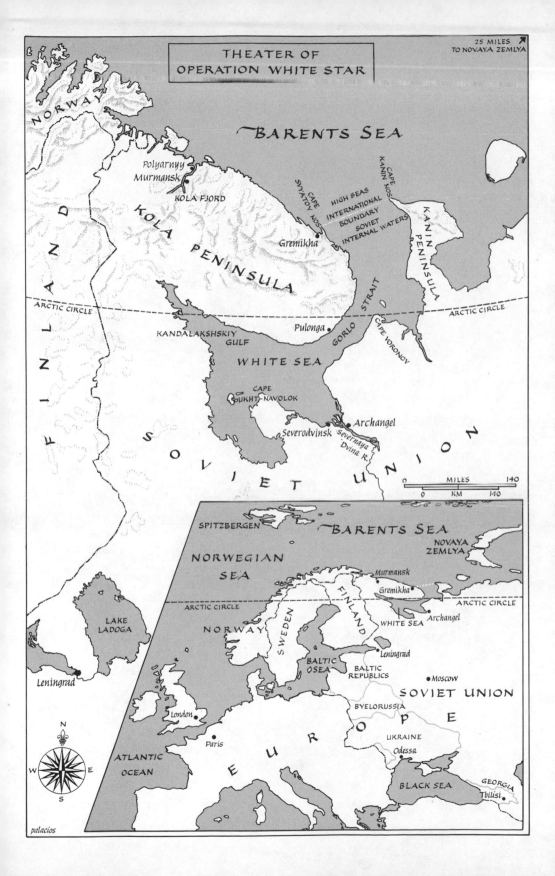

In order to hold their dominions more securely, princes often build fortresses which curb rebellion and provide safe refuge against sudden attack.

—*Niccolò Machiavelli*, The Prince

1

Zenko

A long breakwater sheltered the harbor at Naval Station Gremikha, protecting the Soviet Navy's arctic bastion from the winds and currents of the icy Barents Sea. In April, when sea ice begins to melt, the commander of the station, Vice-Admiral Stefan Zenko, liked to walk the length of the breakwater at night, alone with his thoughts. At the end of his walk he would find a skiff, which, as often as not, he rowed across the harbor.

Zenko was a short, squat, pot-bellied man with big ears and a mariner's compass tattooed on the back of his right hand. Pug-ugly, good-natured, a submariner whose soul was the sea, he enjoyed great affection from the men he commanded. Every night ten sailors volunteered for the honor of taking his boat to the end of the breakwater. Sometimes Zenko found a plump, ripe peach or small bottle of Georgian brandy tucked under the oars. A simple man without pretensions, he was always astonished but pleased by these small gifts.

On this night in late April, wearing black fatigues, floppy rubber boots and a warm fur cap, Zenko settled into the skiff for his nightly journey. Reaching for the oars, he found his own face staring from the cover of *Northern Lights*, the weekly newspaper of the Red Banner Northern Fleet. No doubt the paper had been placed in the boat by a proud sailor. Zenko held the paper at arm's length, turned it sideways and upside down, and wondered cheerfuly if his wife would recognize the picture.

To readers of *Northern Lights*, the commander of Strategic Rocket Submarine Flotilla Six had smooth skin, a stern, closed-mouth smile, a neatly tailored uniform, a tall peaked cap and no ears. When the real Stefan Zenko smiled, which was often, a grin spread across a pockmarked moon face revealing a mouth full of gold teeth. His uniforms never fit and he rarely wore his medals, especially the Hero of the Soviet Union's silver star, so prominently highlighted in the photograph.

Zenko sighed. Being a hero was a bore. The caption under the photo read, "The Man Who Conquered the Ice." Well, that much was true, Zenko thought, but it sounded like an epitaph. While most of his fellow officers had spent their careers preparing to fight the U.S. Navy, Zenko had made war on the ice, the frozen bars of Russia's naval prison. Throughout history Russia had faced many hostile maritime nations—Sweden, England, Germany, Poland, Japan, the United States—whose fleets marauded on the high seas while Russian sailors remained shorebound through long winters, chained to port by relentless ice. In summer, when the ice melted and ships could move from Archangel, Odessa, Leningrad and Vladivostok, the fleets were restricted by narrow, easily blockaded straits. For centuries one spectacular naval defeat after another had resulted in an agony of frustration and humiliation.

Zenko remembered the day forty-six years ago when, at age eight, he fell through the ice at Murmansk and survived, an exceedingly rare event. From that moment on, ice became his obsession. As he studied and learned, he became fascinated with sea ice, its complex nature and physical properties. Later, as a naval cadet, he wrote papers on the geopolitical and military significance of seasonal ice. Rejecting the fatalistic view that ice was an impossible obstacle, he believed arctic ice could be turned to Russia's advantage. In his final thesis he presented a design for a huge atomic-propelled submarine that could travel, hide and fight beneath the ice. Five hundred sixty feet long, eighty feet across the beam, the size of a World War II aircraft carrier, his sub had twin pressure hulls welded side by side surrounded by a third hull, an outer skin. The principal feature of the design was immense size, large enough to create sufficient buoyancy to burst through ten feet of solid pack ice and fire long-range ballistic rockets from the surface.

A visionary, stubborn and relentless as the ice itself, Zenko had badgered and cajoled the Admiralty for twenty years until the Ministry of Military Industry finally built his iceship, the largest, most powerful submarine ever constructed. He called his ship *Taifun*, the Russian, like the English *Typhoon*, derived from the Mandarin *Dai Fung*, the biggest wind. Like an atomic cyclone, *Taifun* transformed the Soviet Union into a great maritime power. Unlike previous generations of Soviet submarines, *Taifun* was extraordinarily quiet. On patrol, hiding in silence under the ice, she was undetectable by NATO sonars or satellites. With this ship, and the five more of her class that followed, the Soviet Navy achieved parity with the U.S. Navy as a first-line seaborne strategic atomic threat. Armed with terrible weapons, Zenko's Typhoons had seized the northern seas, transforming the Arctic Ocean into a Russian lake.

Now, at age fifty-four, he could claim without vanity or modesty to have achieved the impossible. He had indeed conquered the ice, and in the process struck terror in the hearts of Russia's enemies. For this service he had earned a Hero's star, and from time to time his picture appeared in *Northern Lights*.

Zenko lay the newspaper on the stern seat and began to row toward the cliffs of Gremikha. Rising majestically three hundred feet straight up, the steep granite bluffs had served generations of sailors as guideposts, marking the entrance to the White Sea. No more. With the establishment of Naval Station Gremikha, the harbor had been purged from charts and a notice to mariners posted throughout the world: Any vessel approaching within twelve miles of Gremikha would be seized or sunk.

He pulled hard on the oars. Facing the stern and the sea to the north, he checked the compass tattooed on his hand and laughed at his little superstition. A thousand feet beneath the sea, in a world without light, Zenko could look at his hand and never feel lost. Yet here, in the protected harbor of his home port, pushing against benign waters with a pair of comfortable old oars, he felt his bearings slipping away.

The things he loved most, the Soviet Union, the Navy, the

Typhoons, which all his life had been as firm and predictable as pack ice in December, had melted into a marginal ice zone laced with dangerous floes and bergy bits. Political and economic instability were tearing the country apart. Ethnic strife and republican separatism threatened to erupt into civil war. Like a riptide, the conflicting forces of union and secession pulled at the Navy itself.

Zenko's commanding officer, the commander of the Northern Fleet, Admiral Ivan Deminov, had circulated a letter of support for the Union and the Party among the fleet's senior officers. On the surface the letter was a declaration of patriotism, but Zenko perceived a more sinister purpose, a thinly disguised threat to those who would destroy the Soviet Union, and had refused to sign.

As a countermove, Deminov had imposed his authority by naming his son-in-law, Captain First Rank Vladimir Malakov, as commander of the sixth and last Typhoon, the newly commissioned *Sovyetskii Soyuz*. Zenko rankled but could do nothing. Malakov was eminently qualified and had the highest rating of any sub commander in the Northern Fleet save Zenko himself. Then, over Zenko's objections, Deminov had ordered Malakov, on his first patrol in *Sovyetskii Soyuz*, to execute a test shot of an SS-N-20 ballistic rocket. The orders were countersigned by no less an authority than Admiral of the Fleet V. J. Valotin, commander in chief of the Soviet Navy. In the spirit of glasnost, the Admiralty had suggested that film of the test shot be broadcast on the nightly news, American style. Zenko thought that was the stupidest thing he had ever heard, but, in spite of an admiral's stripe and Hero's star, he was only a flotilla commander and didn't make policy. He followed orders.

He rowed on. Patches of new ice speckled the harbor. In the dark arctic night the string of lights along the breakwater resembled a beacon pointing north. Farther out, a seascape of purplish foam and blinking buoys bespoke open water. In the warm spring the pack ice had retreated twenty miles off the coast and into the White Sea.

Zenko realized his tough, triple-hulled subs were products of the Cold War and had outlived their usefulness. The Typhoons were relics of history, derelicts that had foundered on the rocks of communism. He had vanquished the ice and freed his country from the shackles of geography, but the ultimate result of his life's work had been to place unfathomable power in the hands of men whose motives and ambitions he didn't trust.

The article in _Northern Lights_ celebrated the commissioning of _Sovyetskii Soyuz_, the last Typhoon. Like her predecessors, _Sovyetskii Soyuz_ was armed with torpedoes, mines, antiship rockets and twenty long-range ballistic rockets with multiple atomic warheads. A single Typhoon could devastate any nation on earth.

Five nations sent ballistic rocket submarines to sea—the Soviet Union, the United States, Britain, France and China—and every sortie by these vessels presented the possibility of atomic holocaust. With every passing day the threat of international conflict lessened, but as long as these weapons existed, they offered an almost irresistible temptation to anyone, or any faction, with a lust for power.

Lost in thought, Zenko continued to row and presently approached the base of the cliffs. He knew full well he was being observed, and as the skiff came within ten yards of the rocks, a breach opened in the wall. In eerie silence the cliffs parted. Moving on noiseless gas bearings, cleverly disguised doors slid back revealing an immense grotto hidden in the rock. Dynamite and drills had tunneled three thousand feet into the granite, creating a cavern a half-mile deep, five hundred feet wide and one hundred feet from high tide to the concrete ceiling.

Zenko rowed his tiny boat through the narrow opening and the sea gates closed behind him.

The sailors called it Zenko's Cave, and the dreamlike splendor of the cavern always took his breath away. All six Typhoons were in port, which seldom happened. Zenko was surrounded by his ships like a sea turtle swimming among a pod of whales.

Directly ahead, tugs were turning _Lenin_, which had returned from patrol the day before. The colossal sub was a wall of steel, an atomic leviathan. Sailors moved like ants over the decks. As _Lenin_ turned, he could see _Rodina_—the Motherland—resting like a beached sea monster on the floor of a dry dock. Welders crawled over the mottled grey hull repairing dents and bruises from innumerable clashes with pack ice. To his right, a giant crane rolled down quay number two, an SS-N-20 ballistic rocket slung between its spidery steel legs. At the near end of the quay, *First of May* was lashed to the pier, her rocket silos open as she underwent a minor refit. On the far side of the cavern the wall seemed entirely of plate glass. Behind the windows, cut into the rock, were offices, a half-dozen trade shops, a hardened bunker for atomic weapons storage and a secure communications center.

To his left another crane lifted a hull section from the starboard reactor compartment of *The Great Patriotic War.* Behind her lay *Taifun,* which Zenko still commanded. Astern of *Taifun* lay *Sovyetskii Soyuz*—the Soviet Union. A bright red pennant, symbol of a Soviet ship ready for sea, flew from the stern of the new ship. In a few hours Captain Malakov was going to sail into the White Sea and fire a test shot down the rocket range to a target in Siberia.

Zenko shook his head in dismay. The rocket booster would flare on video screens in a dozen NATO commands. In the West the vapor trail would appear as a sudden reminder of Soviet power. Or did Admiral Deminov and Admiral of the Fleet Valotin have some other purpose in mind? Zenko could only wonder at the folly of such an exercise.

Aboard *Sovyetskii Soyuz,* a hatch near the stern popped open and the ship's quartermaster, *Mishman* Vadim Sorokin, pulled himself onto the deck. He silently closed the hatch cover and stood erect, breathing the cool, still air and surveying the deck. Lashed to the pier under the bright lights of Zenko's Cave, the impossibly vast hulk of *Sovyetskii Soyuz* looked more like a factory ship than a man-of-war.

Twenty-eight years old, with high, wide cheekbones and tattoos from shoulders to knuckles, Sorokin lit a cheap Bulgarian cigar and took a few steps forward toward the stubby sail, feet soundless on the rubbery anechoic deck tiles. Forward, the rocket compartment the size of a block of Moscow flats dissolved into a mist. *Sovyetskii Soyuz* exuded raw power. Feeling the grip of her atomic magic, Sorokin sat down directly above the portside reactor compartment and changed into exotic Nike running shoes, red shorts and a white tank top emblazoned with the Soviet naval ensign.

Four circuits of the deck from stern to bow equaled one kilometer. Sorokin thought he would run three kliks, then go ashore and guzzle one last bottle of vodka before the ship sailed. He clamped the cigar between his teeth, pulled a tank commander's leather cap down tight over his ears and began to run. He pounded over the deck, ritually naming the compartments beneath his feet. Portside reactor compartment, aft trim tanks, around the sail on the cusp, forward trim tanks, enlisted mess, galley, command compartment, starboard rocket compartment, turn back toward the stern, portside rocket compartment, command compartment. At sea Sorokin ran inside the boat, round and round the bright yellow silos in the rocket compartments. In port he preferred to run on deck, even in the coldest weather. Around the sail again, aft over the trim tanks, reactor compartment, slope down now over the engineering compartment, splash through the cold water at the base of the rudder, which towered fifteen feet above the deck. Don't stop, don't slip.

Over the rocket compartments Sorokin silently counted cadence: New York, Washington, New London, Charleston, Norfolk, Omaha, Seattle, San Diego, Honolulu—twenty strategic targets, twenty firestorms, twenty times eight million dead. Who cared where they were? Every day Sorokin jogged through the floating rocket field and contemplated its ultimate purpose. A regular Shiva, making the world safe for communism. But weapons were not his province. His job was to keep the crew working smoothly, and he would do his duty even if the silos were filled with cement.

He noticed Zenko's boat drifting close by, stopped running and waved at the admiral thirty feet below.

"Evenin', Captain."

As commander of *Taifun*, Zenko always preferred to be addressed as captain, rather than admiral, which he found too honorific.

"Good evening to you, Vadim. Taking your nightly usual, I see."

"And you too, sir."

Mishmani, or warrant officers, formed the backbone of the

Soviet Navy. Ten years earlier Sorokin had come aboard *Taifun* as a conscripted sailor and never left. Captivated by Zenko's charisma, he had served on the core team that trained each crew in the flotilla. When *Sovyetskii Soyuz* was commissioned, Zenko had asked him to remain as quartermaster of the new ship. Sorokin didn't relish the idea, preferring to remain on *Taifun*, but orders were orders.

Sorokin pointed at the newspaper and said, "I noticed your picture, Captain."

"Did you put this in my boat, Vadim?"

"I'll confess."

"Then where the hell's my brandy?"

"Minski drank it."

They had a good laugh. Picking up the oars, Zenko prepared to resume rowing. "I suppose this is your way of saying you'd like to be reassigned to *Taifun*, eh?"

"Captain Malakov runs a tight ship," Sorokin said. "I can't make as much money as I'm used to."

Zenko chuckled. "Sorokin, you're the only man I know who thinks the Navy can make him rich."

"Yes, sir. I take that as a compliment, only I won't get rich if I can't run my betting pools in peace."

"I need you on *Sovyetskii Soyuz*, Vadim," Zenko said with sudden seriousness. "I need men I can trust on all the ships in the flotilla."

"I understand, Captain."

"I'm sure you do. Don't worry about the money. I'll take care of you."

"I appreciate that, sir."

"Keep your eyes and ears open during the rocket test, and I'll see you when the ship returns."

"Yes, sir. Good night, Captain."

Watching the skiff disappear behind the bow of *Sovyetskii Soyuz*, Sorokin decided to pack away his running clothes and find that last bottle of vodka.

2 *Sovyetskii Soyuz*

Early next morning Zenko stood in his office in the secure communications center inside the cavern, staring through a wall of plate glass at the ships tied to the quays. A pair of tugs stood off *Sovyetskii Soyuz*. High tide was in forty-five minutes, time for the sub to pass through the doors and out to sea. The weather was overcast, visibility five miles, a fine day to dive beneath the ice.

The office, like the man who occupied it, was simple and unadorned. A picture of his wife, Margarita, decorated a plain metal desk. Zenko's true home was the master's cabin aboard *Taifun*, but his ship, like the others in the flotilla, spent only two weeks at sea every three months.

Protected by three hundred feet of solid granite, the secure communications center housed the most advanced radios and cryptographic computers in the Soviet Union. From there Zenko had instant communication with his subs, the Admiralty, the Kremlin and Margarita in Leningrad. All communications with Typhoons originated in the soundproofed, air-conditioned rooms carved from the rock. Extremely low frequency (ELF) signals that could penetrate a thousand feet of seawater were transmitted by a huge antenna aboveground. Very low frequency (VLF) messages that could be received fifty feet under the surface were radioed over scrambled channels to airplanes for retransmission to ships at sea.

Radio signals could be duplicated by other transmitters in the Soviet Union, but the secret code work required for every phase of a strategic sub's operations could be done only at Gremikha. A staff of thirty cryptographers generated communication codes and, equally important, the codes needed for the handling of atomic weapons.

Zenko picked up the phone and called in the center's chief duty officer, Major Boris Riziov from GRU, Soviet Military Intelligence.

The blond, thirty-year-old intelligence officer knocked, entered and waited respectfully.

"Good morning, Boris. How's your family?"

"Just fine, sir, thank you."

"Is comrade computer ready to generate codes for *Sovyetskii Soyuz?*"

"Indeed he is, sir."

Accompanied by Riziov, Zenko passed through two security checks, showing his ID card like every staff member, and entered the cryptography room. He sat down, unlocked a computer terminal, keyed in his password and produced unique algorithms, which in turn conjured up a specific set of codes to be used by one ship for one patrol.

The computer automatically bused the communication codes to the radio room where another computer checked and verified the sequences. Then Zenko printed two sets of communication and weapons codes on special paper, returned to his office, still in the company of Major Riziov, and locked one set in his safe. He placed the second set in a briefcase, and, escorted by Major Riziov, hand-carried the printed sheets down onto the quay to *Sovyetskii Soyuz*. Armed naval infantrymen piped the admiral and Major Riziov aboard, and they clambered through a hatch directly into the sub's command center.

Compared to most Soviet Navy vessels, *Sovyetskii Soyuz* was a luxury liner. Deep red industrial carpeting covered the command center deck and bright fluorescent lighting illuminated the control consoles. Dominating the forward bulkhead, a sixty-inch Mitsubishi navigation monitor displayed an electronic chart of the Barents Sea and the Gremikha roadstead. A blinking red light marked the ship's position. Quartermaster Sorokin stood by the navigation table, ready to depart.

For better or worse, the Admiralty had decided machines were more reliable than men, and all six Typhoons incorporated advanced automation technology requiring the huge ships to carry a crew of only 150. While men monitored display screens, computers and robots did the real work, turning valves, adjusting steam flow from two reactors to propulsion systems and keeping the ship in trim.

Extreme redundancy had been built into the Typhoons, twin pressure hulls, twin reactors, and twin propellers, reflecting the parallel structures that existed thoughout the Soviet Union. The Party paralleled the government, the port reactor paralleled the starboard reactor, and, similarly, all Soviet warships had twin commanders. Captain First Rank Vladimir Malakov, a naval line officer, shared command of _Sovyetskii Soyuz_ with a _zampolit_, or political officer, Captain First Rank Alexi Sergov.

The two commanders awaited Zenko and Riziov in the captain's cabin. As Zenko entered, he felt for the first time a distinct lack of welcome aboard a ship in his flotilla, but he disguised his own antipathy toward Malakov and Sergov behind a cheerful smile. He bustled through the formalities, surrendering a set of codes to Malakov and procuring the required signatures.

"You know I object to this rocket test," Zenko said. "What purpose will it serve? I particularly object to Admiral Deminov's suggestion that film of the test shot be shown on television."

"I respectfully disagree," Malakov said in a stiff and formal manner. "The world needs to be reminded of the Soviet Navy's power."

Blessed with movie star good looks, blond hair turning silver, a strong chin and fiery blue eyes, Vladimir Malakov stood over six feet tall and looked every inch the imperious commander of a strategic rocket sub. He came from an illustrious family of Soviet submariners. In 1917 his grandfather, Andrei Malakov, in command of the Imperial Russian Navy's submarine _Beloye More_, joined the Revolution and torpedoed a czarist cruiser. A generation later, in 1945 during the Great Patriotic War, Malakov's father, Igor, died under the ice with his boat S-99 while trying to escape a German air attack in the Barents Sea. This gallant tradition and his marriage to Admiral Deminov's daughter qualified Malakov as a true Soviet aristocrat, proud and protective of his status and resentful of a man as common as Stefan Zenko.

The zampolit, Alexi Sergov, had sprung from an entirely different tradition. Political officers represented the Party and were the direct descendants of Leon Trotsky's Red cadres. Sergov was a terrorist at heart. A taciturn and humorless man, his existence could be summed up with a long list of hatreds. He despised Zenko for his refusal to sign the letter of support for the Union and the Party. He loathed foreigners and ethnics, and the words perestroika and glasnost sent him into apoplectic fits.

Sergov was not a man to hold his tongue. "It's a new era, Admiral," he said to Zenko. "The Soviet people want to see where their money goes, and we intend to give them a demonstration. They will see a Typhoon, a rocket, the trajectory and the warheads striking a target with pinpoint accuracy. This will only add to the Navy's glory."

Zenko dropped his friendly demeanor. "If that were true," he snapped, "I'd fire a rocket every day. If film of this test is broadcast, within five minutes the streets of Moscow will be filled with protesters."

Sergov shrugged. "There will be just as many celebrating our invincible Typhoons."

Zenko shook his head. "You have permission to depart, gentlemen," he said. "I'll expect a full report on the rocket test when you arrive at Archangel."

Zenko abruptly turned on his heel and left the ship, Riziov scurrying after him. He returned to his office and picked up a telephone.

"Get me my wife in Leningrad, please."

A moment later he heard Margarita's bright voice speaking from the Admiralty Hospital, where she worked as a surgeon.

"Stefan?"

"Hello, Comrade Wife."

Coquettishly, she said, "I saw a stranger's picture in the paper with your name on it."

Listen, can you catch the shuttle and come down here today?" he asked abruptly.

"Is anything wrong?" she asked, detecting a note of tension in his voice.

"No, of course not, but I surely would enjoy your company."

"I already have my seat reserved, Comrade Sailorman."

Zenko replaced the telephone in its cradle and turned to watch _Sovyetskii Soyuz_ through the glass wall of his office.

Soviet subs depart like streetcars. No bands play; no families line the pier to shout bon voyage. Inside the cavern cranes rolled back and forth. A company of sailors from _Lenin_ performed calisthenics on the quay without turning to watch. Only Zenko followed the huge sub as she steamed through the massive doors and out of Zenko's Cave.

In dramatic silence _Sovyetskii Soyuz_ emerged under the grey dome of an arctic sky. A thin crust of new ice covered the harbor, but the sub sliced effortlessly through the glaze and around the breakwater. Above the sail a radar antenna twirled on its shaft. Whitecaps and small ice floes flecked the surface of the sea, reminders of the receding ice cap twenty miles north and east. The early spring had caused an early melt, and along the Kola coast only the Gorlo Strait, the narrow channel that led from the Barents to the White Sea, remained frozen solid.

A wing of antisubmarine helicopters zoomed overhead, preceding _Sovyetskii Soyuz_ as she plunged through the waves. Ten miles out the helos dropped the first of dozens of sonobuoys, searching the waters for lurking subs, NATO spy ships stationed off the coast to observe ship movements from Gremikha. With no need for deception, the sonobuoys went active, loudly pinging the waters and listening for echoes.

Malakov ordered one-third speed and _Sovyetskii Soyuz_ rose and fell gently with the swell.

"Radio to bridge."

"Bridge here. Go ahead, radio."

"Helos report no submerged contacts."

"Very well. Prepare to submerge. Radio Officer, lower masts."

The radio and radar masts retracted into the sail. Malakov

sent the lookouts below, sealed the hatch and descended through the sail.

The navigation monitor displayed an electronic chart of the entrance to the Gorlo Strait. The blinking red cursor representing *Sovyetskii Soyuz* moved steadily east.

Malakov sat down in the commander's comfortable leather chair and adjusted the brightness of his video screens.

"Diving officer, report."

Diving Officer Nordov promptly replied, "All lights show green."

"Very well. Flood forward ballast tanks."

"Flood forward ballast tanks, aye."

"Three degrees down angle."

"Three degrees down, aye."

"Very well. All ahead standard."

"All ahead standard, aye."

Feeling the deck tilt forward, Malakov watched the depth meter as the Barents swallowed *Sovyetskii Soyuz*.

3

Sorokin

Cruising at a slow four knots with the top of her sail a mere ten feet below the surface, *Sovyetskii Soyuz* followed an icebreaker through the Gorlo Strait and passed the sonar station at Pulonga. The sonar operators watched the huge ship as a blip on their screens as she crossed a deactivated mine field designed to keep NATO subs from entering the White Sea.

In the command center, Malakov left the operation of the ship to his junior officers and mishmani. As quartermaster responsible for daily operations, Mishman Sorokin kept records and logs, set watches, organized training programs and ran the command division. When the officer of the deck gave an order, Sorokin had to see it was properly carried out. In essence, he drove the ship, but driving a Red Navy submarine these days was like negotiating a political mine field.

Sorokin could read the Navy's litany of woe on his arms. As a young sailor he had followed the Russian custom of inscribing in his skin the name of every port he visited. On his left forearm an Estonian artist had inked a map of the Baltic Sea and the ports of Klaipeda, Liepaja, and Tallinn. With the probable defection of the Baltic Republics, they would be lost forever. The once grand Baltic Fleet had been pushed back to Leningrad.

Sorokin's right shoulder reminded him of a cruise in *Rodina* to Vladivostok. The ship had laid up for a week in the roadstead outside the port while naval infantry quelled a mutinous riot by non-Russian sailors.

Rebellion was everywhere at once. Sorokin's left shoulder sported a memoir of a trip to Odessa on the Black Sea: the shapely lines of the battleship *Potemkin* in flames, symbol of the Red Navy's part in the October Revolution of 1917. Yet now the Black Sea Fleet was suffering rampant desertions, and the sorry sailors who remained with the fleet were wasting their lives chasing Islamic gun smugglers. Only the wholly Russian Northern Fleet remained intact, but hard-liners like Malakov and Sergov were pushing more and more sailors toward the republican cause.

Sorokin didn't care a damn about politics or what other men believed. To him only the man himself counted. Malakov was an arrogant asshole and Sergov a zealous pig. Only Zenko commanded the loyalty and respect of the veteran mishman. Like Zenko, Sorokin was puzzled by the rocket test, but he would keep his eyes and ears open as the admiral had asked him to do. Beyond that, he wanted only to do his job, run his pools and bring the ship and crew back safe and sound.

As the ship cleared the mine field, Political Officer Sergov ordered the crew to break into divisional assemblies. Sorokin mustered the command division in the ship's library, the Lenin Room, the name given to libraries aboard all Soviet naval vessels. A bronze bust of Vladimir Ilyich Lenin was bolted to the bulkhead and shiny, unread copies of his selected works lined railed shelves alongside technical volumes and well-thumbed works of Chekhov, Tolstoy and Dostoyevski.

Two mishmani, seven ratings qualified in submarines and two conscripts from the submarine school in Murmansk stood at attention under Sorokin's gaze. "Mishman Plesharski," he barked. "Who owns this ship?"

"You, Comrade Boss!" the assistant quartermaster replied.

"Seamen recruits Typov and Bulgakov, take one step forward."

The conscripts advanced one pace. In a written examination the two young sailors had placed highest among the ship's fifteen newly conscripted sailors.

Sorokin stood toe to toe with a tall, dark boy of nineteen and asked in a quiet voice, "Seaman Typov, what is the first duty of a Soviet submariner?"

"To defend our glorious Motherland," Typov answered smartly.

"Is that what they taught you in that hopeless excuse of a submarine school in Murmansk?"

A note of uncertainty crept into the sailor's voice as he said, "Yes, Mishman."

"Define salinity."

"Salinity is, um, salinity . . . the amount of salt in water."

"What is the mean salinity of the Barents Sea?"

"I, I haven't no idea, Mishman."

Sorokin rocked on his heels and said, "If you want to go play hide the sausage in Archangel, you will find the idea."

"Yes, Mishman."

Sorokin addressed the other young conscript, a blond, fair-skinned young man of twenty with an insolent smirk on his face. "Seaman Bulgakov, what is the first responsibility of a Soviet submariner?"

"To follow all orders instantly without question. To preserve the safety and integrity of the submarine."

"That's better. What is the velocity of sound through salt water?"

"The velocity of sound through salt water depends on relative temperature and salinity, but is approximately fifteen hundred meters per second."

"Excellent, most excellent, Seaman Bulgakov. I assign you to the quartermaster's department. You will report to me directly."

"Yes, Mishman."

"Recruit Typov, I assign you to the shit department until you can pass a basic physics test. You'll be the responsibility of Mishman Plesharski."

"Yes, Mishman."

"Step back in line."

Hands locked behind his back, Sorokin paced along the line of sailors. "All of you, understand me well. Some things cannot be repeated too often. We are at war with the most relentless enemy imaginable, the sea. Salt water shows no favorites and forgives no mistakes. Your mothers cannot help you here. Our glorious Motherland, as Seaman Typov so fondly puts it, cannot change the velocity of sound. Komsomol, the Party, the High Command of the Strategic Rocket Forces of the Soviet Union, or even comrade Lenin, don't run this ship. I do!

"My job is to anticipate the orders of Comrade Captain Malakov. Your job is to make sure those orders are carried out. In the command center we have one thought and one spirit. We are the soul of *Sovyetskii Soyuz*. We drive her under the ice, into the deepest sea, and we bring her back. Submariners are called Sons of Neptune. In the command center, helmsman, planesman, communications technician, all of us think like lords of the deep, for we control the most powerful undersea ship in the world, my ship, my personal *Sovyetskii Soyuz*. Except for Typov here, you know your duties. Perform them well, be on time when it's your turn to stand watch and don't hesitate to ask questions. You cannot learn unless you ask, and an error born of ignorance can kill us all in an instant. Any questions?"

"Yes, Mishman, I have a question," Seaman Typov resolutely replied.

"Go ahead, Typov."

"What is our political agenda?"

"Pardon me?"

"We're supposed to have assigned texts for discussion. We're supposed to raise our political consciousness to help build communism."

"Is that so?"

Snickers and rude noises echoed off the bust of Vladimir Ilyich. Sorokin silenced his minions with a stern glance.

"You come from a collective farm outside Minsk, is that not so, Comrade Typov?"

"That's correct, Mishman."

"You were the leader of the local Komsomol brigade, if I'm not mistaken."

"Correct again, Mishman."

"You volunteered for the submarine service. Now you want an assigned text so we can correctly use the analytical tools of Marxist-Leninist thought to solve our problems, build communism and help the Red Navy serve as the vanguard of the people and the Party. Is that it?"

"Yes, Mishman. That is precisely it."

"All right."

Sorokin rummaged through the bookshelves until he found what he wanted. He pulled the volume off the shelf and shoved it into Typov's chest. "Here's your assigned text," he snarled. "Please inform the division of its title."

Typov looked down at the book and then up at Sorokin. His voice climbed half an octave as he squealed, *"The Properties of Saturated Steam Under Pressure."*

"You'll be invited to lead our discussion at the next assembly, Typov," Sorokin said. "That's all. Dismissed. Bulgakov, a word with you, if you please."

Bulgakov stayed behind and spent a few minutes looking through the bookshelves while Sorokin sorted through some paperwork. Sorokin finally looked up from his stack of forms and asked, "What do they call you?"

"Petya."

"All right, Little Petya. You have a Leningrad accent."

"Yes, Mishman."

"You have an educated accent."

"You make that sound like a crime, Mishman."

Sorokin smiled. "It's no crime, simply unusual. On strategic rocket subs we get all kinds of conscripts, a lot of fools with Party connections, ignorant country folk with a few brains, people who think atomic war must be fun, but we don't get university students from Leningrad. That's what you are, isn't it?"

"I started university . . ." Bulgakov didn't finish his sentence.

"But?"

"It's in my records, Mishman."

"I want to hear it from you."

"The administration threw me out for black marketeering, and I was called up."

"Is that what it says in your records?"

"Yes."

"To hell with records. Tell me the truth."

The young sailor looked the mishman in the eye. "I refused to sell videotapes to one of the Komsomol leaders at a discount. She turned me in."

"What else?"

"I wouldn't make love to her."

"That's interesting. Why not?"

"Lovemaking should be erotic, not political, Mishman."

Sorokin laughed and patted Bulgakov on the shoulder. "You lost me there, boy, but you're a sailorman now. I don't care who you fuck and who you don't. I don't care what videotapes you sell or who you sell them to. What I care about is you doing your job and your job is to do what I tell you to do."

"Yes, Mishman."

"You're a sailorman. Say, 'Aye aye.' "

"Aye aye, Mishman."

"That's better. How'd you end up in subs?"

"I don't know. I asked for destroyers."

With a hint of sarcasm Sorokin asked, "So you could call at foreign ports and play the black market?"

"Oh, no, Mishman. I wanted to be stationed nearer to Leningrad."

"Are you going to be a pain in the ass?" Sorokin asked softly.

"No, Mishman. I'm just going to serve my time."

"Let me set you straight on some things you should know, Little Petya. In the rocket compartment, those boys sit with their big firecrackers from the day we leave Gremikha to the day we return. Same with sonar, torpedoes, engineering and the atomheads in the reactor compartment. On the other hand a quartermaster has the run of the ship. In my department we go everywhere. We look and listen, make nice to everyone and don't say much. We learn what everyone wants and needs."

Sorokin lit a cigar and puffed hard two or three times before he continued. "I'm going to be on this ship for the next fifteen years. When I'm through here, I'll retire to a basement flat in a whorehouse in Murmansk, The Gold Ruble, maybe. You're going to be here two and a half years, Little Petya. I can make your time interesting and profitable, or I can make it unspeakable hell."

"I understand, Mishman," Bulgakov said.

"Good. A glimmer of intelligence goes a long way in the quartermaster's department. As of this moment, you're the junior quartermaster in training of this vessel. Come with me. I'm going to teach you how to read a duty roster, so when the watch changes, you can collect watch sheets from each division and check them against the roster. Then, when people know who you are, you can run other errands for me, and make a little money for yourself."

"Money?"

"The squids on this ship bet on anything and everything," Sorokin said. "They bet how far the ship goes, when it goes, how long it will be under the ice. There's cards, dice, hell, some buys bet who has the fattest dick, but nobody makes a bet except through me. You understand?"

"Aye aye, Comrade Boss."

"And nobody buys or sells anything except through me."

"How much do you take?"

"That's none of your damned business, but I'm not going to leave the Navy a poor man with a shitty government pension. Let's get this straight. We have a nice thing going, but none of it works unless we play the Navy game first and play it right."

Sorokin led Bulgakov to the command center and began teaching him the basics of bookkeeping and bookmaking. Perhaps he could turn a few rubles on this cruise after all.

4 Malakov

Twenty-four hours after leaving Gremikha, *Sovyetskii Soyuz* hovered under six feet of ice in the White Sea. A vast inland bay, the forbidding White Sea takes its name from constant fog, snowbound shores, and from September to May, a surface composed entirely of ice. Legend holds the White Sea littoral to have been the homeland of the ancient Rus, Viking progenitors of all the Russians. Since 1922 the Soviet Union has claimed the White Sea as internal waters.

In summer the White Sea teems with fishermen and cruise ships sailing from fabled Archangel, Russia's oldest port. In September when the ice comes, pleasure craft are hauled ashore, fishermen move north into the warmer Barents Sea, and another flotilla steams under the opaque ice. In winter the White Sea becomes a protected refuge for Typhoons. Invisible from the air, undetectable by infrared sensors on satellites, unheard by any sonar, a fully armed Typhoon on a mission of strategic deterrence posed a deadly menace. Unlike land-based ballistic rockets in fixed locations, no enemy could find, let alone destroy the seaborne weapons carried on the huge subs from Gremikha.

On this brief voyage one of the SS-N-20 rockets on *Sovyetskii Soyuz* was fitted with telemetry systems and eight dummy warheads for the test shot. In the command center Captain Malakov stood near the periscope housing directing prelaunch procedures. To Malakov, commanding a Typhoon meant nothing if her weapons lay idle. He regretted the passing of the Cold War, which had brought him honor and prestige. But now he believed the *nomenklatura*, the ruling class of the Soviet Union, faced an even greater danger, not from abroad but from within its own borders. Like a virulent disease, anti-Soviet, anticommunist republicanism had infected the nation and threatened to bring down the political and military institutions that gave him his exalted status. Like a czarist prince, Malakov hated republican separatists who would deny him his birthright. His mind wandering for a moment, he imagined the damage his ship could inflict on the republican cause.

Whoosh, one rocket takes out the Baltics. Whoosh, a second rocket wipes out the incorrigible Trans-Caucasians, the Georgians, Azerbaijanis and Armenians. A third takes care of the damned Muslims in the southeast. Whoosh whoosh, bam bam, bye bye. Was he crazy or a loyal Soviet patriot? If Malakov had his way, another rocket would have Zenko's name on it. Whoosh. The mere thought of Zenko drove him to fury. The fat little man not only had a beautiful young wife, he wore a Hero's silver star, the trinket Malakov coveted more than anything in the world. If the republicans had their way and the Union ceased to exist, Malakov would have to barter for a medal in a flea market. Zenko, who commanded the most potent force in the Soviet Union, had proclaimed politics to have no place in his command. The son of a bitch had refused to sign Deminov's letter of loyalty and opposed the rocket test, claiming it would antagonize the West and stir up antimilitary sentiment. So what? Fear and intimidation could accomplish what talk could not. Politics, thought Malakov, is bullshit. Let the military run the country and there would be no politics. One party, one Union, one heart, like in the days of his father and grandfather.

The mishmani and sailors—bosses and squids in Russian sub-talk—aboard *Sovyetskii Soyuz* were neither republicans nor unionists, patriots nor rebels; they were boys and young men who lived for sex, rock and roll music, decent food and gambling, especially gambling. If the rocket test went well, the crew had been promised a week's liberty in Archangel, a splendid treat. Most of the conscripted sailors at Gremikha had never visited a liberty port. To reach Archangel the squids would murder the first of their brethren who erred.

Mishman Sorokin studied his chronometer and leaned toward the assistant navigator, Mishman Plesharski. "We're going to blow off this useless bird in less than ten minutes," he said in a whisper. "If we're on time, you win the pool, you lucky boy."

A short, thick bulldog of a man, Plesharski whispered back, "Fuck me, Vadim, if we launch on schedule, it'll be the first time in history."

"It's a thousand rubles, man. You can buy a lot of pussy in Archangel if you win."

"Ten to one it'll hit the target," Plesharski said with confidence.

"Make it twenty to one on five rubles."

"You're on, Comrade Boss."

Malakov interrupted this quiet exchange. "Sorokin," he ordered. "Prepare a bridge party."

"Aye, Captain."

Sorokin punched Plesharski in the ribs. "Get your boots on, sailorman," he said. "Hey, Little Petya, you know how to wear arctic gear?"

"Yes, Comrade Boss."

Well, thought Sorokin, at least you know my name.

"Then put it on."

Zampolit Sergov reported to his launch station in the portside rocket compartment 150 feet forward of the command center. To fire a rocket he and Malakov had to turn launch keys simultaneously to arm the warheads and release the launch computers.

Marching down the center of the cavernous, cylindrical two-hundred-foot-long compartment were ten bright yellow canisters festooned with wires, pipes, no smoking signs and arrays of instruments. Black, fire-resistant synthetic rubber lined the compartment, and hundreds of cables and pipes and two levels of catwalk ran the length from the bow to the rear bulkhead where the fully automated fire-control systems were located.

Rocket Officer Lieutenant First Rank Mikhail Minski sat at the launch control terminal. Twenty-three years old, born and raised in Archangel, Minski had chosen rocketry as his specialty because the division offered quick advancement. The psychological barriers were formidable for the man whose finger was on the ultimate button. It was not the president, nor the admiral of the fleet, nor even the captain of the ship who would launch an atomic weapon; it was a red-haired, blue-eyed, freckle-faced lieutenant from Archangel who missed his dog and was embarrassed by masturbation jokes in the junior officers' mess.

"Portside rocket division on station," Minski announced.

"Log in," Sergov commanded.

Each of four mishmani at control panels punched in his military ID number.

"Run diagnostics."

Each man checked his computer, determined that it functioned properly and sounded off in a loud, clear voice.

"Station one, ready."

"Station two, ready."

When all had declared themselves ready, Sergov clicked on his intercom headset and announced, "Portside rocket compartment to command. Ready for launch."

The men studied digital clocks on their computer screens. In the thousand-ruble launch pool everyone had opted for a delayed launch. As a man they shrugged. The launch would be on time. Some lucky bastard would win.

In the command center Malakov asked, "Sorokin, is your bridge party ready?"

"Yes, Captain."

"Sound the pipes. I'm going to address the crew."

Taped chimes sounded through the ship. Malakov drew himself up to his full height and spoke into a microphone. "Attention, men of *Sovyetskii Soyuz*, this is the captain speaking. As you all know, the ultimate defense of our nation rests with the Typhoons. Today we will demonstrate to all our enemies, wherever they may be, that the Union will survive any adversity. Our duty is clear. The test of a rocket is also a test of our will. All divisions, prepare to surface. That is all."

Aroused with almost erotic excitement, Malakov looked around the command center. In arctic gear Sorokin, Bulgakov and Plesharski stood near the commander's chair. The radio and radar officers leaned over their electronic countermeasures control terminals.

The chonometer ticked over.

Malakov ordered, "Bridge party, into the sail."

Sorokin, Bulgakov and Plesharski rushed up the ladder and prepared to open the hatch into the arctic night.

"Blow all ballast tanks. Emergency surface."

"Blow all ballast tanks," the diving officer repeated. "Emergency surface."

Diving Officer Nordov rapidly pushed a sequence of buttons on his board and high-pressure air expelled water from the ballast tanks. The ship's buoyancy suddenly doubled. A tremendous prolonged screech filled the command center as the huge sub strained against the ice. Malakov caught himself looking up as if expecting a jagged icicle to penetrate the double hull and pierce his heart. With a stomach-wrenching surge and thunderous crash the ice yielded. *Sovyetskii Soyuz* broke through and bobbed on the surface.

"Bridge party, open sail hatch," Malakov commanded.

"Hatch open," Sorokin reported. "Going up."

A draft of cold fresh air wafted into the command center. The trio of sailors climbed through the hatch and stood atop the sail. Scanning the horizon, they saw glaring ice surrounding the ship in all directions, the bleakest seascape on earth. Two hundred meters away a large camera on a tripod rested on the ice. A mile and a half west a large helicopter hovered.

With the temperature barely a degree above freezing, Sorokin thought his eyeballs would pop. He pressed his hands against his face, trying to shut out the cold.

"Command to bridge. Report," Malakov said into his microphone.

"Sail is clear," Sorokin replied calmly. "Launch tube number one covered with a large block of ice."

"Radar Officer. Raise radar mast," Malakov ordered.

"Mast going up now."

"Very well, report."

"I have one stationary target, a helicopter, range three kilometers, bearing two seven one, altitude five hundred meters."

"That's Admiral Deminov in the observation helo," Malakov said. "He's where he's supposed to be, a good sign."

"I have a second target, range fifty kilometers, bearing one seven eight, speed three hundred kilometers. He's circling."

"Very well," said Malakov. "The instrumentation plane is in position. Excellent. Radio Officer, raise telemetry mast."

"Telemetry mast going up now."

The radio officer punched buttons on his console and *Sovyetskii Soyuz* began to send radio and radar signals to the circling airplane.

"Weapons Officer, raise ice cannon."

"Raise ice cannon, aye."

Forward of the sail, just behind the rocket silos, a small hatch slid open and an electric motor lifted a small wide-muzzled gun.

Sorokin announced, "Bridge to command, ice cannon ready."

"Fire," said Malakov, and the weapons officer pushed a black button.

A low-velocity shell whistled out of the gun and shattered the block of ice that obstructed rocket silo number one.

The intercom crackled from the bridge party.

"Bridge to command, launch tube number one is clear."

"Very well. Weapons Officer, lower ice cannon."

"Ice cannon lowering."

"Rocket Officer, open launch tube number one."

"Opening tube number one, aye."

"Bridge party report."

"Bridge to command, hatch open and clear."

"Radio Officer, report."

"Radio reports contact with instrumentation plane. Telemetry systems on line."

"Captain Sergov, prepare to arm rocket."

In the portside rocket compartment, the political officer inserted a red key into a launch control console. "Prepared to arm," he said into the intercom.

Malakov inserted his key and said, "Very well. Arm rocket."

Both men turned their keys.

"Rocket armed in aft control," Malakov said.

"Very well," Sergov announced. "Rocket armed in forward control."

"Command to bridge party, come below. Seal the hatch."

On the bridge Sorokin said, "That's it. Let's go down."

Plesharski dropped through the hatch. Bulgakov took one more look around. "I want a souvenir," he declared.

"You what?"

Before Sorokin could grab him, the young sailor scrambled over the sill of the bridge and prepared to jump ten feet to the deck. Sorokin lunged, grabbed Bulgakov's jacket and pulled him back. "There's no ladder!" he shouted.

"Oh, man," said Bulgakov. "A chunk of ice from here must be worth something."

"You idiot," Sorokin said with a grin. "Go below."

A moment later the three shivering men came down the ladder into the command center.

"Rocket Officer, unlock launch key."

Minski fumbled a moment as he read the numbers off the file card and punched in the computer code that released the launch button. A panel on his console slid back revealing a small blue button.

"Launch key unlocked."

Malakov drew in his breath and calmly ordered, "Rocket Officer, launch rocket."

Minski pushed the blue button. The ship shuddered once as high-pressure gas pushed the rocket from the tube.

"Rocket away!"

The rocket's solid-fuel booster motor instantly flamed to life and a terrifying thunder rattled through the entire ship. In the rocket compartments all eyes were straight up. More than one sea-launched rocket had exploded and crashed back into its ship. Some men prayed. Others sweated and tried not to spew their breakfast onto the computer consoles.

In the command center a monitor showed the forward deck of *Sovyetskii Soyuz* glowing golden as the stubby, bullet-shaped flying bomb roared into the sky. Within ten seconds the rocket had penetrated the cloud cover and disappeared south down the rocket range.

Malakov felt a tremendous, climactic release. All the exhortations, ideology and patriotism came down to correctly soldered wires and hatch seals that held. For a successful launch a million details had to go right simultaneously. The crew let out a shattering war whoop. Starting in the command center, cheers reverberated fore and aft as the entire crew howled in celebration.

Sorokin kept his eyes on Malakov and saw a wave of bliss pass over the captain's face. Malakov looked like a man who had just seen paradise.

At the navigation table Plesharski grinned like a lunatic. Sorokin slapped him on the back and kissed his cheeks. Seeing his men react with such exuberance, Malakov felt he would burst with pride, unaware that the crew didn't care about the successful launch. They were going to Archangel.

Archangel! Women! Vodka! Life! A week ashore. No Navy, no stripers, no Typhoons.

5   Deminov

From his helicopter, Admiral Ivan Deminov found the rising
Sovyetskii Soyuz and rocket launch a profoundly satisfying spec-
tacle. A camera crew in the rear of the helicopter had filmed the
launch, and the chief photographer was signaling thumbs up.

The exercise had been Deminov's idea. The commander of
the Northern Fleet hoped to turn glasnost upside down. If the
people wanted "openness," they should have it. Submarines are
intrinsically secret, and Soviet submarines so profoundly ringed
by security that most citizens had never seen even a photograph
of one. Deminov had persuaded his friends on the Defense
Council to change that perception. After all, he had argued, the
Americans watched every test shot from satellites, and the Typhoons certainly impressed and frightened them. "Let the people see where their rubles go," he had declared. "Let them take
pride in the power of their country."

Strapped into the seat next to Deminov, the chief of Northern
Fleet security, Colonel Anatoly Ludinov, pulled cotton balls
from his ears, wrinkled his nose at the acrid odor of rocket
exhaust and replaced his headset to listen to telemetry reports.
"We have a true trajectory," he said to Deminov. "Rocket on
course. Warheads separating now."

Expecting nothing less, Deminov nodded his approval. If the
rocket failed, the stocky, thug-faced GRU officer would happily
go aboard the sub and shoot the rocket officer.

"Impact on target in thirty seconds," Ludinov said. "Ground cameras in place."

A thousand miles south batteries of Navy cameras aimed lenses toward the sky. At three thousand miles per hour, eight streaking warheads produced stunning tracerlike images on infrared film as they slammed into the frozen Siberian permafrost, digging craters thirty feet deep.

"Impact!" Ludinov reported.

A smile flickered across Deminov's face. "Order the camera crews in Siberia to seal the film cases and fly them to Leningrad without delay."

Ludinov relayed the order over the radio and Deminov directed the pilot to land on the ice. The photographer jumped to the frozen surface and ran to retrieve the remote camera that had filmed the launch from the ice.

"I'll be five minutes," Deminov said. "Inform Leningrad that I'll arrive in Murmansk in two hours."

"Aye aye."

Alone, Deminov descended from the helicopter and walked toward *Sovyetskii Soyuz*. He was a robust officer of sixty with bristling grey eyes and hair the color of fresh snow, but his healthy appearance concealed a ravaged inner man. His world was crumbling. The Soviet Union, the mightiest power the world had ever seen, was suffering the agony of self-destruction. Yesterday, Moscow's rule had stretched from the Elbe to the Pacific, from the Arctic Ocean to the Black Sea. Today, the Union was breaking into warring tribes.

A former strategic sub commander, Deminov had spent his life defending the Union. A passionate ideologue, he believed in the Communist party as the glue that had held the Union together since the Revolution, but the Party had lost its way. He believed in the Navy, which had protected the nation from overseas attack since the end of the Great Patriotic War, but with the Cold War winding down the Navy had lost its mission. All that remained intact was his belief in History, to Deminov a tangible, mystic force that few understood and even fewer had the courage to control. The idiots in Moscow had lost control.

From his headquarters in Polyarnyy, Deminov had watched the horror unfold in the Kremlin. Gorbachev and his damnable poison arrows of perestroika and glasnost had opened the flood-gates of discontent. Anarchy and chaos were rampant in the land. With each day's news of riots, strikes, demonstrations and open rebellion, Deminov descended deeper into despair, anger and ultimately, a fierce and determined hatred for the enemies of the Union.

Many senior officers shared his distress. After months of lobbying, he had persuaded the commander in chief of the Navy, Admiral of the Fleet V. J. Valotin, that the ultimate existence of the Soviet Union was at stake. Only the military could restore order among the republics. The rocket test was the first step in a larger plan that had taken shape in Deminov's mind. A public demonstration of invincible force by the Northern Fleet could restore the military to its position as vanguard of the nation. When the Soviet public witnessed the massive shape of a Typhoon smash through the ice and hurl atomic death a thousand miles, every anti-Soviet republican, ethnic separatist, anarchist, Pamyat nationalist, Jew, Christian and Muslim in the USSR would be served notice that no one anywhere in the Union was invulnerable to attack from the depths of the sea. If there were riots and protests, the dissenting elements of the population could be drawn into the open and smashed.

As Deminov neared the sub, Malakov climbed down a rope ladder to the ice, walked out a few yards and saluted his father-in-law. Then the two men hugged and kissed and slapped each other on the back. Deminov noticed the glaze in his son-in-law's eyes, the bittersweet look of a man who had expended his lust in an expensive whorehouse and had come away feeling spent but less than satisfied.

"Congratulations, Vladimir. The shot was perfect."

"We had a little trouble with the prelaunch procedures, but everything seems to have gone all right."

"I envy you," Deminov said. "I miss my days at sea."

"I hope your cameras were working," Malakov replied.

"Also to perfection. The film will be broadcast to the nation and the world before you arrive in Archangel. I'm afraid you'll miss it."

"Zenko was very angry about this," Malakov said.

"Yes, but his star is falling. Unfortunately, he thinks the Typhoons are his personal property. The Navy thinks otherwise. Don't concern yourself with the little admiral from Gremikha. He has a big reputation, a larger-than-life mystique, but he's no hero to the Admiralty, I assure you."

Deminov stomped his feet, rubbed his gloved hands together and gazed with satisfaction at _Sovyetskii Soyuz_.

"How soon will you arrive in Archangel?" he asked.

"I reckon sixteen hours. I'm giving my crew liberty."

"Very well," said Deminov, "but keep your officers and mish-mani on board, and keep steam up."

Surprised, Malakov asked, "Why?"

"Just follow orders, Vladimir, and be quiet about it. Tomorrow night you and I will share a few toasts at the officers' club in Archangel. We'll have plenty to talk about."

"Aye aye, Comrade Admiral."

"And congratulations again, Vladimir. Well done."

Deminov trudged back to his helicopter. Ludinov helped him aboard and the helo lifted off the ice with a noisy roar. Malakov watched it disappear into the clouds, climbed the rope ladder to the deck over the rocket compartments, pulled the ladder after him and slipped through a hatch. A few minutes later _Sovyetskii Soyuz_ disappeared once again under the ice.

Deminov flew to Murmansk. On the tarmac at Polyarnyy Naval Air Station he stepped from his helicopter into an executive jet that carried the discreet markings of the commander in chief of the Soviet Navy.

Admiral of the Fleet V. J. Valotin was partial to meetings aboard his private plane. Tipping a friendly scale at 310 pounds, he didn't like to squeeze his considerable bulk into automobiles or elevators more often than necessary, and he enjoyed his creature comforts. Before Deminov arrived, he locked his mistress in his stateroom, dispatched his officers to the lounge and arranged vodka and liqueurs in the comfortable office in the forward cabin.

A consummate politician, Valotin had decided early in his career to fight his battles in the Admiralty in Leningrad rather than on the high seas. Although he had achieved the highest rank in the Navy, he remained a shadowy figure, preferring to let others like Zenko stand in the limelight, and still others like Deminov and Malakov wield the daggers he kept carefully concealed. Valotin believed in nothing save power and position. Cynical, decadent and eccentric, he lived for intrigues and conspiracies like an old-fashioned oriental despot.

An orderly announced Admiral Deminov and disappeared.

"Aperitif, Ivan?"

"Vodka, Admiral. Thank you."

"You have the film, I presume."

"Yes, of course. The film from Siberia should be arriving at the Admiralty right about now."

"Excellent, excellent. I'm amused by the irony of using one of Zenko's ships for this venture. He's a most unlikely agent provocateur."

"And a most unwilling one," Deminov replied. "I can relieve him from his command, Admiral."

"That may be necessary if we're to proceed to the next step," Valotin said. "Send him to sea in *Taifun* with a pair of attack subs from Squadron Seven as escorts. Brief the commanders. If Zenko leaves his assigned sector, sink him. He will die a hero."

Squadron Seven, the Grey Ghosts of Murmansk, another of Deminov's inspirations, was a unit of four fast Akula class attack submarines officered and manned exclusively by politically correct sailors, staunch Party members devoted to Deminov and his pro-Union faction. Before joining the Typhoon flotilla at Gremikha, Malakov had commanded one of the Grey Ghosts, *Minsk*.

"I take it all arrangements have been made in Moscow."

Valotin smiled. "In Moscow, Leningrad, Kiev, Minsk, Odessa, Archangel, Murmansk. You'll be amazed at how many loyal Soviet citizens suddenly discover they absolutely must go into the streets to protest this wanton display of force. You do your part and look after Zenko's flotilla."

"And the Americans?" Deminov asked. "Have any of their damned Los Angeles class subs been reported in the Barents?"

Valotin shook his head. "No. In anticipation of our operation, we've pulled dozens of ships off regular patrols. We're in a stand-down mode and so are they. After all," Valotin chuckled, his jowls quivering, "the Cold War is over. The main enemy is no longer the U.S. Navy."

That evening a sixty-second film clip appeared on *Vremya*, the nine o'clock news. By ten the first protesters appeared in the streets of Moscow, banners aloft denouncing the Navy. At midnight twenty thousand Soviet citizens had assembled in Red Square, their numbers swelling by the minute. Demonstrations erupted in the capitals of every republic and at dawn, convinced by Admiral Valotin that protests would spread nationwide and could lead to civil war, the Defense Council secretly authorized Admiral Deminov to initiate Operation White Star, the Northern Fleet's contingency plan to counter armed rebellion.

When the Defense Council's session ended, Valotin phoned Deminov at his headquarters in Polyarnyy to give him the order. "Do you have a bottle of vodka handy, Ivan?"

"Of course, Admiral."

"Then fill a glass."

"Aye aye. It's done."

"To Operation White Star," Valotin said.

"To White Star," Deminov echoed and emptied his glass. When the brief conversation ended, he stepped to the window and looked down on the Kola Fjord. Below him the might of the Northern Fleet spread as far as he could see. Hundreds of ships lined the docks: destroyers, cruisers, frigates, aircraft carriers and attack submarines. And soon the Typhoons at Gremikha would be under his direct command. History! It was his for the taking.

6 USS *Reno*

A monstrous storm raced south from the Arctic Ocean and drove deep into the Norwegian Sea. Gusts of ninety-mile-per-hour wind smashed the frozen sea, fracturing the ice and causing giant floes to rise and fall like frothy mountains. Under the ravaged ice, each oscillation agitated a water column three thousand feet deep, stirring the upper isotherms and exciting the fishes.

Fifty miles south of the island of Spitzbergen, the USS *Reno*, SSN 777, quietly patrolled an assigned five-thousand-square-mile sector of ocean, listening for any Soviet submarine venturesome enough to steam south into the Atlantic. Inside, 110 men had surrendered their souls to the boredom of arctic patrol and the high-tensile steel of the pressure hull.

Following a northerly course at twelve knots, *Reno* was so rock steady only two sonarmen and the captain were aware of turbulence overhead. Four hundred feet beneath the surface pressure muted the violence of the cyclone. At four hundred feet there was neither weather nor time. No light penetrated the primal depths where blind predators hunted by sound, guided through the blackness by echoes and the smell of blood. Two miles ahead lay the edge of the European continental shelf and the Barents Sea, home waters of the Soviet Navy's Red Banner Northern Fleet, where *Reno* would spend the next seventy days under the ice spying on Soviet subs.

In the control room *Reno*'s captain, "Plutonium Jack" Gunner, stole surreptitious glances at the navigation monitor, feigning indifference to the boat's location. He lit a Lucky Strike and glanced at his watch. In a few minutes the crew was going to hold a traditional "bluenose" ceremony in the mess, a heady rite of passage for arctic sailors. The captain was expected to pretend ignorance of the pending ritual, and Gunner was delighted to play his part.

Thirty-nine years old, an inch shy of six feet, with black hair and sparkling black eyes set in a long, narrow face, Gunner radiated the confidence of a man who knew his place in the world. He had the best job in the Navy and suffered from neither ambition nor moral uncertainty. As with most commanding officers in the Submarine Service, *Reno* was his first and last command, and he had relished every minute of his three years aboard. On his sixth and final patrol he felt his identity had meshed with the boat almost as if the anechoic tiles that covered her hull were his own skin, her sonars his ears, her missiles and torpedoes the rocks he had hurled at childhood enemies.

With decks hardened by extra plating and torpedoes calibrated for shallow water running in the littoral seas of the Arctic Ocean, *Reno* had been designed and built specifically to fight under pack ice. Bow-mounted forward diving planes enabled her reinforced sail to crack unobstructed through an ice canopy. Built as a weapon of the Cold War, *Reno*'s sixteen Tomahawk cruise missiles, six Harpoon antiship missiles and twenty-four torpedoes, some with nuclear warheads, could decimate the Soviet Navy's Northern Fleet.

Command of *Reno* was the apex of Gunner's career. All he had ever wanted from life was to skipper a nuclear sub. At the end of this patrol the Navy planned to promote him to squadron commander, but Gunner had no interest in commanding a squadron or even a fleet. Instead, he intended to resign his commission, retire to Hawaii and learn to speak with dolphins.

Gunner had been born and raised in Vallejo, California, home of Mare Island Naval Shipyard. Son of a Navy welder who spent thirty years cutting steel for nuclear submarines, he had grown up immersed in the mystique and tradition of nuclear subs and their role in combating communism. In the fifties and sixties the Cold War had been an omnipresent fact of life, and Gunner had been taught to hate and fear the Russians. As a young man attending the Naval Academy and then passing through the ranks of the Submarine Service, his ardor for submersible ships never lessened, but his desire to fight the Russians had waned. The war that was no war had mined deeply in Gunner's soul. The captain loved his ship and crew, but command of *Reno*'s awesome firepower provided no solace. If he ever had to fight his ship, humanity would have failed as custodian of the planet.

Now, in the nineties, the polarities of the Cold War had been altered by upheavals in central Europe, war in the Persian Gulf and instability in the Soviet Union. Pundits and wishful thinkers believed the Cold War had ended, but Gunner knew it surely wasn't over under the sea. Twenty-four hours a day, 365 days a year, Soviet Typhoons and American Tridents prowled the oceans, weapons of mass destruction poised for delivery. To counter the threat of sea-launched strategic missiles, both navies maintained fleets of fast attack subs like *Reno*, hunter-killers that sought out the huge missile-bearing "boomers" in their lairs. In the far north, under arctic ice, the deadly game of hide and seek continued unabated. In secret, far from prying television cameras, the Cold War had been carried to its coldest venue.

Gunner had no qualms about *Reno*'s mission of spying on Soviet submarine maneuvers in the Barents Sea. Ethnic and ideological struggles within the Soviet Union had created a volatile situation in a nation with thirty thousand nuclear warheads. At any moment the Soviet Union could fracture into fifteen separate republics, and the result could be civil war with nuclear weapons. If the Northern Fleet became involved in an internal conflict, *Reno* could move swiftly and silently into Soviet waters to counter any threat projected beyond Soviet borders.

At the moment, however, Gunner's mind had strayed from the Russians. Four hundred miles from the Soviet naval bases on the Kola Peninsula, the captain believed conditions warranted a party.

The control room tingled with anticipation. Illuminated by

bright fluorescent lights, the jumble of men, instruments and sensor screens hardly resembled a room. Kitchen linoleum lined the floor, cables and pipes obscured the ceiling, and banks of monitors were stacked against the bulkheads. In the center, behind the conning station, a double periscope housing hung upside-down. To Gunner's right, looking more like an aircraft pilot than a ship handler, the helmsman gripped a joystick. Next to him, the planesman held fast to his controls, and both glanced every two seconds at the navigation monitor. In a semi-circle around the conning station petty officers manned the combat information center, diving panel, internal communications console and navigation table.

"Sonar to control. The bottom is rising. Range one thousand yards to the continental shelf."

"Very well, sonar," Gunner replied. "Activate ice scanners."

In the blue-lit sonar room near the bow, Chief Sonarman Mike Morrison relayed the order to the operator. High-frequency low-power sound, beamed from transducers mounted on the upper surfaces of the boat, painted a computer-enhanced picture of the ice. Gunner watched the bottom of the ice field unfold on the sonar repeater, a video display that duplicated the screens in the sonar room. The ice appeared as a chaotic array of blips as the storm savaged the pack and broke off massive floes.

To Gunner, ice formed an unnatural umbrella over the top of the world. When hell freezes over, he thought, it'll look like this.

"Sonar to control. Depth nine hundred feet."

In near-perfect silence *Reno* slipped into the Barents Sea. On the sonar repeater the visual display of the storm's turbulence appeared as sharp peaks and valleys representing movements of the shifting ice canopy. No bells rang, no ice crystals appeared on the bulkheads, nothing changed. A supremely arrogant, self-contained military vessel, a submarine was indifferent to her surroundings. Only Gunner felt the subtle difference; *Reno* had entered the Russian zone.

He noticed red-haired Lieutenant Miles Sharpe standing in the passageway, stifling a yawn. Was he sleepy or merely bored? Gunner thought the latter. Sharpe had volunteered to stand watch and forgo the bluenose ceremony. Gunner knew his young combat officer still smarted over having missed the war in the Persian Gulf. *Reno* had been cruising the Norwegian Sea while Sharpe's Academy classmates were flying sorties, launching Tomahawks at Baghdad and earning promotions. Before *Reno* left Norfolk on patrol, Sharpe had applied for a transfer to the surface Navy and resented Gunner for recommending a denial.

Gunner caught Sharpe's eye and motioned him to approach. "I'll tell you a secret, Miles," he said, leaning close to the lieutenant.

"What's that, sir?"

"I hate fucking ice. It's cold and Typhoons hide in it."

"Well, Skipper, I guess that's why we're here. This is the happy hunting ground." Then he asked formally, "Are you ready to be relieved?"

"I am," Gunner answered, stepping down from the conning station. Sharpe seated himself in the comfortable black leather chair. "I relieve you of the conn, sir."

"You have the conn, Lieutenant. Drive carefully." Then Gunner added, "I hear there's a poker game in the wardroom."

"That's correct, sir. Watch out for Lieutenant O'Connell. He's on a hot streak."

With a quick look around the control room, Gunner headed for officers' country.

As *Reno*'s executive officer, Lieutenant Commander Augustus Trout was saddled with endless paperwork. Once, when *Reno* had rested on the bottom of the Sea of Japan outside Vladivostok, he had calculated that eight of his sixteen years in uniform had been spent filling out forms, reading forms filled out by others and requesting new forms. With pleasure he anticipated the revenge he would wreak when he earned an admiral's star. He would design new forms to torment junior officers.

His tiny desk had disappeared under stacks of watch billets, supply orders, maintenance and alteration lists—all the documents required by the Navy to prove a ship was at sea. Trout stood and stretched, his bulky frame filling the closet he called home. Grabbing the phone, he punched a button labeled "Maneuvering, Chief of the Watch."

A crisp, resonant voice answered, "Engineering, Adams."

"Willie," Trout said, "I don't have documentation for the new silver brazing on the secondary condenser piping."

"We're working on it, Mr. Trout. You'll have it by the end of the watch."

"All right."

Trout hung up the phone and stared thoughtfully at his image in the small mirror behind his desk. As always, his round face reminded him of a chocolate cake. The Navy had been good to Gus Trout. Pinching a fat brown cheek, he thought, maybe too good. What the hell, his wife had left him, but the Navy had never let him down. The Navy was Trout's country and he played the Navy game to perfection. Equally comfortable at sea or maneuvering through the Pentagon, he wanted an admiral's flag and had no doubt he would have it.

Hearing a soft rap on the door, he opened to find Gunner in the passageway, cigarette dangling from the corner of his mouth. In contrast to Trout, Gunner's disdain for Navy politics was notorious. The captain was a pure sailor with no use for bureaucracy, promotions or the niceties of refined behavior. A pirate at heart, sly and self-contained, Gunner had the mix of caution, audacity and resourcefulness required of an attack boat commander, but he was no politician. Trout believed his captain worked harder at his job than any man he had ever known. If he had a flaw, it was driving his crew so hard that more requests for transfer came from *Reno* than the rest of the squadron put together.

"Almost time for the party," Gunner announced. "Let's go."

Reno's tiny wardroom served as the officers' dining room, conference chamber, card room and lounge. The commanding officer established the tone of his wardroom, and Gunner had defined his priorities by posting a portrait of the great English admiral Sir Francis Drake, the queen's own brigand. When Gunner and Trout entered, the boisterous card game quieted for a moment.

"Good afternoon, Skipper, Mr. Trout," said Lieutenant (j.g.) Eddy O'Connell, shuffling a deck. A huge pile of chips had accumulated before the young lieutenant, the only officer not yet qualified in submarines. O'Connell was trying unsuccessfully to hide his excitement about his first bluenose ceremony.

"What's the game, gentlemen?" Gunner asked as he and Trout took seats.

"Five-card draw, jacks or better."

Hands trembling, O'Connell dealt a hand of draw. A heavy billow of smoke hung over the table. Gunner grinned at his officers. Seated by rank and seniority, each was a product of the Naval Academy and a "nuc," a graduate of the Navy's nuclear power school. Looking around the table Gunner saw earnest, eager faces, young men full of romance anxious to test their courage in dangerous waters. *Reno* was going north, into the Russians' backyard, and Gunner and his men were about to mark their passage with a solemn rite.

"Open for two blue chips," said Trout in a gruff voice.

Chips rattled in the center of the table.

"Two cards," said the XO, adding, "I hear the Russians have a rednose ceremony when they reach the North Pole."

"Oh, yeah?" said Gunner. "How does that go?"

"They take all the non-Russian sailors, see, Latvians and Georgians and whatnot, and cut off their noses, whap! Like that! And feed 'em to the polar bears."

Frowning, Lieutenant O'Connell looked at his cards, then at Trout. "But I thought only pure ethnic Russians were allowed on Soviet subs," he said.

A huge, booming laugh exploded from Trout's throat. "Now you know why, young man. Now you know why."

7 Bluenose Sailors

The sailors in the radio room had cut a deck of cards to determine who would stand watch during the bluenose ceremony. Petty Officer First Class Frederick Wu had drawn a lowly three of clubs and cursed his bad luck.

Alone with a half-dozen teletype machines and banks of sophisticated communication gear, most of which was useless at depth, Wu sipped coffee and studied an electronic engineering manual. At a depth of four hundred feet, *Reno* could receive communications only on ELF, extremely low frequency, but the excruciatingly slow transmission rate of one digit per minute restricted its use to short, coded messages. At fifty feet, the boat could receive more elaborate messages on VLF, very low frequency, without exposing a radio mast to hostile radar.

In Wu's opinion arctic duty had raised boredom to new heights. A cruise to the Barents Sea offered no ports of call, few messages, nothing but cold salt water and ice, shifting, crashing, unbelievably stultifying, never-ending ice. As a native of San Diego, just thinking of ice made Wu shiver, a purely psychic phenomenon, since the temperature inside the boat never varied. He cupped the coffee mug in his hands, letting it warm his palms, and daydreamed of the beach at La Jolla. The barren arctic reminded him of a desert, which is exactly what the frozen arctic regions are.

.   .   .

In the sonar room Chief Petty Officer Mike Morrison and Sonarman First Class Billy Stewart faced display screens and computer keyboards. Signals from the icepack, the storm, and the rich biosphere of the Barents Sea flashed across the screens, but sensitive listening arrays mounted in the bow and along a cable trailing the stern revealed no machine presence in the depths.

Morrison rose from the supervisor's chair and studied the screens. Bushy eyebrows, a pair of steel-rimmed glasses and an old-fashioned salt-and-pepper beard gave him the look of a submariner from the First World War. At forty-five the eldest man aboard, he felt as old and tired as the bloody twentieth century, a quarter of which he had spent in the sonar rooms of the Atlantic Fleet's submarine force.

Ordinarily, four watchstanders manned the sonar room, but an exception had been made for the bluenose ceremony. Burly arms folded, an expensive but unlit Cuban stogie jammed in his mouth, Morrison held an ancient billet unique to the Submarine Service, chief of the boat. Part chaplain, part shrink, part section boss, the chief of the boat was required to fix things before they broke, make peace among diverse racial and ethnic groups, kick ass when asses needed kicking and run a bluenose ceremony when one was in order.

He turned to Stewart. "You're our ears for the next hour, Billy," he said. "Keep awake."

Twenty years younger and built like a prizefighter, Stewart smiled and waved. "Go ahead and make a fool of yourself, as if I give a shit. My nose is already blue."

"The computer will hear anything before you do, anyway," said the chief, not deprecating Stewart's ability but stating a fact.

Morrison left, and Stewart wondered idly if the chief would bring him a bowl of ice cream.

Morrison made his way aft to engineering. In the maneuvering room, where nucs operated the boat's reactor plant, he found Master Chief Willie Adams, *Reno*'s chief nuc. Every few seconds Adams's eyes flickered over dials and gauges that covered every inch of bulkhead in the small compartment.

"Ain't you a bluenose today?" Morrison asked.

"I'm minding the store, thank you," said Adams. "Go on back. Garrett is holding a preparty party."

Morrison passed through a hatch into the engine room. A turbine whirring on silent bearings poured thirty-five thousand horsepower through whispering reduction gears, pushing _Reno_ farther into the Barents Sea. Morrison stepped discreetly into a small storeroom where Chief Torpedoman Darrell Garrett greeted him with a paper cup filled with gilley, a fiery red liquid. Garrett had brought aboard several gallon jars of maraschino cherries, replaced the syrup with potable ethyl alcohol used to clean torpedo tubes and let it age a week.

Morrison drank and smacked his lips to show proper appreciation. "Splendid. It ain't cold beer but it'll do."

"That'll be two dollars, Morrison."

Morrison fished two crumpled bills from his pants and Garrett poured another pair of gilleys.

"Here's to the Cold War," Garrett said. "May it last forever and keep me employed."

"Yea, brother," Morrison intoned. "Peace on earth, good will toward men."

Garrett replaced the lid on the jar, stowed it in a locker and said, "Let's do it."

A heavy knock sounded at the wardroom door.

"I'll get it," said Gunner. Morrison was waiting in the passageway. A wad of bubble gum crammed in his jaw failed to disguise the smell of gilley, which Gunner politely ignored.

"What can I do for you, Chief?"

"Skipper, request permission to convene the bluenoses in the enlisted mess."

"Say what, Chief?"

"With all respect, Captain, since we're under the ice, I thought now would be an appropriate time. We're well north of the Arctic Circle."

"No shit?"

A chorus of surprised exclamations erupted from the officers around the card table.

"I shit you not," said Morrison.

"Well, I'll be damned. Permission granted. You may address the crew. We'll be along in a few minutes."

In the control room Morrison switched on the ship's intercom and said into the microphone, "Attention all hands, this is the chief of the boat. All members of the Noble Order of Bluenoses are requested to muster in the enlisted mess for an initiation ceremony."

Lieutenant Sharpe ordered speed reduced to dead slow. In the maneuvering room Chief Adams cut steam flow to the turbines and the ship began to lose way.

"Secure the trim," Sharpe ordered. "Maintain depth of four hundred feet."

Ten minutes later the senior chiefs assembled in the mess. None wore insignia of rank and each had applied a daub of blue paint to his nose.

A long chain of sailors lined the passageways forward of the mess. In solemn silence the queue filed past the officers of the order and Morrison painted each man's nose blue. Gunner went through with the rest. Each bluenose had passed north of the Arctic Circle on a previous voyage. When all were appropriately marked, the bluenoses fell back into a curving, haphazard line.

Morrison proclaimed, "The Noble Order of Bluenose Sailors, USS *Reno* Chapter, is now in session."

"Hear hear," eighty men shouted in unison.

"Bring out the ice bucket," Morrison commanded.

Trout and Gunner went into the galley and returned with a large corrugated-steel tub filled with blue whipped cream, green apples and ice cubes made from water tinted with blue cake coloring.

The previously anointed began to clap rhythmically, stomp their feet and chant, "Bluenoses, bluenoses, bluenoses . . ."

"All cherries may now approach," Morrison shouted over the din.

Stripped to the waist, regardless of rank, twenty-four young men formed a second line that snaked through the passageways from the torpedo room, up the ladder to the galley and into the mess.

"Cherry number one, come forward."

Giddy with anticipation, O'Connell stepped before Morrison.

"What are you, cherry?" Morrison demanded.

"I am nothing, less than nothing, O Master."

"Where do you come from?"

"The disgusting, meaningless land of sunshine."

"Where are you now?"

"In the realm of ice and darkness."

"Are you a virgin, cherry?"

"Yes, O Master, I am."

"Would you fuck a polar bear and eat her young?"

"If commanded, O Master."

"Would you cut off your dick and feed it to King Neptune?"

"If commanded, O Master."

"Dunk, cherry, and be anointed or drown."

O'Connell dropped to his knees and plunged his face into the icy brew, snatched an apple with his teeth and came up sputtering. Blue cream dribbled down his chest.

"Stand and be anointed."

O'Connell scrambled to his feet and Morrison smeared blue paint on his nose. "What are you now?" he demanded.

"A Noble Bluenose, O Master of the icy deep."

"Take your place among your brothers, Bluenose, and know that you have passed into the frozen wasteland where few have gone before."

Intoxicated with the glory of his new status, O'Connell fell into line grinning like an idiot.

"Cherry number two, come forward."

The ritual continued until all twenty-four neophytes on their first arctic voyage had been inducted into the order. By the end of the ceremony the floor of the mess was awash in melting blue ice and whipped cream.

"Who are we?" Morrison bellowed at the company.

The crew took up the cry, chanting, "Bluenoses, bluenoses, bluenoses," until they were hoarse and could shout no more. Cooks began setting up tubs of blue cake and ice cream.

In the radio room Frederick Wu sat at a typewriter composing a letter to his parents. "With the Cold War ending," he wrote, "I think I'll have a better chance at learning new technologies in Silicon Valley. More money, too! My enlistment is up in . . ."

Suddenly the ELF message alarm beeped with shocking volume. Wu jerked his head around, spilled his coffee and swore, "Damn!" A red light flashed insistently on the main teletype, which clacked three times in slow sequence.

B2D.

Wu took a deep breath, stepped to the crypto decoder, checked to see the date was set properly and typed in the code.

The machine spit out the decoded message.

```
ASCEND TO VLF RADIO DEPTH FOR
IMMEDIATE TRANSMISSION.
```

"The whole damned crew is eating ice cream and cake like a bunch of kiddies," Wu muttered to himself, "and the Navy decides to say hello."

Sitting at the conning station, dreaming of Tomahawk launches from the Red Sea, Miles Sharpe heard Wu's anxious voice in his headphones. "Radio to control. We have an ELF transmission from Norfolk."

Startled, Sharpe asked, "Say again, radio?"

Wu repeated his announcement and recited the order to take the boat up to receive a message.

Sharpe felt a twinge of excitement. Maybe the war had resumed in the Gulf. Maybe the Russians had gone off their rockers and started something. Maybe this wouldn't be another boring arctic cruise after all.

Sharpe punched in the number for the enlisted mess. A cook answered. "Give me the captain," Sharpe shouted urgently into the phone.

The celebration in the mess had reached a crescendo of high hilarity. Soaked with paint and blue cake coloring, a chorus line of new bluenoses stumbled through a ragged can-can. At the center table an ice-cream–eating contest was degenerating into a sophomoric food fight.

Gunner took the phone from the cook, listened and said to Sharpe, "Take her up, Miles. Sound general quarters."

Alarm lights flashed and Sharpe's voice announced through the loudspeakers, "Attention all hands, general quarters, general quarters."

A brief moment of confusion prevailed before the rowdy bluenoses were transformed into a disciplined crew. The boat began to tilt upward, causing several men to slip on melted ice and fall to the deck as they scrambled toward their battle stations. Muffled curses echoed off the bulkheads.

Wiping paint from his face, Gunner raced toward the control room. On the ladder to the deck above he heard Trout's heavy footsteps right behind. On the run Trout asked breathlessly, "What do we have, Jack?"

"VLF message coming in."

"Jesus, their timing is terrific."

When they reached the control room, Gunner relieved Sharpe and began to relax. Filing in, bluenoses tracked wet splotches on the deck and dripped blue paint on the consoles. To Gunner the men looked like savage ancient Britons who had just discovered a Roman legion marching across the sward. Only Miles Sharpe, standing in a clean uniform before the combat information console, looked as if he belonged in the elec tronic environment of a nuclear sub.

Gunner laughed out loud.

"What's so funny?" Trout asked, annoyed.

Gunner spread his arms in a sweeping gesture around the control room. "Look at these guys in Halloween paint," he said. "If you were the Russians, what would you think?"

Trout didn't see anything funny at all.

8

Blue Lights

Ascending at a slight angle, *Reno* encountered the icy turbulence of the weather front. The storm penetrated fractures in the marginal ice zone and roiled the waters. For the first time since submerging outside Norfolk, the boat rolled. Ever so slowly, like a whale at play in the deep, the sub rotated three degrees to starboard.

In the control room Gunner smiled, bemused by the look of terror that passed over the blue-stained face of Lieutenant O'Connell.

"What the hell was that?" O'Connell asked.

Sitting in the comfortable leather conning chair, left ankle propped on right knee, ship's log spread on lap, a Lucky burning between fingers, Gunner pretended to speak into his microphone. "Sonar, did we hit a whale?" he asked deadpan.

Startled, O'Connell uttered a strangled, "What?"

"Thank you, sonar," Gunner said gravely. "It was no whale, Lieutenant. Sonar says maybe it was a Russian sub. Those things happen and nobody knows, nobody sees."

O'Connell blanched. "Why didn't we get a collision alarm? How could the Russians make the ship roll?"

After eighteen years sailing under the oceans, Gunner had experienced dozens of heart-stopping incidents. By comparison, a storm amounted to a nonevent. He shook his head in mock despair. He understood the young officer's confusion but couldn't resist a taunt. "Haven't you heard? Ivan has a new secret ship-rolling electromagnet. At five thousand yards they can electrocute *Reno* and everyone on it."

"The bastards," O'Connell spat through clenched teeth.

Gunner remembered when nuclear submariners were hard-core blue-water sailors who could smell a storm from a thousand feet down. Now, the young ones were bright technicians with no salt in their veins. In Gunner's opinion O'Connell probably could design the best raft ever made but couldn't sail it across the Mississippi. When you got right down to it, the whole damned crew on *Reno* was like that. Whenever the boat surfaced in a swell and really rocked and rolled, half the crew got seasick.

Gunner looked directly at O'Connell. "Has anybody on this boat told you the Cold War is over? If there's a Russian boat in these waters, they'd invite us aboard for vodka and caviar." Then he softened and added, "It's only a storm."

"A storm?" O'Connell's face clouded with puzzlement.

"There's a big storm on the surface," Gunner explained patiently. "Forget it. Think of the marvelous technology required to send us a message. Thousands of scientists in hundreds of laboratories spending billions of dollars to master the black arts of cryptology, rocketry, electronic engineering, satellite station keeping, low-frequency radio transmission. Wow. This massive infusion of hardware has been assembled so a weather officer in Norfolk can tell me what I already know: a big storm is overhead and the Navy wants to make sure we know it's up there."

"VLF depth," Trout announced from the diving panel.

"Very well," said Gunner. "Level her off."

Twenty-six thousand miles above the North Atlantic a satellite in geosynchronous orbit sent a highly compressed and enciphered stream of data to a Navy plane circling slowly over Norway. Computers aboard the plane converted the data to VLF and transmitted a continuous stream of VLF messages to the Atlantic Fleet's submarine force.

"Radio to control. Receiving VLF."

"Very well, radio."

In the radio room computers picked *Reno*'s message from the general broadcast. A portion of the message remained scrambled to be decoded by the captain. Gunner took the message into the cryptography room, keyed his personal code into the crypto machine and a few minutes later the digital code groups were rendered into plain English.

```
TO CO USS RENO: SOVNAV TYPHOON CLASS
LAUNCHED UNANNOUNCED SS-N-20 TEST
FROM WHITE SEA THIS DATE 0900 GMT.
SOV TV BROADCAST FILM OF LAUNCH.
ANTISOVNAV DEMONSTRATIONS THROUGHOUT
USSR. POLITICAL IMPLICATIONS UNCLEAR.
PROCEED IMMEDIATELY TO GREMIKHA AND
MONITOR TYPHOON ACTIVITY. COMSUBLANT
SENDS.
```

Typhoon! In Gunner's mind the word conjured up an image of a nuclear monster that chilled his heart. At 360 feet *Reno* was a big ship, as long as a football field. By comparison a Typhoon was the whole damned stadium. *Reno* had been built for the express purpose of tracking the huge subs under the ice, but Typhoons were elusive prey, operating almost exclusively in the restricted waters of the White Sea. In five previous arctic patrols, *Reno* had not made a single contact with a Soviet boomer.

Gunner easily imagined what had happened in the Pentagon when an unexpected missile flared out of the White Sea. Alarms, bells, buzzers, ten seconds of panic until the trajectory was determined; angry phone calls on the hot line to Moscow; a quick debate over a response; which sub is closest to Gremikha? USS *Reno*, SSN 777. Send in Gunner. If the Russians want to play games, he'll know what to do.

Gunner felt his heart sink. Soviet TV? Demonstrations? Political implications unclear? What the hell did that mean? Was this an unauthorized launch? Did some fool Russian sub commander decide to blow off a missile just to watch the contrail? Was the Cold War heating up? What was the Pentagon sending him into?

Gunner returned to the control room. "Mr. Trout," he asked, "will you join me in my cabin?"

. . .

Sparse, unadorned with sentiment, the captain's minuscule quarters barely held two men. Gunner sat at his desk and read the brief message aloud while Trout paced around the small space.

"These fucking Russians don't know when to leave well enough alone," Trout exploded when Gunner finished. "I swear to God, Jack, the bastards don't want the Cold War to end. They did this to provoke us."

Accustomed to Trout's tirades, Gunner waited a moment to make sure his XO had vented his spleen. "Doing a little Soviet strategic planning on the side, Gus?" he asked.

"Hell, yes."

"We test missiles, they test missiles," Gunner said with a trace of annoyance. "So what?"

"We announce our tests like we're supposed to so nobody gets excited," Trout protested belligerently.

"Like Russian demonstrators, or like you?" Gunner asked mildly.

Chastised, Trout made a visible effort to calm down. "Looks like the Russians are getting a dose of the sixties thirty years late," he said. "Soviet launches on TV and demonstrators in the streets. I couldn't wish it on a nicer bunch of guys."

"The world has changed, Gus," Gunner said. "The simple truth is the Russian Empire is finished. The Soviet Admiralty just doesn't know it yet. One missile test won't change that. Relax. At least we won't be patrolling an empty Barents Sea. We'll be sitting outside Gremikha, and you'll get your fill of the big, bad Russians."

Trout sat down on Gunner's bunk and massaged his scalp for a moment. "The Cold War isn't over, Jack," he said. "You know that as well as I do."

"So what? We can have a Cold War forever as long as it doesn't turn into a shooting war. Jesus, Gus, we've been over this a hundred times. The Russians will never attack because they have nothing to gain and everything to lose. Even if their politicians catastrophically miscalculate, their military knows they can't compete. They can't fight us, not in a million years, and they know it. If they truly threatened us, we'd waste 'em in a hot minute."

"Perhaps," said Trout, "but the Soviet Union is falling apart, and some of their big guys don't like that. Trout's axiom: No one relinquishes power willingly. The easiest way to divert attention from domestic troubles is to find a foreign enemy."

Gunner tapped a Lucky from the pack and lit it. "No shit, genius. That's what Bush did with Noriega and Saddam. Panama and Iraq are third-rate Third World countries, but the Russians have a first-rate Third World country. They're not going to screw around outside their borders. Not now. Not anymore. Those days are over."

An unreconstructed cold warrior, Trout retained anti-Soviet opinions shared by hundreds of officers. "No?" he asked. "Did they magically turn into good guys overnight?"

"Gus, I don't make policy. I'm a sub driver and I go where I'm ordered. Nobody says you have to like the Russians, but I don't think it does much good to hate them."

Trout paused, as if reflecting on a profound truth. "I don't hate them," he said. "I just don't trust them."

"Fair enough," Gunner said, trying to be conciliatory.

Trout gazed longingly at Gunner's cigarette and fought the urge to bum one and light up himself.

"Hell," Gunner said, "after this cruise they'll give you a Trident. Count on it. You'll command a boomer, and if you still don't like the Russians, you can blow them to hell."

Trout considered his captain as something of an enigma. Gunner talked like a peacenik but Trout knew "Plutonium Jack" would never hesitate to pull the nuclear trigger if he had to. Gunner had no apparent interest beyond his command. Ashore, most submarine officers acted like other complex, intelligent men with warts, flaws, and funky, half-rotted sailboats. Trout had married, divorced, raised children, gone fishing, climbed mountains and sailed his old Triton around Chesapeake Bay, but not Gunner. The captain had never married. In Norfolk he hadn't joined the officers' club, never participated in Navy social events, never did anything but prepare himself for patrol in arctic waters. He had even attended the Armed Forces language school at Monterey, learned Russian, and frequently read Russian books, newspapers and military journals. For a man who didn't want to fight the Russians, he had assiduously followed the first rule of combat: Know thine enemy.

Gunner unlocked his safe, took out a red-jacketed folder labeled Top Secret, and withdrew a series of satellite photos and a detailed analysis of recent Soviet naval operations. He spread the documents around the cabin.

"Take a look at this, Gus," he said. "An unusual pattern of Red Navy ship movements has been developing. The Soviets rarely have more than 15 percent of their ships at sea at any one time. That figure is now down to 10 percent and decreasing. Ships on patrol are returning to port without being replaced at sea. In the Baltic, Black and Caspian seas, virtually no ships are on patrol."

"Those are pretty much non-Russian ethnic areas," Trout interjected. "The main Black Sea port, Odessa, is in the Ukraine."

"Correct," said Gunner, "but the Pacific and Northern fleets are pulling back as well. The Red Navy is the most independent of their services and, frankly, there's no love lost between the civilian government in Moscow and the Admiralty in Leningrad. With the ships in port, there's no question of who's in command. With ships at sea, especially subs, specifically strategic missile subs, the answer grows fuzzy."

"Are you suggesting Moscow is afraid of the fleets?"

"That's one interpretation, and it may or may not be valid. At the moment Moscow is afraid of everything. Hell, the Soviet Union may cease to exist any minute. The point is the Russians could well be struggling over who's in command of their armed forces. All we can do is watch the situation develop and determine if anything threatens us. That's only prudent."

"I consider an SS-N-20 a significant threat," Trout said.

"Agreed," Gunner sighed. "This bird flew out of a Typhoon. Only one man could have conducted this test."

"Zenko!" said Trout.

"Yes, Zenko. The Typhoons are his life. In a civil war his squadron could lay waste to everything from the Ukraine to China. We need to know what Zenko's doing with his boats and how he's going to deploy them. Maybe that's what this missile test was all about, Gus—a message to Moscow."

"What do we tell the crew?" Trout asked.

"The truth. We're going to Gremikha, and we may sit on the bottom with quiet in the boat for weeks. Rough duty for everyone. They're all bluenoses now. They can take it."

Gunner got up to open the door for Trout's exit. "Lay in a course for a point one hundred fifty miles north of Gremikha," he said. "We'll come down on them from the north and get as close as we can."

"Aye aye, Skipper."

Gunner gently shut the door and lay down on his bunk, knowing he wouldn't sleep. Whenever he closed his eyes, he saw bright blue lights, tiny specks glowing above a vast white sea. One by one they rushed into the sky and disappeared. From the moment *Reno* had sailed from Norfolk, the lights had grown in intensity until now, after twelve days at sea, each light pulsed like a star going nova right behind his eyeballs.

Sometimes, as the lights ascended, Gunner imagined they were human souls streaking toward the heavens, but the trajectories curved back to earth, and the souls plunged into the hellfire of exploding plutonium. Sixteen ignitions, sixteen blue lights, sixteen Tomahawk cruise missiles rocketing across the universe, signifying the end of civilization. The lights pulsed, grew fat, then faded away. On this final patrol, Gunner had given up hope of exorcising these hellish private demons until he was off the boat forever.

He felt the darkness of the deep, cold ice covering him like a cloak of invisibility. He felt the sub accelerate, striking like an assassin's dagger deep into hostile waters. Ahead lay a sea of Typhoons and Akulas, cyclones and sharks, a mariner's most ancient enemies, and Plutonium Jack Gunner was afraid.

9 The Barents Sea

If the Barents Sea were a bathtub full of water, the ice canopy would be the soap scum floating on top. Even the deepest ice keel makes barely a dent in the basin, which averages 750 feet deep. By steaming at four hundred feet, *Reno* removed ice from the equation of arctic navigation.

Before the advent of nuclear submarines, voyages under the ice were restricted to a few hours. A diesel-electric sub requires oxygen and must retreat from under the ice to replenish its air. A nuclear sub makes breathable air by desalinating sea water and subjecting the resultant fresh water to electrolysis. Thus a nuke can remain below the ice until her food runs out or the men go insane. To *Reno*, crossing an ice-covered sea posed no greater problem than transiting the Atlantic.

Aside from ice, the major obstacle to precise navigation in northern latitudes is the effect of the north magnetic pole on a magnetic compass. Early arctic explorers quickly discovered their compasses spinning wildly, creating what mariners call longitude roulette. In the long polar night celestial navigation by sextant and stars is impossible where no discernible horizon exists and the heavens revolve around a north star directly overhead. In the equally long polar day the sun lingers interminably above an indistinct horizon. The first brave adventurers who sought to conquer the North Pole traveled in circles, became lost and froze to death on the shifting, maddening, spectacularly wild surface of the ice.

The Arctic Ocean remained the last maritime frontier until 1958, when the first nuclear submarine, the USS *Nautilus*, completed the first undersea transpolar voyage. Equipped with an inertial navigation system, three gyroscopes that accurately measure movement in three directions from a known starting point, *Nautilus* was unaffected by the magnetic pole.

Now, satellite or Loran fixes can check the accuracy of inertial navigation gyros. A second check can be made by measuring distances from known geological features on the seabed. After more than thirty years of submarine navigation, the bottom of the Barents Sea has been thoroughly charted. Seamounts and troughs are well known. Thus *Reno* crossed the Barents Sea under the ice and arrived precisely on course midway between the coast of the Kola Peninsula and Novaya Zemlya, a large island of permafrost and tundra used by the Soviets for nuclear tests. An extensive array of sonars stretched between the island and the Kola mainland, 150 miles south.

Commander Trout reported, "We're almost on top of the Soviets' outer sonar array, Captain."

"Quiet in the boat," Gunner ordered.

"Quiet in the boat, aye." The command echoed softly through each compartment.

"All stop."

"All stop, aye."

The steam flow stopped, the prop ceased turning and the boat drifted forward on momentum.

"Control to sonar, report."

The full-array sonar screen showed ice crashing above and reverberations bouncing off the bottom. Ice scanners showed anchored ice—undersea stalagmites resembling inverted icicles—near the island shores. The processed signal showed nothing. The sonar computers detected no mechanical or electronic sounds.

"Sonar reports all clear, Skipper."

Gunner stroked his chin. "Where is he, Gus? Where's our old friend, Ivan?"

"Not looking for us, apparently."

"They used to be so damned predictable," Gunner snorted. "Are they getting smarter or quieter or both?"

"Maybe they scuttled the fleet and sent their sailors out to plant potatoes."

"Wouldn't surprise me," Gunner said. "If I were hungry, that's what I'd do."

Gunner switched on the ship's intercom and dialed to low volume. "Attention all hands," he announced. "We are entering hostile Soviet waters. We'll have quiet in the boat until further notice. You're all good submariners and know your jobs. From this moment on, we're pirates. Our mission is to steal secrets from the Red Navy, and we can't do that if they know we're here. So keep it quiet. That is all."

"Bravo," said Trout.

"Thank you," said Gunner. "Control to maneuvering."

"Maneuvering."

"Engage propulsors."

"Propulsors, aye."

Chief Adams increased steam to the turbogenerator and fed electric power to a pair of hydropropulsors mounted behind the stern planes.

"Maneuvering to control. Propulsors ready."

"All ahead on full propulsors."

The small but powerful electric hydroturbines silently jetted seawater sternward, pushing the boat quietly through the sea at six knots.

From the beginnings of submersible craft in the nineteenth century, submariners have been outlaws. In the First World War submarines demonstrated that war was no longer waged by gentlemen but rather by pirates who used invisibility to wreak terror. Under water no rules exist.

An admiralty court would call the Barents international waters, but Gunner knew he had entered the private preserve of the Northern Fleet. From here on, he too was an outlaw, and the Soviet Navy would consider any movement south an act of aggression.

Proceeding with extreme caution, Gunner stopped every

thirty minutes to listen to the water. Each time Morrison announced no contacts. After the third report Gunner began to suspect the Russians had abandoned the Barents Sea.

"Where are they, Gus? Where the hell are they?"

Reno moved in absolute silence, wrapped in stealth like a thief in the night. No machinery noises registered on the Soviet sonars. The elaborate system of bottom arrays designed to detect undersea incursions near the Kola coast failed completely.

Unseen, unheard, an underwater stealth fighter, *Reno* crept through inner space toward the Soviet Union. No vibration rattled the decks. Only the ship's inertial navigation system detected *Reno*'s passage through the dark waters of the Barents Sea. With no weather, no sky, no horizon, no changes in temperature, night and day disappeared. Time was marked every four hours by the changing of the watch. Each enlisted man had four hours on watch followed by eight hours to sleep, eat, play cards, study for rating and promotion exams or find more creative ways of preserving his sanity. Every six hours the cooks laid out one hundred meals, rapidly depleting their stock of salad greens and fresh milk. Every twelve hours the quartermaster announced the date and hour in Greenwich Mean Time over the ship's intercom, but few sailors took interest, an attitude that would change as the patrol lengthened. The date mattered as little as the latitude or depth. The real world was far away, replaced by a steel tube exactly thirty-three feet four inches in diameter.

In the sonar room Morrison allowed Billie Stewart to open his dirty book store.

Each sailor was permitted to bring two seabags of personal goods aboard the ship. Instead of clothes Stewart had filled his bags with hundreds of cheap pornographic novels and a formidable collection of laminated photographs displaying female anatomy provocatively posed.

Chief Torpedoman Garrett was among the first to express interest in Stewart's library. He appeared in the sonar room and said to Stewart, "I hear you got books."

"Yeah. So?"

"And plastic pictures."

"I got them, too."

"Lemme see a book."

Stewart opened one of his bags and handed Garrett a paperback entitled *One Night in Hamburg*. The lurid cover showed a dark street lined with windows where barely clad women lounged under red lights.

Garrett opened the novel, read a page at random and twitched his nose. "Lemme see a picture."

Stewart handed him a four-by-six color print of a nude young woman lying on a bed, knees spread apart. "I wanna buy a book and some pictures. How much?"

"These books are not for sale," Stewart explained. "They're for rent. You want fun and games, you gotta get on the program."

"Howzzat?"

Stewart let Garrett hold the book and look at the picture while he spelled out the deal. "I got three hundred different books and six hundred pictures. You take a book and two pictures, keep them as long as you like, then bring them back and I give you another set. You can get two sets a day every day on patrol and never duplicate. Variety, my man, continuous reading pleasure for the duration and friendly pictures you can take into the shower."

"How much?"

"For you, Garrett, two bills."

"How much izzat?"

"What planet are you from, Garrett? Two hundred dollars."

"That's highway robbery!"

"It is? Gee whiz. Maybe you can find another dirty book store on this boat, pal."

"I'll think about it."

"You do that. And if you don't like pictures of girls, I got boys, too, ones with big torpedoes."

"I ain't no fag."

"Do I care?"

Garrett was back in five minutes, a wad of crumpled twenties in his hand. On a good patrol Stewart could clear five thousand dollars, most of which he squandered in poker games. Morrison made him put 10 percent into the Sonarman's Fund, cash that went toward a major blowout for the sonar gang at the end of each patrol.

A few hours later when the watch changed, Morrison burst into the chiefs' mess wearing a Soviet submariner's black cap and waving a miniature Soviet naval ensign. His huge, booming laugh echoed off the bulkheads and filled the crowded space with manic glee.

"Ivan ho!" he roared, punching Chief Garrett in the shoulder and yapping in a mock Russian accent. "Imperialist swine! You miss me? You gonna miss me. Da. I go home now."

He drew a forefinger across his throat and said, "Cold War over. Finito. Kaput. Now whatta we gonna do for fun?"

"I don't see what's so funny, Morrison," Garrett said, a frown twitching the edges of his lower lip.

"For chrissake, Garrett. Peace on earth, good will toward men."

"You weenie, Morrison. Go fuck yourself."

"C'mon, man. Lighten up. All your life you've been told the Russians are the enemy, the bad guys, the evil empire and all that crap. Now, the iron curtain has disappeared and peace has broken out. Oh dear, what's a dedicated cold warrior to do?"

Garrett thought for a moment, poking at his food. "If the Cold War is over, how come we're here? Answer me that, smart guy."

Morrison grabbed a tray, helped himself to meatloaf and mashed potatoes. "Good question. Why are we here on the good ship *Reno* with all this deadly ordnance pointed straight at the heart of the Soviet Union? Because we're the good guys and they're the bad guys? Is that it? Did you ever see *Waiting for Godot?*"

"Listen, egghead," Garrett said. "I know damned well why I'm here, even if you don't."

"You got a mouth on you, Garrett, but I'll bite. Okay, why?"

"Because the Cold War gave me the most fun I ever had. I don't give a damn about communism or the Russians. Playing subs with Ivan is the best game in town."

"Maybe it was," said Morrison, "but the clock is running

down. Tick tick tick, tock, the final whistle." He stuck his fork into a piece of meatloaf and held it up in the air. "The Soviet threat is like your lunch hanging naked on your fork. Now you see it"—he paused to cram the greasy morsel in his mouth— "and now you don't."

"You're full of shit," Garrett said, shaking his head.

"No I ain't." Morrison laughed. "I'm full of meatloaf, same as you." He looked around, whipping his head left and right and snapped, "Where's that cocktail waitress? I thought I ordered me a vodka and lime. What's got into the Navy, anyway? Jesus, I wish I was drunk."

"Shut up, Morrison. Just shut the fuck up and let us eat."

Morrison ate several bites of meatloaf in silence and thought about the Barents Sea. The monstrous Typhoons lived here under the ice, guarded by squadrons of fast, quiet Akula class attack subs. Why the fuck were they here? As _Reno_ inched toward Gremikha, Morrison suspected the Navy was putting a torch to the Cold War and heating it up all over again. Garrett would have his chance to play with the Russians, but somehow, Morrison thought, the Russians wouldn't consider an American sub in their waters a plaything.

10   Archangel

Aboard *Sovyetskii Soyuz*, Mishman Sorokin descended to the enlisted men's quarters to call the first watch and discovered seaman recruit Typov, the boy from Komsomol, sitting in a passageway studying his assigned text on saturated steam. "How's it going?" Sorokin asked, pleased to see the young squid taking his duty seriously.

"It's difficult," Typov answered with naive honesty, "but interesting."

"Didn't you learn in Komsomol that socialism is science?"

"Yes, Mishman, but in Babayevo we have no reactors. No one ever heard of saturated steam. It's not like Leningrad."

"Do you truly want to be a sailorman?"

"I don't know, but I don't want to be an idiot."

Sorokin turned away, then stopped and asked, "Why aren't you in your bunk? It's more comfortable than the passageway."

"Go inside. You'll see," Typov mumbled, returning to a page of equations.

Sorokin pushed into the compartment and discovered two dozen squids having an illicit party. Rock and roll music pulsed from a tape deck as young sailors swayed and bopped to "Dancin' in the Street" by Martha and the Vandellas.

Petya Bulgakov danced over to Sorokin and said, "Hey, Comrade Boss. Rock on."

"Rock on, my ass. Is that your music machine, Little Petya?"

"Yeah. Ain't it beautiful!"

"I thought you had some brains, you little shit," Sorokin said sternly. "Shut it down. If an officer comes in here, you're in big trouble, all of you."

"Why? We launched our ridiculous rocket, comrade. What can the stripers do to us that's worse than being on this ship?"

"They can take away your liberty, cloudbrain," Sorokin shouted over the music. "We're going to surface in fifteen minutes. Don't you understand? If you want to dance and chase women in Archangel, turn it off."

Shaking his head, Sorokin about-faced and returned to the command center. Behind him, the music died.

At high noon *Sovyetskii Soyuz* surfaced in a long swath of ship-broken ice five miles outside Archangel. Lookouts could see a pall of brown air over the ancient city. Archangel! The name alone excited the crew. The lookouts held up their thumbs and grinned.

From the bridge Captain Malakov saw only two small ice-breakers and a white ferry motoring across the usually bustling harbor. In the most vile winter freeze, numerous tugs with barges moved around the busy port, but not today. The rocket officer, Lieutenant Minski, a native of Archangel, invited up to the bridge by the captain, commented on how quiet and subdued the city looked.

Presently the great smokestacks of the Ministry of Military Industry Shipyard 402 at Severodvinsk came into view. Minski noted an absence of smoke emanating from stacks that normally operated 365 days a year, another ominous sign.

"Radio to bridge," the radio officer said through the intercom. "The shipyard commander is on the horn and wants to talk to you, Captain."

"Patch him through."

"Captain Malakov?" said a nervous voice. "This is Colonel Volostov from the Ministry of Military Industry. We have a problem here at Severodvinsk. Our civilian workers called a wildcat strike this morning and walked off the job."

Malakov felt murderous urges rushing through his veins, but he asked calmly, "Can you arrange berthing?"

"Yes, but . . ."

"But what?"

"It would be better if your ship returned to Gremikha."

"Impossible! You have naval personnel on the yard, don't you?"

"Yes."

"Then unless they deserted en masse, put them to work. Malakov, out!"

Two Navy tugs came alongside and gently pushed *Sovyetskii Soyuz* toward Severodvinsk. As the sub moved closer to shore, Malakov saw green trolley buses rolling along the waterfront, but little other traffic. A few trucks and a lone militia patrol car with blue lights and police markings rolled down White Sea Boulevard. Archangel had gone to sleep.

The tugs guided the ship into one of the covered berths built to protect the Navy's assets from fierce northern weather. As the sub moved under the roof, the bridge party felt an eerie silence. Instead of the usual cacophony of rolling cranes, roaring blowtorches and steam hammers, the shipyard was quiet.

From the bridge Malakov watched a makeshift shore party of naval infantry assist his crew with mooring procedures. At the end of the dock a single figure, the forlorn shipyard commander, Colonel Volostov, stood fidgeting and wringing his hands.

When *Sovyetskii Soyuz* was made fast to the quay, Malakov scrambled down from the bridge screaming furiously, "What the hell has happened here?"

"Captain First Rank Malakov, please, the ironworkers demanded a wage increase and called a wildcat strike this morning, and the rest of the workers walked off in sympathy. There was an anti-Navy demonstration at the main gate today. The workers want more money and the demonstrators say they get too much. They had a fight, and when the militia came, the workers and demonstrators fought them together."

Malakov glared at the man. "This is a military shipyard! You son of a bitch, you can be shot for this."

"It's not my fault, Captain, please. The civilians will be back on the job in a few days, perhaps even tomorrow. I assure you . . ."

"Your assurances are worthless," Malakov hissed. "Have you informed the Admiralty?"

"Of course."

"And Northern Fleet headquarters?"

"Yes, Captain, you've been at sea. We have nothing but problems."

Malakov realized flailing an unfortunate functionary constrained by forces beyond his control served no purpose. This was Russia, hopeless, helpless, paralyzed. "What a way to run a navy," he said. "Comrad Shipyard Commander, we need your equipment and parts from your stores for routine maintenance. We can take care of our ship ourselves."

"Our stores are depleted," the wretched commander complained. "The railway workers walked out in support of the shipyard workers. Things are as fouled up as can be, Captain."

"Is anything working in this godforsaken town?"

Brightening, Volostov answered, "The bars, Captain. The vodka is flowing."

"That's wonderful," Malakov said with a sneer. "Go on strike, get drunk, go home and watch television. That's modern Russia. I'll use naval infantry to unload railroad cars if I have to."

"I don't understand what's happening in this country," Volostov whined. "I swear I don't."

"I do," Malakov snapped. "Assholes like you are running shipyards. Get out of my sight."

Volostov slunk away, thinking only of the vodka bottle hidden in his office desk. Between the unions and the Navy a man might as well drown himself. When the ice melted in another month or two, he might try.

Malakov summoned Sorokin and ordered him to arrange for shore power. An hour later power lines snaked over the quay and into the ship. Sergov posted naval infantry as guards and dispatched engineers to scour the shipyard for supplies. In the reactor compartment Malakov commanded the operators to hold the reactor at 10 percent and maintain steam.

With the ship secure, Sorokin mustered the crew and marched 105 sailors off the ship. Toting seabags, the squids crossed the shipyard to a long, low, dilapidated, uninsulated building that served as barracks. Each sailor had brought bedding from the ship and claimed a bunk. Cooks broke into a long-unused kitchen, but finding no provisions, returned to the ship to raid the galley.

Sorokin formed the men in ranks and announced liberty call.

"How long will we be here, Boss?" asked Petya Bulgakov.

"Three days," Sorokin answered.

"The stripers said we'd get a week."

"Shut up, Little Petya. Don't be a pest. You've got liberty. Enjoy it. Play music as loud as you like."

"Do we have to wear uniforms in town?" another sailor asked.

"No. Stay in groups and keep the hell out of trouble. No fights, no bullshit."

"Can we call home?" Typov asked.

"If you find a phone that works and can pay for the call."

"What happens when we run out of food?"

Questions and complaints assaulted the quartermaster from all directions. Finally, Sorokin held up his hand and said, "You're sailormen, for God's sake. Stop whining like children and take care of yourselves. You," he pointed at Petya Bulgakov, "don't screw up."

"Aye aye, Comrade Boss."

Sorokin returned to the ship hoping the mishmani would get a day ashore. He had an old friend or two he could look up in Archangel, former squids who might want to hoist a bottle of vodka. On the other hand, if he didn't get into town, it wouldn't break his heart. He had plenty to keep him busy.

The ship was quiet. Still shiny and new, *Sovyetskii Soyuz* had been built here at Severodvinsk on the ways of the adjacent shop. Sorokin recalled sailing with Zenko and a crew of twenty during the sub's first sea trials, and several months later they had delivered her to Gremikha. He remembered the day in Zenko's Cave when Malakov had taken command, coming aboard with seven officers from the notorious, fanatic pro-Union Grey Ghost Squadron Seven at Murmansk. Sorokin ordinarily tolerated officers, but Malakov and his comrades were hard-edged and political in what had been a distinctively apolitical flotilla.

An exception was Lieutenant Minski, the rocket officer, who

had showed signs of being human. Now, Sorokin thought he might sound Minski out, befriend him, and perhaps discover the secret black market shopping lists of the other officers. Sorokin could make a little money and even uncover some important information in his capacity as Zenko's spy.

He found Minski huddled over the navigation table with Plesharski discussing the test launch. Just as he was about to strike up a conversation, Malakov called an assembly in the Lenin Room. Forty-five men squeezed through the door, and Political Officer Sergov passed out glasses of tea.

"Do we get liberty like the squids?" Plesharski whispered to Sorokin.

"Shut up, fool. Put your thousand rubles away for your old age."

"I'm already old."

"Gentlemen," said Malakov, "I regret to tell you that for us officers there will be no liberty. We're required to keep ourselves in a state of readiness."

The stoic faces around the table revealed nothing. Minski thought, readiness for what? World War III?

Malakov continued with a long speech about patriotism and the glories of naval service. Sorokin struggled to keep awake. When the captain finished, Sergov harangued the officers and mishmani about the political responsibility of divisional commanders. Plesharski kicked Sorokin under the table.

"Wake up, Boss."

Sorokin scanned the faces in the room as if they were blank spaces without features. Corrupting them with bottles of imported brandy, razor blades and jeans from Levi Strauss didn't seem like fun after all.

Sergov read an interminable list of quotations from Party ideologues, demonstrating his grasp of Marxist-Leninist thought. When he finally finished, Malakov said, "I'm going into Archangel to meet with Admiral Deminov this evening. I expect a unit citation for our successful rocket launch will be forthcoming. That's all. Dismissed."

The officers and mishmani returned to their quarters. Sorokin went up on deck, then wandered over to the barracks. The squids were gone. He wondered how many would come back.

11

White Star

At eight o'clock, with a free hour before his meeting with Deminov, Malakov dismissed his car and driver and strolled through the cobbled streets of Archangel. Grateful like any veteran sailor for a breath of shore life, he hoped to see a green sign of spring. Within a few minutes he regretted his decision. Like grit on the windows, a terrible malaise lay over the ancient city.

In the center of town he saw clusters of angry shipyard workers, a few tired women with string bags lightly laden with meager goods, and gangs of strange youths with wild hair and white-washed faces. Along the central waterfront dirty snow covered the ground and the smell of burning coal fouled the air. He passed decrepit boatyards and ferry slips and old men watching the ice from benches along the seawall. After several blocks he turned inland once again and stopped to read posters slathered on the side of an apartment building. Among theater notices and offers to sell used furniture he found a crudely printed call for a general strike to support the shipyard workers, another for a rally to support an independent Russian republic, and a third demanding free bread and the abolition of the Communist party. A fourth poster urging citizens to support the Union was defaced with a swastika. Malakov felt the urge to rip it down, but then saw another across the street and yet another down the block.

Around the corner he encountered a breadline three blocks long. A cheeky mime worked the queue, provoking waves of laughter and a shower of coins with caricatures of Gorbachev, Yeltsin, a commissar and, when he saw Malakov, a naval officer. The mime puffed out his chest, arched his back and goose-stepped. The crowd howled and Malakov's face burned with rage. He wanted to pummel the mime with his fists and assault the crowd, but there were so many, so many.

"Take our money," yelled a man tossing a coin to the mime. "We have nothing to spend it on." Turning on Malakov with a malicious smile he added, "The Navy has taken everything to fire useless rockets at Siberia."

The crowd applauded and several citizens openly jeered at Malakov. The mime picked up the fifty-kopek piece, tried to crunch it between his teeth, scowled and flipped it over his shoulder. The crowd clapped and whistled. A moment later he scrambled after the coin and dropped it in his boot.

Malakov walked on, catcalls from the crowd stinging his ears. Everywhere he saw closed shutters and gates as if Archangel were oppressed by a blizzard, but the windows and doors were locked not against the long winter, which had passed, but against the malignant, palpable threat of violence and anarchy in the air. When people have no bread, Malakov thought, they storm the bakeries. When they have no hope, they burn the bakeries to the ground.

By nine o'clock he had seen enough. A cold wind blew off the harbor as he crossed White Sea Boulevard toward the brightly lit naval officers' club. Music wafted from the entrance. Cars pulled up, discharged officers in shining uniforms with sharp epaulettes, then pulled around the corner where the drivers parked and shivered in the cold. Before 1917 the club's ornate waterfront building had been headquarters of the Imperial White Sea Flotilla. During the Great Patriotic War the American Land-Lease Commission had occupied the structure. How things change, thought Malakov, and how they will change again.

Malakov mounted the wooden steps and reached for the brass handles on the doors. The enlisted guard promptly barred his way. "Members only, Comrade Officer."

Malakov fished his military identification card from his wallet and flashed it briefly at the guard.

"Sorry, sir," the guard said with sudden deference. "Didn't recognize you. Open up, Dmitri! This is Captain First Rank Malakov."

"Malakov? From *Sovyetskii Soyuz?* Welcome, sir. Welcome! We saw your ship on television, sir, and what a sight it was!"

The guards saluted smartly and swung wide the doors. Inside, bright chandeliers glowed above the foyer and grand staircase. A three-piece string ensemble playing Mozart ambled through the drinking rooms. With few ships at sea the club was crowded with aviators from Wing Archangel and destroyermen from the Northern Fleet's ice-bound White Sea squadron. Spirits were high. The scene reminded Malakov of Russia in 1917, just before the Revolution. While privileged officers ate and drank and danced, the old regime crashed down on their heads.

The main bar was jammed. Malakov found Deminov presiding over a corner table attended by a half-dozen officers. Sitting next to the admiral, the fleet's security chief, the granite-faced Colonel Ludinov, flicked his eyes over the company like a shark studying a school of tuna.

Deminov jumped to his feet and forced a glass into his son-in-law's hand. "Gentlemen, a toast," he bellowed. "To the commander of *Sovyetskii Soyuz,* who yesterday demonstrated the might of our modern Navy."

"To Malakov," shouted the officers, swallowing vodka as though it were fresh spring water. Already drunk, they were willing to toast the queen of England as long as the liquor flowed.

"I wish to propose a toast of my own," Malakov said, raising his glass. "Gentlemen," he said in a voice thick with sarcasm, "a toast to the loyal shipyard workers of Severodvinsk. May they get their just reward."

"To the workers!" roared the officers.

Hot-blooded anger poured like sweat from Malakov. Deminov did not like his son-in-law, but his anger could prove useful. He clapped his arm around Malakov's shoulders. "Vladimir, I have a room reserved upstairs. Colonel Ludinov, will you stand in for me as toastmaster?"

"Of course, Admiral," Ludinov replied.

"By your leave, gentlemen," Deminov said to the company of drunken pilots and destroyermen, then turned and led Malakov toward the grand staircase.

The table for two in a private dining room was laid with pre-Revolution silver, crystal and gilded china. Vodka cooled in sterling ice-buckets. Mounds of caviar and sweet butter and baskets of bread occupied the center of the table. A gold-jacketed naval steward stood at attention in the corner. Deminov allowed the steward to pour vodka, then motioned for him to disappear.

Malakov stared at the luxurious table and remembered the breadline and the mime. Suddenly, he drew his arm back and hurled his glass against the wall.

Amused, Deminov shouted, "What the hell is the matter with you?"

Malakov leaned over the table and hissed, "No, Ivan, what's the matter with you? Have you been in the town? Have you seen the people, the posters on the walls? They looked at my uniform with pure loathing and would've stoned me if they thought they could get away with it. I never thought I'd ever see such hatred."

Alarmed by the sound of breaking glass, the steward knocked and entered, and Deminov violently waved him away.

"Look at this!" Malakov ranted, his voice trembling with outrage. "Caviar and white bread! A rat's nest of drunks downstairs!"

"Control your temper, Vladimir. Or make a pretty gesture. Go ahead and smash everything."

"You're a decadent man, Ivan Ivanovitch."

"I should hope so. Since the Cold War has been declared over, I have a fleet with no mission. An admiral's red stripe should be good for something, so I enjoy myself. I don't need to visit the wretched people of Archangel to know what's happening in this country. I'm neither blind nor ignorant." He spread a spoonful of black sturgeon eggs on a sliver of bread. "You should try the caviar, Vladimir. It's quite good. No point in wasting good caviar, just as there's no point in ranting at me because no one in the street hailed you as a hero."

"There's chaos in the streets," Malakov shouted. "Someone must reestablish order."

"Indeed," Deminov agreed. "Order, that's our old bugaboo, isn't it. Lenin established order, Stalin imposed order, even Brezhnev forced a corrupt order. The truth was known and all questions answered by the rigorous application of Marxist-Leninist thought. Even decadence had its place in the order of things."

Malakov poured a fresh glass of vodka and gulped it down.

"Decadence and weakness have brought us to this sorry state of affairs."

"Ah," Deminov said. "So I'm weak as well as decadent."

"Your notion of glorifying the Navy proves it," Malakov said with contempt. "Your television show backfired. People are cursing the Navy, exactly the reaction Zenko predicted."

Deminov smiled. "Yes, isn't it marvelous?"

Malakov shook his head in disbelief. "You mean, this is what you wanted?"

"Of course. I even helped the demonstrations along here and there."

"But why?" Malakov asked, still incredulous.

"Admiral Valotin has authorized Operation White Star."

Every officer in the fleet was familiar with White Star, one of dozens of military contingency plans prepared by the Defense Council. Malakov shared the common perception of White Star as a thinly disguised campaign strategy for civil war. Military convention held that a Soviet civil war would be fought between North and South. White Star was the war plan for the North, a variation of an old Soviet scheme for the invasion of Norway and Finland from the Kola Peninsula, modified to attack south instead of west. White Star mobilized the Northern Fleet for an assault on European Russia, Byelorussia, the Ukraine, and the Baltic Republics.

Phase One was the deployment of two Typhoons, one in the White Sea, another in the Barents. Should republican rebels seize atomic weapons, the Typhoons could deliver a swift and devastating response anywhere in the Soviet Union.

Phase Two gradually and secretly mobilized thirty attack submarines and sixty surface ships arrayed for land attack. Phase

Three activated the Northwest Theater of Operations, an elemental Soviet war-fighting command that unified the forces on the Kola Peninsula under the commander of the Northern Fleet. In Phase Three Admiral Deminov would take control of two parachute divisions, six motorized infantry battalions, eight tactical air wings, two strategic bomber wings and twelve regiments of spetsnaz special forces.

"Phase One of the operation goes into effect immediately," Deminov said, watching his son-in-law's reaction closely. "You, of course, will command *Sovyetskii Soyuz*."

Malakov's sullen mood began to change. For the first time he flashed his brilliant smile. "And who will command the second Typhoon?" he asked.

"Zenko," Deminov answered. "Stefan Zenko is a loyal Party member, a leader of the group that resisted the movement to disband the Political Administration. He agreed with the decision to use naval infantry from the Pacific Fleet to suppress the riots in Vladivostok. He's shown no tendencies toward favoring the republics. His refusal to stand with us on the Union makes no sense, no sense at all. Nevertheless, he will follow orders. If he does not, I'll remove him from his command."

"He's a republican," Malakov stated as if it were a fact. "Even if you remove him from his command, he'll object to White Star, and he has many powerful friends in Moscow." Malakov paused to drink another half-glass of vodka. An idea began to form in his mind. "When I studied tactics under Zenko at Frunze, he reminded us constantly that surprise is the essence of submarine combat. Surprise, silence and stealth win the day. Why don't we give Zenko a surprise?"

Deminov had been waiting for this. Arching his eyebrows, he asked, "What kind of surprise, Vladimir?"

"If I take *Sovyetskii Soyuz* to sea tonight, Zenko will be faced with a fait accompli."

"That's a bold suggestion, my boy. You'd put yourself and your ship at considerable risk. The *Soyuz* is under Zenko's command."

"And Zenko is under your command," Malakov replied smugly. "There is no risk. No one can find a Typhoon under the ice. No one."

"Isn't your crew on liberty call?" Deminov asked.

"I don't need a crew. With forty officers and mishmani I can operate the ship. Cut my orders and I'll sail tonight."

Deminov appeared to reflect and consider. "Yes," he said finally, "that would be within the scope and meaning of White Star." He reached into his pocket, removed an official Navy order form and pushed the sealed red folder across the table. "An icebreaker is waiting off Severodvinsk now."

Malakov broke out laughing. "You sly old son of a bitch."

"I should hope so," said Deminov. "Now will you eat a little caviar?"

Grinning, Malakov heaped a spoonful onto a crust of bread and savored the salty richness.

Deminov watched him for a moment and then spoke, measuring his words carefully. "We are presented with an opportunity, Vladimir."

"To get rid of Zenko?"

"To go much further than that."

"What do you mean, Ivan?"

"The Defense Council has authorized White Star, but I doubt if Valotin is prepared to push them to continue to its logical conclusion."

"Which is?"

"The elimination of all opposition to the Union and the establishment of a military government."

"A coup d'état?"

"No less," Deminov said.

"Now who's being bold?" Malakov said playfully.

"With a Typhoon, we can be as bold as we dare," Deminov said. "History is ours! With *Sovyetskii Soyuz* at sea, I can deliver an ultimatum to the president."

"And demand what?"

"That he resign and surrender power to Valotin. He will then authorize Phase Two and Phase Three of White Star, and I will be in complete control."

"What if Valotin balks?" Malakov asked.

"He'll be too dazzled by the prospect of supreme power. If he hesitates, you will launch a warning shot."

"Another dummy warhead?" Malakov asked.

Deminov slowly shook his head. "No," he said. "A war shot. A single atomic warhead."

Malakov looked pleased. "What's the target?" he asked.

"Tbilisi, Georgia. You will tell your officers the Georgians have commenced a full-scale armed rebellion, precisely the event White Star was designed to interdict."

"Atomic blackmail," Malakov said softly.

"The salvation of the Union."

For a long time Malakov stared at his father-in-law, trying to read his expressionless eyes.

"Do you have reservations, Vladimir?" Deminov asked.

Malakov didn't hesitate to answer. "Certainly, but I have only to consider what will happen if we fail to act. If I launch, I'll kill hundreds of thousands of people, but if I don't pose a credible threat to the government, millions will die in a civil war."

"That may occur anyway," Deminov said.

"So be it. History will judge us."

"No," said Deminov. "We are History. We are the judges, the two of us alone in this room, and, of course, your officers. Do you think Sergov will cooperate?"

"Without doubt. Alexi hates republicans perhaps more than we do. But one question remains. How do we deal with Zenko?"

"I'm going to Gremikha in the morning," Deminov said. "He'll have no choice but to consent to White Star. Are we agreed?"

Malakov beamed. He was being given license to fire atomic weapons. His path to glory was clearly marked. He grabbed his father-in-law's hand and shook it eagerly. "We are agreed."

12 Petya

Less than a mile south of the officers' club, Seaman Recruit Petya Bulgakov took to the streets of Archangel alone in a studded leather jacket, black t-shirt, Italian sunglasses with rose-colored lenses, Levis and his prize possession, the Leningrad look. I'm hip, Petya said to himself. I'm from Leningrad and I'm a stud and this is my worldly, cynical, drop-dead James Dean I'm cool Leningrad look.

The scattered citizens on the desolate streets scarcely gave the twenty-year-old sailor a second glance. Archangel, like all Russian cities, trembled in the twilight of the Revolution. The long journey from 1917 to perestroika had run into the blind alley of strikes, inflation, famine and the grim specter of civil war.

Indifferent to history and politics, more concerned with style than substance, Petya wanted only to catch a whiff of Afghan hash and roll over some little Katarina in a miniskirt. Trekking briskly along White Sea Boulevard, he was searching for an underground rock club called Placebo where, he had heard, the drinks were cheap, the music loud and the girls friendly.

The club moved weekly, changed its name and opened at odd hours. Tramping along the waterfront, almost ready to give up his search, Petya felt his big-city Leningrad arrogance dissolve into the forlorn shivering of a cold and lonely young sailor. To his left the ice-shrouded White Sea glowed luminescent purple.

The temperature had risen a few degrees above freezing and the ice was breaking up, filling the midnight with weird scrapes and crashes. Ten miles west, beyond the islands in the harbor, he could see the lights of the shipyard at Severodvinsk. Two and a half years would pass before his national service ended and he could grow hair again. Damn, the Navy was all right, good food, righteous brothers, but the officers, especially the political officers, made him want to puke. We must build communism! We must preserve the Union! What a load of crap. The Union was falling apart and he couldn't have cared less.

From the apex of a bridge over the mouth of the Dvina River, Petya saw a disorderly line of people a block away. The collection of longhairs and punks looked like the object of his quest. He adjusted his sunglasses, ran his hand over his closely cropped hair and cursed the Navy. In Leningrad he had worn his hair to his shoulders until the day he was conscripted. He hoped the girls wouldn't notice what the military butchers had done to his hair.

"This the line for the Placebo bar?"

"Yes, brother, but it's not called the Placebo anymore. Now it's the No Name."

Petya joined the line, which ran ten yards to the corner and turned into a narrow side street. The redheaded sister in front of him looked eighteen, dressed in nice leathers with four jeweled rings in her left ear.

"Waiting long?" Petya asked.

"A few minutes."

She looked him up and down. "Hey, brother," she said, offering Petya a cigarette, "you Navy?"

"I guess it's pretty obvious," Petya said, color flowing into his cheeks. He took the smoke and struck a match.

"I'm Petya. What's your name?"

"Melissa."

"That's not a Russian name."

"It's Greek."

"You Greek?"

"Not many Greeks in Archangel," she said with a grin. "Someday I want to go to Greece and live naked on an island."

"Is that what the Greeks do?"

"Yes."

"It must be warm there. Not like here."

"What's the name of your ship, navyman?"

"Sovyetskii Soyuz."

"Oho, an undersea man. A squid."

"How do you know one ship from another, a girl like you?"

"What do you mean, a girl like me? I work at the shipyard in Severodvinsk, for your information. Or I did, 'til we went on strike."

"You on strike?" Petya asked.

"Sure. Everybody is," said Melissa. "Power to the workers."

"You sound political, Melissa. A new restructurist."

"I am. Everybody at the No Name is."

"I'm more interested in music than politics," Petya said.

"They go together. Even Navy guys from Old Peter should know that. I like your accent."

The line moved, slowly at first, then surged around the corner. The club had opened and people were disappearing one by one into a hole in the sidewalk.

"Oh, just like Alice in Wonderland! C'mon, Petya, my little sailorman, buy me a rum and Pepsi-Cola."

Petya thought he had struck gold. Melissa took his hand and pulled him toward the subterranean entrance. Blue light and smoke drifted up from the manhole. Petya heard the seductive beat of a scratchy James Brown tape.

Cheap blue velvet covered the walls of the foyer. As they entered, an enormously fat woman in whiteface and red muu-muu handed each patron a printed flyer. Distracted by the woman's thick white stage makeup, Petya took a flyer without a glance. Then a tiny bell tinkled in his head—whiteface, white-face—that meant something but he couldn't remember what. Behind the woman, a man in whiteface and a striped jumper intoned, "Two rubles, two rubles, two rubles."

Impulsively, Petya paid for the redhead and himself, receiving a squeeze on his forearm for his generosity. They followed the queue through a curtain into a dark, damp room crowded with ghostly figures, many in whiteface. Clouds of incense billowed from a corner. James Brown continued to beat a song to death while backstage guitars tuned up. In the dim light Petya stumbled into a table, found a chair and sat down, rubbing his shin.

"Give me some money and I'll find us a drink," said Melissa.

Petya dug into his pockets, pulled out a crumpled banknote and handed it over, and the girl disappeared into the crowd. Petya's eyes adjusted to the dark and he read the flyer he had been handed at the door.

"The State Is The Enemy Of The People," he read. "The Party Is The Enemy Of The People. The Army Is The Enemy Of The People. Support The Severodvinsk Strike. Power To The People. Support The Afghan Vets Against Communist Fascism. Soldiers! Sailors! Desert! Mutiny! Refuse To Obey Orders! Kill Your Officers! Revolt! Long Live Rock And Roll! Freedom Forever!"

Shaking his head, Petya crumpled the flimsy paper and dropped it on the floor. Politics. Radical crazies in Archangel, of all places. Suddenly the whiteface makeup on so many people fell into place. Whiteface was the symbol of the Anarchist Commune, the craziest of the crazies.

The whitefaces would draw police like moths to a flame, Petya thought. He felt like bolting for the door but lost his resolve when Melissa returned with a pair of clinking glasses.

"Cuban rum and Pepsi Cola," she said, sitting down with a smile. "The all-Union drink."

"Are you a member of the Anarchist Commune?" Petya asked.

Melissa's smile remained, but her eyes turned guarded. "Why do you ask?"

Like every Russian, Petya recognized her look of fear and suspicion. "I'm not an informer," he said. "My blood is red but my heart is white."

"You're military, little sailorman."

"I sure am. It's a military labor brigade for me if I'm caught in here," Petya answered.

"Are you afraid?"

"A little."

"Well, you're honest. That's good. That's almost as good as cute. What's your opinion of the Anarchist Commune?"

"I don't know much about it. All this shit has happened while I've been in the Navy. I'm a little out of it."

"I'm not a member," Melissa said. "But two of my flatmates are. I'm thinking of joining. I'm sick of this country. I'm sick of struggling for a bowl of soup. Did you hear about the whiteface mutiny at Polyarnyy?"

"No."

"Six sailors on the aircraft carrier _Kiev_ refused to attend a compulsory political indoctrination meeting. They were charged with mutiny and showed up at their court-martial in whiteface."

"Oh, shit. What happened to them?"

"Nobody knows. I don't think it matters. There'll be more and more. All you guys in the military will have to decide for yourselves. Whose side are you on? Are you Soviets? Are you Russians? Or are you human beings with allegiance to humanity and the planet? The guys from the _Kiev_ made their choice, and they were only the first."

Jesus Christ, thought Petya, I'm being proselytized. What the hell, that must be the price of love. "I'd like to meet your flatmates," he said.

"I can read your mind, navyman," Melissa said with a coquettish smile. "Drink your drink."

With a crash of drums the stage curtains opened and the band roared into a rock and roll whirlwind. One of the guitar players stepped to the microphone and screamed, "Hit them, hit them, hit them where they hurt!" Bodies hurled onto the floor, knocking over tables and chairs and bouncing off one another like bumper cars.

"What the hell is this?" Petya asked.

"I can't hear you," Melissa shouted, her eyes glistening. She leaned over and yelled in his ear. "This dance is called the New Revolution. It's fantastic. Let's do it."

She jumped to her feet and began gyrating wildly, hand in the air, pelvis rotating, legs kicking toward the ceiling. Petya started doing the Leningrad shuffle, moving his feet and whirling his arms like a windmill. Melissa slammed into a young woman in whiteface and they sprawled together to the floor, laughing with delirious glee. The band jumped crazily around the low stage, knocking into one another. Blue sparks fizzled from one of the amps and a guitar died in electric blue flame. The musician began smashing his instrument into the blown amp. Feeling like a kid in a sandbox free-for-all, Petya let himself go, his intoxication rising with every bump and bash. He lost sight of Melissa, then seemed to lose himself.

"Hit them, hit them, hit them where they . . ."

The power abruptly died. For a moment the singer continued to scream. The drummer, standing on his stool kicking a cymbal, looked around, confused, his foot in midair, and keeled over. There were cries, catcalls, then silence.

Petya, who had caught a glimpse of Melissa on the far side of the floor, turned toward the entrance and saw police uniforms. A militia captain in jackboots raised his eyes from the political flyer and surveyed the room. "Segregate the ones in whiteface and take them to Central," he said loudly. "Take the others to Station Fourteen. All right, you scum. Line up. Let's see ID cards."

The captain moved down the untidy line examining IDs. When he came to Petya, he said, "What have we here?"

"Seaman recruit," Petya mumbled.

The captain studied Petya's Navy card. "Says here you're on *Sovyetskii Soyuz*. That ship's over at Severodvinsk, isn't it?"

"Yes, sir."

"I heard Vadim Sorokin was assigned to that ship."

"Mishman Sorokin? Yes, sir. He's my boss."

"You wouldn't lie to me, boy."

"No, sir."

The policeman put his arm around Petya's shoulders and drew him out of the line.

"What the hell are you doing in an anarchist's club?"

"I'm just trying to get laid," Petya said. "I didn't know what it was."

"Bullshit. You're not a rube, not with that accent."

"I swear, Captain. I'm not a political."

"Sit down and be quiet. Any of your shipmates in here?"

"I haven't recognized anyone."

"All right. I'll call Sorokin. If he vouches for you, maybe we can work this out. Got any money?"

"Not much. Fifty rubles maybe."

"That's a lot for a sailorman. Maybe you do work for Sorokin. Sit tight."

The captain turned back to the room. "Sergeant, call the wagon. Get these people out of here. Someone find me a telephone that works."

Aboard *Sovyetskii Soyuz* Sorokin stepped onto the deck for his nightly jog. The ship's brief cruise under the ice had left slashing scars in the hull. Dents and patches of mottled white streaked the flat grey paint. *Sovyetskii Soyuz* bore no numbers, no name, no marking of any kind.

Overhead, a pair of huge cranes loomed above the sub. Above the cranes the roof replaced the sky. Sorokin didn't miss the stars. Unlike surface sailors, he rarely glanced at the constellations. What he missed were the sounds of the shipyard's graveyard shift, the clanging of metal, the roar of welders' torches, the shouts of men at work. The laboring masses of Severodvinsk had forsaken the sacred duty of building communism and had shut down the shipyard. Sorokin didn't blame them. Forced to work double shifts, faced with crippling inflation and price increases, thousands had refused to report for work. The silence reminded him of a cemetery, the graveyard of communism, he mused to himself. Sorokin thought of himself as neither a communist nor anticommunist, but rather uncommunist. He was an arctic sailorman, a patriot of the ice.

"Sorokin!" Political Officer Sergov, on duty in the command center, was shouting through the open hatch.

"Yo!"

"You know a militiaman named Zharzharskiev over in Archangel?"

"Yeah, I know him."

"He wants you on the phone."

Sorokin dropped through the hatch into the command center and took the phone.

"Mishman Sorokin speaking."

"Hello, Vadim. Roman Zharzharskiev here. Can you drive over here right away?"

"It's two o'clock in the morning."

"I have one of your men here, Bulgakov. I think you'd better come get him before the military police find out he's here."

"You're a good man, Roman. I'll be there in an hour. Give me the address and I'll see if I can find a vehicle."

Sorokin hung up. "I have to go into Archangel and retrieve a wayward squid," he said to Sergov.

The political officer looked at his watch and said, "Be back in two hours, no more."

13

Minski

A light shower pelted Malakov as he waited outside the officers' club for his car. He captured a few drops, licked his palm and tasted the rain. The car arrived and he climbed into the backseat.

Twenty kilometers of bad road separated Archangel from the shipyard. April had been unseasonably warm and the highway, frozen solid since October, had been transformed into a nasty, rutted river of mud. Twice the car got stuck, but Malakov ignored his cursing driver.

The enormity of what he had agreed to do had been swept away by the myriad of operational details. Over borscht in the private room at the officers' club, Malakov, Deminov and Colonel Ludinov had refined their plan. To ensure the secrecy of the operation, Colonel Ludinov was to follow in an hour with a platoon of spetsnaz special forces to secure the shipyard and sequester crew members left behind when *Sovyetskii Soyuz* sailed. Thirty-six hours later, Deminov would present his ultimatum to the Kremlin, giving the government twelve hours to respond. Ideally, the result would be a bloodless coup. After the resignation of the government, if the republicans rebelled, the full force of Operation White Star would be brought to bear. If rebels seized atomic weapons, Malakov could strike any appropriate target.

But what if, despite his protestations to the contrary, Malakov's officers refused to launch, or even mutinied? What if something happened to Deminov? No plan was foolproof, but a great cause requires great risk. If the plot failed, he would be shot. If it succeeded, he would take his rightful place in the pantheon of Soviet heroes.

As the car approached the shipyard, a battered old truck emerged from the gate and roared down the road toward Archangel. Malakov caught a fleeting glimpse of Sorokin at the wheel. "Was that one of my men who just passed through?" he asked the sentry at the gate.

"Yes, sir. I believe so."

"How many sailors have gone into town?"

"Maybe seventy, eighty. A dozen have come back."

"Drunk?"

"Fucked up beyond all recognition, Captain."

"All right," said Malakov. "Assemble your entire unit of naval infantry here at the gate and wait for Colonel Ludinov from GRU to arrive. He'll identify himself and give you further orders."

"Aye aye, sir."

The infantryman blew his whistle and shouted toward the shed where his mates huddled out of the rain.

The car dropped Malakov at the foot of the quay. Tiny wavelets lapped at concrete pilings and a light sheen of oil shimmered on the water. *Sovyetskii Soyuz* lay against the pier like a sleeping giant.

Assistant Quartermaster Plesharski stood at the foot of the accommodation ladder, an assault rifle slung over his shoulder.

"Evenin', Captain."

"Having a quiet night, Mishman?"

"It's like a tomb in here, sir."

"Where's Sorokin off to?"

"Collecting a squid from the militia."

"I see. In that case, Plesharski, I appoint you acting quartermaster of *Sovyetskii Soyuz*."

Startled, Plesharski stiffened to attention and saluted. "Thank you, sir."

"Quartermaster, prepare to make way in one hour."

"One hour, sir?"

Malakov gave Plesharski a look that would stop sharks in a feeding frenzy.

"Yes, sir. Aye aye, sir."

Malakov went aboard. In the command center he found Sergov with dossiers spread over the navigation table.

"Alexi?"

"Hello, Vladimir. How was dinner?"

"The club has an excellent cook. Come to my quarters. It's going to be a long night."

In his cabin Malakov hung up his tunic and cap, unlocked an old wooden cabinet, a present from Katarina, and pulled out a bottle of pepper vodka.

"Drink, Alexi?"

"Only if it's a large."

"Right."

Malakov poured pale pink fluid into a pair of tall glasses. "What shall we drink to?" he asked, flashing a smile. "The honorable Stefan Zenko?"

Sergov snorted. "I'll eat pigshit before I do that."

Malakov raised his glass. "To the Union," he said.

"To the Union," Sergov repeated solemnly.

"We should get drunk, Alexi," Malakov said. "Just you and I like good sailormen, right here in the captain's cabin of *Sovyetskii Soyuz*."

"I'm for that," said Sergov, reaching eagerly for the bottle.

"But instead, we're going to sea."

"What? Now?"

"Yes. Right now. We're shoving off."

Malakov handed Sergov the orders signed by Deminov and Valotin. Leaning on his elbows, Sergov carefully studied the documents. "So, the Defense Council has finally come to its senses. This is something that should've been done years ago," he said.

"Then you agree that these are legal orders?"

"Since they're not signed by Zenko, no, not legal, but valid orders, which I'll obey," Sergov said, making a fine distinction. "Such drastic action is absolutely necessary, otherwise the Revolution is lost forever and communism dies, the Union dies, our lives become meaningless and worthless. This way, we derail the republican train before it gets rolling."

"Then let's drink. To *Sovyetskii Soyuz*, the Soviet Union."

They drained their glasses and Malakov locked the bottle in the wooden cabinet. "Are the officers and mishmani on board?"

"All except Sorokin."

"Good. To hell with Sorokin. We're better off without him."

"What about the crew?" Sergov asked.

Malakov looked at his watch. "The local militia has orders to round them up and keep them under wraps until the operation is over."

Sovyetskii Soyuz had been in port only fourteen hours and was ready to make steam without delay. Throughout the sub forty-three men, more than enough to stand watches and sail the automated ship, turned dials and studied gauges.

Malakov ordered Quartermaster Plesharski to lay in a course for Kandalakshskiy Gulf, the deepest part of the White Sea. As Plesharski set to work on the computer, Seaman Recruit Typov wandered into the command center and stood near the navigation table rubbing sleep from his eyes.

"What the hell are you doing here?" Plesharski demanded. "You're not supposed to be on the ship."

"I didn't want to go into town and I came back to get something to eat. I guess I fell asleep. Where's Comrade Boss?"

"Guess he took the wrong night off," Plesharski answered.

"Why're we leaving in such a hurry? Where's the crew?"

"Shut up, Typov," Plesharski snarled. "You're here, so just keep out of the way."

"Why didn't the captain post our orders?"

"Sometimes he does, sometimes he doesn't."

"Is there a crisis? Did something happen? Are we at war?"

"Shut up, shut up, shut up."

Shore power was disconnected, bow and stern lines cast off, hatches sealed. Colonel Ludinov stood on the quay surrounded by black-uniformed spetsnaz commandos. Special forces now manned the shipyard gates and were arresting any sailors who wandered in.

The captain of a small icebreaker radioed that he was in position. On the bridge Malakov squared away his fur hat. "Give me steam," he ordered. "All ahead slow."

Twin propellers churned the water and the great sub moved. The space between the ship and the pier widened and *Sovyetskii Soyuz* steamed away from the covered dock. In the gentle rain Archangel's halo glowed under the wispy clouds, softening the hard edge of Soviet Russia.

"Radar to bridge. Icebreaker dead ahead, Captain. Range five hundred meters."

Malakov stared through binoculars at the half-meter-thick ice. The icebreaker smashed ahead, breaking the ice into huge floes. The irregular surface shifted and bobbed.

"Flood stern tanks."

"Flood stern tanks, aye!"

Water vented into the stern tanks and *Sovyetskii Soyuz's* bow rose higher, just enough for the nose to skid over the edge of the first ice floe. Then thirty thousand tons of steel exploded the floe. A massive shudder rolled through the hull from bow to stern. The downward motion stopped and buoyancy forced the bow to rise again and splinter the next floe from underneath. *Sovyetskii Soyuz* smashed out of Archangel like a submersible atomic icebreaker.

The hull was tough, but hydrophones embedded in the steel around the bow were delicate. Malakov knew that each collision with the ice threatened the sub's vital ability to hear underwater, but this was no time for timidity. He felt as if he was riding a bucking whale. The lookouts clipped safety lines to the rails and hung on for their lives.

Three kilometers from shore the bottom dropped away, giving Malakov sufficient depth to submerge under the ice. He sent the lookouts below, sealed the hatch and descended into the command center.

"Command to sonar, damage report."

"This is sonar. We knocked out two side-array hydrophones but the main dome is undamaged."

"Diving Officer, damage report."

"A few dents on the outer hull, Captain."

"Depth under the kneel."

"Twenty-seven meters."

"Take her down."

With one last bump of her sail on the ice, *Sovyetskii Soyuz* submerged.

The command center was quiet and tense. Malakov switched on the intercom. "Men of *Sovyetskii Soyuz*," he said. "We have been given a secret mission by direct order from Admiral De-minov, commander of the Northern Fleet and the Northwest Theater of Operations. A full-scale rebellion by anti-Soviet forces is imminent. Nationalist rebels in the republic of Georgia have seized the city of Tbilisi. Loyal Soviet citizens have been ordered to evacuate. The Union will no longer tolerate the de-structive, separatist tendencies that have been racking our na-tion. Within forty-eight hours we will know if we will be called upon to do our duty to preserve the Union. That is all."

"I don't understand," Typov whispered to Plesharski. "What duty?"

Plesharski desperately missed Sorokin. Comrade Boss would know what to say, what to do. "This is a Typhoon, Typov," he said. "Our duty is to launch atomic rockets."

An hour out of Archangel Malakov assembled the officers in the Lenin Room. When Lieutenant Minski squeezed through the door, Political Officer Sergov was passing out glasses of tea.

Malakov cleared his throat. "As you know, gentlemen," he said, "the Union is in great danger. As loyal officers our duty is to prevent an attack on the Soviet Union from any quarter. To that end the uncompromising commander of the Northern Fleet, Admiral Deminov, has prepared a plan to deal with an uprising. Captain Sergov, hand out the documents, if you please."

Sergov distributed copies of a single page stamped "Secret" and labeled "Operation White Star."

"Read the document," Malakov ordered, "sign the security restriction statement at the bottom and return your copies to Captain Sergov."

Minski quickly skimmed through the paragraphs, which he recognized as a highly edited version of a much longer set of operational orders. He felt disheartened but not surprised by what he read. According to the edited sheet, *Sovyetskii Soyuz* was putting to sea as part of Phase One of Operation White Star. But the young rocket officer thought Operation White Star with its massive deployment of forces looked like something more than a plan for the suppression of rebellion in a distant republic. The single-warhead rocket in Silo Six was to be retargeted for the city of Tbilisi. To Minski, threatening the capital of Georgia with an SS-N-20 seemed like smashing a gnat with a hammer.

He signed his copy and returned it to Sergov. "The document seems to lack an analysis of opposing forces," he commented.

"Correct," Sergov said. "White Star is a contingency plan. The assumption is that mutinous army and militia units may fall under republican control. The rebels may seize strategic centers and perhaps atomic weapons. We're not concerned with mere riots in the streets, but with a full-scale rebellion by military forces. To be frank, not all our forces are as loyal as the Northern Fleet."

"I see," Minski said. "Thank you, Comrade Political Officer."

Discussion of the plan continued until morning. The officers from the Grey Ghost squadron were respectful of authority and accustomed to following orders. No one seemed alarmed or surprised. Minski, however, remained mute, his suspicions unvoiced. Unanswered questions gnawed at his mind. What if the Georgians refused to lay down their arms? What if *Sovyetskii Soyuz* actually received orders to launch atomic rockets at the rebellious republic? Who would give the order? Not Zenko, he was certain of that. There was no love lost between Zenko and Deminov, whose signature was on the orders. Was this a power struggle between Zenko and Deminov? Had Deminov ordered *Sovyetskii Soyuz* to sea as part of a secret plan to wrest control of the Typhoons away from Zenko? He had no answer to those questions, but Minski was positive of one thing: If the order came to launch, Malakov would devastate Tbilisi without batting an eye. But why? What would be the purpose of such a monstrously evil act?

As *Sovyetskii Soyuz* steamed northwest through the White Sea toward Kandalakshskiy Gulf, Minski felt a growing horror at the nature of her mission. How, in the name of all that was good and holy, could she be stopped?

14 Zharzharskiev

On the muddy road to Archangel Sorokin pulled the leather tank commander's cap tight over his ears and pushed ahead. Approaching the suburbs of Archangel, he manhandled the truck around potholes and broken concrete and over a narrow bridge. To his left the melting ice of the White Sea rumbled like distant cannon. To his right a pine forest drifted away into the Russian heartland. Ahead, the city glowed blue-white like a giant reactor whose heat had initiated the spring thaw.

Ordinarily even-tempered, Sorokin crashed gears and cursed the road, the battered old truck, the Navy, the wicked city of Archangel and most of all, Petya Bulgakov, who had gotten himself arrested by the militia. Zharzharskiev had not told him what Petya had done. The kid was only twenty but seemed to have what passed for brains in the Navy. Sorokin thought Little Petya might have the makings of a submariner if he learned to keep out of trouble.

He crossed a second bridge over the main fork of the Dvina River and entered the city proper. Twelve-story apartment buildings lined the streets. Blockhouses, thought Sorokin, prefab icebergs for the masses. He despised Archangel and all cities. People spent twenty hours a week waiting in line for bread and shoes. Imagine! The only escape was to go to sea.

He found the address he was looking for and descended into

the subterranean nightclub. The black marias had come and gone, and all that remained of the No Name Bar was the lingering odor of incense and hashish. In a back room a subdued and scared Petya Bulgakov drank hot tea with Captain Zharzharskiev.

"What did he do?" Sorokin asked the militiaman.

"This is one of those roving whiteface clubs. He says he didn't know what it was when he came in. Is he a political?"

"No, he's just a wise-ass kid. Here." Sorokin peeled off fifty rubles.

"Thanks, Vadim. How's Navy life?"

"Same as when you were in, I expect. How's things with you?"

"The usual, only worse," said the militiaman with a wide smile. "The strike has things screwed up, but strike or no strike, people will steal and swindle and run illegal clubs. Nothing changes."

"I know what you mean." Sorokin turned to Bulgakov. "What do you have to say for yourself, you little prick?"

"Sorry, Boss."

"Sorry boss, sorry boss. You could be in real trouble here, boy. You're one lucky squid. Let's go."

"Wait a minute, Vadim." Zharzharskiev took Sorokin aside and said quietly, "Orders have just come through to detain all crewmen from *Sovyetskii Soyuz*."

"Why? What's up?" Sorokin asked.

"I don't know. My dispatcher said the orders came from the GRU unit at Air Wing Archangel."

"Oh, shit. You gonna take us in?"

Roman Zharzharskiev had spent ten years in the Navy, the last two on *Taifun* with Sorokin. As shipmates, they had drunk, gambled and whored together like millionaires.

"Once a squid, always a squid," Sorokin said.

"Okay," said the militiaman. "I never saw you. Get outta here and be careful. You got civilian ID?"

"No. Even if I did, I look like a recruiting poster."

"Right," said Zharzharskiev, reconsidering. "Look, I'd better drive you back to the ship. Otherwise, you'll never make it."

"You sure?"

"Yeah. Let's go."

The militiaman hustled the two sailors outside to a Lada police cruiser.

"What's happening, Comrade Boss?" Bulgakov asked.

"A free ride home," Sorokin answered, turning to face Bulgakov, who settled in the backseat. "You cost me fifty rubles. You owe me."

The rain finally stopped. On the way to Severodvinsk Sorokin and Zharzharskiev talked over old times and new times. Zharzharskiev had started a family and settled down.

"Not me," said Sorokin. "I'm a blue-water bum."

"You and Zenko, that old fart," Zharzharskiev said with a laugh.

"He got married," Sorokin said.

"You're kidding."

"To a woman twenty years younger than him. A doctor."

"Some guys are just born lucky," Zharzharskiev said. Then he asked, "How's the new guy, Malakov? Isn't he your captain now?"

Sorokin nodded. "He may be a first-class sailor, but he's one hard-nosed son of a bitch. I think he loves the rockets in a rocket sub a little too much."

"One of those, hey? An itchy trigger finger? How'd he get past Zenko?"

"He married Deminov's daughter. Connections, man, that's the passport to command of a Typhoon."

As they approached the shipyard, two trucks loaded with commandos passed going in the opposite direction.

"Spetsnaz!" Zharzharskiev exclaimed. "Jesus."

"I don't like the looks of this," Sorokin said, turning to watch the trucks roll off into the distance. "Something's wrong here. Is there another way into the shipyard?"

"Yeah," said Zharzharskiev. "I'll show you."

From the backseat Bulgakov whined, "Will one of you guys tell me what's going on?"

"We don't know yet," Sorokin told him.

The road curved around the shipyard's shop buildings. A half-mile from the main gate and out of sight of the sentries, Zharzharskiev stopped the car and asked Sorokin, "You want to slip in there and take a look?"

"Give me ten minutes. C'mon, Little Petya. Come with me and don't make a sound."

The two sailors slipped through a gap in the fence and tramped across the darkened shipyard, past deserted shops and stacks of huge brass ship propellers. As they approached the enlisted men's barracks, Sorokin's ears picked up a strange quiet. On liberty the squids should have been making a drunken racket. Crouching behind a shed, he put his finger to his lips and whispered to Bulgakov, "Stay here out of sight and be quiet."

Sorokin circled behind the barracks and peeked around the corner. He could see through the open-ended covered dock to the quay where *Sovyetskii Soyuz* had been moored. A thick hawser dangled off the quay into the water. The ship was gone. Among the spetsnaz commandos lounging on the dock, Sorokin recognized Colonel Ludinov from fleet security.

A minute later he collected Bulgakov and returned to the hole in the fence. Looking through, they saw Zharzharskiev talking to a spetsnaz officer. When the officer got into a truck and drove away, Sorokin pushed Bulgakov through the fence and into the police car.

"What did that guy have to say?" Sorokin asked.

"Not much, only that any squids who turn up are to be taken to Air Wing Archangel. He didn't say why."

"I'll tell you why," Sorokin said. "The ship is gone, man, disappeared. My guess is they want the crew locked up so no one will know."

"The Navy does shit like this all the time," Zharzharskiev said with a shrug. "So what?"

"Just get me to a long-distance phone," Sorokin said, then asked, "Does your department have a plane?"

"A plane! What the hell for?"

"How much is a ticket to Gremikha?" Sorokin asked.

"I can't do that. You're crazy. That's restricted airspace, Sorokin. They shoot down anything that comes close."

"If I fix it with air traffic control on the base, can you arrange it on the quiet?"

"Oh, man, you're asking a lot."

"Look, old pal, Captain First Rank Vladimir Malakov just

sailed in a Typhoon loaded with ballistic rockets. You understand? Spetsnaz assholes are crawling all over the shipyard. I don't know who's involved or what it means, but I do know one thing. I have to get back to Gremikha and tell Zenko."

Zharzharskiev took a deep breath and let it out. "Okay," he said. "We can use the phone at my substation."

Zharzharskiev pulled into the rear of the small police station. Inside, three militiamen in wet uniforms and muddy boots drank tea and smoked cigarettes.

"Hey, Zharzharskiev, what ya got there?"

"Squids," Zharzharskiev said. "Ain't it great doing the Navy's dirty work? I'm taking these two into my office for interrogation."

Zharzharskiev shut out the sounds of vulgar laughter, telephones and teletypes and pointed at the bank of phones on his desk.

"The green phone is a direct line to the long-distance operator in Archangel," he said. "Be careful, it's an open line."

Sorokin retrieved a slip of paper from his pocket. When he picked up the phone, an operator came on immediately and Sorokin read off the long number. Miraculously, after two rings he heard, "Secure communications."

Sorokin said, "Give me 75-43-22. Authorization 2BC."

"Wait one."

For a moment Sorokin heard nothing but static, then a series of clicks, then a voice said, "Riziov."

"Sorokin here."

"Hey, Vadim. Where the hell are you?"

"Archangel."

"Lucky boy."

"Listen, Boris, I want to come home. I have a sick sailor here, a seaman recruit."

"For Christ's sake, put him in the hospital there."

"Boris, I want to come home."

After a long pause Riziov finally said, "I see."

"Good," Sorokin said. "I have what I need at my end if you can clear it with air traffic control."

"Yeah, sure."

"I'll give you the numbers."

When Sorokin hung up, Zharzharskiev said, "Let me make a call."

Forty-five minutes later Sorokin and Bulgakov crossed the tarmac at Archangel Municipal Airport to a Navy surplus twin-engined Seagull flying boat. The plane belonged to the regional militia but was painted Coast Guard colors.

The pilot was another old Navy hand. Without a word Sorokin peeled off two hundred rubles from his roll and stuck the bills in the man's breast pocket.

"You sure you got the clearance codes?" the man asked.

"Yeah, I got 'em."

"They damn well better work. You must be somebody pretty special to get clearance to fly into Gremikha."

"We're just a couple sailormen trying to get home," Sorokin said.

With a roar of turboprops the plane taxied toward the runway. Sorokin looked back but Zharzharskiev was already gone.

"You don't get airsick, do you, Little Petya?"

"I don't know. I never been in a plane before."

The pilot took off. Far to the east a faint line of dawn appeared, but in the west the White Sea was as black as the night above. Sorokin stared down at the ice and thought of the malignant force hiding under the surface. Malakov, he thought, you bastard. You stole my ship.

Within an hour the plane entered Gremikha's airspace. The pilot picked up a microphone, gave the clearance codes he had obtained from Zharzharskiev and received permission to land.

Bulgakov pressed his nose against a window and announced excitedly that he could see harbor lights. Hemmed in by the dark Barents on one side and the darker Kola Peninsula on the other, the naval station glowed in the blackness.

Sorokin laughed. "Be glad you're not seeing flak, Little Petya," he said.

The pilot pushed on the steering yoke and the Seagull descended toward the cliffs of Gremikha.

15 A Hole in the Water

Forty miles northeast of Gremikha, *Reno* crept just below the ice canopy seeking a place to hide. So much tension permeated the control room that Gunner thought the bulkheads would start to sweat. "Are we going to find an ice keel?" he asked Trout. "Or is Ivan going to find us first?"

"Don't even think like that, Kemo Sabe," Trout replied. "We're in Soviet waters as deep as we can go."

In the radio room the VLF teletype began to print.

"Radio to control. Receiving VLF transmission."

"Very well, radio. I'll be right in." He turned to Trout. "Call me if you find an ice keel."

Gunner locked himself in the crypto room and decoded the message.

```
TO CO USS RENO: SOVNAV HAS
REDEPLOYED A TYPHOON IN THE WHITE
SEA. INCREASED ACTIVITY AT POLYARNYY
AND MURMANSK. TWO SSN AKULAS SAILED
0600 GMT THIS DATE. MORE DEPLOYMENTS
EXPECTED. ENTRY INTO WHITE SEA
AUTHORIZED AT YOUR DISCRETION.
CINCLANT SENDS.
```

At your discretion. In other words, commanding officer, USS *Reno*, if another Typhoon comes out of Gremikha and goes into the White Sea, stick to his tail like glue and follow him in.

The White Sea. Putting *Reno* into a shipping lane to Archangel was like a Soviet sub sneaking into Puget Sound, as aggressive a provocation as Gunner could imagine. As an exercise in dangerous tactics, tracking a Typhoon into the White Sea posed interesting problems. U.S. Navy VLF and ELF communications couldn't penetrate the White Sea. If he took *Reno* in, Gunner would be incommunicado unless he surfaced through the ice. Even though he spoke Russian, he couldn't pretend to be a fishing boat in the middle of a frozen sea. And what would happen if *Reno* were discovered? At the moment, when tensions were rising in the Soviet Union, an incursion into Soviet waters could be a fiasco. He could create the *Pueblo* disaster and KAL Flight 007 rolled into one.

Gunner reentered the control room and handed the message to Trout, who quickly scanned the typed sheet. "Christ almighty," Trout said. "Looks like we can go deeper."

"Looks like," Gunner said, putting on a headset. A moment later he heard, "Sonar to control. Double ice keel dead ahead, range one thousand yards."

"All stop," Gunner ordered.

On the sonar repeater the image of the double ice keel looked like two prongs of a fork forty feet apart hanging eighty feet into the sea.

"What do you think, Gus?"

"We can hide in there for days," Trout said. "There's six feet of ice above and a quarter-knot current running south. Looks good to me."

Gunner nodded in agreement. "All ahead dead slow on propulsors for five seconds," he ordered.

Reno crept forward until her bow poked between the two jagged submerged icicles and the boat came to a stop.

"Secure propulsors."

"Secure propulsors, aye."

"Reduce reactor to twenty percent."

The command was relayed to the maneuvering room in a quiet whisper. Chief Adams pushed the control rods deeper into the reactor core, reducing power and noise from the nuclear power plant.

"Bleed trim tanks," Gunner said. "Easy now."

Trout punched buttons on the diving panel and compressed air slowly bled into all _Reno_'s trim tanks simultaneously. The boat rose until the sail gently bumped the underside of the ice.

"Securing trim tanks," said Trout.

"Pass the word," Gunner said. "We might sit here for days. No metal, no nothin'. We're a hole in the water and we'll keep it that way. Take the conn. I'll be in my rack."

Gunner had slept little during the voyage. At odd hours he snatched catnaps, but his dreams were still interrupted by visions of lethal blue lights. Instead of sleeping, he sat at his tiny desk studying maps and charts. He believed no sonar yet built could detect _Reno_ sitting dead quiet between two ice keels, yet the captain was bathed in sweat. He was a spy and his submarine a spy-ship. In war, hot or cold, spies are shot.

Reno hunkered in silence forty miles off the coast of the remote Kola Peninsula, a thumb on the hand of Scandinavia. The size of West Virginia, a rugged landscape of low mountains, frozen lakes, salmon-rich rivers and permafrost, the Kola extends from the Soviet Union's borders with Finland and Norway three hundred miles southeast to the White Sea.

During the Cold War the Northern Fleet, headquartered at Polyarnyy near Murmansk, had been built into a force of three hundred ships including over one hundred nuclear subs. To protect the fleet, by the late 1980s the Kola Peninsula had been transformed into the most heavily militarized region in the Soviet Union. The original population of reindeer and nomadic Lapps had been ruthlessly displaced by hundreds of thousands of ethnic Russian troops, many of whom were transferred from former Warsaw Pact bases. Radiating south and east from Murmansk a vast complex of air bases, naval ports, army posts, missile batteries, radar stations and communication networks guarded the USSR's vulnerable northern flank.

Most important were the ballistic missile submarine bases, the core of Soviet strategic defense. Two hundred miles southeast of Murmansk lay the jewel of the Kola complex, the Typhoon base at Gremikha. Billions of rubles, millions of man-hours, and an entire fleet had been established for the single purpose of preventing American subs from doing exactly what Gunner had done. *Reno* now lurked deep inside the forbidden zone. Any miscalculation or error of judgment could result in a sunken ship and 110 dead men, no questions asked.

Hunched over his desk, Gunner examined satellite photos of Gremikha Naval Station, a jumble of low-rise buildings, radar arrays, antiaircraft missile batteries, an airfield with hardened hangars for antisubmarine helicopters, a huge radio transmission complex, but no subs. The Typhoons, and all their awesome ordnance, were underground, hidden in a cavity blasted into the sheer granite cliffs.

Without leaving Gremikha's small harbor, a Typhoon could fire long-range missiles that could obliterate North America. With no need to range far from home, Typhoons hugged the coast under the ice, invisible to satellites and away from the prying sonars of NATO antisubmarine aircraft flying out of Norway. Normally, a pair of Akula class attack subs escorted a Typhoon on patrol, creating a submerged task force of immense firepower. Typhoons used the ice and the security of the White Sea the way American trident missile subs used the vastness of the Atlantic and Pacific to conceal their movements. Under the ice within the easily protected White Sea, Typhoons were virtually invulnerable to anything except a massive nuclear attack or a silent, stealthy hunter-killer in the hands of a daring pirate.

As a warm-blooded Californian, Gunner had to bend his mind to comprehend what the arctic meant to the Russians. To them the frozen north was neither remote nor obscure. It was their backyard, the source of boundless riches as well as centuries of frustration. Ironically, the event that catapulted the Russians toward the conquest of the Arctic Ocean had been provided by the U.S. Navy. When *Nautilus* first steamed under the North Pole, the Soviet Admiralty quickly understood that nuclear submarines were the key to arctic navigation, but it took the vision and determination of a single man to build a squadron of giant ice-subs. The Typhoons were the brainchild of the legendary commander of Naval Station Gremikha, Vice Admiral Stefan Zenko.

Gunner had read Zenko's dossier so many times he had memorized the details. After a brilliant career at the Frunze Higher Naval War College, Zenko had joined the Red Navy's submarine service at age twenty in 1962. Two decades later *Taifun* slipped down the ways at Severodvinsk. During the next few years five more colossal subs were built, and construction of Naval Station Gremikha was completed in 1989.

Mentally reviewing Zenko's history, Gunner searched for a clue to the man behind this formidable achievement. What kind of man was Stefan Zenko? Gunner knew he was a short, rather pudgy little guy with bad teeth who drank French brandy by the gallon. In 1978 he had commanded a Yankee class missile boat that suffered an engine-room casualty and surfaced thirty miles outside the American submarine base at Charleston, South Carolina. The U.S. Navy had never known he was there until he popped up like a sea monster. While his boat was being towed across the Atlantic, Zenko broadcast a continuous stream of American pop music he had recorded while sitting off the Carolina coast. He seemed to have a unique combination of humor and audacity which Gunner admired. If the Cold War truly ended, if the Soviet Union did not explode into murderous agony, if the world still contained a glimmer of sanity and justice, Gunner would like to buy Zenko a drink, maybe more than one, and talk all night of subs and ice and dreams.

But now, as always, reality interfered with wishful thinking. The latest satellite photo of Gremikha showed twenty miles of open water between the coast and the marginal ice zone. Should a Typhoon emerge from Gremikha and head north into the Barents, Gunner had a chance to stay on her tail. But if the Soviet boat went south through the Gorlo Strait into the White Sea, how could *Reno* follow? On regular patrols icebreakers preceded Typhoons through the strait. To follow, Gunner would risk bumping *Reno* on dangerous floes. Moreover, in the narrow, shallow waters, Soviet sonar barriers were certain to be effective. *Reno* was the quietest boat in the water, but was she quiet enough? Skill would take him only so far. He would have to sneak in like a thief and trust to luck.

Once through the strait, he believed, he could successfully follow a Typhoon in the White Sea, but in the next thirty days much of the ice would melt and antisubmarine frigates would begin to patrol. What would he do if the Russians detected *Reno* in their waters? He couldn't shoot his way out. He would have to surface and say, "Well done," a hell of a way to end his career. Was that what the Navy wanted? Was he just a spy or had he been sent on a kamikaze mission to provoke the Russians and prolong the Cold War? He was a good officer, a competent master of his ship but nonetheless as much a pawn in the grand scheme of things as the newest recruit.

Gunner had no reason to believe the giant Typhoons and their missiles threatened the United States. They were merely there, like Everest, like the moon, like America's own Tridents, and he was certain the Russians no longer possessed the will to use them against the West. The last act of the Cold War was shaping up exactly like every preceding act, a nuclear standoff by posturing giants.

He lay down on his bunk. Tossing and turning, he closed his eyes and tried to sleep but once again was tormented by blue lights. Like a machine that couldn't be turned off, his mind played out one scenario after another.

Suddenly, the telephone light flashed in urgent silence. Gunner shook his head clear of jumbled thoughts and picked it up.

"Gunner."

"Trout here, Skipper. Sonar reports a submerged contact."

"How close?"

"Approximately thirty miles, bearing two six nine, speed six knots, depth two hundred feet, course one two six."

"Identification?"

"Not yet, but it's not a Typhoon."

Gunner stuck a cigarette in his mouth. "Tell sonar I'm on my way down," he said. "Get Morrison in there, and order absolute silence in the boat. Nobody breathe."

In three minutes Gunner was in the sonar room leaning over the operators and their screens. Chief Morrison was right behind him, rubbing sleep from his eyes.

"What do you think, Chief?"

"I just got here, Skipper. I gotta listen to him."

Morrison put on a headset and stared at the screen. "Okay," he said, "we've got an icebreaker heading south toward the Gorlo Strait with a convoy of three ships." He punched several buttons on his console and filtered out the surface shipping noises. "And we have a sub running quiet but I can hear him. He's quiet, but not that quiet. See, there he is on the screen, a steady line."

"Computer is working on his signature," Stewart said. "Akula class, Skipper, possibly _Gorky_, possibly _Odessa_."

Stewart's screen filled with data on the two Soviet attack subs, _Gorky_ and _Odessa_, specs, histories, records of known contacts, position in order of battle, and commanding officers.

"_Akula_ means shark," Morrison said, "and that's what we got, Skipper, a real hunter-killer, just like us."

"What's he hunting, Chief?"

"Dunno, but we're a hole in the water. I don't think he's after us."

"Stay on him, Chief. I'll be talking to you."

Gunner hurried to the control room, relieved Trout of the conn and together they watched the sonar repeater. Submerged, the Akula stayed in the ice-ridden southbound shipping lane from Murmansk as she headed toward the Gremikha roadstead.

"Is he part of a Typhoon escort?" Trout asked. "Or is he looking for us?"

Gunner shook his head. "He doesn't know we're here."

"You're sure he hasn't detected us?"

"Yes," said Gunner. "If he knew, he'd come at us full bore. I think he's doing exactly what we're doing, lying off Gremikha waiting for a Typhoon. I think we've stumbled onto a Typhoon deployment."

"Sonar to control. We have a second contact."

"That settles it," Gunner exclaimed. "Morrison, did you ID the first contact?"

"Yes, sir. Positive ID on Akula class _Gorky_."

"The Grey Ghosts of Murmansk," Gunner muttered. "Squadron Seven, regular duty: Typhoon escort."

For two tense hours sonar operators and control room personnel watched the two Soviet subs maneuver. _Gorky_ inched close to Gremikha, finally coming to a halt twelve miles outside the harbor. The second sub, another Akula identified as *Minsk*, also from Squadron Seven, passed between *Reno* and Gremikha and continued east into the White Sea approaches. Thirty miles from *Reno* she shut down her engines and went quiet.

"Sonar to control. We lost *Minsk*."

"You'll get her back," Gunner said. "Now we wait. Gus, pass the word. Tell the crew we have two little Ivans around us waiting for Big Ivan. No one make a sound."

16 Margarita

Wrapped in an old flannel robe, Stefan Zenko sat in the kitchen of his modest apartment at Gremikha unable to sleep, afraid to dream. It was four-thirty in the morning, and he had spent the night calculating rocket trajectories, plotting currents and salt water densities, filling the hours with busywork. In a few hours he was scheduled to take his ship, *Taifun*, on regular patrol in the White Sea. Rocket test shots and absurd television broadcasts notwithstanding, the essential mission of the flotilla, strategic deterrence, must continue. He expected a quiet patrol. No NATO subs had been reported in the Barents for over a month, but Zenko knew the quiet American Los Angeles class boats were able to slip past the sonar barriers with impunity. Throughout his career he had relished playing tag with the U.S. Navy, testing his wiles against clever American commanders, but this morning he was not looking forward to a three-week patrol. Political instability in Moscow seemed to increase hourly, and in three weeks the Soviet Union could turn upside down.

He listened to the low moan of a foghorn roll over Gremikha, warning ships away. To Zenko the deep bass note sounded like the voice of the Rodina, the Motherland, wailing out for her lost children. Above the foghorn he could make out faint, irregular staccato cracks, the sound of distant ice floes crashing in the slow current. Much closer, a noisy truck clattered over cobblestones two stories below. From the next room he heard his wife make soft cooing sounds in her sleep. Ah, Margarita, perhaps dreaming of Leningrad in the springtime. Zenko resisted the urge to wake her and tell her of his fears and nightmares.

A nameless dread pounded at his soul. He closed his eyes and let his mind drift. Suddenly, he saw a flash of orange and for a brief moment he was gripped by terror. But no shock wave reduced his apartment to rubble. Instead, only soft orange light filtered through the window from clock-triggered mercury vapor lamps outside.

He leaned back in his chair, laughed softly at himself and rubbed his ample belly. For ten years he had worried himself sick imagining an American attack on Gremikha Naval Station. In a conflict Gremikha would have been target number one. Flash, boom, atomized. That fear had never materialized, and he felt certain it never would. Why, then, did he have a hollow feeling in his gut? What did he have to fear?

He stretched and stepped to the bedroom door, where he lingered, studying his sleeping wife. Margarita was like an animated pastiche of old Petrograd. She walked fast, talked fast, had opinions on everything and spewed forth ideas like a fountain. She had come from Leningrad with a bouquet of delicious smells, sounds, a bottle of good cognac and erotic intentions. Her beauty amazed him. At thirty-four, she was still firm and high-breasted, with fashionable blond curls, a quick smile and Mongol's eyes as bright as icicles. A staff surgeon at the Admiralty Hospital in Leningrad, she journeyed to Gremikha on weekends, bringing delicacies and a welcome boost of good cheer to that cheerless place. Zenko often wondered how he had courted and won such a lovely woman, twenty years his junior. She surely hadn't fallen for his looks.

He went into the sitting room and gazed through the double-paned window. In the courtyard below, a spotlight illuminated the Soviet naval ensign that flew day and night in front of the building. On this dark morning the upraised shaft of light caught the flag draped around the pole so Zenko could see only the red star on a white field over a broad blue stripe. The hammer and sickle were hidden in the folds. As he had done for forty honorable years, he raised his hand in a long, solemn salute.

Beyond the flagpole lay the black Barents Sea and the ice. Frozen images swirled through his head. Like an Eskimo, he had more names for ice than he could count. Frazil, slush, shuga, dark nilas, light nilas, young ice, grey ice, grease ice, new ridges, relict ridges, hummocks, bummocks and keels. As a cadet he had had visions of America's famous under-ice subs *Nautilus*, *Skate* and *Seadragon* and the Red Navy's own *Leninskii Komsomol* crashing into the blue haze of the midnight sun. Since childhood he had feared the cold, the terror of frozen death with lungs full of razor-sharp air, but he had defeated his fear of ice by building the Typhoons. Now, he had discovered worse fears, terrible forebodings, specters that he couldn't even name.

"Good morning, comrade sailorman."

He felt warm arms circling his belly, cutting short his black reverie.

"Good morning, comrade wife."

"Did you sleep, Stefan?"

"Not much."

He turned and kissed her cheek. Fresh from the shower, she was wet and naked under a terrycloth robe. Lost in thought, he hadn't heard the showerhead.

"Is it time for you to go?" Margarita asked.

"Soon, yes. How are you feeling?"

"Better than I have a right to."

She went into the compact kitchen, rattled his old samovar and made tea. He sat at the small table, chin in his hands.

"We've had a good weekend, Stefan. We ate and ate and drank and drank and made love and made love, but we didn't talk much."

He took her face in his hands and said, "So talk."

"Is Deminov going to take away your command?" she asked.

Zenko's soft round face took on a sharp edge of annoyance. "What kind of question is that, Margarita?"

"The kind people in the Admiralty are asking these days, Stefan. I want to know what I should do."

"What you should do, dear woman, is what your conscience compels you to do."

"Stefan, this is serious. Ugly rumors are going around."

Leaning on his elbows, he said, "Russia has fed on rumors for centuries. Without rumors we would suffocate."

"But the rumor in Leningrad is that Deminov wants you replaced," Margarita said, sitting down opposite her husband.

"Is that what they say?"

"Yes. Since you refuse to sign his dirty little letter, the implication is you favor the republicans, and that infuriates Deminov."

"I don't lose much sleep over Ivan Ivanovitch Deminov."

"Nonsense." Margarita became agitated. "After you watched *Sovyetskii Soyuz* on *Vremya*, you spent the entire night festering. Deminov is a Nazi who wears a red star. He's spoken openly of a military government. He commands thousands of atomic warheads."

"Do you think he'll drop them on Moscow?" Zenko asked with a quiet laugh. "That certainly would solve our bureaucratic problems."

Exasperated, Margarita declared, "Stefan, I love you but you're an impossible ass. Deminov is a powerful man, and he's waiting for the right moment to seize control of your flotilla. He's a genuine threat to you, and I want to know what you're going to do about him."

"Should I shoot him in the head like they do in the American movies you like so much? Jesus Christ, life is not black and white, good and evil. Spare me your moralisms, Margarita. The Defense Council has to deal with Deminov."

"And what if he orders you to sign his bloody letter or surrender your command? Are you going to let him get away with it."

"Darling wife, you above all others should know that I follow orders. Whatever happens, the issues are complex and classified and I can't discuss them, so please, shut up," he commanded with a gentle pat on her bottom. "I don't like to talk politics with a naked woman. Come back to bed."

"Not so fast, Comrade Admiral. You can't hide from me behind classified this and secret that, not with your Typhoons paraded before the entire country on television after a rocket test you wanted canceled."

"Margarita, please. I simply cannot discuss it."

"Stefan, I can't believe you're going to sit on your butt and let Deminov roll over you."

Zenko watched orange light pour through the window. Reality was there, just beyond the double-paned glass. Perhaps that was what he feared, reality compressing him the way the sea compresses a submarine, pressuring and ultimately crushing him if he ventured too deep. He took Margarita by the hand and led her toward the bedroom. "What do the pundits in the Admiralty have to say about my chances of keeping my command?" he asked.

"That Deminov wants to smash your image as a hero and make you swear fealty to him."

"Fealty? Is the Navy some kind of medieval kingdom?"

"Of course."

"Are they giving odds?"

"Three to one in your favor," she said as they lay down side by side.

"That's all?" he asked, idly circling her nipple with his thumb. "Last year it was five to one."

"Deminov is out to get you, famous Admiral Zenko, and everybody knows it."

Laughing, Zenko slowly drew his finger back and forth like a swaying cobra. "And you, comrade darling, did you bet?"

"Gambling is capitalistic decadence," she scolded. "Didn't you know?"

Zenko nuzzled his face between her breasts and caressed her thighs. With a shriek of laughter Margarita rolled over on her back and they began to make joyful, sweet love.

The phone rang.

"Damn!" Swearing, Zenko pulled himself from the bed, stomped into the sitting room and picked up the receiver. "Zenko!"

"This is Major Riziov, sir. Mishman Sorokin from *Sovyetskii Soyuz* is here in secure communications and . . ."

"Sorokin? He's supposed to be in Archangel."

"He's escorting a sick sailor."

"For God's sake, send them to the infirmary."

"He wants to see you, sir. He says it's urgent."

Zenko's mind raced furiously. Sorokin wouldn't journey from Archangel to Gremikha—how the hell did he manage that?—to trouble him with a trivial matter. Something must have happened on *Sovyetskii Soyuz*.

"All right," he said. "I'll see him in my office in half an hour."

"Very good, sir."

"Send a car around and hold a seat on this morning's shuttle to Leningrad for my wife."

"Yes, sir."

Zenko replaced the phone and returned to the bedroom.

"What is it?" Margarita asked.

"I have to go."

"Things were just getting interesting, comrade lover."

"I know, I'm sorry, but I must leave."

He quickly showered, shaved and dressed in his sea uniform. His silver star lay slightly cockeyed against his breast, a dozen lesser honors stacked below in untidy rows.

Margarita put on a flowery robe, made more tea and watched her husband. He was a man who tried to fill each day as if it were his last. He loved sex, booze, sitting up all night telling stories, walking in the snow and growing vegetables in his tiny garden, but Margarita knew that nothing could stand in comparison to the way he loved going to sea in submarines. His crew was his real family. Some day, she thought, when the Navy finally did take away his subs, she would have a miserable old man on her hands.

"How long will you be gone this time, Stefan?"

"Standard patrol. Three weeks."

"I want you to visit me in Leningrad when you return. I want to roast a goose and play music."

"That sounds wonderful."

"Something is wrong. I can feel it."

"Margarita, please."

He pulled on his boots and rummaged around a closet for his greatcoat. Margarita fussed over him, straightening his lapels and adjusting his medals. Putting on a stern face, she demanded. "Now kiss me, comrade hero, and I'll send you off to make war on the arctic ice."

"Kissing is done, darling Margarita. Heroes don't kiss, they rape and pillage. They turn the frozen sea into crushed ice for the commissar's drink."

"Then come plunder me in Leningrad, Stefan. I'll be waiting."

Reaching for the door, Zenko uncharacteristically stepped back, took Margarita in the arms of his massive greatcoat and kissed her passionately.

"For luck," he said. "For love." And he was gone.

17 Secure Communications

Rank and position notwithstanding, Zenko had to pass through a security check and show identification before he could step into the personnel elevator and drop three hundred feet to the submarine pens of Gremikha. Impatient and irritated, he hustled smartly down the quay and entered the secure communications center. As he passed the main desk the duty officer, Major Riziov, jumped to his feet and announced, "Admiral Deminov's plane just radioed, sir. He's in the air en route from Archangel and should arrive in thirty minutes."

Zenko stopped in midstep and turned slowly to the young, blond GRU major. "Did he send any orders?"

"Only that you were not to put to sea before his arrival."

"Indeed."

No protocol, no warning, and, Zenko thought, no mercy. "Gremikha is a popular destination this morning," he said. "Where's Sorokin?"

"Waiting outside your office."

Zenko found the two sailors on a bench in the hall. Little Petya had fallen asleep, and Sorokin had littered the floor with cigar ashes. Looking angry and bleary-eyed, the mishman rose slowly to his feet and saluted.

"What's this?" Zenko asked, eyeing the sleeping sailor.

"Seaman Recruit Bulgakov, Captain," Sorokin answered.

"Is he ill?"

"No, sir."

"I see. Well, let him sleep. Come in, Vadim."

Zenko unlocked his office, pushed through the door and waved Sorokin toward a seat. The mishman remained standing.

"What are you doing here, Vadim?"

"Sir, it may not be my place to ask, but I want to know why they're arresting the crew of the *Soyuz*."

"What the hell are you taking about, Mishman?"

"After the ship left, the shipyard was—"

"What do you mean, after the ship left? What ship?"

"Why, the *Soyuz*, Captain."

Zenko was stunned. "*Sovyetskii Soyuz* sailed from Severodvinsk?"

"Yes, sir."

"When? Who was in command?"

"At approximately two o'clock this morning, Captain Malakov commanding. Sir, didn't you order the ship to sea?"

Zenko felt his skin crawl. Margarita was right. He could sense Deminov maneuvering around him, like an invisible sub. His mind began to boil. *Sovyetskii Soyuz* couldn't sail without direct orders from the flotilla's commanding officer or someone higher in the chain of command. And with Deminov's imminent arrival, Zenko wondered if his tenure in Gremikha might be measured in minutes.

"No, I issued no such order. Please, sit down."

Sorokin sat stiffly on the edge of a chair. Zenko offered him a cigarette and lit one himself. Sorokin noticed a slight tremble in the admiral's hands as they held the match.

"Tell me exactly what happened," Zenko said, his voice low but steady.

Sorokin recounted the story of Bulgakov's arrest, his trip into Archangel to rescue him and Zharzharskiev's largess. "When we got back to Severodvinsk, the ship was gone, spetsnaz were in control of the shipyard, and the militia was arresting crew members left ashore."

"Did you see anyone you recognized at Severodvinsk?"

"Colonel Ludinov from fleet security."

"Deminov's hatchet man," Zenko said. "When was the last time you saw Malakov?"

"Just before he went ashore to meet with Admiral Deminov. He gave a speech, spouting patriotic slogans, glorious this and glorious that. I watched him launch that SS-N-20, Captain. He had a look on his face I'll never forget."

"You did the right thing coming here, Vadim. Thank you."

"What's happening, sir? Is there anything I can do?"

"Yes," Zenko replied. "I'm reassigning you immediately as quartermaster of *Taifun*."

"Thank you, sir. That's like a homecoming for me. What should I do with Bulgakov?"

"Is he an able seaman?"

"He's learning."

"Take him on board and tell him to keep his mouth shut. Go ahead and get squared away. We sail with the tide."

"Aye aye, Captain."

Sorokin left the office and collected Little Petya. Through the big window Zenko watched them walk down the quay, Sorokin in full stride, Bulgakov a step behind.

A red pennant hung from the stern of *Taifun*, but Zenko doubted he was going to sea today, and perhaps never again. His instinct for survival told him his loyalty was about to be tested. Loyalty to whom, to what? For ten years his first loyalty had been to his ships and crews. Beyond that he had remained loyal to the Navy, the Party, the Union and the Rodina. Now he had to search deeper inside himself. He wasn't too old to change. The Navy had been built to fight a war with the Americans that would never happen. The Party had betrayed the Revolution and the Union had been revealed as a mask for the Russian Empire. What remained? The Rodina, the Motherland, the Russian people.

Valotin and Deminov had cut him out of the loop and dispatched Malakov into the White Sea. Whatever his superiors' intentions, Zenko had grave doubts about Malakov, who saw his ship only as an extension of himself, a weapon to be used for his own aggrandizement. Take a handful of enriched uranium, enough steel to bridge the Gorlo Strait, two hundred thousand X-ray–tested welds, one hundred kilometers of cable, a thousand man-years of training, a lifetime of corrosive ideology, and a man with a lust for glory, and what do you get? Captain Nemo

gone mad, an atomic maelstrom, a monster from the ice age
with atomic tusks.

Zenko picked up the phone. "Major Riziov," he said, "get me
Admiral Valotin in Leningrad."

"Yes, sir."

Holding his head in his hands, Zenko could feel the pressure
building behind his eyes like ridges in pack ice.

The phone buzzed.

"Admiral Valotin is on the line, sir. I'll put you through."

"Zenko?"

"Yes, Admiral. I understand *Sovyetskii Soyuz* sailed with a
short crew without my being informed."

"That's correct. Has Deminov arrived there yet?"

"He's due shortly."

"Then you might as well hear it from me, Stefan Grigorivitch.
I've authorized Operation White Star. Deminov will have your
orders."

Valotin's voice was cold, formal and distant. Zenko realized
it was useless to protest. "I see," he said. "Very good, sir."

The line clicked and went dead.

White Star. He should have guessed. Alone among the Typhoon commanders, Malakov could be counted on to fire a
rocket. With the ordnance aboard *Sovyetskii Soyuz,* he could
level the capital of every republic and even Moscow itself. Was
that what Deminov and Valotin were up to? Were they using
White Star as a cover? With Malakov's finger on an atomic trigger, they had the muscle to bring off a coup. Margarita had said
they were waiting for the right moment. Now they were creating
that moment.

Zenko felt mired in deceit and treachery. Valotin and Deminov didn't have to remove him from command. They had only
to order him to sea and keep him incommunicado under the ice
while they blackmailed the government with *Sovyetskii Soyuz.*
Or they could simply lock him in the brig at Gremikha. Somehow he had to stop the bastards, but he needed help. He picked
up the phone. "Major Riziov, come in here, please."

The major knocked and entered. Zenko had to trust someone
with access to the radio transmission systems and he didn't have
time to interview and screen the fifty people working in secure

communications. He studied the blond, thirty-year-old officer and made a snap decision.

"Sit down, Boris."

"Thank you, sir."

"You've been here four years, if I remember correctly. Last year you had an opportunity to go to Polyarnyy to fleet headquarters, but you chose to stay here."

"That's right, sir."

"Did Colonel Ludinov from fleet security ask you to remain at Gremikha?"

"No, sir. He wanted me at Polyarnyy."

"Why did you stay on? Gremikha is isolated, there's nothing here. You have a little boy who's growing up here in a frozen desert."

"Admiral, our living standard is the best in the Navy. Our shops are full. We don't wait in lines or go without."

"That's not a good enough reason for most men. They leave."

"We do important work here," Riziov said. "What can be more important than deterring atomic war?"

"I agree wholeheartedly," Zenko replied. "But you're GRU, major, not regular Navy. You're a specialist in military intelligence, in short, a spy. I've wondered if you remained here to spy on me."

Riziov flushed and his lower lip trembled. He took a deep breath and said, "Yes, sir. That's part of my brief."

"And to whom do you report?"

"Colonel Ludinov."

"I see. Have you reported to Ludinov that Mishman Sorokin arrived here from Archangel?"

"No, sir."

"Why not?"

"I report as little as possible, Admiral. Sometimes I go months without filing with Polyarnyy."

"When did you last file?"

"Three weeks ago. Ludinov wanted to know why you didn't sign the letter of support for the Union and the Party. He also wanted to know if you've ever expressed republican sentiments. I told him you are the most patriotic officer I've ever been privileged to serve under. Frankly, sir, I think you believe politics have no place in a military command."

"I believe patriotism is more important than politics. Would you agree, Boris?"

"Yes, sir," Riziov answered, wondering where this questioning was leading.

"When do you go off duty?" Zenko asked.

"After *Taifun* sails."

"*Taifun* is scheduled to depart in two hours," Zenko said. "When I'm gone, Admiral Deminov will be in command of the base. Admiral Valotin has authorized Operation White Star. Are you familiar with it?"

"Only in general terms, sir. It's a contingency plan to suppress armed rebellion."

"Yes, but it may also be a blueprint *for* an armed rebellion." Zenko paused a moment, then said, "Now, what I say may shock you, Major, but Admiral Deminov may send a signal from this base to *Sovyetskii Soyuz* to launch a rocket, and this one will be a war shot, not a test."

Riziov's bright young face turned dark. "Against whom, sir?" It was the only thing he could think to ask.

"I don't know, but probably against one of the republics."

Major Riziov's jaw dropped. "It's civil war, then."

"Yes," said Zenko. "Deminov and Admiral Valotin are using *Sovyetskii Soyuz* for their own purposes. I feel it's our duty within the flotilla to stop them." He saw the major was frightened and confused. "Are you all right?" he asked.

"Yes, sir. It's just a lot to absorb all at once."

"I need your help, Major."

"What can I do, sir?"

"I'm afraid that, once I'm gone, Deminov may deploy another Typhoon for strikes against the Motherland. You and I can establish a simple series of codes so you can keep me informed while I'm under the ice."

Riziov hesitated. "I'm not sure, Admiral. The security systems are very efficient."

"How well I know," Zenko said. "If Deminov discovers you, you'll be shot. You can count on that."

Riziov still hesitated. He understood Zenko was appealing to his personal loyalty.

"Major, I have to trust you," Zenko said. "You can agree with me now and report me to Deminov when he arrives in a few minutes. My purpose is to prevent my ships from attacking our country. You must choose sides, Major. Right now."

"What do you intend to do, Admiral?"

"I think it best if you don't know precisely." In fact, Zenko himself didn't yet know what he was going to do.

The phone buzzed and Zenko answered.

"This is air traffic control, sir. Admiral Deminov's plane is touching down now."

"Thank you. See that he has a proper escort and bring him here."

"Yes, sir."

Zenko replaced the phone and turned to Riziov. "Well, have you decided?"

"I'll help you, sir. I'll do my best."

"All right. If Deminov issues a launch order to *Sovyetskii Soyuz*, you signal *Taifun* with double letter B. If he prepares to deploy another Typhoon, double letter K."

Riziov nodded. "Double letter K. Yes, sir."

Zenko led Riziov through the security checks into the cryptology room, sat down at a terminal and produced codes for *Taifun*'s patrol. The radio room computers checked and verified the sequences and Zenko printed two sets. Following procedure, they returned to Zenko's office and locked one set in the safe.

"Is there anything else I should know?" Riziov asked, an anxious expression on his face.

"You probably know too much already," Zenko said. "But cheer up, Boris. Deminov may not send me to sea at all. I may spend the next few days in the brig. If that's the case . . ." He shrugged and locked a set of codes in his briefcase.

18 Command and Control

In full dress whites Ivan Deminov swept into Zenko's Cave like a reigning prince. With an entourage of twenty staff officers, he paraded down the quay past subs, cranes and gawking squids. Holding his military identification card at arm's length, he quick-stepped past the naval infantry guards and into the secure communications center.

Standing behind the main desk, Major Riziov watched with apprehension as Deminov approached, a whirlwind of flashing red stripes on white trousers. One step behind the admiral, dressed in intimidating black, came Colonel Ludinov, the stone-faced GRU chieftain to whom the major reported.

Deminov presented himself at the desk and announced, "This facility is now under direct control of the Northern Fleet."

Riziov stiffened to attention and saluted. "Yes, sir. Duty Officer Major Riziov, at your service."

Deminov returned the salute. "Where is your commanding officer?" he demanded.

"In his office, sir. Shall I call him?"

"No. I know where to find Stefan Grigorivitch Zenko."

As Deminov strode down the hall, Ludinov stepped to the desk and leaned close to Riziov. "Hello, Boris," he said. "I haven't heard from you for a while."

* * *

Admiral Deminov wore a golden dolphin, the insignia of a submarine officer. During his long career he had spent fifteen years in submarines and once commanded a flotilla of Delta II class strategic rocket subs. But his years underwater only made him restless and wanting. Unlike Zenko, he had no love for the sea or ships. To him Typhoons represented naked, intoxicating power—power he had finally wrested from Zenko and now controlled. For thirty years he had resented Zenko's genius and blunt honesty. In many previous confrontations, Zenko had emerged the winner. This time would be different.

The door to Zenko's office was open. Standing behind his desk, Zenko waited, his uniform rumpled but his dignity intact. If Riziov reported their conversation to Ludinov, he knew his career would terminate within five minutes. On the chance that Riziov was more than a GRU weasel, Zenko hoped to keep Deminov slightly off balance and extract as much information as possible without arousing his anger or suspicion. He needed to know *Sovyetskii Soyuz*'s precise location and Deminov's plans and intentions.

When Deminov stepped inside the office, a smug look on his face, Zenko said, "Welcome to Gremikha, Ivan Ivanovitch. Come in." Before Deminov could reply, he added, "Sit down. Take off your hat. I expect you're going to stay a while."

Zenko walked around his desk to an old samovar and began making tea. Caught off guard by Zenko's informality, Deminov watched his nemesis rattle spoons and glasses. Zenko smiled and loosened his collar, acting quite unlike a man whose career was in jeopardy. Years before, as young officers serving together on a long patrol, they had almost become friends, but by the time they returned to port, Zenko had come to realize Deminov was a hollow man with no vision, only a hunger for power.

"I will not mince words with you," Deminov declared, "Vice-Admiral Stefan Grigorivitch Zenko, I hereby relieve you of command of Strategic Rocket Submarine Flotilla Six."

The words hung in the air like moths. Deminov waited for Zenko to break, to curse and shout, but he merely returned to his desk carrying a glass of tea.

"Do you accept?"

"Of course I accept. I have no choice, Ivan, and I've never disobeyed an order."

"You will surrender to me all weapons and communications codes for the ships in your flotilla."

Zenko bent over his desk and wrote the combination to his safe on a notepad. "Major Riziov has access to all pertinent files. I have an excellent staff. They'll serve you well. Shall I call them together and introduce you?"

"In due course."

Zenko opened his briefcase and removed *Taifun*'s weapons and communications code sheets. "I presume you'll assign a new commander to my ship. Here are codes for the patrol generated this morning by Major Riziov and myself." He looked at his watch and reached for his cap. "Ivan, I've been here ten years. Suddenly it's over and that's that. If I hurry, I can join my wife on the shuttle to Leningrad. I'd rather not spend any more time here than absolutely necessary."

Deminov had expected outrage. He had seen Zenko angry, a formidable sight. Having anticipated that Zenko would refuse to accept his orders, he had taken the precaution of warning Ludinov that they might have to lock him in the brig. But instead of protesting vehemently, Zenko was acting like a servile recruit. "Not so fast, Stefan Grigorivitch," Deminov said. "You will continue in your assignment as commanding officer of *Taifun* and participate fully in Operation White Star."

"You strip me of my command and then expect me to participate in an operation I detest? Go fuck your mother, Ivan."

This was the Zenko Deminov knew, the man he would bring to his knees. "You can't refuse. I'll order your arrest!"

"You wouldn't dare."

"I can and I will. You and your entire crew, if I have to, and every son of a bitch on this base who refuses to obey orders from the commander of the Northern Fleet!"

Suddenly subdued, Zenko seemed to crumple before his eyes. Deminov placed a sealed red folder on the desk. "Here are your orders. You will proceed in *Taifun* directly to Sector 6122 in the Barents Sea and remain on station until further notice. *Taifun* will be escorted by *Gorky* from attack submarine Squadron

Seven. *Gorky* is commanded by Victor Lorinski. Do you know him?"

"Of course. I know all the Grey Ghosts. I taught them tactics at Frunze."

"Be aware, Zenko, that you are to sail directly to your assigned sector. Deviate by one meter and Lorinski has orders to blow you out of the water."

"And did you send *Minsk* into the White Sea to ride herd on Malakov?"

"*Minsk* is patrolling the entrance to the Gorlo Strait."

"I see."

"I'm sure you do."

Zenko broke the seal, opened the red folder and studied his orders. "There is no mention of the deployment of *Sovyetskii Soyuz*. If I were in command, I'd send Malakov to the Kandalakshskiy Gulf."

This location was a guess, which Deminov accepted as a compliment. "You seem exceptionally well informed," he said.

"I spoke to Valotin a few minutes ago."

"Then you know the Union has reached a crisis."

"So it would seem," Zenko said. "White Star presumes armed rebellion. Pray tell, where is the rebellion?"

Deminov looked at him with scorn. "You've been isolated down here in Gremikha for too long, Stefan. The whole damned country is in a state of rebellion. We're even having strikes at military shipyards."

"And you counter with rocket tests, which provoke protests, which in turn give you an excuse for military intimidation."

"What are you implying?"

"Only that your response to the current political situation may be out of proportion."

"Have you become a republican?"

"Are you questioning my loyalty?" Zenko answered mildly. "It's no secret that I've always kept politics out of my command, whatever my personal opinions."

"This is not politics. This is survival!"

"Whose survival?" Zenko demanded. "Yours? Mine?"

"The Soviet Union's," Deminov replied hotly. "Things have gone too far. The so-called reformers have brought us nothing but anarchy and disorder. The Baltics and Georgia are in total chaos. We could lose the Ukraine and Byelorussia next, and by God, Russia herself! We're being ravaged by Rasputins with computers and their damned perestroika! Before Gorbachev we had peace among the republics. We had stability and no doubt as to our mission in the world. We're losing everything, and I won't stand by and let that happen."

"So there is to be no further discussion? The issue is settled?"

"It is."

"You may provoke a civil war," Zenko said darkly.

"So be it," Deminov declared. "My goal is to preserve the Union. Consider the alternative: If the Union is destroyed, Russia will be surrounded by independent republics armed with atomic weapons and bent on revenge. That is a prospect no one wants to face. We must crush our enemies before they turn on us. If one has a will, the path is easy to follow. It's always been so, Zenko. We won't allow history to pass over us like a cold wind. We're going to be history. We must have order!"

Yes, thought Zenko, the history of Russia has been written in blood by saviors who wanted to establish order. "And while you're saving the Union," he said, "I shall be under the ice counting my fingers and toes. What is my role?"

"To remain in your sector and await orders, no more, no less."

"And Malakov?"

"The same."

"What about the Americans?" Zenko asked. "When you suddenly deploy dozens of ships, they'll take notice. If civil war breaks out, they'll get nervous."

Deminov snorted. "The Americans are of no significance. They'll make noise, issue statements, recall their ambassador and in the end do nothing. They won't go to war just because we happen to change governments."

"Is it your intention to change governments?"

"It's inevitable."

So, Zenko thought, you traitorous sons of bitches are really going to do it. "I agree we can't continue our present course," he said.

Now feeling supremely self-confident, Deminov produced

two documents and handed them to Zenko. "This," he said, "is the order relieving you of command of Naval Station Gremikha. And this is a statement of your intention to comply with all the directives of Operation White Star. Please sign both."

Zenko glanced at the documents and signed with a show of heavy-hearted resignation. "My command is yours. Wait here a moment and I'll introduce you to the staff of the center."

He left the office and found Riziov. A single glance from the major told him his ally had not caved in to Colonel Ludinov. Riziov assembled over fifty technicians, radio operators, cryptologists and clerks in a conference room. Zenko entered with Deminov at his side and introduced him with deference and respect. "The Admiralty has initiated Operation White Star," he said. "You are now under the direct control of the Northern Fleet and Admiral Deminov. Until the conclusion of this operation, Naval Station Gremikha is to be sealed off from the outside world. You are on alert status. Admiral Deminov will command the fleet from here. Until further notice, all fleet communications will be directed from this center, so you'll be busy for the next several days. I remind you that all terminal entries and radio signals are recorded for the sake of security. Your performance will be subject to review. Major Riziov will be in charge of communication security. That is all. Carry on and good luck."

Zenko and Deminov returned to Zenko's office. Deminov watched the deposed master of Gremikha put on his greatcoat and set his cap upon his head. He extended his hand. Zenko shook it with no display of emotion, then left the communications center. Through the plate-glass window Deminov watched him begin the long walk up the quay to his ship, his shoulders slumped in the posture of a broken man. Deminov grunted with satisfaction. The first obstacle to his plans had been overcome with surprising ease.

He returned to the communications center and issued his first order to Major Riziov. "Send a message to *Sovyetskii Soyuz*."

Two hundred miles southwest of Gremikha, *Sovyetskii Soyuz* hovered motionless under nine hundred feet of water in the Kandalakshskiy Gulf, the deepest part of the White Sea. Malakov had taken the extra precaution of secreting his ship at depth rather than the usual Typhoon procedure of hiding just below the ice. He certainly didn't expect a prowler, but any sub looking for *Sovyetskii Soyuz* would find a surprise.

The command center was quiet. Malakov paced back and forth between the sonar repeaters and the radio room, anxiously awaiting a signal from Gremikha via ELF.

Finally, the incoming alarm flashed and the slow ELF message came in, one digit per minute. Twenty-five minutes later the scrambled transmission was decoded and Malakov read, ZENKO TO SEA DEMINOV SENDS."

Zenko had submitted. Malakov experienced a moment of deep satisfaction. Now he had only to wait. The next signal would be a declaration of total victory or an order to launch.

19

Taifun

As Zenko walked down the quay, he could feel Deminov's eyes burning into his back. Ivan Ivanovitch is a fool, he thought. He has presented me with the one weapon that can stop this treason, my ship.

As he approached *Taifun*, he saw a commotion on the deck forward of the sail. Men were scrambling through hatches and forming ranks. Sorokin paced in front of the crew and bawled parade ground commands. When Zenko reached the side of the sub, the mishman stopped in front of the assembly and faced his captain.

"Attention!"

Behind him 150 pairs of heels snapped together.

"Salute!"

One hundred fifty hands saluted in unison.

"Proclaim!"

"Vice-Admiral Stefan Gregorivitch Zenko, we salute you, master of *Taifun!*"

Zenko returned the salute, thinking, my God, how can I tell these men we have to fight our ship? His eyes flicked from man to man, sturdy young faces almost cherubic in their youth, sailors who would be remembered for a thousand years if he succeeded; forgotten in an instant if he failed. His gaze lingered over the rocket compartments charged with plutonium. Were

Valotin, Deminov and Malakov the madmen or was it he who had built these engines of destruction?

He took one step forward and shouted, "Men of *Taifun*, are you ready to sail?"

"We are!"

"Well then, Sons of Neptune," Zenko roared at the top of his lungs, "kiss the sky good-bye!"

The crew roared back, "Kiss the sky good-bye!"

Zenko's ship, Zenko's signature. The captain crossed the accommodation ladder, tossed his greatcoat onto the deck and disappeared down the hatch.

Taifun was an old friend. The command center was trimmed in dark blue which Zenko preferred over the red of the newer ships. He watched the command division file into the compartment. Sorokin took his quartermaster's station at the navigation table and ran his eyes over a bank of monitors. Everything was in order. The ship was ready.

In the radio room Zenko found *Taifun's* political officer, Captain First Rank Sasha Kugarin, preparing crypto sheets. Having served together for fifteen years, Zenko and Kugarin were wedded more closely than either with his wife. Zenko had no use for zampolits like Sergov on *Sovyetskii Soyuz*, who couldn't turn a valve or monitor a steam feed. The sea didn't care if a man had read Lenin, nor did a reactor need a quotation from Karl Marx. Kugarin had attended the submarine school at Murmansk and next to his party pin proudly wore a submarine officer's golden dolphin.

Effusive, excitable, with wild curly hair and thick glasses, Kugarin warmly shook Zenko's hand. "Greetings, Comrade Stefan. How's Margarita?"

Zenko spread his short arms wide, "Like a glass of champagne. No, make that a bottle, three bottles. Gad, I should've married a woman my own age."

"Want to trade? I'll take Margarita, you take Vadya."

"No, thanks, Comrade Hero Father." On every Soviet naval vessel the man with the most children was called the Hero Father. "You can keep your fat old woman," Zenko chided. "Is she pregnant again? Tell me, Sasha, how are your seven little communists?"

"You want to hear about my kids? I'll tell you. Ivan paints his face white and is stoned on hashish every night. Alexi wants to be in a rock and roll band. Katarina has joined the Green party and tells me I'm an enemy of the people. Got that? From my own child. She also demanded that all forms of atomic energy be banned and the Navy abolished. She's a lot of fun at dinnertime. Georgi watches TV all day and talks on the telephone. Maia is the leader of her Pioneer group and comes home crying every day because the other kids say communism is a big lie and Lenin was an ass. She and Katarina scream at each other like Georgians. The twins are in kindergarten and too little to cause much trouble yet. I tell you, Stefan, the world is crazy."

Zenko listened patiently to the zampolit's recitation, then asked, "Are you ready to sail?"

"I can't wait to get the hell out of here. Three weeks of peace and quiet under the ice sounds perfect to me."

Zenko folded his arms across his chest. "Have you been aboard all morning?"

"Yes. I spent the night on board."

"Been on deck?"

"No."

"Did you see Sorokin?"

"Good old Vadim? He came aboard an hour ago and took charge of the crew like a wizard, just as if he'd never left."

"Did he tell you why he's here?"

"I didn't ask."

"We aren't going on regular patrol. I had a little visit from our friend Ivan Deminov this morning."

"I suppose he fed you his usual line of garbage," Kugarin said, his voice dripping with contempt. "Solidarity with the Union, kiss his ass. What does he want? Another rocket test?"

Zenko leaned back against a counter. "He removed me from command of the flotilla," he stated flatly.

Kugarin blinked in surprise. "He what?"

"Yes," said Zenko. "And Valotin has authorized Operation White Star."

"I'm speechless," Kugarin sputtered. "I don't know what to say. I'm not sure I even want to ask why."

"And Malakov put to sea last night in *Sovyetskii Soyuz* under Deminov's orders without consulting me first."

Suddenly pale, Kugarin trembled. "Malakov? Malakov is the kind of man who goes out of his way to step on bugs."

Zenko showed the zampolit his orders. "This is horrendous," Kugarin blurted. "We're supposed to reprogram ten rockets for domestic targets?"

Zenko merely nodded, his eyes turned to slits.

"I'll report these bastards to the Party," Kugarin said.

"The Party!" Zenko exclaimed, fury rising in his throat. "Do you think we can stop Deminov with a phone call to the Party? I swear, sometimes you think like an *apparatchik* instead of a naval officer. You stop a fleet with torpedoes. You defeat a mutiny by killing the mutineers."

The truth exploded in Kugarin's mind like a bomb. "What do you propose, Stefan?"

"I'm going to hunt down Malakov and sink *Sovyetskii Soyuz*."

Thunderstruck, head swirling, Kugarin saw the future erupting in a violent maelstrom. Zenko had drawn the line. "So it's come to this," he said. "We go to war."

"That's right," Zenko said, his calm returning. "And we fire the first shot."

"We'll be one ship against the fleet."

"Yes. Not very good odds, are they? I need you, Sasha, but you can stop me now by walking off this ship. You're free to join Deminov and his mad rebels. Think of your children and their future. Do you want them to live in a military dictatorship for the rest of their lives? If Deminov has his way, the Cold War will resume, or worse. We'll have another Stalin."

"Does Sorokin know?"

"Not yet. I wanted to tell you first. Without you, I don't have a chance. Are you with me?"

Without hesitation Sasha Kugarin stepped over the line. "Of course, but my God, how in the world do you expect to run the Gorlo Strait?"

"I'll find a way," Zenko said with a sly smile. "Now, let's get this tub under the ice before Deminov changes his mind."

. . .

A few minutes later, swaddled in arctic cap, goggles, jacket, headset and binoculars, Zenko stood on the bridge of *Taifun* with Sorokin. Feet wide apart, a broad grin showing off his gold teeth, Zenko shouted and swore like a common seaman. "My God, this is an ugly fucking boat. She's so ugly she even makes me look beautiful."

Sorokin pushed his cap back on his forehead. "The ocean is blind, Captain. He don't care."

"Blind but not deaf, Comrade Mishman. Two Akulas are waiting for us just inside the ice line."

"Escorts?"

"Or assassins," Zenko replied. He turned to face Sorokin. "We're going to war, Vadim."

"Malakov," Sorokin stated, unfazed.

"Yes, if I can find him. I'll need your help with the crew."

"Aye, Captain." Sorokin nodded. "Tell the men the truth and they'll fight for you. Me, you don't even have to ask."

"Then let's get under way. Bridge to command," Zenko ordered. "Both engines, slow speed."

"Slow speed, aye."

White water roiled under the stern. With a deep shudder *Taifun* inched away from the quay.

"Helm, steer left ten degrees."

"Turning now, left ten degrees."

"Open the sea gate."

The heavy steel doors began to slide apart and a wave of cool air rolled through the cavern.

As *Taifun* steamed past *First of May*, Zenko noticed a group of young officers assembled on the forward deck. He waved, but none of the second- and third-rank lieutenants returned his salute. Zenko felt a stab in the heart, then realized the young men had been informed of Operation White Star, and that Zenko had agreed to participate.

They felt betrayed. Zenko was their hero, not because he wore a silver star, but because he had always gone his own way, refusing to cooperate with the Admirality's political schemes. Now, in their eyes, perhaps to save his command or for some reason they couldn't guess, Zenko was showing himself to be as crass and cynical as the rest of the bastards who ran the Navy.

He could do nothing but stare straight ahead and hold his sorrow. The civil war had taken its first casualties, and he hadn't yet reached the harbor.

Taifun slipped out of Zenko's Cave like a waking sea monster. Her 560-foot length seemed to take forever to pass through the gates, as if she were unwilling to come into the light. From the bridge Zenko watched the first wave of antisubmarine helicopters appear above the cliffs, race out to sea and begin dropping sonobuoys in the water. He filled his lungs with sea air and shouted at the lookouts, "Keep a sharp eye for ice floes!"

"Aye aye, Captain."

Sorokin turned to look back at the cavern doors closing behind the ship. Gremikha, his home for ten years, seemed alien and hostile, the way it would appear if an American sub had ever been this close to Zenko's Cave.

They passed the breakwater. Zenko's skiff had broken loose from its moorings and drifted helplessly in the harbor. A sheet of newsprint blew out of the boat and landed in the water, sinking immediately.

Overhead, radio and radar masts twirled on their bearings and above them seabirds fluttered and dove toward the water. Small ice floes drifted by. Zenko smelled the ice, the sea, the salt and, sniffing harder, his own fear.

Taifun plunged into the sea, as reluctant a man-of-war as ever sailed the deep blue, yet more potent than a thousand navies. Behold the furies of Russia, thought Stefan Zenko. See what ye have wrought.

20 Big Ivan

Aboard *Reno* air-conditioners were set at minimum and showers prohibited. The interior had begun to smell like a pigboat from World War II.

A Nintendo tournament in the torpedo room had reached the quarterfinals. In the maneuvering room the nucs had passed through the far side of boredom and had begun designing a nuclear electric magnetohydrodynamic propulsor. Throughout the sub men had tired of silence, dirty books and one another's company and roosted in sweaty bunks dreaming of home.

In the control room Gunner watched the inertial navigation display click over. *Reno* was drifting south in the quarter-knot current and in twelve hours Gremikha would fall beyond sonar range. If no Typhoon appeared, Gunner would have to fire up the propulsors, move north and find another ice keel, a risky if not downright suicidal maneuver with two Soviet attack subs nearby.

In the sonar room Morrison daydreamed of walking across the ice to Archangel. On the waterfront a flock of Russian beauties cavorted in bikinis. Cold war, hell. Cold love, that's the ticket, on the ice, in the snow. Bring on the polar bears and bluenoses.

Billie Stewart slapped Morrison on the knee. "Wake up, Chief."

"I ain't asleep."

"You sure snore when you're awake."

"Jesus, okay. Any sign of Big Ivan?"

"Not yet."

"Well, screw 'em."

Suddenly, the screens lit up like Times Square on New Year's Eve. The lethargy that had infested the sonar room vanished. Morrison felt an instant rush of adrenaline.

"Ye gods. Sonobuoys."

Fear thrashed Billie Stewart's face. "Have they detected us?" he squawked.

"No," Morrison answered. "This is Russian standard procedure when Big Ivan comes out." He switched on his headset. "Sonar to control. Active sonars in the water."

In the control room Gunner's eyes locked on the sonar repeater. A series of peaks and valleys moved across the screen indicating pinging sonobuoys dropped from helicopters. This was the crunch. Cold War or no Cold War, a Typhoon was about to steam out of the harbor at Gremikha and *Reno* would follow wherever she went.

"I read you, sonar. What's the range, Chief?"

"Thirty to thirty-five miles, Skipper. Looks like a standard search pattern. We should be too far away for them to pick us out. If they read us at all, they'll think we're part of the ice keel."

"Sit tight, sonar," Gunner said. "Big Ivan will be on your screens in a few minutes."

Morrison switched off his intercom microphone. "And we might be on his," he reminded the operators. "Fun and games time."

Throughout the boat whispering speakers announced, "All hands, general quarters, general quarters."

Still on the surface, *Taifun* plunged into the swell, splashing the bridge party with cold spray.

"Bridge to command. Increase speed to two-thirds," Zenko ordered.

"Two-thirds speed, aye."

"Radio to bridge."

"Go ahead, radio."

"Helos report submerged contact, bearing zero one one,

range twenty-five kilometers. Identification Akula class, probably *Gorky*."

"You're positive of his location?"

"Yes, Captain."

"Bridge to helm, steer course zero zero zero."

"Course zero zero zero, aye."

A second wave of helicopters roared past, a swarm of sinister mechanical wasps, each carrying a rack of spherical depth charges under its fuselage.

On *Reno*, Gunner demanded, "Control to sonar. Where's the second Akula, *Minsk?*"

"She hasn't moved, Captain," Morrison answered. "I don't know where she is, but she can't be far from her last position if she's drifting at the same rate we are. She has to be about twenty-five miles southeast. If Big Ivan heads into the White Sea, he'll pass right across her bow."

"Morrison, what's it like down in sonar?"

"It stinks, sir. We sure could use some coffee."

"Hang in there. Big Ivan is coming out any minute."

"We'll hear him, Skipper."

Gunner thrummed his fingers on the periscope housing. A few feet away Trout rubbed his eyes and yawned. Crewmen scratched and fidgeted.

"Damn," Gunner said. "I'd give anything to poke a mast up and listen to their radios."

On the bridge of *Taifun* Zenko ordered Sorokin and the lookouts below.

"Bridge to diving officer, lower masts."

The radio and radar masts slipped down into the sail. Zenko paused a moment, watching the sea roll over the bow. An ice floe half the size of the ship drifted nearby, pushed by wind and current. He sealed the hatch and descended through the sail.

The big navigation monitor displayed an electronic chart of the Gremikha roadstead. A blinking red cursor marked *Taifun*'s position and steady blue lights represented *Gorky* and *Minsk*.

Zenko sat down in the commander's comfortable leather chair and adjusted the brightness on his video screens.

"Diving Officer, report."

"All lights show green."

"Very well. Flood forward ballast tanks."

"Flood forward ballast tanks, aye."

"Three degrees down angle."

"Three degrees down, aye."

"Very well. All ahead standard."

"All ahead standard, aye."

Feeling the deck tilt forward, Zenko watched the depth meter. _Taifun_ sank beneath the surface. Twenty, thirty, forty meters of water lay above.

"Bring her level at fifty meters."

"Fifty meters, aye."

"Sonar, set the ice watch."

"Setting ice watch, aye."

Monitors blinked as sonarmen turned on high-frequency, low powered ice scanners.

"Maintain standard speed."

"Standard speed, aye."

"Helm, steer three four zero degrees true."

Zenko turned his ship northwest, following the course laid out by Deminov and doing precisely what Captain Lorinski in _Gorky_ expected him to do.

In _Reno_'s sonar room Morrison leaned forward, elbows digging into knees, eyes flickering over a half-dozen screens. _Reno_ continued to drift slowly in the current, requiring the operators to make fine adjustments to the array.

"Focus on the bearing," Morrison said. "That's it, that's it. Wait. Hold it right there. Turn on the audio."

The computer filtered out ice noises and marine life, leaving a low-pitched, complex, mechanical throbbing whoosh. "That's him. He's submerged," Morrison said, flicking on the intercom. "Sonar to control. I have cavitation in the water. Big Ivan has come out of his hole."

In the control room a crowd mustered around the sonar repeater to watch a blip slide across the CRT. Although advanced technology had quieted Soviet machinery, a Typhoon displaced thirty thousand tons and movement of that volume of seawater made noise. At depths shallower than four hundred feet her props cavitated, and *Reno's* hydrophones, far more sensitive than any Soviet sonar, picked up every nuance of sound emanating from the Typhoon.

A wave of vertical lines moved across the screen ahead of the blip. "High-frequency, low-powered ice scanners," Gunner said. "He's taking a picture, and giving another to us. Lieutenant Sharpe, run a mock attack program. We don't get a chance like this very often."

"Aye aye."

"He's turning northwest," Trout said, "course three four zero true."

"Control to sonar. Identification, please."

"*Taifun*, Skipper."

"Zenko's boat," Gunner said. "The fat little bastard himself. And he's heading *away* from the White Sea."

A half hour from Gremikha *Taifun's* sonar officer announced, "Approaching the ice, Captain. Range two thousand meters."

On the navigation monitor the moving red cursor blinked across a line representing the marginal ice zone. The image changed to a three-dimensional graphic of the ice above. Near the edge new ice was only a foot thick. Pieces broke away with a roar and floated off as islands. Wind and current pushed relentlessly against the pack, compacting the edge and creating tremendous pressures that stacked blocks of ice into ridges above the surface and keels below.

The shifting and crashing of the slowly melting ice masked quiet machinery noises, making *Taifun* difficult but not impossible to locate. As the sub moved north toward the interior of the pack, the ice thickened. With three feet of ice above and the shallow Barents below, *Taifun* drove straight ahead as if she were the Golden Horde racing across the steppe.

Aboard *Gorky*, the sonar officer reported, "*Taifun* approaching, Captain. Range twelve kilometers and closing. Speed twenty knots."

"All ahead standard," Captain Lorinski ordered.

Steering a parallel course, *Gorky* slowly accelerated until she matched *Taifun*'s speed.

On *Reno*, Morrison almost shouted. "Got him! Sonar to control. We have *Gorky* on the screen. *Taifun* is approaching our maximum range."

"Sit tight," said Gunner. "As long as we have one, we have both, and we can't move until both *Taifun* and *Gorky* are almost beyond sonar range."

On *Taifun* Zenko ordered the officers and mishmani to assemble in the Lenin Room. Standing before forty-five men while the ship steamed dead ahead on automatic pilot, he decided to take Sorokin's advice and tell them the truth.

"Gentlemen," he said, his voice resonant with sorrow, "I would like to read *Taifun*'s orders as they were given me by Admiral Deminov." He read the long, complex operational orders in their entirety, and ended with, "Paragraph seventeen: Upon receipt of coded signal 77M9 you will launch Rocket Seven, Starboard Silo, target coordinates forty-four degrees fifty minutes east, thirty-seven degrees nineteen minutes north." He looked up from the document and faced his men. "Those coordinates are for the city of Tbilisi."

Shock moved through the room like a wave from a violent blast. Before the men could recover, Zenko declared, "I do not intend to follow these orders."

A riot of voices broke out as the men began to argue among themselves. After a moment Zenko called for quiet. "Gentlemen," he said, "as you know, Operation White Star was prepared by the Defense Council to counter civil war. The Union suffers discontent and unrest, but there is no civil war. I believe Admiral of the Fleet Valotin and Admiral Deminov have put the plan into operation in order to execute a coup d'état. They intend to threaten the government with the rockets on *Taifun* and those aboard *Sovyetskii Soyuz*, which is already on station in the White Sea. Their goal is to replace the civilian government with a military dictatorship. If the government does not submit to their demands, both Captain Malakov and I will receive orders to fire rockets. As I have stated, I will not comply, but I have no doubt that Captain Malakov will launch atomic weapons at our homeland."

He paused and scanned the room, trying to read the expressions on the faces of his men. They knew Malakov, and he could see they believed him. "No one in the Navy has a stronger belief in the Union than I," he continued, "but using atomic weapons against one of our own republics is unconscionable and cannot be allowed. Admiral of the Fleet Valotin, Admiral Deminov and Captain First Rank Malakov believe their actions will preserve the Union. I believe they are madmen whose crimes will bring only death and destruction to our homeland. Men of *Taifun*, we're going to stop them. We're going to fight our ship."

Voices assailed him from all sides until he asked for quiet. "You have many questions," he said, "many doubts and fears, but we have no time for debate. If any man chooses not to join the fight, let him say so now. No dishonor will befall a man with courage to speak out. I ask you to undertake a perilous voyage. We must run the Gorlo Strait and perhaps fight the entire Northern Fleet before we're finished."

Zenko looked around the room, holding one man's gaze, then another's: Assistant Chief Engineer Borznov, Reactor Officer Gandanov, Diving Officer Ludnov and the mishmani, computer technicians, rocketmen, torpedomen, radiomen.

Suddenly Sorokin stepped forward, dominating the company with his presence. He raised his fist and sang out loud and clear, "Kiss the sky good-bye."

Kugarin took up the cry and repeated Sorokin's words like a chant, then another man followed and another. The Lenin Room shook with Zenko's war cry.

Heart pounding with emotion, Zenko held up both hands and achieved instant silence.

"Men of *Taifun*, man your battle stations."

21 Deception

"Prepare for maneuvering," Gunner ordered. "Looks like we're going to miss our cruise in the exotic White Sea. All hands, maneuvering stations."

The news that *Reno* was about to move from her hiding place under the ice traveled swiftly through the boat. Sailors tucked plastic-coated photos under pillows and took their stations.

"Five more minutes," Gunner said. "Just five more minutes."

On *Taifun* the word was passed to the squids. Sorokin mustered the command division around the navigation table. "Some of you don't know me," he said. "I served on this ship for five years, and I've spent the last five on different Typhoons. My last assignment was on *Sovyetskii Soyuz* along with seaman Bulgakov here. Last night Captain Malakov put to sea in *Sovyetskii Soyuz* on a secret mission to overthrow the government. His crew has been rounded up and thrown in jail by the GRU. Our mission is to find *Sovyetskii Soyuz* and put an end to Malakov's treason. I can tell you personally that Captain Malakov is stone crazy and must be stopped. We are now in a state of war so I expect you to act accordingly. Man battle stations."

Confused but compliant, the young sailors accepted their orders without grumbling. As they took their stations, one conscript asked Bulgakov, "Is it true? Is Malakov crazy?"

Bulgakov nodded sagely. "They're all crazy," he replied. "Every last one of them."

From the commander's chair Zenko ordered, "Torpedo room, load a decoy in tube one."

Using a silent hydraulic hoist torpedomen lifted a torpedo-shaped decoy and loaded it into a tube. Running free in the water, the decoy was programmed to simulate the sounds of *Taifun*.

"Torpedo room to command, decoy loaded."

"Program the decoy to follow our present course and speed," Zenko ordered.

"Present course and speed, aye."

The weapons officer fed navigation data to the decoy's computers. "Decoy programmed and ready."

Zenko then ordered, "Maneuvering, prepare for all stop."

"Prepare for all stop, aye."

"On my mark, stop all engines and fire decoy. Three, two, one, mark."

The engines shut down, the propellers stopped turning and simultaneously the decoy shot out of the tube.

"Sonar to command. Decoy is in the water and running clear."

"Report on *Gorky*," Zenko barked.

"Maintaining course and speed."

Zenko glanced at Kugarin who was staring at the sonar monitors. "What do you think, Sasha?"

The zampolit recited what he hoped to be true. "Red Navy commanders are trained to trust their computers instead of their heads. If the computer tells Lorinski the decoy is *Taifun*, he'll believe it."

On the screen two blips moved steadily northwest on parallel courses. *Gorky* had taken the bait and was steaming abreast the decoy. "Helm, turn hard right," Zenko ordered. "All ahead slow."

The decoy deceived the sonars on *Gorky*, but not the more sophisticated arrays carried by *Reno*. On the control room repeater, two blips became three and the third turned sharply 180 degrees and headed south.

"Belay maneuvering," Gunner ordered. "Quiet in the boat. What the hell is going on here? Control to sonar. Morrison! What do you make of this?"

"One of them is a decoy, Skipper."

"Which one, for chrissake?"

"Want me to flip a coin?"

"Don't be a wiseass. Sort it out."

"They're awfully far away, Captain," Morrison said, "but I think the one coming back toward us is the sub. I think he fired a decoy to deceive the Akula."

"Why would he do that?" Gunner asked.

"It's probably an exercise, Skipper. Zenko might be putting these attack boat commanders to some kind of test. Too bad we can't ask him."

"Has *Minsk* moved?"

"She hasn't budged," Morrison answered. "I haven't heard a peep, but she's there, Skipper. I can smell her."

Gorky ran parallel to the decoy for an hour. When batteries powering the decoy's electric motor finally gave out, the motor died and the decoy sank. The sonar officer reported to Captain Lorinski that *Taifun* had disappeared.

Lorinski protested. "A submarine can't disappear unless her commander makes her disappear."

"I don't want to contradict you, sir," said the sonar officer, "but *Taifun* has vanished. She's not on the screens."

Lorinski didn't hesitate. "Reduce speed to one-third, start a search pattern, and find me thin ice," he ordered. "We're going to surface and send a message to Gremikha."

At Gremikha Admiral Deminov was in secure communications introducing Major Riziov to a group of staff officers from Polyarnyy. Holding a three-inch stack of signal orders, Riziov felt overwhelmed by the scope of Operation White Star. The communications center was accustomed to maintaining radio contact with no more than two or three ships at one time, but the Northern Fleet was preparing to deploy several squadrons of subs and surface ships.

At that moment a technician ran out of the radio room. "A

message from *Gorky*, sir," he said breathlessly to Deminov. "Coded for your eyes only."

Deminov took the flimsy into the code room and unlocked the cipher machine. A minute later he was in a state of total outrage, ranting curses at the dead walls of the tiny sound-proofed chamber. He rushed from the code room to Zenko's office and called Valotin in Leningrad on a secure, scrambled phone line. "Admiral," he said, trying to conceal his rage, "Zenko has betrayed us. He slipped away from *Gorky*. God know's what he's up to, but he may try to run the Gorlo and then go after *Sovyetskii Soyuz*. We must take precautions."

"Son of a bitch," Valotin hissed, and then the line remained silent for several seconds. "Find him and destroy him," Valotin finally ordered, "and do it quickly with minimum force. Minimum force, you understand. We have to keep this under wraps, Ivan. We can't let the Defense Council know anything has gone wrong with White Star."

"We can stop *Taifun* at Pulonga," Deminov said. "No one can get through the narrows in a Typhoon, not even Zenko."

"Minimum force," Valotin repeated. "No squadrons of helicopters. We can't set off every radar screen between Gremikha and Moscow."

Deminov slammed down the phone. He had let Zenko go. If the coup failed, his head would be the first to roll. "Major Riziov," he shouted. "Signal *Gorky* and tell Lorinski to proceed toward the Gorlo Strait, then signal Kuznetsov in *Minsk* and tell him Zenko may be heading for the strait in *Taifun*. The bastard will wish he'd never seen the inside of a submarine. Colonel Ludinov, assemble a security team. You're going to the sonar station at Pulonga on the strait. I'll speak to the helicopter crew myself." He turned to his staff officers and said, "Gentlemen, we have our first crisis."

The current flowing south continued to push *Reno* and her ice cover toward the White Sea. Finally, the inertial navigation monitor clicked over and read sixty-eight degrees twenty minutes north, forty degrees ten minutes east.

"We're over the line," Trout announced. "We're in Soviet internal waters."

"We surely can't move now," Gunner replied. "Big Ivan is breathing down our neck."

The approach of *Taifun* mesmerized the Americans. The Soviet sub had made a wide, sweeping turn, reversed course and had come back parallel to the shipping lane that led toward the Gorlo Strait. *Gorky* had blinked off the screens, joining *Minsk* as unknowns in a frightening situation. *Taifun* was steaming for the strait and *Reno* was drifting into the middle of a convention of Northern Fleet submarines.

In the sonar room tape-recorders rolled and screens flickered. "Don't breathe, don't sneeze, don't hiccup," Morrison whispered to the operators. "With a good arm you could hit Big Ivan with a rock." He switched on his intercom and said, "Sonar to control. *Taifun* is passing three miles off the port bow. He's running very quiet, Skipper."

Gunner felt a tightness in his chest. *Taifun* was so close he wanted to reach out and touch her to convince himself she was real.

Taifun glided by, apparently unaware of the American sub. So far, quiet and stealth had protected *Reno* from detection, but for how much longer? Soviet VLF radio traffic was increasing. Gunner assumed Gremikha was communicating with *Gorky* and *Minsk* as well as *Taifun*, but he had no way to decode the signals.

He closed his eyes and saw blue lights, nuclear sea monsters and the mysterious figure of Stefan Zenko.

After two hours of steaming at slow speed *Taifun* reached a point fifteen miles off Cape Orlov-Terskiy Tolstyy, a mile outside the shipping lane through the Gorlo Strait. Zenko ordered all stop and *Taifun* hovered near the western shore of the Gorlo, the "Throat," the frozen waterway between the Barents and White seas. Twenty-seven miles wide at the narrowest point off Pulonga, the Gorlo freezes first and melts last. During the brief ice-free summer, Red Navy subs pass through submerged. In winter when six feet of ice jams the Gorlo, Typhoons follow nuclear-powered icebreakers through the strait.

Zenko stepped to the sonar station and briefly reviewed the sonar "picture" of the ice taken shortly after leaving Gremikha, a three-dimensional representation of densely packed ice drifting south at a quarter-knot.

"Diving Officer, take her up."

Diving Officer Ludnov punched a series of commands into his console and the diving computer went to work. High-pressure air slowly forced seawater from the fore and aft main ballast tanks. The high-frequency low-powered sonar array sent information to the computer, which automatically adjusted dozens of trim tanks between the inner and outer hulls. *Taifun* rose slightly and nestled up against the undersurface of the ice canopy.

Zenko glanced at the ship's chronometer. "Sonar," he commanded, "stay alert for icebreakers. *Arktika* is due any moment."

In *Reno*'s control room Gunner caught himself thinking of Custer at Little Big Horn. Custer's loss had ennobled American sacrifice, revealed a powerful enemy and justified the conquest of the West. *Reno*'s loss under the arctic ice would contain nothing noble. A sudden, violent battle between submarines no longer carried the portent of World War III. Yet here they were playing out fossilized Cold War roles, flirting with a disaster that ultimately meant nothing. Existential submarines, Custer's last stand, bad microwaved coffee, arctic ice, what a life. Gunner glanced at Trout who had not taken his eyes from the sonar screens for hours. "You like the Red Sox this year?" he asked quietly

Trout didn't follow baseball and Gunner knew it. Without looking away from the screens he said, "Knock it off, Jack."

"You worried about the Russians?" Gunner asked with a touch of mockery. "They don't know we're here."

"You sure?"

"Yes, but if Zenko turns toward us, the game is up, and I'm wrong."

"This is one hell of a game of hide and seek," Trout said. "If one of these Russian boats cranks up an attack sonar, she'll paint a pretty picture of *Reno*."

"Them's the breaks," said Gunner. "Then we trust to anechoic tile, ice and faulty Russian sonars, I'd say the odds are even."

Aboard _Minsk_, Captain Boris Kuznetsov read the message from Gremikha and profaned mightily. Zenko had been on course for the central Barents when he had disappeared. Presumably, _Taifun_ was headed for Kuznetsov's sector.

The first Northern Fleet commander to sign Deminov's letter of support for the Union, Kuznetsov had volunteered to guard the strait. The prospect of sinking _Taifun_ and demolishing Zenko's illustrious career brought him no joy, but he justified that action by reminding himself that no officer could put himself above the Navy, and the Navy was solidly for the Union. If Zenko tried to run the strait, he would die.

Northern Fleet doctrine held that a Typhoon with her enormous size needed an icebreaker to precede her through the strait. To maintain security, Kuznetsov knew civilian shipping was never alerted to the presence of subs in and around the strait. Zenko would have to slip into the wake of one of the three or four icebreakers that passed daily through the narrow waterway. "Command to sonar," Kuznetsov ordered. "Post an icebreaker watch. Zenko won't waste time. He'll follow the first breaker through the strait and _Arktika_ is due."

Kuznetsov studied his sonar screens. His orders were straightforward, the plan simple. When _Taifun_ passed across his bows, probably not more than ten kilometers away, he would slip into her baffles directly astern and follow. If all went according to plan, the sonar defenses at Pulonga would be primed and ready. Antisubmarine helicopters would attempt the kill. If the helos' ordnance failed to penetrate the ice, Kuznetsov was ordered to destroy _Taifun_ with torpedoes.

At Gremikha Deminov and Colonel Ludinov hurried across the base to the airfield. In the main helicopter hangar Ludinov loaded a squad of spetsnaz commandos into a command helo while mechanics fitted spherical depth charges and two Type 533 torpedoes under a smaller gunship.

Normally, Deminov would have deployed dozens of antisubmarine helicopters and fixed-wing aircraft to locate and destroy a sub, but Valotin had insisted on minimal force. Under the circumstances, he mustered the most experienced crew from the antisubmarine helicopter squadron. Three young men in flight gear stood in a hangar listening to an unfamiliar admiral tell them the world was on fire.

Speaking in grave tones, Deminov said, "Comrades, we are faced with a crisis that threatens the national security of the Soviet Union. For more than thirty years the fleet has deployed strategic submarines armed with atomic rockets. The commanders of these ships enjoy the greatest trust of any military officers in our armed forces.

"It is my solemn duty to inform you that one of our commanders has violated his trust. We have a rogue ship. To put it bluntly, one of the commanders from this naval station has gone insane and threatens the Union with ballistic rockets."

Attentive now, drinking tea and smoking cheap cigarettes, the airmen shuffled their feet and slid sideways glances at one another. Zenko? Malakov? Both?

"For the first time," Deminov continued, "you're going to kill a sub, and when you've done your job, you'll receive medals you will never be allowed to wear. You will never speak of this mission to your fathers or your wives. We are not going to have a general alert. You men alone will find this pirate and sink him. You will be under the command of Colonel Ludinov operating out of the sonar station at Pulonga. Good luck and good hunting."

Deminov formally shook hands with each young warrior, the mechanics declared the helo ready for combat, and the tiny sub-killing armada took off for the short flight to Pulonga seventy miles south on the shores of the Gorlo Strait.

22 _Minsk_

Every fifteen seconds the powerful hull of the nuclear-propelled icebreaker _Arktika_ rose up and crashed like the hammer of Thor through the yard-thick ice of the Gorlo Strait, creating the same rhythmic blip on the sonar screens of _Taifun_, _Minsk_ and _Reno_. Leading a convoy of three ships on the last leg of the westbound Great Northern Sea Route from Vladivostok, _Arktika_ plowed toward Archangel at a stately six knots.

In _Taifun_'s command center, Zenko watched the sonar screen with rapt attention. To Zenko, any ship that could assault the ice with impunity was a powerful entity that deserved respect. Icebreakers owned the northern ocean. "Sorokin," he said, "put the Gorlo on the big screen."

The electronic chart changed from the small-scale White Sea to a larger-scale Gorlo Strait. The blinking red cursor indicated that the sub and the ice above had drifted a quarter-mile south since _Taifun_ had nested.

"Sonar Officer," Zenko commanded, "feed _Arktika_'s position and course to the navigation computer."

The passive sonar suite in the bow of the ship fed the machinery noises of the icebreaker and her convoy to the signal-processing computer which separated out the cacophonous thrashing of the ice. Four yellow dots representing the slowly moving _Arktika_ and her convoy popped onto the screen.

"Now feed the same information to the decoy in the torpedo

room. It worked once. Maybe it'll work again. We'll set the decoy to follow the last ship, *Tamyr*, and slowly accelerate under all the ships and break free into the White Sea."

Aboard *Minsk* Captain Kuznetsov watched the icebreaker on his sonar screen pounding through the drifting floes in the Gorlo Strait.

"If Zenko is coming through, now's his chance. Keep alert, sonar. You may be hearing *Taifun*'s engines any moment."

In *Reno*'s control room Gunner watched the convergence of ships the way a mountaineer watches an avalanche. If Zenko conformed to Soviet Navy practice, *Taifun* would fall in behind the last ship in the convoy. Gunner would then pilot *Reno* into *Taifun*'s baffles and become the caboose at the end of a submarine train. Time for a sanity check, he told himself.

"What are these Russians up to?" he asked Trout.

"Beats the shit out of me, Skipper," Trout replied, his eyes glued to the screen. "And where the hell is *Minsk?*"

"Release the decoy," Zenko ordered.

Hydraulic pressure quietly pushed the long, thin projectile from the torpedo tube. The decoy ran on quiet electric motors toward the southbound shipping channel and three minutes after leaving *Taifun* began emitting sounds duplicating the sub's machinery noises.

"Contact," said the sonar officer on *Minsk*. "It's *Taifun*."

"Run a computer check," Kuznetsov ordered.

"It's the computer that identifies *Taifun*, Captain."

Kuznetsov never argued with computers. Life was safer that way. "All ahead slow," he ordered.

Minsk began a slow turn that would put her directly behind the contact identified as *Taifun*.

"Sonar to control," said Chief Morrison. "Two contacts. One is positively ID'd as *Minsk*, but I'm not sure of the other, Skipper. The computer says it's *Taifun*, but I think it's another decoy."

"Why, Morrison?" Gunner asked.

"It's running too steady. Look at the line on the screen, Captain, steady as a rock. No sub runs under the ice like that at shallow depth. Now look at the line of the ship following, not quite so steady. The one ahead is a small decoy, the other behind is a much larger craft."

"So why," Gunner asked, "is _Minsk_ acting as if the lead contact were _Taifun?_ Her captain should know the difference."

"There's no accounting for taste," Morrison said. "Perhaps these are maneuvers and he's supposed to follow a decoy."

"What do you think, Gus?" Gunner asked Trout.

"I think if I could stop breathing," Trout said, "I would."

A fierce wind blew over the strait, whipping snow off the ice and creating the impression of a blizzard. A weak sun shone on _Arktika_ and her convoy loaded with oil-drilling machinery and a disassembled Japanese sawmill. _Arktika_ smashed through the ice, her mission one of peaceful commerce, while below, unseen and silent, like the dark underside of a split personality, deadly war machines sailed toward conflict and tragedy.

Piloting the convoy's last ship into the narrows, the master of _Tamyr_ watched an attack helicopter suddenly appear off his stern. An old Navy man, he recognized the antisubmarine armament slung under the aircraft and knew what it meant.

"Typhoons," he said to his first mate. "War games again."

Ten miles west of _Taifun_'s position, Colonel Ludinov's command helicopter landed near the Yakut fishing village of Pulonga on the northern shore of the Gorlo Strait. In a low rocky depression next to the village, the Navy had constructed a quonset hut jammed full of electronics. Ludinov led a squad of spetsnaz into the hut and found the commanding lieutenant, Igor Tarinski. A generator for the electric heaters had failed and the temperature inside was barely above freezing. Ludinov pulled a fur cap tight over his ears and blew on gloved hands as he spoke to Tarinski.

"We have a delicate situation here, Lieutenant. One of our Typhoon commanders has gone berserk and will try to run the strait. We're going to kill him right here, and we must maintain tight security."

"Yes, sir," said Tarinski, concealing his shock. "We have orders from fleet headquarters to prevent any submarine passage, but we weren't told why."

Ludinov walked over to the banks of radio equipment. "The first order of business is to establish a secure, scrambled channel to Gremikha."

"Yes, sir."

A moment later Ludinov had Deminov on the line from Zenko's office. "Any contact?" the admiral asked, his voice distorted by the scrambled radio frequency.

"No, sir. Not yet."

"Keep this line open."

Ludinov paced, urging the radar, radio and sonar operators to operate their equipment despite frozen fingers. The intimidating presence of the Northern Fleet's security chief set their hearts racing.

The bottom of the strait was seeded with mines which were deactivated with an icebreaker and convoy in the strait. Along with the mines were a dozen anchored sonars which performed erratically in the harsh water conditions. Mortars in shore batteries stood by, but their shells would only punch holes in the ice without significant effect below. Ludinov knew defense of the strait rested with the single attack helicopter from Gremikha and the torpedoes aboard *Minsk*.

"Colonel," the station's senior sonar officer announced, "icebreaker *Arktika* has entered the narrows with a convoy of three ships. I have a possible submerged contact behind the last ship."

Ludinov picked up the scrambled phone and reported to Deminov in Gremikha. "That's him," Deminov said with jubilation in his voice. "That's *Taifun*. Only Zenko would think he could sneak a Typhoon undetected through the Gorlo. Put Lieutenant Tarinski on the line."

When Tarinski heard Deminov's voice, he instinctively drew himself to attention. "Admiral," he said, "we don't have positive identification. Are there other subs in these waters?"

"It's *Taifun*," Deminov declared with conviction.

Tarinski glanced at the sonar screen, looked at the scowling Ludinov and wondered why he bothered to make a professional judgment. "Should we activate the mines?" he asked.

"No," Deminov said. "Mines will sink *Arktika* and the convoy and block the strait for months. Put Colonel Ludinov on again."

"Ludinov here, Admiral."

"Order *Arktika* and the other ships to keep moving no matter what and to observe radio silence. Jam all frequencies except the secure channels to the helicopter and to me."

"Yes, sir. Very good, sir. I'll keep you posted."

Ludinov set down the phone and turned to Tarinski. "Order the helo to drop a dipping sonar and verify the contact."

"Yes, sir."

Ludinov longed for the time when men warred with cannon aimed at the enemy's colors flying in the breeze. He hated depending on electronic gadgets to fight an enemy he couldn't see. Despite the cold he signaled one of his commandos to accompany him and stepped outside. Raft ice and fog lay over the shore. Ludinov walked along the rocky beach, kicking at the ice and muttering to the consternation of his heavily bundled escort.

"You're trapped, Zenko. No escape," he shouted into the wind.

"Pardon me, Comrade Colonel?" the soldier inquired politely.

"That bastard," Ludinov hissed, breath pumping from his lungs like exhaust from a steam engine.

The guard kept his mouth shut and remained a respectful distance away.

"Give me your gun," Ludinov ordered.

The spetsnaz unslung his Kalashnikov. Ludinov checked the clip, flicked off the safety and unloaded thirty rounds into the ice. Gunfire echoed over the frozen sea. "I hate ice," Ludinov said, returning the rifle to the startled soldier. "Don't you?"

The doors of the quonset hut burst open and men rushed outside. Voices rang over the rocks, "Colonel?"

"Nothing! Nothing! It was nothing!" Ludinov shouted back.

The guard stared at him, mentally calculating the days until his enlistment was completed. He had served with bad crazies in Afghanistan and he had just seen enough of this maniac.

Ludinov returned to the hut. The radar screen showed the icebreaker and convoy and the helicopter hovering over the strait.

"Jammers operating," said the radio officer.

Tension rose swiftly in the freezing quonset hut. The blinking red lights of the chronometers reflected off the faces of men beginning to show fatigue in the cold. The soldier who had gone outside with Ludinov stood in the corner wondering if the admiral would really put on a show and shoot up the video screens. That would be something to tell the boys in Polyarnyy.

"Helo reports positive contact!" shouted the radio officer.

Ludinov rushed to the screen. With data from the helo, the sonar operators detected submarine machinery noises in the southbound channel. Wind, thrashing ice and four surface ships contributed to signal interference, giving the operators an unclear image of the sub. Within a few seconds it appeared ahead of or behind itself, then as a scattered double image.

"It might be two contacts," the sonar officer said. "I don't have a good image. Ice conditions are very bad."

"Do you hear one prop or two?" Tarinski asked. A Typhoon had twin propellers, an Akula only one.

"I can't tell." With no positive identification, the sonar officer looked to Tarinski, but the lieutenant shrugged and said nothing.

Ludinov grabbed the phone. "Positive contact, Admiral."

At Gremikha Deminov could feel the jaws of the trap about to snap shut. "Is the helo in position?" he asked.

"Yes, sir."

Deminov understood the risk and had a moment of doubt. Kuznetsov would not have taken *Minsk* into the strait unless he were following *Taifun*, and the sonars at Pulonga should have two submerged contacts. But the sonars were unreliable. He could order *Minsk* to surface and then wait, but if *Taifun* was already inside the convoy, Zenko would escape.

On *Minsk* the sonar officer was beginning to have his own doubts about the contact identified by the computer as *Taifun*. The contact had advanced to within one hundred yards of the last ship in the convoy and was about to run under her stern. A Typhoon was too big for that, wasn't it? The officer said nothing and *Minsk* crept forward.

"Fire," Deminov ordered.

"Fire!" Ludinov commanded.

"Fire," repeated the radio operator to the helicopter crew.

In the helicopter the pilot turned to the sonar and weapons officer sitting behind him. "Here we go."

"I can't believe we're trying to kill Zenko," the weapons officer said, "if that's who it is."

"Shut up, Mikhail. Just do your job."

On the bridge of _Tamyr_, officers and men watched in awe as a lone helicopter dove at the broken ice in their wake and dropped small spherical bombs. The captain lit his pipe. "Must be an American trying to sneak into the White Sea," he said with mild distaste. "That's why they've jammed the radio."

"I thought the Cold War was over," said the first mate.

"Those are depth charges," the captain said, puffing on his pipe. "I don't think the Navy has started killing fish."

The first depth charge landed on _Minsk_'s sail, bounced off and exploded a meter off the starboard side, knocking out three hydrophones. His eardrums ruptured, the sonar officer screamed, ripped off his headphones and writhed in pain on the deck.

The crew of young conscripted sailors panicked. Discipline in the command center dissolved in turmoil. Terrified men ran amok. In the confusion someone tripped over a sonar console, pulled loose a wire and plunged the sub into darkness. Close to panic himself, Kuznetsov screamed, "Emergency surface. Get power back on in here!"

The second charge exploded over the stern, blew off the rudder and prop and punctured the pressure hull. Water gushed into the engineering compartment. Circuits snorted, fires started and black smoke filled the compartment.

In the command center the emergency power system popped on the lights.

"Emergency service. Blow all tanks."

The diving officer kept his head and punched buttons on his control board. High-pressure air forced ballast from the forward ballast tanks but the stern controls failed to respond. The bow rose swiftly and breached the surface of ship-broken ice like a maddened whale.

Men and equipment began to slide aft. Kuznetsov pulled himself to the sonar station, crawled over the unconscious sonar officer and looked at the single functioning screen. The contact he had been following continued south behind the convoy and was almost through the narrows. "Zenko!" he screamed. "Radio! Let them know *Taifun* is getting away."

"All frequencies are jammed," the radio officer shouted.

The water was 150 feet deep, less than the length of the ship. The stern would hit bottom and Kuznetsov hoped *Minsk* could dance on her tail long enough to save the crew. Water began to seep into the command center, then a series of explosions aft rocked the hull.

"Abandon ship!" Kuznetsov shouted, but his voice was inaudible in the din. The captain lunged for the ladder that led to the top of the sail. Terrified sailors clustered at the top.

"Open the hatch!"

No one moved. Kuznetsov knocked the men aside and turned the wheel. Water poured in, men screamed and tumbled back into the sub. The bow began to sink as Kuznetsov swam up through the freezing water.

At Pulonga a radar officer shouted, "Sub on the surface, Colonel. We got him." Then he paused, listening to his headphone. "The helo pilot says it's not a Typhoon. It's an Akula," he said, his voice dry and quaking. "She's sinking."

Frantically searching the room for someone to blame, Ludinov grabbed the phone. "Admiral," he said tersely to Deminov, "we attacked the wrong sub. *Minsk* is sinking in the strait."

Deminov didn't care a damn about *Minsk*. Mistakes happen in war. He shot back, "Then where the hell is *Taifun?*"

Minsk was going down fast by the stern. Fire and smoke poured into the forward compartments and blackened sailors scrambled out the forward hatches. Three inflatable life rafts bobbed in the freezing water. Then the bow slid under. Thirty men were in rafts and a dozen in the water dying of exposure. Captain Kuznetsov died trying to drag a seaman recruit out of the sail. The bodies of ninety men, drowned or burned to death, drifted in the waters of the Gorlo Strait. Struck by ice floes, one raft capsized immediately, spilling men into the deadly cold sea.

In shock, sailors on *Tamyr* stood helplessly on the fantail watching the death throes of *Minsk*. A second raft was foundering.

"Captain," said the first mate, "we should put a boat in the water. Those men are in Soviet uniforms."

A man of the sea, the captain knew his duty was to rescue men in peril. He couldn't fathom the reasons for the travesty he was witnessing, and with his radio jammed he couldn't ask, but he had no doubt *Tamyr* would be sunk if she stopped. He drew on his pipe and shook his head.

At Pulonga Ludinov was still on the phone when the sonar operator sang out, "Submerged contact. I've got *Taifun* back. She's ahead of the icebreaker and heading for the open sea."

Stunned, Ludinov repeated the announcement to Deminov.

Sitting in Zenko's office in Gremikha, Deminov held the telephone at arm's length and stared at it in horror. Zenko had broken through into the White Sea. Rage pounded through Deminov's temples and for a moment he was speechless. He should have shot Zenko in the head right here in his office. He should have gone to Pulonga himself. He should have picked a more competent commander than Kuznetsov. After a minute he regained his composure and barked orders at Ludinov. "Send the helo twenty kilometers south of the strait with orders to drill through the ice. If the crew hears anything, understand, anything, they are to launch torpedoes through holes in the ice. Place two men on *Arktika* and each ship in the convoy to maintain radio silence. The ships are to proceed fifty kilometers into the White Sea and circle in the ice."

"Yes, sir. There appear to be survivors from *Minsk*."

"Bring them to Gremikha," Deminov ordered. "Leave part of your squad as guards at Pulonga. Tell Lieutenant Tarinski to expect *Gorky* to pass through the strait in a few hours."

"Yes, sir."

The admiral slammed down the phone and stormed into the communications center. Now Zenko's intentions were crystal clear. The treacherous little bastard was stalking Malakov. "Major Riziov," Deminov shouted. "I need to contact *Sovyetskii Soyuz*."

23
Tamyr

"Depth charges in the water!"

After days of enforced quiet, Morrison's shout had reverberated in Gunner's ears. Explosion after explosion had reduced *Minsk* to electronic debris on *Reno's* screens.

No one on the American sub ever had witnessed the sinking of a ship in combat. The ugly noise of submarine death, the screech of metal and roar of water rushing into sacrosanct spaces came clearly through the sonars. Long after the last echoes died away, the sounds remained, burned forever into the memories of the men who heard them.

Every man in the control room had the same thought: That could have been us.

"Now we know what's waiting in the strait," Trout said quietly.

Gunner struggled to remain clear-headed. "What in God's name is going on here, Gus? Why would the Russians sink one of their own subs?"

"It sure as hell isn't an exercise," Trout said.

"*Minsk* thought she was tracking *Taifun*," Gunner said. "If they sank *Minsk*, they're trying to protect *Taifun*, but I swear, I can't tell the good guys from the bad guys. Where's *Taifun* now? Control to sonar. What happened to the decoy?"

"It's gone, Skipper," Morrison said in a dead voice. "There's so much noise and confusion I can't tell. They may have blown it up."

"Everything all right in sonar?" Gunner asked.

"We're having a party here, Skipper. We—"

"Can the smart remarks, Chief. Not appreciated right now."

Gunner switched off the intercom, rubbed his eyes and tried to imagine the scene above. Helicopters, planes, the sonar station at Pulonga, half the Northern Fleet. Had *Minsk* been a rogue ship? Would *Reno* be next if he moved? If he didn't move? Where was *Gorky*? Where was *Taifun*? He could drive himself crazy with questions.

"Jack, we need to talk."

Gunner looked up to see Trout leaning over him like a concerned uncle. "This'll give the Pentagon something to analyze for the next ten years," he said. "Jesus Christ, I don't know what we got ourselves into. *Taifun* is still out there, waiting. Maybe Zenko's not going through the strait at all."

Trout pulled Gunner into a corner of the control room. "Jack, you've got to report the sinking of *Minsk* to Norfolk," he said. "That's why they sent us here."

"I sure as hell can't stick a mast up now," Gunner said. "If Zenko moves his boat, I'm going with him. I'm not going to turn tail and run."

"They're killing each other," Trout insisted. "We could be next."

"Gus, I'm scared, you're scared, any sane man would be scared, but our orders are to follow a Typhoon wherever she goes."

"At your discretion," Trout reminded his captain. "You're authorized to go into the White Sea, but you're not ordered in."

"Same difference, and you know it." Gunner felt anger rising in his voice and tried to hold it in check. "Listen, Gus," he said, "I don't like being inside Soviet waters with the Russians sinking each other, but we're here and we'll stay. If *Taifun* goes to Archangel, so will we. That's a command decision."

"Aye aye," Trout replied curtly and returned to the navigation table.

On *Taifun* the reality of civil war shocked the command center into silence. After all the speeches and threats, posturing and polarization, Russians were killing Russians. *Minsk* had been destroyed, but every man knew *Taifun* had been the intended target.

Zenko stood before the commander's console, his face an inch from the screen. "They were waiting for us," he said quietly to Kugarin. "I knew most of the officers on *Minsk*. I taught tactics to Kuznetsov. He should have paid more attention."

"Do you think the decoy made it through?" Kugarin asked.

"I doubt it. Sorokin!"

"Yes, sir."

"Put up a chart of the mines and sonars in the strait."

The chart appeared on the monitor, red dots for mines, blue for the sonars lining the shipping channels north and south. Zenko studied the screen. "Deminov didn't use mines for fear of sinking the convoy," he commented. "The depth charges and explosions on *Minsk* may have destroyed some sonars, but we must assume all are operational. Sonar! Report on the convoy."

"All four ships are still moving south at six knots," the sonar officer replied. "They never stopped."

"What are you going to do, Stefan?" Kugarin asked.

Zenko answered decisively. "Go through immediately while they're confused. If we follow directly behind *Tamyr*, we should encounter no difficulty with the ice. Once we pass through the narrows at Pulonga, the water deepens and we can break away from the convoy. We can't get at Malakov sitting here, can we?" He switched on the ship's intercom. "Men of *Taifun*, prepare to run the Gorlo Strait. We may be attacked with depth charges, but this ship can survive a dozen depth charge explosions. All hands report to damage control stations. That is all." He turned off the intercom and ordered, "Diving Officer, descend to twelve meters."

"Twelve meters, aye."

The sub slowly dropped away from her nest under the ice. Twelve meters put almost forty feet of water between the top of the sail and the surface, giving *Taifun* clearance to pass under the keel of *Tamyr* should she stop for any reason.

"Depth, twelve meters, Captain."

"Very well. Engineering, give me slow speed."

"Slow speed," rang the acknowledgment.

Taifun began to make way.

. . .

At Pulonga Colonel Ludinov took over the radio officer's terminal and ordered the attack helicopter to fly south, punch a hole in the ice and submerge a dipping sonar. Then he turned to Tarinski. "I'm leaving in the command helo to place men on the ships in the convoy and then collect the survivors from *Minsk*," he said. "Maintain a vigilant sonar watch. The attack sub *Gorky* will be passing through the strait in a few hours. Captain Lorinski will signal before he makes his transit."

Leaving a spetsnaz sergeant and one commando behind with instructions to shoot anyone who attempted to break radio silence, Ludinov packed the rest of the squad into his helicopter and took off. *Arktika* was now four miles from Pulonga, the convoy strung out a half mile behind her.

Once again in command of his station, Tarinski offered tea to his watchdogs.

"It's damned cold in here," said the sergeant.

"The generator's down," Tarinski told him. "We were about to fix it when the colonel arrived."

"Ludinov is gone. Let's get some heat," the sergeant suggested.

"That's a wonderful idea," said the sonar officer. "I'll do it."

No one in the quonset hut was anxious to discuss what had happened. Over the next few days Tarinski knew a lot of frozen bodies would turn up in the strait, and he fervently hoped one would not be his. While the sonar officer tinkered with the generator, Tarinski monitored the sonar screen and saw a flicker of what might be submerged machinery noises.

"Vasily," he said to the sonarman. "Take a look at this."

"What do you see?" asked the spetsnaz sergeant.

"A possible contact in the channel."

The sonar officer took one look and said, "That's a Typhoon."

On *Reno*, Gunner had taken a five-minute break from the control room to eat microwaved macaroni and cheese. The bland food soothed his churning stomach, but the brief respite was ended by a buzzing phone.

"Wardroom, Gunner."

"Big Ivan has started to move, Skipper."

Gunner was in the control room in an instant.

"Control to sonar. Where is she?"

"Bearing two one two. Range six thousand yards."

"Jesus," said Gunner. "She's closer than I thought. Control to maneuvering, give me twenty percent steam."

"Aye aye, Captain. Twenty percent."

Gunner switched on the intercom. "Attention all hands. Rig for silent running."

"Helm, steer one nine two degrees," Zenko ordered.

"Steering one nine two."

"Sonar, what's our range to *Tamyr?*"

"Three thousand meters."

"We want to fall in five hundred meters behind her," Zenko said. "Sing out the range in hundred-meter increments."

"Aye aye, Captain. Twenty-nine hundred, twenty-eight hundred, twenty-seven hundred . . ."

After fifteen minutes the range was reduced to seven hundred meters. Zenko held his breath, waiting for depth charges.

"Range five hundred meters, Captain," said the sonar officer. "Clear water above. We're in her wake."

"Steer two zero five degrees."

"Steering two zero five."

"Steady as she goes. Diving Officer, what's the depth under our keel?"

"Twenty meters, Captain."

"Alert me instantly if the depth falls below fifteen meters."

"Aye aye."

"And remind me to send the master of *Tamyr* a bottle of good Georgian champagne."

"Sonar to control. Big Ivan is moving into the southbound channel behind the last ship in the convoy."

"Maneuvering, give me slow speed on propulsors," Gunner ordered. "Forward ho!"

Like a deadly sea snake, *Reno* slipped out of her secret nest under the ice. Gunner maneuvered the boat into the channel and carefully matched *Taifun*'s course and speed.

"Control to sonar. Stay right with him, Morrison. I want to be no less than five hundred yards behind him in case he jukes."

"It's like following a double windmill, Skipper."

Below the surface behind *Tamyr*, *Taifun* passed into the narrows opposite Pulonga. Zenko ordered a glass of tea. "Sorokin, have the charts for the Gulf of Kandalakshskiy ready, if you please," he said to the quartermaster.

"Aye aye, Captain. They're already in the buffer."

Zenko swallowed a mouthful of tea and tried to project calm.

Ludinov's helicopter hovered over *Tamyr*. The ship began to slow to allow two commandos to be lowered onto the heaving deck. While the helo pilot maneuvered the sling, the radio suddenly squawked on the scrambled channel. "Seabreeze, this is Pulonga."

"This is Seabreeze," Ludinov answered.

"We have two contacts in the channel. Repeat, two contacts."

Astonished, Ludinov realized the full implication of the hasty destruction of *Minsk*. Two contacts had to be *Taifun* and *Gorky*. Deminov had sent the attack helicopter south too soon. Ludinov had never felt so helpless. The command helo's armament consisted of two cannon, antiaircraft missiles and a machine gun, useless against a sub.

"Permission to activate mines, Colonel," Tarinski asked over the radio.

"No! Alert the attack helo that the target will be coming toward them from the north."

"Should I inform Admiral Deminov?"

What's the point? Ludinov thought, but he said, "Yes, I'm afraid so."

On *Taifun* the sonar officer reported, "Sonar to command. *Tamyr* is slowing."

"All stop," Zenko commanded. "Let's not hit him."

"All stop, aye."

"Reverse engines, half speed."

"Reverse engines, half speed, aye."

The sub shuddered as her props strained to reverse her momentum and pull her backward.

"Range to *Tamyr*."

"Four hundred meters and closing."

"How much water underneath us?"

"Sixty meters."

"Diving Officer, take us down another ten meters. All ahead slow."

"Range two hundred meters and closing."

"She's going to reverse," said Zenko.

"One hundred meters and closing."

Above them, trying to maneuver under the helicopter, *Tamyr* stopped dead in the ice. Her prop began to spin in reverse, pulling the stern down toward the vulnerable bow of *Taifun*.

"Flooding forward ballast tanks," said the diving officer, a wavering voice betraying his fear.

Morrison spoke over *Reno*'s intercom with exaggerated calm. "Sonar to control. Big Ivan has reversed his screws."

"Propulsors all stop," Gunner ordered. "Engage shaft. Prepare to reverse."

Reno continued to move forward on momentum. The boat was so quiet Gunner thought he could hear water sloshing in the trim tanks. His hands were trembling. Trout looked as if he wanted to vomit.

"You pay your insurance premium this year?" Gunner asked.

"Are you going to reverse or make jokes?" Trout retorted.

"If I engage my prop now, the Russians will hear me."

"They sure as hell will hear you if you hit them."

"Control to sonar. What's our range to *Taifun*?"

"Nine hundred yards and closing."

The bow of *Taifun* abruptly tilted forward at a shallow angle and the huge sub passed directly under the hull of *Tamyr*, clearing the prop by less than a yard. The entire command center crew stared straight up as if expecting the ship's rudder to burst through the sail. Sounding like a tank division racing through a forest, the roar of *Tamyr*'s engines rattled through the sub. As

Taifun inched forward, the machinery noise was replaced by the sound of crashing ice.

"Sonar to command. We're past her."

A hollow cheer echoed through the command center. The danger of colliding with *Tamyr* had passed, but the danger of striking the bottom of the shallow strait dramatically increased.

Zenko alone looked unworried. He could go to the bottom and wait for the ship to pass overhead, but he chose to press forward. Glancing at the chart he said, "Helm, steer left into the northbound channel and follow the forty-meter line west-southwest."

"Forty-meter line west-southwest, aye."

"We'll go around the rest of the convoy. If they were going to activate the minefield, they would have done it already. Engineering, give me ten knots."

"Ten knots, aye."

"Deep water ahead, Captain," said the diving officer. "We can drop a towed array astern if you like."

"Not yet," said Zenko. "Make our depth fifty meters."

At Gremikha, Admiral Deminov was preparing a message of warning to Malakov when Tarinski's call came through from Pulonga.

"You have what?" Deminov yelled into the phone.

"Two contacts, sir. The lead sub is definitely a Typhoon."

"Has *Gorky* signaled her approach?"

"No, sir."

"Then who is the second sub?"

"We can't get a positive ID under these ice conditions," Tarinski said. "We think it's *Gorky*."

Deminov vented his frustration by screaming over the phone. "Don't tell me what you think! Tell me what you see!"

Tarinski had given up hope of understanding exactly who was involved in this conflict and what it was about. The sonars clearly showed two subs in the strait, he told Deminov. The Typhoon had moved past the convoy and was almost through the minefield.

As Tarinski described each movement, Deminov became increasingly desperate. "Activate the last two mines in both channels," he ordered.

"But, sir," Tarinski said, "the mines might damage the icebreaker and the surface ships."

"Follow my orders, Lieutenant, or I'll have you shot."

"Yes, sir."

Tarinski unlocked the mine control console. A bank of thirty green lights glowed across the panel. The lieutenant threw two switches, expecting two lights to change from green to red, but nothing happened. He tried again with the same result. He tried a third switch and a fourth. Over the long winter either salt water had corroded the cables, or the panel itself had faulty connections and shoddy workmanship. Defective mines were not unknown in the Red Navy. Tarinski slammed the panel with the heel of his hand, gave up and returned to the phone.

"The minefield is dead, Admiral. I think we have a defective control panel."

"Where is the Typhoon now?" Deminov asked.

"Through the narrows, almost in the open sea."

"Then he's trapped in the White Sea," Deminov said. "Contact the attack helo and make sure it's ready. He won't escape again."

On _Reno_ Morrison said, "Sonar to control. Big Ivan is increasing speed."

"Thank you, sonar. Helm, steer left ten degrees. We're going around the convoy. Maneuvering, step on the gas. Give me ten knots."

Reno turned into the northbound channel, picked up speed and steamed into the White Sea. No depth charges ignited the sonar screens, no torpedoes flashed from _Taifun._ Perhaps, Gunner thought, it was only a matter of time.

24   The White Sea

Ninety-five miles southwest of Pulonga the ELF alarm flashed in the radio room of *Sovyetskii Soyuz*. Routine messages from Gremikha had been arriving on schedule every two hours, but for the first time the two-letter ELF message ordered Malakov to ascend to VLF depth.

Only twenty hours had elapsed since *Sovyetskii Soyuz* pulled away from Severodvinsk, but Malakov felt lightyears removed from the past. Somewhere between the glow of Archangel and the murky depths nine hundred feet below the ice, he had made a clean break, achieving in the process a liberation experienced only by outlaws and revolutionaries.

Sitting on the bottom of Kandalakshskiy Gulf with primed atomic weapons had forced Malakov to a new level of introspection. With time to think, he realized he had been chosen for a unique mission. He hoped the government refused to accept his father-in-law's demands. If he received an order to launch, he would experience the thrill of doing what no one had ever dared to do. Only action mattered, not cause or effect. He had surpassed morality, gone beyond good and evil and entered another realm, a forbidden zone where nothing was forbidden.

"Diving Officer, take us to VLF radio depth."

The sub rose; the message arrived. Expecting a launch order, Malakov took the printout into the code room in a state of intense anticipation. Instead he read:

FROM COMMANDER OPERATION WHITE STAR
TO COMMANDING OFFICER SOVYETSKII
SOYUZ: BE ADVISED TAIFUN HAS ENTERED
WHITE SEA AT 1800H. ALL EFFORTS
BEING MADE TO LOCATE AND INTERDICT.
SCHEDULE POSTPONED TWELVE HOURS.
DEMINOV.

Malakov was disappointed, yet he felt a strange sense of exhil-aration. Zenko could have only one purpose in the White Sea, and a duel with such an adversary appealed to the commander of *Sovyetskii Soyuz*. He tried to imagine the scene at Gremikha. Deminov had committed a monumental error in allowing Zenko to sortie. Had panic compounded his blunder? The un-certainty provoked by the message was unsettling but not dev-astating. Before Zenko could attack, he had to find *Sovyetskii Soyuz*. As long as the *Soyuz* remained silent, Zenko's task was impossible. For *Taifun* to approach close enough to launch a weapon, she had to reveal herself and suffer the consequences.

"Diving Officer, take us back to the bottom."

As *Sovyetskii Soyuz* sank back into the depths, Malakov showed the message to Sergov.

"I don't like being hunted by Stefan Zenko," the political officer said, obviously frightened.

"Zenko may think he's hunting us," Malakov said, "but now we have an opportunity to destroy him. To search, he must make noise. All we need do is wait. In a few hours none of it will matter. We'll launch, then we'll kill *Taifun*."

"Do we tell the crew?"

"No," Malakov said. "They may be willing to help us kill a million Georgians, but I think Zenko will scare them as much as he scares you, my brave zampolit."

Sovyetskii Soyuz resumed her silent vigil. Malakov paced through the rocket compartments, checking the computers, testing the circuits, counting the minutes.

Taifun had steamed twelve miles from Pulonga when her radio room computers automatically recorded two messages transmit-ted from Gremikha to *Sovyetskii Soyuz*. Without crypto keys the signals remained undeciphered. Nevertheless, Zenko guessed what they meant. The first, short ELF message was clearly an order to ascend, the second VLF signal a warning.

To Zenko's advantage, Deminov's need for secrecy, for keeping events underwater and out of sight, made the full capability of the Northern Fleet's antisubmarine forces unavailable. As far as Zenko knew, *Sovyetskii Soyuz* was unaccompanied by escorts. She had neither helicopters nor attack submarines for protection. An attacking force relying on sonars would have difficulties distinguishing between *Sovyetskii Soyuz* and *Taifun*. Deminov's people had already made one mistake by sinking *Minsk*. Malakov was alone with a ship rigged for silence and a nervous crew who had probably been told they were doing their patriotic duty. Zenko asked himself, Is Malakov afraid? No, his arrogance makes him unafraid, and that's his weakness.

"Sorokin," Zenko called out. "Gather the division around the commander's chair."

When the men had assembled, Zenko said, "We have no time to search the entire White Sea for *Sovyetskii Soyuz*. We will search in Kandalakshskiy Gulf first. Before we left Gremikha, Deminov as much as admitted that Malakov is there. If he isn't, we may never find him. If he is, with luck we can lure him out of his hole. Division commanders, prepare to man your battle stations. We're going to start combat drills and turn this ship into a hunter-killer. Torpedo drill in five minutes!"

Two thousand yards astern, *Reno* crept through the sea in the Soviet sub's baffles. In every compartment a red fluorescent sign glowed "Silent Running."

In the galley cooks churned out hundreds of microwaved meals and for their efforts earned a running commentary about Bluenose Airways and its lousy food.

In the chiefs' mess Morrison accepted a plastic tray. "What is this, Cookie?" he asked suspiciously.

"Salisbury steak."

"That's a steak?"

"You want tofu, Chief? You want seaweed and raw fish?"

"Up yours. I get that at home. I want sliders," Morrison demanded. Hamburgers.

"Yeah, me too," said the cook. "But we gettin' down with the Rooshins, and there ain't no quiet sliders."

Taking a seat opposite Adams, Garrett and Deuterman, Morrison pushed food around his tray without tasting it. Skin sagged under his eyes. Unmowed bristle decorated his chin. Depth charges reverberated in his ears.

"Where's your black hat now, Morrison?" Garrett asked.

"You look like shit," said Deuterman. "What's the matter with you?"

"No sleep."

"You still think the Cold War is over, Morrison? We got a Typhoon running loose in the water bigger'n shit."

Morrison reached inside his shirt, whipped out his black Russian cap and jammed it on his head. "Ho, Amerikanski, you come in White Sea, you die!"

"Oh, Jesus, here we go again."

In the control room Trout said with genuine pride, "Well, Skipper, you made it into the White Sea. Few men can say that."

"I haven't done a damned thing until I get us out," Gunner replied with a snort.

The narrows of the strait were behind them and _Taifun_ ahead. If Zenko turned on an active sonar, _Reno_ would stand out like a black eye.

"Where's he going and what's he doing, Gus?"

Trout leaned over the navigation table and aligned a grease pencil with a straightedge. "That's the sixty-four-dollar question. He's going to hide under the ice, wait for a message from Moscow and start World War Three."

"You're nuts."

"Somebody is, that's for damned sure. They're not trying to stop Zenko. That's why they blew up _Minsk_. They have two Typhoons in the White Sea now, and they don't want anyone near them, including us. It looks bad to me," Trout said, trying to be perfectly candid. "Typhoons have only one purpose, to blow the world to hell. I think Zenko and company want to start a war, and the other guys are trying to stop them."

Gunner lit a cigarette. "Sounds like you've made up your mind who the goods guys are, and Zenko's the bad guy."

"Seems pretty obvious," Trout acknowledged. "There's no way a Typhoon can be a good guy."

"Then maybe I should put a torpedo right into his props, a baby nuke, say." Gunner let a tiny smile curl his lip. Smoke drifted across his face. "Isn't that why they call me Plutonium Jack?"

"I don't think I'd go quite that far. That would be an act of war."

"Coming into the White Sea is an act of war," Gunner said. "Ask a judge."

From the air the southern reaches of the Gorlo Strait looked like a frozen salt mine. Six miles north of *Reno*'s position, Deminov's attack helicopter hovered five hundred feet above the ice, dropped a small charge of explosive plastic to the surface and blew a thirty-foot hole in the ice.

The sonar operator aboard the helo lowered a hydrophone on a cable fifty feet into the water and promptly heard submarine machinery noises. "Contact," he said to the pilot. "Incredible on the first try."

"What do you hear? One prop or two?"

"Hard to tell. Computer reading, range eleven kilometers. Bearing one eight seven. I have a second contact. Same bearing, range twelve kilometers. We're damn near right on top of two subs."

"Which one is which?"

"How the fuck do I know?"

"We already blew up the wrong sub once today."

"So what? We don't pick the targets. We follow orders."

On *Reno* the explosion almost knocked three sonar operators out of their chairs.

"What the hell was that?" Billie Stewart said. "Sonar to control. Reading one explosion, possibly in the water, possibly on the surface."

"What kind of explosion, Billie?"

"Don't know sir. One sharp report, range six miles, bearing zero zero eight."

Gunner checked his sonar monitor. The screen showed ice

crashing on the surface, reverberations bouncing off the bottom, and _Taifun_ motoring steadily at ten knots. Gunner knew sound waves from the explosion would have echoed off _Reno_ and revealed her presence to _Taifun_. "The game is up," he said and switched on the intercom. "Prepare for high-speed maneuvering. All hands, general quarters."

In the chiefs' mess Morrison stopped in midchew. "Jesus," he swore. "What now?"

Thirty seconds later he burst into the sonar room and took the supervisor's chair. _Taifun_ had stopped. _Reno_ was banking left to avoid ramming the Soviet sub's stern.

On _Taifun_, Zenko heard the explosion and knew what it was.

"They're punching holes in the ice. All stop."

The flow of steam stopped immediately but _Taifun_ continued to glide forward on momentum. The sonar officer took advantage of silent engine compartments to listen to his stern array and was shocked at what he heard.

"Sonar to command! There's a sub directly behind us!"

Zenko dropped a plastic teacup on the command center's blue carpet and stared in amazement at the spreading stain.

"Who the hell is that? Sonar, can you give me an ID?"

"I only got a glimpse, but the computer says it's not an Akula."

"Not an Akula!"

The shock in the sonarman's voice vibrated through the intercom speaker. "Preliminary computer reading is American Los Angeles class, Captain."

Zenko switched the monitor to wide area display and saw a slow blip crawl along _Taifun_'s track. He tapped his fingers on the chart table.

An American!

A turd in the honey.

Kill the son of a bitch. Now.

Shocked into speechlessness, Kugarin walked close to the screen. After a moment he found his voice and said, "You can't sink him, Stefan."

"What the hell is he doing here?"

"What they always do," Kugarin said. "He's a spy."

Zenko pointed at the screen. "In the White Sea?"

Kugarin could feel the specter of Cold War hatred creeping over his old friend. The Main Enemy. The Americans.

Kugarin spoke quickly and with vehemence. "Stefan, forget him. He may have been in the White Sea for months. You know how quiet their boats are. If he was up to mischief, he would have already made a nuisance of himself. You can't shoot him!"

"I don't have to," Zenko said. "Our friends will do it for us."

Above, the helicopter pilot ordered, "Arm torpedo."

Like most Soviet naval forces, the ASW helos of Air Gremikha were armed with old-style, active sonar-guided Type 533 torpedoes. Fast, lethal and reliable, Type 533s were designed specifically to kill American subs. No one had ever considered how effective they might be against Typhoons.

"Torpedo armed," the weapons officer replied.

"Reading only one contact now," the sonar officer announced.

"Our orders are to drop our fish on anything that swims," the pilot said. "Drop torpedo."

"Torpedo away," said the weapons officer.

The fifteen-foot-long Type 533 splashed into the water, sank twenty feet and started its electric motor. Passive sonars in the nose heard *Reno*'s movement in the water and in thirty seconds the deadly fish accelerated to forty knots.

The sound came out of nowhere as if generated by the sea itself. The Soviet torpedo rushing toward *Reno* sounded like a freight train. For the first time in his career Morrison screamed into a microphone, "Torpedo in the water! Range six miles and closing fast. Bearing zero zero seven."

Gunner cursed himself under his breath. You shithead. You pushed too hard and now they've heard you. In the game of hide and seek, you lose.

He grabbed the intercom mike. "Helm, hard left! Maneuvering, give me flank speed."

With a great burst of bubbles the prop clawed at the water. *Reno* jumped forward. In the control room Gunner could smell the acrid odor of fear.

"Sonar to control, we're cavitating."

"I know we are, Morrison. Shut up!"

Banking hard left like an airplane, *Reno* slowly built up speed.

"Sonar to command. Torpedo range four miles and closing."

"I see it on the screen, Morrison," Gunner shouted. "Pipe down. That's an order. Control to weapons. Load a static decoy in tube one. Load Captor mines in tubes four, five and six."

In the torpedo room Chief Garrett and three torpedomen pulled a decoy from the racks, plugged in electronic guidance modules, and drove the shaft into a tube.

"Torpedo room to control. Decoy ready. Loading Captors now."

"Flood tube number one. Open the outer doors. Maneuvering, give me one hundred ten percent steam. Turn on the afterburners."

Zenko watched his screens in utter amazement. The American sub gained speed but clearly couldn't outrun a Type 533. He could hear the sub accelerating into the void.

"How long do you think he's been following us, Sasha?"

"Ever since we left Gremikha."

"And we never heard him. That's frightening. He could have sunk us at any time but he didn't."

"He must have observed the sinking of *Minsk*," Kugarin said.

"No doubt," Zenko replied. "He's caught in a crossfire, and he's going to die without ever knowing why."

Designed for silence and stealth, heavily laden with arms and electronics, *Reno* was no hotrod. With a top speed of thirty-seven knots, she could not outrun the torpedo, and Gunner knew it. When the boat reached twenty knots, he ordered, "Lieutenant Sharpe, fire decoy."

Sharpe punched keys on the fire control console and the static decoy dropped away from a torpedo tube. Emitting sounds similar to *Reno*'s, the decoy remained suspended immobile in the water while *Reno* hurried forward.

The torpedo ignored the decoy and continued to pursue the submarine.

"Sonar to control. Torpedo still closing! Range two miles."

"Torpedo room," Gunner ordered. "Prepare Captor mines for sequential deployment at twenty-, thirty- and forty-second delays."

In ninety seconds Chief Garrett and the torpedo gang had three Captors loaded in tubes. Encapsulated torpedoes, the mines had acoustic activators. When the built in sonars heard machinery, they released torpedoes.

"Torpedo room to control, Captors loaded and armed. Delayed activation set at ten-second intervals."

"Flood tubes."

Lieutenant Sharpe opened the outer doors of the torpedo tubes, flooding them with seawater.

"Release tubes four, five and six."

Compressed air pushed the mines from the tubes. Twenty seconds later the first activator switched on. The mine's sonar heard *Reno* but an automatic cutout disallowed the sub as a target. The sonar continued to search until it heard the Soviet torpedo racing at forty knots now only a mile away. The activator released its torpedo just as the activator in the second mine switched on. The second activator heard the first torpedo, decided it was a target and released its torpedo. Three seconds later the torpedo from the second mine destroyed the first in a tremendous undersea explosion. The third activator switched on and heard the Soviet weapon, locked on and released. The two torpedos charged through the sea and collided at a combined speed of seventy knots.

Shock waves from the two blasts slammed into *Reno*, which bucked like a toy boat and steamed ahead undamaged.

"Sonar to control. I have clear screens. Torpedo destroyed."

"All stop," Gunner ordered. "Quiet in the boat."

As *Reno* slowly deaccelerated, every man in the control room looked as if he had just stepped from a bath. Lieutenant Sharpe clutched the weapons console in a death grip. Terror distorted the cherubic face of Lieutenant O'Connell standing near the radio-room door. Gus Trout was frozen like a statue in front of the sonar screens.

Before paralysis could set in, Gunner flipped on the intercom. "Gentlemen," he said, "we just survived a torpedo attack because every man did his job. For thirty years we've wondered what Ivan could throw at us, and now we know. We're not out of this yet, but we know we can survive. Don't ease up. The Russians are bombing the ice and dropping torpedoes and they may do it again."

The sonar screens showed debris settling to the bottom, but no torpedoes and no *Taifun*.

25 Truce

The attack helicopter still hovered above the ice. "Two detonations," the sonar officer reported, "but no ship breaking up. We missed."

"Arm the second fish," the pilot ordered.

The weapons officer punched keys and waited for the red light to blink. It didn't.

"Arm torpedo," the pilot repeated, his voice rising.

"Torpedo fails to arm. Damn." The weapons officer frantically scrounged inside a tool kit. "Leonid, I'm checking panel light default circuit breaker."

"Don't you test your circuits, Mikhail?" the pilot complained.

"Yes, dammit, but how often do we drop live torpedos, for God's sake?"

"Drop the torpedo anyway. See what happens."

The weapons officer rolled his eyes at the sonarman. "Did you hear him, Nikita? He's ordering me to drop an unarmed torpedo."

"We're almost out of fuel. Get on with it," ordered the pilot. "I'm not going back to Pulonga with a weapons tray half full."

The weapons officer pushed the release button. The Type 533 dropped away, fell through the hole in the ice and promptly started. The pilot grunted with satisfaction. The torpedo's guidance systems switched on. The sonar detected no ship noises in the water, and the torpedo began a spiral search pattern.

. . .

On *Reno* Morrison announced, "Sonar to control. I have a second torpedo in the water. Same bearing, range nine miles."

Instead of trying to outrun the 533, Gunner held *Reno* motionless and listened in silent terror to motor and prop churning through the acoustic maze of thrashing ice. Encased in a machine, at the mercy of a machine, watching machines as pixels on television screens, Gunner wondered if there was a god of machinery who would hear his prayer. The Russian torpedo sounded like an engine of death.

With no target to lock on, the torpedo's sonars became confused by ice noises echoing off the shallow bottom. Four minutes into the search pattern the torpedo attacked a submerged floe. The blip on *Reno's* screens exploded.

"That's it, you son of a bitch!" Gunner shouted. "How do you like that, Gus? The Russian fish got lost in the ice."

"How many more?" Trout groaned. "How did we get into a war?"

A mile from the helicopter a column of ice erupted like a frozen geyser.

"Another miss," the sonar officer said dryly.

"Well," said the weapons officer, "at least the warhead was armed. The problem must be in the panel light."

"We need fuel," said the pilot. "We're gone."

The helo pulled up and away from the hole in the ice. "Something tells me this operation was planned by the same people who distribute rock-hard tooth powder and rusty razor blades to the fleet," the pilot said.

The sonar officer laughed. "It wasn't planned at all. It just happened. Everything just happens."

"What kind of bullshit is that, Nikita?"

"Listen, comrade, I'm a new restructuralist. The world is chaos. Order is an illusion. Atomic bombs will destroy the final illusion and the universe will return to its natural state of entropy."

"Do we have to listen to this?" asked the weapons officer.

"All the way to Pulonga," said the pilot, rolling his eyes.

. . .

Zenko waited fifteen minutes for a third torpedo. In a proper antisubmarine operation, a dozen helos would splash torpedoes into the water generating an attack no sub could survive. Zenko had rigorously trained his ASW crews to locate, track and destroy a hostile intruder, but apparently Deminov had decided to hold back the helo squadron.

Zenko had never expected an encounter with a NATO sub in the White Sea, and found the irony of the present situation extremely unpleasant. In pursuit of *Sovyetskii Soyuz*, he detested the idea of an American intruder meddling in his private war.

"What should we do about this intruder, Sasha?" he asked his political officer.

"Nothing," Kugarin replied.

"I was afraid you'd say that," Zenko said. "This is a bad dream. I understand Malakov and Deminov. Their insanity is Russian, but this . . . I don't know."

"Nothing happens in a vacuum, Stefan."

"The Cold War is over," Zenko insisted. "An American captain has no business in the White Sea. This is a provocation."

"Stefan, we're not at war with the Americans. We're at war with *Sovyetskii Soyuz* and Vladimir Malakov."

"Stop reciting the obvious. I can't ignore this unwelcome visitor. Did you notice how quickly he learns? After the first torpedo, he realized he had to remain still to survive a 533."

"We knew the Americans would be formidable opponents," Kugarin said.

"Ah, yes," Zenko agreed with a smile. "But is he an opponent? He didn't shoot. Why not?"

The zampolit considered his response. "He knows he's not the main enemy," he said.

The main enemy. Throughout the Cold War the Admiralty had referred to the United States Navy as the main enemy.

"He was attacked," Zenko protested.

"But not by *Taifun*," Kugarin replied. "He's a spy. His orders are to observe and report."

"Yes, and if he sees *Taifun* sink *Sovyetskii Soyuz*, what will he report?"

"Stefan, you can't attack him."

"Sasha," Zenko said impatiently, "I'm trying to make a tactical analysis, and you're impeding my thought process with political gibberish. If this Los Angeles threatens _Taifun_, she dies. Can I afford to wait until her commander locks his attack sonars on my propellers? Until his torpedoes are flying through the sea? I can't afford to waste time stalking this bold American. Is he or is he not a threat to _Taifun?_"

"We can't know for sure."

"No, and it galls me. These are our waters!"

"If he is a threat," Kugarin declared, "he won't be easy to sink."

"I fear you're correct on that point, Comrade Political Officer," Zenko conceded. "And we can't sit here. All ahead slow. Steer course two seven seven."

Taifun's propellers began to spin. The huge sub moved and headed west-northwest, obliquely away from the American sub.

"He'll follow," Kugarin said.

"Good," Zenko said. "Then I'll know where he is. Imagine, Sasha, this Los Angeles survived an attack by a 533. That's a hell of a ship and a hell of a captain."

"Perhaps," said Kugarin, "but this is a Typhoon. We carry Type 65s."

"Sonar to control. Big Ivan is moving again."

"What's our range now, sonar?" Gunner asked.

"I reckon nine miles, Skipper."

Gunner rolled a red bandana into a rope and tied it around his head. Cold war, hot war, civil war, he was now a warrior in a fight for his life. Trout raised an eyebrow but said nothing. Lieutenant O'Connell stared awestruck at the captain.

"All ahead one third," Gunner ordered. "Control to sonar. Morrison, we want to stay two thousand yards behind him. Where he goes, we go."

Reno moved. Nine miles ahead, _Taifun_ steamed west-northwest. Gunner felt a bond with Stefan Zenko. The Russian captain had to know he was being followed, but by not killing one another, somehow, at least for the moment, they had bridged a gulf of history and created a truce beneath the frozen sea.

"She's heading for the Kandalakshskiy Gulf," Trout announced from the navigation table.

"Boomerville," Gunner said. "The place where Typhoons go to die."

At Pulonga, Lieutenant Tarinski and the radio officer disassembled the malfunctioning mine control panel, found corroded connections and corrected the problem. The sonar officer repaired the generators and the inhabitants of the quonset felt like warm-blooded creatures again.

The radio cackled, "*Gorky* calling Naval Station Pulonga requesting permission to transit the strait."

"This is Pulonga. Identify by code, please."

"7Z99Z9."

"Permission granted."

Tarinski shook his head with bewilderment. If this was *Gorky*, and two subs had already gone through the strait after the *Minsk* disaster, who was driving the second sub?

Before he could relay the perplexing news to Deminov in Gremikha, the helicopter crew walked in and reported contact with two subs and their failure to sink either.

"You call Deminov," Tarinski demanded of the pilot. "I'd rather have him scream at you than me."

"If Deminov wants to kill a Typhoon, he needs more than one attack helo. That's all I've got to say," said the pilot. "I've seen a lot of screwed-up operations in my time, but this mess is the all-time champion of bullshit."

Tarinski gestured casually toward the opotonaz guards. "Be careful what you say."

"The hell with them. Give me the phone."

At Gremikha, Deminov listened to the helicopter pilot describe his unsuccessful torpedo attack, then heard Tarinski's report of *Gorky*'s radio contact. *Taifun* was hunting *Sovyetskii Soyuz*, *Minsk* was sunk, and now a mystery sub had entered the White Sea. What next? Deminov could sense his plot beginning to unravel. With each fresh catastrophe he felt heat building to the boiling point. Within a few hours *Arktika* and her convoy would fail to arrive at Archangel and civilian authorities would make inquiries. So far, according to Major Riziov, signal security had held and no electronic leak had spilled over for collection by Defense Council receivers. What could he do? If he ordered Malakov to launch immediately, he would defeat his goal of a bloodless coup. He couldn't count on *Gorky* sinking *Taifun* before Zenko found *Sovyetskii Soyuz*. He had no choice. He had to send another Typhoon to sea.

For three hours *Taifun* attempted no evasive maneuvers, no sudden "Crazy Ivan" turns to throw off her pursuer as she steamed due west at twenty knots. On *Reno* minutes passed like drops from a leaky faucet. Sonar screens flickered with blips, lines, graphics, charts, always with *Taifun* a bull's-eye squarely in the middle. Trout supervised computer technicians whose machines collected gigabytes of data from the White Sea and *Taifun*, priceless military secrets, grist for the hungry maws of government spy agencies. Data from the Soviet torpedoes, depth charges and ice explosives were subjected to intense computer analysis, refining *Reno*'s defenses. The ancient military seesaw of offense and defense jogged up and down in electronic brains below the arctic ice.

In Gunner's mind the equation was out of balance. Why was Zenko allowing *Reno* to follow? Why didn't *Taifun* shoot? After two rounds of violence, both the American and Soviet captains had reverted to Cold War rules with a strange twist. Never had the game been played so deep inside Soviet waters.

The crew adopted a siege mentality. After long hours at general quarters, the boat smelled like a locker room. Despite occasional jarring crashes from the ice above, the men tried not to think about where they were, as if the Russians were there but not there, and *Reno* there but not there, cloaked by the opaque depths of inner space, a tiny capsule of America coursing through an alien and hostile sea.

"He's still behind us, Comrade Boss. He hasn't budged."

Gazing in fascination at the image on the sonar screen, Petya Bulgakov tried to imagine life aboard an American sub. His knowledge of America was a mix of propaganda, old movies, rock and roll lyrics and a half-baked smattering of English.

"Gud day, zir and madam. I am likink smashed egg this day for eatink. Yes, tank you. Good golly, Miz Molly, I'm bad to the bone, yes?"

"What the hell are you babbling about, Little Petya?" Sorokin asked.

"What are you, ignorant? That's English."

"How quaint." Sorokin sneered. "Take yourself down to port-side engineering and bring back the duty rosters."

"Aye aye."

Bulgakov sauntered aft whistling "We All Live in a Yellow Submarine."

"Your little friend seems fond of Americans, Vadim," Zenko said.

"He doesn't have sense enough to be scared, Captain."

Zenko smiled. "I envy him. When you're twenty, life is an entertainment, even a war."

Sorokin stepped closer to Zenko. "Comrade Captain," he asked quietly, "how are we going to find Malakov? All he has to do is remain still."

Zenko stroked his jaw and studied the monitor. "I've asked myself the same question a hundred times, Vadim," he said. "We'll use the American as bait."

Aboard *Sovyetskii Soyuz* Captain Malakov showered, shaved and put on a freshly pressed new uniform. Two more routine messages from Gremikha had arrived in timely fashion indicating no change in the status quo. *Taifun* had not been sunk.

In just eighteen hours Admiral Deminov would call the Kremlin and issue his ultimatum. Malakov amused himself by imagining the president taking the call in his apartment. It would be eight in the evening, suppertime. Guests would be present, and security people and all the paraphernalia of power. A light snow might be falling outside the window, melting within minutes. Deminov would cut through layers of red tape and speak directly to the great reformer himself, perhaps standing alone in an antechamber, the phone to his ear. The message from Gremikha would be short and precise. Yield power to the Defense Council or Tbilisi will be turned into radioactive dust. There will be no negotiations. Ashen, confused and forlorn, the president would reenter the dining room, instantly cleared of guests. He would call the Politburo, the Supreme Soviet, and the Army. Alerts would sound, klaxons ring, to no avail. Around him, like frantic wasps in a disturbed hive, politicians would lash out in a frenzy, stinging one another to death. Moscow would panic. Tbilisi would panic. No one would make a decision and _Sovyetskii Soyuz_ would launch the first rocket.

CNN news would go live from Moscow within minutes. Deminov had the luxury of CNN in Gremikha and he would watch the limousines come and go from the Kremlin at a frantic pace. A flat American voice would announce, "Unconfirmed reports indicate the city of Tbilisi in the southern republic of Georgia has been destroyed by a nuclear explosion." Russian subtitles would run across the bottom of the screen. "Back after these messages." Pepsi commercial. The new Russia. Cut back to Red Square, civil defense sirens screaming . . . Malakov abruptly halted his fantasy. Like a slash through a painting, the thought of Stefan Zenko ruined his picture.

Somewhere out there Zenko was hunting in murky darkness. Malakov wasn't going to panic. He had considered moving _Sovyetskii Soyuz_ away from the trench in the gulf, but using the ship's engines would make noise, attracting _Taifun_'s attention if Zenko were nearby. He could remain on the bottom and wait for _Taifun_ to pass overhead, but he reasoned Zenko would search the bottom first. The cruel truth of submarine warfare had never been so apparent—whoever hears first lives longest. The more he turned the matter over in his mind, the more he liked the notion of destroying _Taifun_ and killing Zenko. He resolved to set an ambush.

He returned to the command center, resplendent in his new uniform. "Diving Officer," he commanded, "take us straight up and hold us under the ice. Slow and quiet now. Take your time."

26
Gorky

Twenty miles east of the Kandalakshskiy Gulf, Zenko ordered speed reduced to six knots. At that speed *Sovyetskii Soyuz* had to be within three miles to detect *Taifun*. Astern, the American followed suit, and the two ships in tandem cautiously approached the gulf.

After steaming several minutes at slow speed, Zenko ordered a wide, easy ninety-degree turn to the right, continued north for one kilometer, then ordered another right turn, reversing his original course. He intended to follow a pattern, back and forth, each pass pushing the American a little farther over the deep trench where he suspected *Sovyetskii Soyuz* was hiding. With luck, he would put the American between *Taifun* and *Sovyetskii Soyuz* and draw a shot from Malakov.

Zenko studied the image from his stern array, expecting the first sign of *Sovyetskii Soyuz*'s presence to be an attack sonar lighting up his screens, followed within seconds by Type 65 torpedo motors. Far more sophisticated than Type 533s, Type 65s had complex guidance systems including infrared sensors. If the shot came from the west, Malakov would reveal his position while infrared sensors on *Sovyetskii Soyuz*'s torpedoes would lock on the Los Angeles.

Zenko fought off his most desperate fear, that Malakov was nowhere near the Kandalakshskiy Gulf. In six hours he would have to risk *Taifun* by searching the surface with radar. Malakov would surface only to launch and would not remain above the ice for long. Zenko thought he might be able to sink *Sovyetskii Soyuz* with an antiship rocket, but only after she had launched the first deadly atomic rocket. Hiding under the ice, Malakov had every advantage Zenko had designed into the Typhoons. He feared he had done his work too well.

Gunner followed *Taifun* by making one sweeping turn, keeping two miles between *Reno* and the Soviet sub. At first, he guessed that Zenko had reached an assigned sector where he would patrol quietly while awaiting a launch order, but soon he began to think otherwise.

"Gus," he said to his XO, "this looks like a search pattern. He's fishing for the other Typhoon."

"Why would he do that?" Trout asked. "He may be looking for a lead in the ice so he can poke up a mast and send a message. A message about us, Jack. Then Gremikha signals the other Typhoon and we're caught in a vise."

"Why go to that much trouble?" Gunner replied. "He can take a shot at us anytime. Lord knows we're not hiding from him. Besides, he hasn't turned on his ice scanners."

Morrison's voice on the intercom interrupted the conversation. "Sonar to command."

"Go ahead, sonar."

"Reading a submerged contact, bearing zero eight eight true, range twenty-four thousand yards, speed approximately thirty-one knots, depth two hundred feet. ID Soviet Akula class, probably *Gorky*."

With *Sovyetskii Soyuz* and the American intruder on his mind, Zenko was unprepared for what he heard next.

"Sonar to command, contact dead ahead, Akula class, bearing zero eight seven, range twenty thousand meters, speed thirty-one knots."

Zenko's mind whirred and buzzed. "*Gorky*," he exclaimed. "All stop."

The engines quieted and *Taifun* sliced through the water on momentum. Zenko switched to the forward array and listened to *Gorky* storming through the sea at flank speed, deafening her own sonars as she raced for the Kandalakshskiy Gulf.

Warfare is messy, Zenko thought, messy, and wasteful. Lorinski was charging into a killing field like a saber-waving cossack.

"Command to sonar, where's the American?"

"He stopped when we stopped, Captain."

"We can't ignore this Akula," Zenko said to Kugarin. "I thought Lorinski would stay in the Barents to block our exit from the Gorlo. I was mistaken."

"I don't think he's heard us," Kugarin said. "He's running too fast."

Zenko stole a glance at Sorokin. Grim-faced, the quartermaster drew a line across his neck.

Zenko nodded. "Command to torpedo room, load shallow water torpedoes Type 65 in tubes one, two and three."

The command echoed through the torpedo room. The torpedo officer punched commands into a console and hydraulic lifters pulled three fast, lightweight sub-killers from racks, opened the inner doors on three starboard tubes, pushed in the torpedoes and sealed the doors.

"Torpedo room to command. Tubes loaded."

"Open muzzle doors on tubes one, two and three. Flood tubes."

The doors opened and seawater rushed into the tubes.

"Arm torpedoes, set for minimum array at range three kilometers."

Computers in the torpedo room fed sonar data to the guidance systems on board the underwater missiles. *Taifun* was ready for a snap shot, a quick firing of torpedoes at close range.

"Torpedoes armed, Captain."

Morrison heard an unmistakable combination of sounds: hydraulic flurries followed by the distinctive thump of water slugs plunging into cavities followed by bursts of bubbles. Torpedo doors were opening and tubes flooding.

"Sonar to control. *Taifun* has flooded tubes."

"Control to sonar, say again," Gunner ordered, fighting to keep alarm out of his voice.

Morrison repeated his warning and Gunner switched on the intercom. "Attention all hands," he said. "Man battle stations. Prepare for evasive maneuvers."

Adrenaline rushed through *Reno* like steam through a turbine. In silent frenzy men evacuated the mess, rolled out of bunks and ran to their stations pulling up pants and buttoning shirts.

Sharpe and O'Connell rushed into the control room half-dressed. "What's going on?" Sharpe asked.

"I don't know yet," Gunner said, "but *Taifun* is ready to shoot."

"At us? Good Lord."

"I don't know. Goddamn! I just don't know, but I'm ready to run. Fasten your safety belts. He's either going to shoot at us or at the Akula."

Reno hovered, poised to flee. Gunner ordered reactor power raised, increasing the noise the boat projected into the water.

Suddenly, Morrison was astonished to see a new configuration on his screen. The computer now indicated the Akula was much closer than previous analysis had determined. She was six miles east, four miles from *Taifun* and closing fast at an oblique angle that would carry her to within a few hundred yards of Zenko's ship.

Aboard *Gorky*, Captain Lorinski knew the danger of his gambit. His boat was generating enough noise to reveal his location to any sonar in the White Sea. His goal was to draw Zenko's attention away from *Sovyetskii Soyuz*, a bold but perilous maneuver. He knew both Malakov and Zenko could hear *Gorky* racing into Kandalakshskiy Gulf and hoped each would draw the correct conclusion. Malakov would know Lorinski was there to protect him, and Zenko would be distracted enough by *Gorky* to reveal his location to *Sovyetskii Soyuz*.

Lorinski watched the speed gauge. The Akula vibrated beneath his feet. In ten minutes *Gorky* would be over the deep trench in the gulf and he would stop and listen. Until then, he was blind and deaf and racing through inner space.

. . .

"Comrade Computer, do you have a firing solution?" Zenko gestured to Kugarin who was seated at the fire control panel. "Sasha," he said, "the computer can't answer for himself. You have to do it for him."

"Yes, Captain," Kugarin stammered. "I have a solution."

Gorky was five kilometers off *Taifun*'s starboard bow. If she didn't turn, she would pass close enough to program the torpedo guidance systems without turning on *Taifun*'s active targeting sonar.

Solemn faces populated the command center. No one in *Taifun* had ever fired a warshot, but the crew didn't question the captain's decision to fire on one of their own ships. Zenko saw no anger, only sorrow and bitter resolution.

Gorky drew closer. At three kilometers the cavitation behind her prop became audible through the *Taifun*'s hull.

"Lorinski must know he's committing suicide," Zenko said sadly. "God bless their souls. Fire."

Kugarin hit three red buttons. Three Type 65 torpedoes streaked from the starboard tubes and raced toward *Gorky*. Infrared guidance kept the fish under the ice, above the bottom and attracted to the target emitting the most heat.

Gorky never reacted. When her sonar operators heard the high-pitched whine of fast-spinning electric motors, the lethal high-explosive charges were only one hundred meters away.

"Prepare for impact!" Lorinski screamed.

The first torpedo struck *Gorky* amidships near her greatest heat source, the reactor compartment. The charge ruptured the pressure hull, flooding the compartment. Within seconds, cold seawater washed over the volatile heat exchangers and rapidly expanded into steam, blowing out bulkheads and splitting the sub in two. The second torpedo penetrated the hull aft and exploded inside the engine room, instantly killing the engineers. The third detonated against the sail and exploded the command center into fragments. The bow section immediately flooded and sank. *Gorky* and everyone aboard died within ninety seconds.

The debris slowly settled to the bottom. In *Taifun*'s command center no one cheered. Sorokin kept his eyes fixed on the sonar screens, watching for movement by the American sub. Bulgakov wondered if he could pop a hatch, swim to the surface, punch through the ice and walk to Archangel. He tried to focus his mind's eye on the redhaired girl from the whiteface bar but couldn't remember her name. Kugarin silently prayed.

"Men of *Taifun*," Zenko announced on the intercom, his voice wavering, "we have sunk the Akula *Gorky* from Squadron Seven at Murmansk. One hundred brave sailormen were on that ship. Let us observe a moment of silence."

Men removed their hats and bowed their heads for a few seconds. "Now, let's get the hell out of here," Zenko said. "Steer course two seven zero. Make our speed six knots."

"Holy shit."

"Holy shit."

"Holy shit."

The expletive was repeated by fifteen awestruck men on *Reno*. No sailor who witnessed a Soviet torpedo barrage ever wanted to see one again.

"That looked like a broadside from a battleship," Trout said. "Jesus, now how do you tell the good guys from the bad guys?"

"Damned if I know," Gunner answered, "but I know who the dead guys are."

"Is he done?" Trout asked, "Or are we next?"

"Sonar to control. *Taifun* is picking up speed," Morrison said. "Some show, hey, Captain?"

"I expect you got this travesty on tape, Morrison."

"Yes, sir. A tape for the ages."

Gunner rubbed his eyes with his fists. "Has Zenko gone off his nut?" he asked Trout. "Now I know we're in the middle of a Goddamned civil war."

Thirty miles west, sound waves from the blasts resonated through the sonar systems of *Sovyetskii Soyuz*.

"Sonar to command. Three blasts, Captain, direct hits by Type 65s and numerous secondary explosions. *Gorky* is destroyed, but we're getting some strange shadows."

Malakov went into the sonar room to examine tapes of *Taifun*'s attack. *Sovyetskii Soyuz* had detected *Gorky*'s fast approach, and the sudden appearance of three torpedoes revealed

Taifun's location, but sound from the blasts had echoed off two submerged hulls.

"One is *Taifun*, that's certain," Malakov said. "But who the hell is the other one?"

The sonarmen looked at one another and shook their heads. "We have no idea, Captain."

"What do you hear now?"

"Nothing."

Zenko was close, too damned close. Malakov returned to the command center. "Torpedo room," he ordered. "load all tubes with Type 65 torpedoes, conventional warheads."

"Torpedo room, all tubes, Type 65s, aye."

"Portside rocket compartment."

"Portside," Rocket Officer Minski answered.

"Prepare to launch."

27

The Dance

"Following *Taifun* is not a healthy occupation," Gunner said to Trout. "How did *Gorky* get through the strait after *Minsk* was sunk with depth charges?

"Same way we did," Trout answered. "She snuck through."

"I don't believe it," Gunner said. "I think *Gorky* was the first of many. If Zenko has turned rogue, the Northern Fleet will throw everything they have at him until *Taifun* is destroyed. We've already had one torpedo shot at us, and there'll be more if we stay in the crossfire."

"Is Zenko going to launch?" Trout asked. "We have to stay with him in case he does."

"If he were going to launch a missile, he wouldn't fight his way into the White Sea. He could launch from the Barents. So, he's after something in here. Suppose he's trying to find and destroy the other Typhoon. But if that's true and the second Typhoon is the rogue, why were Akulas and helicopters trying to sink *Taifun*? That just doesn't make sense."

"We can play 'suppose, suppose' all day," Trout said.

"I need information. Washington needs information," Gunner groaned, repeatedly striking a match that wouldn't light. He was almost ready to risk exposing a radio mast, but three feet of frozen seawater separated *Reno* from the satellites whirling above. At any moment another torpedo could drop through the ice or *Taifun* could shoot. More Akulas could appear. If *Reno* were sunk before Gunner reported what her sonars had recorded, crew, ship and captain would die for nothing.

"Sonar to control. Big Ivan is moving west again."

"Thank you, sonar. We're going to follow from farther behind. Let him go five miles, then we'll match his course and speed."

"Aye aye."

"Gus, prepare a report on what we've witnessed so far, our location and the current situation."

"Putting up a mast is a big risk right now," Trout said, surprised.

"Of course," Gunner agreed, "but I want to be ready if an opportunity presents itself."

"Aye aye, Skipper."

"Control to sonar."

"Sonar."

"Morrison, find a lead of open water without activating the ice scanners."

In the sonar room Morrison scratched his head and chewed on a cigar. "The impossible takes a little time, Skipper."

"I know. Do what you can."

"Aye aye."

On *Taifun* Zenko waited for the American to fall into formation astern. *Taifun's* sonar computers were unable to identify the Los Angeles class sub by name, but Zenko had spent the entire Cold War in strategic rocket subs playing hide and seek with American SSNs. From the beginning of atomic submarines the Americans had had the advantage of superior stealth—until the Typhoons matched quiet with quiet. Now, as Zenko was keenly aware, he was attempting what American attack sub commanders trained to do throughout their careers—find a Typhoon hiding under the ice. He envied the Los Angeles her sensitive sonars and quiet propulsors but not her captain's situation. He was deep in hostile waters with former enemies sinking their own ships. Zenko wondered how the American commander interpreted what he was observing.

"Sonar to command. Intruder sub is not moving, Captain."

"He's confused," Zenko said. "Confused, frustrated, frightened and perhaps a little angry. He'll come along eventually, like a recalcitrant puppy. Maintain course and speed."

In the command center of *Sovyetskii Soyuz* all ears were tuned to the sonars, listening for a distant rumble of coolant pumps, the swish of props and whir of reduction gears. Two subs were approaching the gulf. Computer analysis of sonar tapes indicated the Akula had been destroyed by a torpedo barrage from a Typhoon. Zenko lived. *Taifun* was thirty miles away, accompanied by a mysterious ally, presumably another Akula.

Launch or wait? Malakov had to decide. He could punch through the ice and launch his rocket immediately, then engage Zenko and his escort. The situation at Gremikha was uncertain, but if Zenko had the cooperation of another sub from the Northern Fleet, then Deminov had blundered again and lost control not only of the naval station but of the entire fleet. Was *Sovyetskii Soyuz* alone, abandoned? Had the coup failed? Malakov watched blank screens. If *Taifun* was moving, Zenko was proceeding stealthily and with extreme caution. *Sovyetskii Soyuz*'s sonars could not detect another Typhoon steaming at six knots until the target was three miles away. At three knots, sonar range was half a mile.

"Come closer, Hero of the Soviet Union Stefan Zenko. Come right into my bathtub," Malakov whispered.

Two hundred feet forward, in the portside rocket compartment, the atmosphere was thick as smoke. Political Officer Sergov, Rocket Officer Minski and three technicians made the final run-through of prelaunch procedures. Arming circuit tested, check. Liftoff circuit tested, check. Compressed nitrogen system tested, check. Rocket booster fuel system tested, check. Inertial guidance system tested, check. Booster release system tested, check. Warhead trigger mechanism tested, check. One hundred forty-seven different systems checked, double-checked, triple-checked. At the far end of the compartment, in the forward silo, rocket number eleven was programmed to fly 1,547 miles south and explode a single two-hundred-kiloton nuclear warhead five hundred meters above the main plaza in Tbilisi, Republic of Georgia.

The last rapid-fire command dissipated as a hollow echo inside the cavernous compartment. An uneasy silence reigned. The technicians stared at their hands and breathed in short gulps. Their job was to launch a rocket in defense of the Union, not think about the devastation it would cause.

"What time is it in Tbilisi?" Minski asked.

"What difference does it make?" Sergov answered, looking at his watch. "Nine in the evening. Time for the *Vremya,* the evening news."

Sitting at the fire control panel against the aft bulkhead, Sergov swiveled his chair and let his eyes travel down the row of ten bright yellow cylinders numbered eleven through twenty. Blinking red lights illuminated the last canister. Sergov fingered his launch key. A single twist in the lock, one push of a button and liftoff, rocket away. Hiroshima, Nagasaki, Tbilisi. A million would die; the Union would live. Ever since the Civil War of 1917–1922, communism had survived by ruthlessly exterminating its enemies. Sergov considered incinerating a rebellious city the logical next step in an honorable tradition of political terrorism. "Continuous revolution by any means" meant precisely by "any" means.

Smug, consumed by zealotry, excited by the idea of perpetrating immense violence by remote control from a great distance, Sergov assumed the other men in the compartment felt exactly as he did. To him, they were ideological tools, not people.

A few feet away, Rocket Officer Minski began to tremble. "This is wrong," his mind screamed, "unforgivably, unspeakably wrong." Sweat poured from his body and pooled in his crotch. He tugged at his underpants and felt queasy. So far he had followed the prelaunch procedures like a robot, but now he didn't know what he should do, wasn't sure what he could do. Sergov wore a sidearm and would shoot him if he made a false move. Frightened and sick, he stood up from his terminal and bolted for the latrine.

In the torpedo room directly below the command center, red signs hung over all six torpedo tube doors, "Warning: Warshot Loaded." _Taifun_ was so quiet at slow speed that Malakov knew his only chance would come at such close range that an atomic warhead would destroy _Sovyetskii Soyuz_ as well as the target. All six tubes were loaded with Type 65 torpedoes armed only with conventional high-explosive warheads, and the outer muzzle doors were open to the sea.

None of the seven officers and mishmani in the torpedo crew had ever fired at a live target. Shortly after leaving Archangel, Malakov had announced that rebels had seized Soviet Georgia, but since then the captain had disclosed nothing about their mission or the situation ashore. Mysteries were a way of life in the Red Navy, but not in Zenko's flotilla. Typhoon commanders were instructed to explain their orders, but no one had explained how Georgians hundred of miles away could threaten _Sovyetskii Soyuz_ in the White Sea. A feeling of unease permeated the compartment, but no man dared speak first. The torpedomen smoked cigarettes, drank tea and fought private battles in their minds.

On the deck above the torpedo room, Malakov sat absolutely immobile in the commander's chair. The full catastrophe of an atomic explosion over a city of three million people struck him with a flash more brilliant than the sun. The potency of the image intoxicated the captain of _Sovyetskii Soyuz_, and he drank full measure from its cup. From Einstein to Stefan Zenko, countless men had labored to place him in a submarine with his finger on an atomic button, and he wanted to thank each one. He was the fruit of their grand endeavor. He loved them for their theoretical physics and rocket science, their atomic reactors and computerized fire control. He loved the six kilos of plutonium in rocket number eleven. He loved his wife, Katerina, their children, Andrei and Natasha, and his father-in-law, Ivan. His parents were long dead, but he loved them, too. He felt overwhelmed by love and thought he might weep.

Around him several officers noticed Malakov had gone rigid, speechless and frozen, as if in a trance. The moment passed and the captain blinked and settled into his chair.

"Sonar, report."

"Screens clear, Captain."

"Diving Officer, put the ship up against the ice canopy, prepare to surface."

"Prepare to surface, aye, Captain."

On *Reno*, Gunner listened to *Taifun* proceed steadily west. When five miles separated the two subs, he ordered, "All ahead slow on propulsors." *Reno* slipped through the water with barely a gurgle.

In the sonar room Morrison and the operators listened to lively bursts of noise from the White Sea's rich biosphere. Perceiving the arrival of spring, millions of starfish crawled south toward the shallows off Cape Zhizhginskiy, starfish capital of the world ocean. Crabs, shrimp and schools of herring feasting on starfish spawn rustled the water, creating a constant background of marine noise. In this pool of sound *Reno*'s sonars detected a hole of silence surrounding the huge submarine steaming slowly through the biosphere five miles away. Even when she stopped, creatures fled from a Typhoon. Giant sturgeon disappeared, herring darted away and crabs hid under rocks. The sea fell silent the way a forest quiets when a tiger stalks the night.

After two hours of following *Taifun* at six knots, *Reno*'s sonars detected a second region of silence seventeen miles ahead, twelve miles west of *Taifun*.

"There he is," Morrison said. "The other Typhoon. Sonar to control, reading a possible stationary contact sixty-five degrees forty-two minutes north, thirty-five degrees twelve minutes east."

"What do you have, Morrison?"

"A hole in the water, Skipper. Computer rates a seventy percent probability it's a submarine hull scaring off the fish."

"Bingo," Gunner crowed. "All stop."

On *Taifun*, sonarmen no longer heard the American, nor could their sonars detect the subtle difference in background noise that revealed *Sovyetskii Soyuz* to *Reno*. Blind and deaf, Zenko closed on the deepest waters in the White Sea, the stan-

dard Typhoon operating area and most logical place for Malakov to hide.

He had to assume the next message from Gremikha to _Sov-
yetskii Soyuz_ would be an order to launch. "We don't have time
to make a thorough search," Zenko said to the command division. "We have to flush him out by drawing his fire."

"Do you mean exposing ourselves to the same fate as _Gorky?_"
Kugarin asked anxiously.

"I hope not. I'm going to launch four torpedoes in a 120-
degree spread. Maybe one will find him, if he's here at all,"
Zenko said with a fatalistic shrug.

"Stefan," Kugarin reminded him, "a single Type 65 with a
high-explosive warhead won't sink a Typhoon. The only way to
destroy Malakov in one shot is with an atomic device."

"That's right."

Shocked, Kugarin asked, "You're going to fire four atomic
weapons blindly into these waters?"

"No," Zenko said. "Conventional warheads, but if Malakov
hears them, he'll have to assume they're hellfire. If he activates
his defenses, we have him."

"And he has us, too," Kugarin said.

"Weapons, prepare to fire torpedoes. Load Type 65 HE in
tubes one, two, three and four. I want a 120-degree spread."

Orders echoed from the command division to the torpedo
room. Sailors loaded, armed and programmed the weapons.
"Torpedoes ready, Captain," said the torpedo officer.

"Fire one, fire two, fire three, fire four."

The weapons exited the sub's angled tubes and streaked west
in a fan-shaped pattern. Zenko ordered the tubes reloaded and
turned sharply to the right, steaming north, distancing _Taifun_
from the torpedo release point.

"Jesus Christ," Gunner said into the intercom in the control
room of _Reno_. "Sonar, what the hell's going on? What do you
make of this, Morrison?"

"A new type of torpedo, Captain. Never seen it before. I hear
no active guidance system, but she's making fifty-five knots."

"Infrared," Gunner exclaimed. "Bad news."

Trout made a series of quick calculations. "He's shooting blind, but with infrared guidance he may get a hit."

Aboard *Sovyetskii Soyuz*, Malakov noted the terror in the sonarman's voice through the intercom as the young officer reported the course, bearing, range, speed and depth of four Type 65 torpedoes speeding through the water from the east. "Captain," he said, his voice constricted with fear, "the northernmost weapon will pass five thousand meters south, and at that range overpressure from the detonation of a standard atomic charge will rupture the pressure hulls."

"Your comment is insubordinate," Malakov snapped.

The officer was more afraid of torpedoes with atomic warheads than of Malakov. "Sir," he demanded, "who's shooting at us? I respectfully submit that those are Soviet torpedoes. Someone has made a terrible mistake."

Malakov looked around the command division and stopped at Quartermaster Plesharski. "Plesharski, go down to sonar and relieve the sonar officer. Replace him with the senior sonar mishman."

"Aye aye, Captain."

Plesharski entered the sonar room and found four men staring in unmitigated terror at the screens. "I'm to relieve you of your station, sir," he said to the sonar officer.

"Look at these screens, Plesharski," the officer said hoarsely. "Tell me what you see."

Plesharski had only to read the scrip that ran across the bottom of each screen: torpedo type, speed, range, course, bearing, all the pertinent numbers. "Mother of God," he exclaimed.

"You can relieve me, but you can't relieve Type 65s with atomic warheads!" shouted the sonarman, crossing the line between conjecture and fact. "We're going to die unless those torpedoes are destroyed."

"Where'd they come from?" Plesharski asked.

"We don't know."

Panic shattered Plesharski's mind into disconnected pieces. In one stroke his ability to process information disintegrated. "What can I tell the captain?" he wailed. "What the hell can I say?"

"We'll support you," the sonar officer said. "Tell him you relieved us all. Take me to the torpedo room. I can persuade the weapons crew to override the command center and fire decoys. It's our only chance. Malakov is lying. He's going to get us killed."

"This is mutiny," Plesharski stammered. "You're relieved, sir."

Malakov's voice came through an overhead speaker. "Sonar, report."

No one lifted a finger to the microphone key.

"Answer him," Plesharski demanded.

"I'm relieved," said the officer.

"You!" Plesharski pointed at the senior mishman.

"Yes, sir!" the mishman replied smartly and reached over and hit the torpedo collision alarm button.

Whooping klaxons blared in every compartment, transforming _Sovyetskii Soyuz_ from a quiet hole in the water into a sonic beacon.

 **Broken Ships**

In the command center Malakov was jolted by the howling klaxons. "Son of a bitch!" he swore. "Turn off that alarm!"

All hands scrambled for the cutoff switch and the alarm stopped.

"Bridge party into the sail!"

Three mishmani in goggles and coats hustled up the ladder.

"Surface!" Malakov shouted.

Functioning on remote control, the diving officer punched buttons on his panel and *Sovyetskii Soyuz* strained against the ice canopy. The sail punched through.

"Bridge party, report."

"Bad weather, Captain. Rain and sleet."

"Run up the ECM mast!"

"ECM mast, aye."

"Report."

"No radar, Captain."

The hull cracked the ice. The missile silo doors lay exposed to cold, arctic air.

"Bridge to command. Forward deck is clear."

"Rocket compartment, prepare to arm rocket."

On *Taifun*, *Sovyetskii Soyuz*'s position nineteen miles distant suddenly appeared on the sonar screens. Zenko struggled to remain calm. Never had he felt so helpless since the day he fell through the ice as a boy. Miraculously, *Taifun*'s four torpedoes were racing toward *Sovyetskii Soyuz*, but Zenko knew they would never reach her in time.

"She's too damned far away," Kugarin said dejectedly. "The torpedo run will take close to eighteen minutes. She can launch in six minutes or less."

"Malakov can launch in four," Zenko said. "He's always been good at rocketry. We'll go in closer and take another shot. Maybe he can launch one rocket, but not two. Helm, hard left. Full speed ahead."

"Sonar to command. Reporting contact with intruder sub."

The Los Angeles had reappeared on the screens.

"The hell with him," Zenko said.

On *Reno*, Gunner's worst nightmare unfolded on the sonar screens. He had come into the White Sea determined not to fight. His mission was to spy, not to involve the United States in a foreign civil war, yet suddenly he was faced with a scenario from deepest Cold War hell, a Soviet ballistic missile sub in launch posture.

"The bastard is going to launch. Zenko is trying to stop him, but those torpedoes will never get him. Prepare to surface. Weapons, prepare to fire a Tomahawk, antiship configuration, nuclear warhead. Now! We're going to take this boomer out. Sonar, ice conditions."

Morrison switched on the ice scanner. "Thick ice, Skipper," he reported. "Six feet."

"Jack, we don't know what's up there," Trout exclaimed.

"We know what will be," Gunner snarled. "In five minutes an SS-N-20 will blast into the sky. That's not allowed."

Red bandana wrapped around his forehead and eyes glistening, Gunner would tolerate no debate. He had issued the ultimate command—prepare to fire a Tomahawk with a nuclear warhead—and there was nothing more to say. Training and discipline overcame shock and the crew set about the task of arming a Tomahawk.

Reno's sail strained against the ice. The canopy flexed but refused to crack.

. . .

In *Sovyetskii Soyuz*'s torpedo room, the torpedo alarm abruptly quit. The lieutenant in command of the torpedo crew dialed sonar and shouted, "Feed me the targets directly."

Targeting screens popped to life. The first torpedo had passed but the other three had detected *Sovyetskii Soyuz* and were coming directly at the ship. Suddenly, *Taifun* appeared on the screen.

The lieutenant frantically started the process of unloading three torpedoes in order to reload with decoys. "We don't have time to unload. This is insane. Program tube one to lock on *Taifun*."

"It's not atomic," said the mishman.

"It's all we can do," replied the lieutenant.

In the portside rocket compartment Lieutenant Minski rushed from the latrine to his console, a fresh stain down the front of his uniform. Just as he sat down, Sergov turned his key to arm the warhead. "Rocket armed in forward control," he said into his microphone.

"Rocket armed in aft control," Malakov said from his station in the command center.

Sergov walked to the weapons terminal to unlock the blue launch button and fire the rocket himself. Minski's crib sheet from the test launch was still taped to the panel. Sergov punched in three numbers and the panel slid back, exposing the button.

In the torpedo room the lieutenant gave up trying to load decoys into the torpedo tubes. Three torpedoes armed with conventional high-explosive warheads were locked on *Taifun*, now running toward *Sovyetskii Soyuz* at twelve knots. The lieutenant didn't bother with commands. He pushed the appropriate buttons himself and the first Type 65 leaped from the tube and zeroed in on *Taifun*.

On *Taifun*, the sonar officer shouted, "Torpedo in the water, bow on."

"Load infrared decoy in tube six," Zenko calmly ordered. "Evasive maneuvers. Helm, hard right. Maneuvering, give me flank speed."

. . .

Seventeen miles away *Reno's* sail finally cracked through the ice but the hull failed to breach the surface. An ECM mast at the top of the sail popped up and revolved.

"No radio traffic, Skipper. No radar. Nothing."

Gunner put on a headset, charged up the ladder into the sail, spun the hatch lock, and thrust his head into the open air. Rain and sleet whipped his eyes and lashed his face. Visibility was no more than fifty feet, but over the bow he saw a huge hummock of stacked ice that blocked the hull from pushing through.

"Launch rocket," Malakov ordered.

Sergov stood at Minski's panel and pushed the button. In the bow of *Sovyetskii Soyuz*, compressed air lifted the SS-N-20 from silo number eleven. The ship trembled slightly.

"No!" Minski screamed, lunging for the terminal. Caught by surprise, Sergov fumbled for his pistol, pulled it from the holster at his belt, clicked off the safety and shot Minski in the arm. Undeterred, Minski swatted Sergov aside, took a deep breath, punched commands into the terminal and hit the abort button.

Pushed by compressed air, the rocket's tail cleared the silo just as Minski's command broke the ignition circuit. The rocket booster sputtered but failed to ignite. For a moment the SS-N-20 hovered in midair, guidance vanes extended, pressure valves exuding steam, a sleek arrow poised for madness. Then the thirty-five-foot, eighty-thousand-pound mass of titanium, rocket fuel, gold-plated wiring and plutonium warhead teetered, keeled over and crashed back onto the deck, splitting open both pressure hulls. A deep peal like the bells of hell rang through the ship. The bow plunged under the surface, and the hatches at the rear of the rocket compartments automatically sealed. Minski groaned. Sergov picked himself off the heaving deck and unloaded his pistol into Minski's head.

A torrent of seawater poured into the compartment. Sergov clawed in vain at the hatch. The technicians were swept under violently until their lungs filled with water and their bodies caromed off the rocket silos. Shattered into pieces, the rocket slipped through the broken ice and sank. Sailors in both rocket compartments were lost, claimed by the sea.

Aft of the rocket compartments a rash of sudden electrical fires ignited a tank of stored oxygen, which exploded, blowing pieces of bulkhead like jackhammers into the sonar room, crushing the operators. In the command center Malakov felt the deck slide away under his feet as the ship began to sink bow-first. Heavy black smoke billowed through the hatches from the forward compartments followed by flames and a surge of sea-water. Plesharski tried to climb the ladder to the bridge and fell backward, splitting his skull on a control panel. Malakov could see men's mouths screaming but heard nothing. Electric circuits crackled and popped. Lights flickered and then more explosions ruptured the forward bulkheads. A wall of water and sea ice deluged the ship, flooding the torpedo room and command center. Grasping the railing of the ladder to the bridge, Malakov could see through the open hatch to a tiny patch of dark sky. The bridge party had disappeared. Then flying debris knocked him from his feet, the ship tilted to a steeper angle, and Malakov slid forward, drowning in the cold water of the White Sea.

Storage batteries exploded. Tanks of light fuel oil and flammable gases burst into flames. *Sovyetskii Soyuz* plunged bow-first toward the bottom of Kandalakshshkiy Gulf, jammed her shattered prow into the mud and settled slowly on her starboard side. Attracted by the heat of the explosions, the infrared guidance systems on two of *Taifun's* torpedoes locked onto the hot ruins of the great sub. The underwater missiles nosed over and smashed into the lifeless hulk, blowing the aft compartments to bits.

From *Reno's* bridge, Gunner expected to see the flare of a rocket booster, a light bright enough to be visible from seventeen miles in any weather. Instead, in his headset he heard Morrison say, "Sonar to bridge, I'm reading underwater explosions and a ship breaking up."

"*Taifun?*"

"No, Skipper, the other one."

"I'll be damned!"

Gunner slammed the hatch and climbed down to the control

room. Explosions rumbled like distant volcanoes through the sonars. Awed, he watched the screen as *Sovyetskii Soyuz* self-destructed. "Jesus Christ, she blew up," he said. "Belay surfacing. Flood tanks. Take her down to one hundred feet. Secure that Tomahawk."

Reno stopped pushing against the ice and descended below the pack.

Gunner thought his heart would burst. He had been minutes from firing a nuclear weapon at a Soviet ship. His mind was one bright blue light. "I didn't see an explosion," he said to Trout. "I don't know what the hell happened, but she didn't launch." He took a deep breath. "That was too damned close." He took another breath. "Control to sonar. Where's *Taifun?*"

Morrison answered with a series of numbers. "He'll take a torpedo hit in thirty seconds."

"It's time to get the hell out of here," Gunner said. "All ahead two-thirds. Make our course zero nine zero."

Reno turned and accelerated east, away from *Taifun* and toward the Gorlo Strait.

Taifun banked like a giant airplane through a hard right turn away from the charging torpedo. Explosion after explosion from *Sovyetskii Soyuz* splayed electronic chaff across the sonar screens. The computers couldn't tell exactly what had caused the first explosion, but it wasn't *Taifun*'s torpedoes. Zenko knew he had failed but felt as if he had been saved by luck or a merciful God. Malakov had been thwarted.

On the main screen he watched a single torpedo charging at forty knots from the left.

"If it's an atomic warhead, we're dead," Kugarin said.

"Shut up, Sasha," Zenko snapped. "Sometimes you're a pain in the butt."

"Sonar to command. Torpedo impact in thirty seconds."

"Weapons officer, fire decoy."

"Decoy away."

The infrared decoy, a heat bomb loaded with magnesium shards, jetted from the tube and hovered motionless in the water two hundred yards from the ship.

"Command to engineering. Give me more speed."

Possessed of vast inertia, her props spinning like pinwheels, *Taifun* tried in vain to put the stationary decoy aft of her rudder.

In portside engineering six engineers sweated like old cheese. Raw heat from myriad steam pipes turned the machinery-jammed space into a sauna. Cold seawater circulating through condensers cooled a layer of hot air and created ankle-deep fog on the rubber deck.

When Zenko called for more speed, Assistant Chief Engineer Borznov keyed the throttle command for the portside turbine. Superheated steam from heat exchangers pushed the turbine to its design limit, whining like a hyena. In starboard engineering next door, the same conditions obtained, but the air-conditioners worked better and temperatures remained relatively cool. In portside, the temperature rose to 110 degrees Fahrenheit and six dripping men stripped off shirts, fashioned headbands from rags and urged on the throbbing machinery. The noise level jumped as valves, gears, pumps and shafts turned faster and faster. Hot oil under high pressure ran through pipes everywhere in the compartment. Stripped to the waist, Borznov wiped his brow and leaned closer to his terminal, carefully watching temperature readings in the lubrication systems.

Two hundred yards outside the pressure hull, sonar on *Taifun*'s infrared decoy picked up the rapidly closing torpedo. As the huge ship glided by at an excruciatingly slow pace, the decoy exploded. Shards of white hot magnesium created a rapidly expanding steam bubble, which instantly attracted the infrared sensors in the torpedo guidance system. The rudder turned slightly, the diving vanes adjusted, and the torpedo homed in on the hot spot in the water. When the nose hit the bubble, the warhead exploded and the blast slammed into the side of *Taifun*.

In portside engineering, every head jerked toward the deafening sound. The explosion in the water directly outside the compartment buckled the pressure hull, which flexed and snapped back into place with a thunderous crack. Time stopped for the engineers as they waited for the sea to stream into the compartment in a lethal jet that could cut a man in two.

The welds held. The steel remained intact and no leaks appeared, but a pipe carrying lubrication oil to the main turbine cracked, spewing a flammable brown geyser into the compartment.

Without hesitation Borznov reached for the electrical cutoff switch. With no power, the oil pumps stopped, pressure in the lines dropped and the gaping pipe stopped spurting oil, but the compartment was plunged into darkness. Borznov hit the alarm and screaming klaxons blasted the entire ship with an insistent wail. Low-power emergency lighting flicked on and chaotic shadows danced across the bulkheads. Shouts and curses echoed off the machinery.

Temperature in the turbine surged. Borznov cut off steam and the turbine immediately stopped spinning.

"Command to portside engineering, report!" Zenko ordered. The engineer heard him but the captain had to wait.

"Everyone into respirators," Borznov bawled. "Damage control team, get into your gear and spray everything with foam."

Three sailors scrambled into asbestos suits, turned on respirators and began spraying foam on the hot oil. Borznov struggled into a respirator mask, strapped an oxygen tank to his back and sealed the hatch. Two more engineering squids at the rear of the compartment ran forward toward the emergency breathing apparatus hanging from a bulkhead.

"Engineering to command," Borznov said into the radio built into the mask. "We have total turbine lubrication failure in portside engineering. I'm evacuating the air from this compartment. Oh, Jesus."

"What's happening?" Zenko shouted, alarmed by the fear in Borznov's voice.

"We're afire!"

Nothing aboard a submarine is more terrifying than fire.

With no lubrication, the temperature of the turbine bearings flared high enough to ignite the spilled oil. To his horror Borznov saw a sailor engulfed in flames. Swearing madly, he keyed his terminal and in seconds powerful air-conditioners replaced the oxygen-rich atmosphere of the compartment with inert nitrogen. The flames died as rapidly as they had started, but the compartment was full of smoke. A sailor with no respirator stumbled through the smoke-laden nitrogen atmosphere and collapsed at Borznov's feet. Three sailors in asbestos suits loomed out of the smoke, wild-eyed but alive. Black oily mist swirled into the air-conditioning vents. Emergency lights flashed. Soot covered the bulkheads and the faces of desperate men.

In the command center Sorokin dashed for a cabinet, pulled out a white asbestos coverall and struggled into it as he ran forward. Klaxons wailed like grieving widows. Officers fought their fear as they quickly broke out fire extinguishers and organized damage control teams.

Fire could kill *Taifun* and every man in her. With great effort Zenko remained calm and repeatedly called the engineer on the intercom, his voice crackling in Borznov's radio. "Command to engineering. Can you hear me, Borznov?"

Finally, he responded, "I can hear you, Captain."

"Any injuries?"

"Two dead. I have pure nitrogen in here. We're coming out."

"How many with you?"

"Three in hotsuits with respirators."

Sorokin reached the hatch between the reactor control room and portside engineering and called the captain.

"Get them out," Zenko ordered.

Sorokin spun the wheel, pulled open the hatch, and four burned and half-asphyxiated engineers stumbled out in a billow of smoke. Sorokin slammed the hatch, leaned against the wheel and thought waiting in bread lines in Murmansk didn't sound so bad.

Slowly, the hull's momentum played itself out and the sub stopped moving.

"Sasha," Zenko shouted. "Turn off the klaxon."

The captain took several deep breaths and realized his breathing was the loudest sound in the command center.

Taifun lay quiet in the water, the top of her sail one hundred feet below the ice. When fire broke out in portside engineering, discipline among conscripted squids in other compartments bent without breaking. Zenko knew the most comprehensive training ever devised couldn't simulate the emotional assault of submarine combat. You never saw the enemy who was trying to kill you. You never saw the ocean that was trying to kill you. You rarely saw your officers, who were probably trying to kill you. In fact, you saw little except the compartment you were in and the terrifying images conjured by your imagination. Fire. Depth charges. Torpedoes. The sea crashing through the pressure hull. Encapsulated by an atomic behemoth twisting and turning like a storm-tossed toy boat, you sweated inside an asbestos fire-fighting suit steamed to Saharan temperatures. Men's faces distorted by fear appeared and disappeared, and then the blast, so loud and close your heart stopped. Zenko himself could barely master such terror.

Only when the last echo of the torpedo died away did 150 hearts resume beating, tentatively, hopefully, and finally with normal cadence. Fear dropped from a crescendo to manageable proportions.

In the command center a rapid check of the ship's systems revealed the portside sonar array destroyed. The diving panel showed only green lights, indicating the pressure hull had not been breached.

Zenko switched on the intercom. "Men of *Taifun*. The fire in portside engineering has been extinguished. The ship is safe. Secure from damage control stations."

Adrenaline nausea swept through the crew Nervous lines formed outside latrines.

"We can't stay here," Zenko said. "The explosions must have attracted attention. Helm, give me slow speed. Make our course zero eight zero."

The ship began to move under starboard propulsion. Zenko quelled his private demons and walked through the ship, talking quietly to young sailors, calming fears and inspiring confidence with his concerned attention. Presently, he entered the infirmary where the ship's physician was treating Borznov and the surviving engineers for burns and shock.

"What happened to *Sovyetskii Soyuz*, Captain?" Borznov asked.

"She's sunk."

"Then my boys died for something."

"Yes," Zenko said. "I don't know what's going to happen to us, but I know what you deserve."

Zenko removed his Hero's silver star, pinned it to Borznov's shirt and saluted the assistant chief engineer.

On *Reno* Morrison reported, "Sonar to control. *Taifun* is moving. I can barely read her. Range twenty-eight miles. I think she's running on only one engine, Skipper."

"Mark his course and bearing, Chief," Gunner ordered. "Let's hope Zenko beelines for the strait. Helm, all ahead one-third."

Gunner thought three tequilas would go just fine right now. The problem with being captain of a spy-ship deep inside hostile waters was that you had to act like a captain, a staunch upholder of the national interest, stiff upper lip and all, a symbol of tradition and a role model for junior officers. Gunner was those things, and proud of it, but he was also a man who surely could use a drink. How deep into shit did you have to get before you understood why you were there? How deep into his own shit was Zenko?

Taifun had taken a hit and survived. That would send the weapons designers back to their drawing boards. In an emergency situation *Reno* had failed to puncture thick ice. More design work. Russian Type 65 torpedoes apparently had infrared guidance systems. Gunner had information overload on the one hand and a complete lack of information on the other. Drinking a cup of tepid coffee, he felt as if his soul was being scrutinized by angels. He had almost popped off a nuke.

In the center of the control room Trout toyed with the periscope controls.

"There's nothing to see up there," Gunner said.

"You should've raised a radio mast and sent a message, Jack."

"If I had, the GRU would've intercepted my transmission, and they'd be shooting at us again by now. And what if my message got through channels? Our idiots in Washington would be calling their idiots in Moscow. Our guys would say, How come your people are killing each other? Their guys would say, None of your goddamned business. How come your boat is in our waters interfering in our affairs? I don't want to start a war, cold or hot."

"You were ready to nuke that boomer, Skipper."

"Damned straight. I'm not going to let the Russians start a missile war, either." Gunner lit another cigarette. "What the hell. We came to the party. It's too late to call a cab and go home."

Lucky Strike butts littered the deck. Trout felt so edgy he took one of Gunner's cigarettes, lit it and took a deep drag.

"I thought you quit smokin'," Gunner said, astonished.

29

Riziov

Deminov was becoming aware that replacing Zenko at Gremikha was more difficult than simply declaring himself commander of the base. Ferociously loyal to Zenko, the base personnel resented the occupation of their village by a hostile army in black fatigues. Shopkeepers had closed their stores, the telephone system broke down, and the motorpool ran out of gas. Gremikha slowly ground to a halt under a wave of passive resistance.

In Zenko's office, Deminov stood before the plate-glass window fuming at four giant submarines, none of which was ready to put to sea. *First of May* was without a crew, *Rodina* was in dry dock, *Great Patriotic War* had a large section of hull removed over the portside reactor compartment and *Lenin* had been partially disarmed.

During an inspection of the ships, Deminov had encountered one frustrating problem after another. The engineering compartments were in perfect condition, but the rocket compartments were beset with difficulties: faulty computers, recalcitrant electrical systems, rocket fuel chemistry deficiencies—the logs were crammed with fix lists. Furthermore, Zenko had enhanced and expanded Northern Fleet weapons security directives. As soon as a ship returned from patrol, all weapons were removed, disassembled, and stored in hardened bunkers at the rear of the cavern. Atomic weapons were broken down and components stored separately. As a result, the flotilla had a net combat readiness of zero. Deminov shuddered to imagine what would have happened if Gremikha had ever been put on red alert. The Soviet Union's most potent strategic weapons were inert and useless.

Zenko's legacy ran deep. The master of Gremikha had ensured that World War III could not occur on his watch without careful deliberation. Sudden changes of command in the Soviet Navy were commonplace, and Zenko had been prepared. Before leaving his office, he had replaced the genuine sets of weapons codes locked in his safe with fakes.

Deminov couldn't rearm _Lenin_ without the codes. He called in Major Riziov, who appeared red-eyed and yawning.

"What is our state of readiness, Major?"

"The orders to the fleet have been programmed, sir. We can send them all in a single burst whenever you're ready."

"Your efficiency is remarkable," Deminov said. "Zenko trained you well."

"Thank you, sir."

"Sit down."

"Thank you, sir."

"Major, I need to know what I must do to send _Lenin_ on patrol."

Riziov felt a stab of fear and yawned to cover his expression. "First, you need weapon release codes to get the components out of storage, then another set of codes to assemble the weapons, and a third set to arm and fire them."

"Who has access to the codes?"

"The commanding officer."

"Anyone else?"

"The commander of the base."

"Admiral Zenko neglected to leave the proper codes in his safe."

Riziov endured an uncomfortable silence before Deminov formulated his next question.

"Can you reconstruct the codes, Major?"

"Yes, sir, there's a procedure, but it's slow and tedious."

"Do it."

"Yes, sir."

Riziov left the office and Deminov summoned *Lenin*'s commanding officer, Captain First Rank Emile Rubicoff. Arriving in Zenko's office in an angry and uncooperative mood, Rubicoff stood before Deminov like an enraged bulldog. "Why has Zenko been relieved of his command?" he demanded.

"As part of Operation White Star. In any case, that's none of your concern, Captain."

"It sure as hell is. I'm next in seniority."

"I'm in command now, Rubicoff. Be reasonable."

"Go to hell. GRU people are running all over my ship and questioning my officers."

"Sit down," Deminov said. "Would you like a glass of tea? Vodka?"

Rubicoff leaned over the desk and shoved his face close to Deminov. "No. I prefer to stand."

Deminov didn't flinch. "Rubicoff," he said, "you've always been loyal to the Union, but it seems as though everyone on this station belongs to Zenko's personality cult."

"Are you questioning my loyalty?"

"Yes. That is the issue here. I intend to send you to sea in *Lenin*."

"On your own authority?"

"Yes."

"Without Zenko's approval?"

"Yes."

"Go to hell."

"Your career is on the line, perhaps your life," Deminov threatened. "If you won't sail your ship, I order you to surrender the weapons codes."

"You're stepping beyond your authority, Admiral."

"You're a brave man, Rubicoff. You're entitled to an explanation. Zenko has turned rogue. He defied his orders and is in the White Sea trying to sink *Sovyetskii Soyuz*."

Rubicoff laughed, a short, ugly bark. "I don't believe you. Even if it's true, it's no reason to give you the codes. You don't need Typhoons. If Zenko has turned rogue, you need ASW helicopters."

"Give me the codes, Captain, or I'll have you shot."

"What use do you have for weapons codes?" Rubicoff taunted. "Are you planning an atomic attack?"

"Unless you change your mind, you have one minute to live." Deminov picked up a phone and said, "Send in Colonel Ludinov."

Rubicoff refused to believe Deminov was serious. Ludinov entered the office and gently shut the door.

"Shoot him in the knee," Deminov ordered.

Ludinov calmly unholstered a nine-millimeter target pistol and fired a bullet into Rubicoff's right knee. Rubicoff fell backward, grabbed his leg but remained defiant.

"Give me the combination to the safe on your ship," Deminov demanded.

Rubicoff had commanded _Lenin_ for three years. During his months at sea he had had plenty of time to reflect on the terrible effects of atomic weapons and his responsibility as their custodian. He had spent nights drinking with Zenko, discussing Typhoons, sea ice, starfish in the White Sea, mermaids, the women of Moscow and atomic weapons. Wonderful nights, never to be repeated. If Zenko had defied Deminov, so would he, whatever the cost.

"Never," he uttered. "Go to hell."

Ludinov shot him twice in the chest and holstered his pistol. "Everyone on this base is like Rubicoff," he said without emotion. "It would be a nuisance to kill them all."

Deminov ignored the crumpled body on the floor. "Call Squadron Seven at Murmansk and tell the commanding officer to assemble a crew of Grey Ghosts with Typhoon experience and order them here at once. I'll take the damned _Lenin_ to sea myself."

"Aye aye, Comrade Admiral."

Major Riziov saw Captain Rubicoff go in to see Deminov. A few minutes later Ludinov followed, and to his horror, Riziov heard muffled shots.

The killing had begun. Until that moment Riziov had not been absolutely sure Zenko had told the truth, but now he understood that Deminov was a traitor and a desperate man. Rubicoff must have refused to give him the weapons codes, which meant Riziov had to produce the necessary digital combinations or suffer the same fate.

Riziov was not a brave man, but he didn't want to die for nothing. If Deminov shot enough people, eventually one of the technicians would retrieve the codes from the computers. Nothing could prevent Deminov from arming *Lenin*. The only thing Riziov could do was stall for as long as possible and warn Zenko.

No one else had heard the shots. Riziov saw Deminov and Ludinov emerge from Zenko's office, lock the door and go out on the quay to inspect *Lenin*.

With both senior officers absent, the manic pace of the communications center quieted a notch. For three hours Riziov diligently pursued his duties, putting his top cryptanalyst to work on the weapons codes, monitoring routine communications to *Sovyetskii Soyuz* and answering a stream of questions from Northern Fleet staff officers.

During a quiet moment Riziov entered the transmission room where two operators worked the ELF and VLF broadcasting equipment. A bored naval infantryman lounged in the corner, fingering his rifle.

"I have a message for *Sovyetskii Soyuz*," Riziov said.

"Let's have it," said the senior operator.

"I'll send it myself. Why don't you take a break?"

"Be sure to log in as sender, Major."

"No problem."

Riziov sat down, keyed in his personal code, logged onto the ELF system, punched in the three-digit code for *Taifun*, hit the "K" key twice, the signal that would inform Zenko that another Typhoon was being armed and prepared for sea, and logged off.

The second operator sitting next to him opened his mouth to say something and gagged on the words.

"Kiss the sky good-bye," Riziov whispered.

Aboard *Taifun* the command center speaker announced, "Radio to command. Receiving ELF."

Surprised, Kugarin asked, "From Gremikha? Impossible."

"I'm afraid it's all too possible," Zenko said.

Ten minutes later, message in hand, Zenko walked out of the

radio room feeling like an old man. He gestured for Kugarin to follow and retreated to his cabin.

Zenko had filled the spacious stateroom with books and old charts, transforming the modern, plastic cabin into a bastion of tradition. He glanced at an eighteenth-century chart of the White Sea and ran his fingers over a bookshelf. He picked up a paperback of _The Brothers Karamazov_, thumbed it and replaced it on the shelf. "Ah, the human soul," he said, almost to himself, "the Grand Inquisitor, the tangle of good and evil. Perhaps we've gone beyond good, but evil is very much with us. Let's have a drink, Sasha." He opened a bottle of pepper vodka. "I think we can bend Navy regulations a little."

"By all means. What shall we drink to?"

Zenko raised his glass. "To the memory of the Typhoons."

Startled, Kugarin asked, "What's that supposed to mean?"

"Drink up, Sasha. Salute Strategic Rocket Submarine Flotilla Number Six, and let's mourn her passing with respect."

"I don't understand."

"You will. Drink up."

"To the Typhoons," Kugarin saluted, and they drank.

"You know," Zenko said, "the squids say the ocean is blind, but I don't believe it. Underwater I can see more clearly than when I walk on solid ground under the sun."

"You've been saying that for so many years I think you believe it."

"I do believe it, and I'll tell you why. When I was a boy, I fell through the ice in the Kola Fjord at Murmansk. I should have died, I suppose, but I looked up and saw the sun from under the ice, and I knew I was going to live. A man with a rope pulled me from the river, and for weeks afterward all I could think was, 'I could see through the ice. I could see the sun.' I couldn't have been under more than a few seconds, but that was long enough."

Kugarin had heard the story many times but now asked a new question. "Who was the man?"

"I don't know," Zenko said. "A citizen, an ordinary man. After I was dry and he saw I was all right, he disappeared. Perhaps because of him, I have faith in ordinary people. Or perhaps I learned that from you, my political friend."

"I'd like to think you learned something from me, but I know you better than that," Kugarin said.

"Don't underestimate yourself, Sasha. You've taught me many things. You've protected me from the Party and the Admiralty for years. You made it possible for me to fulfill my life's dream, building these wonderful ships that can travel under the ice. You have a right to express your judgment."

"I'm no judge."

"Of course you are," Zenko replied. "That's your job as zampolit on a rocket sub. Captains of these vessels are the only commanders of strategic weapons beyond the reach of the general staff. Underwater, I'm on my own, and your duty is to prevent me from overstepping my bounds. That's the first thing they teach you at zampolit school."

Kugarin knew his friend would get around to the message from Gremikha. Finally, Zenko said, "Deminov is going to deploy another Typhoon."

Kugarin gulped his vodka and cursed. "But he can't fire a rocket without weapons codes."

"Believe me," Zenko said, "he can get the codes. In time the computers can reconstruct the algorithms."

"What are you going to do, Stefan?"

For a moment Zenko's eyes closed and he was lost in thought. Then he laughed at a private joke. "Russia doesn't need thirty thousand atomic warheads," he said. "No Hitler or Napoleon threatens us. I built the Typhoons to conquer the ice. I wanted the ships, not the weapons, but I had no alternative. No one builds atomic submarines except the Ministry of Military Industry. I fear I made a bad bargain. I wear an admiral's star, Sasha, but I've never been a warrior."

"We're warriors now, whether we like it or not," Kugarin said. "You haven't answered my question, Stefan. What are you going to do?"

A few minutes later Zenko mustered the officers, mishmani and as many squids as could fit into the Lenin Room. Loudspeakers carried the captain's words to duty stations thoughout the ship.

"Men of *Taifun*," Zenko said, "*Sovyetskii Soyuz* is sunk, but the danger to the Motherland posed by Admiral Ivan Deminov has not been put to rest. I have just received a message from the secure communications center at Gremikha sent by Major Boris Riziov, a very courageous officer. Deminov is preparing another Typhoon for sea duty, probably _Lenin_, which will be loaded and armed approximately eight hours from now. Others will follow. That is why, after much consideration and soul searching, I've decided to attack Gremikha."

A chorus of groans and protests greeted the announcement. Zenko raised his hands for silence. "I know your families are there, our friends and shipmates are there, but we must consider them hostages. If Deminov is able to deploy _Lenin_ into the Barents Sea, millions may die. I'm prepared to sacrifice the things I love most to prevent such a monstrous event. I built the Typhoon flotilla to protect the Motherland, never thinking that my ships might be turned against her. This is the saddest day in the history of the Red Navy. We're at war with our brothers. Three proud ships and three hundred seventy brave sailors have died today, including two on this ship, but we cannot stop until the threat is destroyed at its source. I promise you this: I won't use atomic weapons if I can avoid it. I wish to destroy only the ships in the grotto, not the surface structures. Your families will be safe."

The sorrow in Zenko's voice drove straight to the hearts of the men jammed into the Lenin Room. Sorokin sensed the mood of the crew, and in a shaky baritone began to sing a slow, mournful sailors' lament. In twos and threes, and then by divisions, the entire crew joined in.

30 *First of May*

A big military transport taxied to a stop on the tarmac at Gremikha's airfield and disembarked 150 submarine sailors from Squadron Seven, the Grey Ghosts of Murmansk, and fifty heavily armed spetsnaz commandos. The sailors immediately filed into vans, drove to the personnel elevators and dropped down to Zenko's Cave. With packs, assault rifles and black berets, the commandos quick-marched through the base, deliberately intimidating off-duty squids and their families.

In the secure communications center, Major Riziov watched Colonel Ludinov lead the Grey Ghosts from the elevator to *Lenin*'s berth where Deminov waited. The cryptanalyst had broken the weapons assembly codes, and warheads for three rockets were being reassembled in the bunkers. Deminov appeared on *Lenin*'s bridge and began shouting and gesturing at the crane operator.

Beyond *Lenin*, *First of May* was moored to the outer berth, closest to the sea gates. Concentrating on *Lenin*, Deminov and his officers had ignored *First of May*. Checking the duty roster, Riziov saw his comrade in vodka, Lieutenant Yevgeni Zharinski, was assigned as *First of May*'s officer of the deck. Riziov went into his office, closed the door and phoned the wardroom.

With no senior officer aboard *First of May*, the three junior officers on the sub were looking forward to a day of light duty.

First of May had 5 percent power in her reactors, enough for an emergency start, but the young officers didn't expect to go to sea for at least a month. Anything that needed doing—updating maintenance lists, requisitioning small parts, sending fittings to the machine shop—could be handled by four engineering mishmani on duty aft. The captain and zampolit were in Leningrad, the engineering officers in Murmansk and the crew aboveground enjoying the open air.

Illegal vodka flowed in the wardroom. The young officers filled small glasses over and over again. Assistant Weapons Officer Lieutenant Second Rank Yevgeni Zharinski had been drunk ever since he watched Zenko steam through the gates in *Taifun*. Disillusionment and vodka had pushed the young officer into fierce depression and revolutionary thoughts. He held up a measure of spirits and toasted, "Here's to the Russian Republic!"

His brothers-in-arms shared his sentiments but were not so prone to express their feelings aboard a Soviet warship.

"Stow it, Yevgeni."

They drank and Zharinski poured again. The phone rang and he picked it up. *"First of May*, Lieutenant Zharinski."

"Riziov here, Yevgeni," said the major in a hoarse stage whisper. "Who's on the ship with you?"

"Nicholai and Alexander and four atomheads. Why?"

"Are you drunk?"

"Only a little."

"Can you make steam?"

"Can I what? Speak up!"

"I can't," Riziov said. "I'm in my office and people are listening."

Zharinski laughed. "What do you want? Come down and have a drink."

"Can you make steam?"

"Why? You planning a cruise to Norway?"

"Yevgeni, pay attention. We need to discuss something serious. Did you see Zenko leave in *Taifun*?"

"How could I miss him? The fat little prick kissed Deminov's ass and sailed off to blow up the world. He betrayed us, Boris. I'd rather not hear his name."

"No, Yevgeni, you've got it backward. Deminov is the traitor and Zenko is trying to stop him. Deminov called in Captain Rubicoff from *Lenin* and shot him to death in Zenko's office just a few minutes ago."

"What?"

"Yes."

"You're crazy."

"Yevgeni, I'm not joking. Off-base communications are restricted. We can't radio Zenko or anyone else. Deminov is using White Star to overthrow the government. He's putting a new crew on *Lenin*. His men will probably be inspecting *First of May* in a few minutes."

Zharinski covered the mouthpiece. "Get rid of your drinks," he said to the others in the wardroom, then said to Riziov, "Thanks for the warning."

Desperate, Riziov said, "Zharinski, he's going to send *Lenin* to sea. You must stop him! Take *First of May* into the channel and sink her. Block his exit, for God's sake." ·

"Now I know you're crazy," Zharinski sputtered.

"Listen to me! Malakov is in the White Sea in *Sovyetskii Soyuz* with a rocket targeted for Tbilisi. I swear. I saw the codes. Deminov is using Typhoons to blackmail the government. He's trying to start a civil war. With Zenko gone we've got to stop him ourselves. Wait a minute. Someone's coming in here."

Zharinski heard a voice shout, "Get off that telephone!"

The line went dead. Zharinski tried to shake off the vodka. Tbilisi. He had cousins in Tbilisi. "You're not going to believe what Riziov just told me," he said to his mates.

Ludinov stood in the doorway to Riziov's office, pistol in hand. "Who were you talking to?" he asked angrily.

"My communications are classified, Colonel."

Ludinov held up a printout of Riziov's transmission to *Taifun*. "Like this one? You're under arrest, Major."

"By whose authority?" Riziov blustered. "I demand to call directly to the Admiralty in Leningrad."

Ludinov laughed in his face. "Put your hands on your head and we'll go have a chat with Admiral Deminov."

Riziov reluctantly obeyed. They left the office and started

down the hall. As they neared the communications center, where a dozen people were watching, Riziov banged his elbow into a red fire alarm button. A deafening roar of clanging bells erupted throughout the communications center. Witnesses to Riziov's act dove under desks. Elsewhere in the center, clerks and technicians, believing a fire had started, abandoned their terminals and jammed the exits. Below, inside Zenko's Cave, a siren screamed and security doors automatically slammed shut.

Startled by the bedlam careening around him, Ludinov swore, then shot Riziov four times in the back.

"Stop them!" Riziov screamed at the cowering technicians with his last breath. "They're going to . . ." Ludinov silenced him with another shot to the head.

Three hundred feet above the communications center, the company of spetsnaz arrived at the high-speed elevators amid the blare of fire alarms. The commanding captain approached the young naval infantryman standing sentry duty and demanded, "Open the elevator doors!"

The sentry snapped to attention. "The doors have locked automatically," he said. "I can't open them from here."

"Break them down!" the captain ordered.

"Can I see your authorization, sir? No entry without authorization."

"Stand aside, sailor!"

A siren warped the air with a loud scream. Lights flashed. A naval infantry lieutenant came rushing across the concrete. "What's going on here?" he shouted.

The sentry answered, "These men are demanding entry to the submarine pens, sir."

"We have a fire downstairs. No one can go down," said the lieutenant.

"I order you to shut off the alarms and unlock the elevator doors," the captain demanded.

"I can't do that, sir."

"If there's a fire, it's sabotage," the captain shouted. "My men have to get downstairs."

The captain turned his back on the infantrymen and nodded

to a sergeant. A spetsnaz assault rifle hissed and the sentry and lieutenant slumped to the floor, blood spurting from their wounds.

"Work your way down the staircase," the captain ordered. "Shoot anyone who resists."

Alarms inside the cave were loud enough to penetrate the wardroom of *First of May*. Zharinski ran forward to the command center, popped a hatch to look out and was confronted by pandemonium. Explosions and machine-gun fire echoed down the stairwell. Klaxons wailed. Officers and men ran up and down the quays. Suddenly, the alarms stopped. A few seconds later the elevator doors burst open and spetsnaz troops rushed onto the quays toward the ships. Deminov appeared on the bridge of *Lenin*.

Zharinski dropped back into the command center, threw the helm over hard left and locked it.

Dazed, the two other on-duty officers stumbled into the command center. "We're under attack," Zharinski shouted.

"Attack?" one asked, drunk and confused.

"The Americans?" asked the other.

"Renegades are trying to steal *Lenin*," Zharinski yelled. "We have to block the channel."

He raced aft to the portside maneuvering room where he bowled over the mishman standing watch and hit the reactor emergency power button. Hearing shouts rattling through the passageways, two startled engineers came through a hatch from the portside engineering compartment and were surprised by a wild-eyed Zharinski, face gone white as ice. Before they realized what he was doing, he force-fed the residual heat in the reactor into the heat exchangers and created a "bullet" of superheated steam. He hammered at the computer terminal and within a few seconds the portside main propulsion turbine began to spin madly.

With a sickening lurch the ship moved. The portside propeller sprayed the quay with water and the bow swung toward the channel. An immense hawser tensed and straightened and with a thunderous crack ripped away the mooring cleats.

Instead of trying to stop Zharinski, the two engineers ran for the hatches. The other two, much farther aft in the engineering compartment, simultaneously shouted over the intercom.

The bow of *First of May* swung into the channel. The rudder smashed into the quay, shattering concrete and bending steel. The stern line pulled loose a thirty-foot section of pier, tumbling several soldiers into the water. A squad of spetsnaz jumped from the quay onto the deck of the sub. An overanxious commando shot the first engineer whose head appeared from the hatch. The spetsnaz pushed his body aside and leaped into the command center. Two drunk, terrified officers stood by the diving panel and an engineering mishman sprawled on the deck.

"Go aft," shouted the engineer. "One of the officers went crazy."

When the ship had moved fifty feet from the pier, the shore power cables snapped with a crackling flash of sparks. Zharinski rushed into the portside engineering compartment, reached the seawater valves and yanked the levers.

Water gushed into the compartment. Screaming in panic, the two remaining engineers jammed through the hatch and ran headlong into a hail of spetsnaz gunfire. The ship began to tilt toward the stern. The commandos stepped into knee-deep water and found Zharinski grinning like a fool next to the turbo-generator. As water met electrical power, sparks flew and fires started. Black smoke billowed in the air.

In a fine baritone Zharinski began to sing the "Internationale." A burst from a Kalashnikov cut short his recital.

Standing on the bridge of *Lenin*, Deminov watched aghast as *First of May* sank by the stern until her rudder rested on the underwater concrete floor. Black smoke roiled through her open hatches and drifted toward the ceiling of the grotto.

The sea gates were blocked. *Lenin* couldn't exit until the sunken ship was moved. "Damn you, Stefan Zenko," Deminov muttered to himself. "You'll pay for this."

31 Breakthrough

A small buoy floated to the surface in a narrow lead of open water and extended an antenna into the air.

"Reading no radio signals, Captain."

"Periscope up."

A slim search periscope slid up through its housing and broke the surface. Zenko leaned into the eyepiece. "Rain and sleet," he said. "There'll be no helicopters aloft in this weather. Down scope. Make our speed twenty knots. We're going to run the Gorlo Strait!"

The defiant command rattled through the ship. The atomic power train rumbled and uranium atoms committed suicide by the billions to propel *Taifun* under the ice. Shafts spinning in bearings strained against the gross bulk of the hull and the resistance of the sea, pushing the great ship faster and faster until she reached twenty knots, her maximum speed on one engine. *Taifun* ripped through the water, ice scanners blazing a path under the frozen mantle, starboard turbine whizzing, coolant pumps churning, propeller cavitating like an eggbeater, sending waves of sound bouncing off the ice and reverberating from the bottom.

"We're making more noise than a destroyer," Kugarin said, his face creased with worry and fear.

Zenko laughed. "You're an astute observer of acoustic phenomena, Sasha," he chided.

"Would you mind explaining just what the hell you're doing?"

Zenko ordered Sorokin to put up a chart of the strait on the big Mitsubishi. "No matter how slowly we proceed," he said, "anchored sonars in the strait will pick us up. We can't avoid that. This time there's no convoy, so the gunners can fire mortars. At slow speed they can zero in on us, punch through the ice and we take hits. But naval mortarmen have never heard a submarine steam through the Gorlo at speed and don't train to shoot at fast-moving targets. Their shells will explode harmlessly on the ice."

"Maybe," Kugarin said doubtfully. "But what about the mines?"

Zenko keyed the navigation console and an array of red lights appeared on the electronic chart. "There's your minefield," he said. "We know where they are. These weapons were installed to stop an American sub, not a Typhoon whose captain knows their locations. For years I taught submarine tactics to the Northern Fleet, Sasha. I preached quiet, quiet, quiet, and that's what they expect. I'm going to do the opposite and catch them by surprise." Zenko called to Sorokin.

"Sir!"

"What odds will you give on us making it through the strait?"

Sorokin scratched his face and frowned at the navigation monitor showing a formidable array of sonars, mines and mortar batteries. "Six to one against," he declared.

Zenko dug in his pockets and came up with a fistful of bills. "Here's five hundred rubles that say we'll make it. That's a year's pay for a sailorman."

"Captain, if you lose," Sorokin said ruefully, "I won't be around to collect."

"Sonar to control," Chief Morrison said. "*Taifun* is increasing speed. She's still running one engine and one prop. Looks like she's headed for the Pulonga narrows."

"Goddamn!" Gunner swore. "If there ever was a Crazy Ivan, this guy is it. Control to maneuvering. Give me more speed."

Anxiety churned Gunner's stomach. Ripping open a fresh pack of Luckies, he said, "The channel runs one hundred twenty feet deep to the point off Pulonga where Zenko fooled them with a decoy on his way in. At Pulonga the bottom comes up to eighty-five feet which gives us thirty-five feet of clearance. I'm not worried about hitting bottom or striking the ice, but suppose Zenko catches them by surprise and runs right through. Then we come along and helicopters unload on us. Caught in the crossfire again. Big fun."

"Shouldn't we slow the hell down?" Trout asked.

"We'll lose him."

"Better we lose the Russian than lose *Reno*," Trout reasoned.

Gunner studied the navigation chart and looked at his watch. "At twenty knots Zenko is forty minutes from the narrows, and we're thirty minutes behind him. We'll slow down and take a good listen in twenty mintues."

"The shore-based sonarmen will have us on their screens by then," Trout said.

"Yes, but they won't know who we are."

Thirty-five minutes later *Taifun* was eleven miles from the narrows.

"Load decoys," Zenko commanded.

In the torpedo room the automated system loaded five decoys in tubes, opened the outer doors and flooded the tubes.

"Torpedo room to command. Decoys ready."

The first decoy was programmed to run ahead of the sub directly into the minefield, the second to run on the course Zenko intended to follow, the third and fourth to go left and right to confuse the gunners. The fifth was a reserve.

Zenko took a deep breath and said quietly, "Fire decoy number one."

Sorokin hit the button. "Decoy away."

"Cut engines."

The flow of steam stopped immediately but *Taifun* continued to surge forward on momentum. In the sonar room the operator took advantage of the silent props to activate his stern array and once again was surprised by what he heard.

"Sonar to command! The American has returned!"

"What's his range?"

"Thirty-five kilometers and closing."

"Damn," Zenko cursed, tapping his fingers on the chart table. "I've had enough of this turd in the honey."

Kugarin repeated his refrain. "You can't sink him, Stefan. When we finish with Deminov, we'll need all the friends we can get, especially the Americans."

"You're right, Sasha, but I can't have him on my tail any longer. Command to weapons, reprogram decoy five to simulate a Type 65 and prepare to fire it back along our track."

The weapons officer feverishly punched commands into the weapons computer, made a programming error and had to repeat the keystrokes. A green light popped on.

"Decoy ready."

"Fire."

"Decoy away."

"All ahead full!"

"Torpedo in the water!" Morrison shouted from the sonar room. "Type 65."

Hurtling through the water at fifty-five knots, the speed of the Soviet decoy imitating a torpedo combined with *Reno*'s twenty knots to make the closing speed eighty-five miles per hour. Morrison made a series of rapid calculations in his head. "Impact in sixteen minutes," he said. "Recommend we come about, Skipper."

Gunner cursed himself under his breath. Zenko wasn't trying to sink him—the range was too great for that. The Russian was trying to deflect the American from following *Taifun* through the strait. Jesus, Gunner thought, I can't play chicken with a Type 65. "Helm, hard left," he ordered. "Maintain speed. Bring her about one hundred eighty degrees."

"We can outrun it!" Trout shouted.

As *Reno* turned, the torpedo continued straight on course. "I'll be damned," Trout said. "The guidance system is defective."

"We don't know that," Gunner said. "Control to weapons. Prepare a Captor."

In the torpedo room Chief Garrett and three torpedomen pulled a Captor mine from the racks, plugged in electronic modules, and guided the shaft into a tube.

"Torpedo room to control. Captor ready."

"Sonar to control. Torpedo noises have stopped. The fish is dead in the water."

"You sure, Morrison?"

"I can't hear it anymore, Skipper. It's gone."

"I hope you're right. Maybe it is defective. Torpedo room, belay Captor. Helm, turn right ten degrees, back to your course."

"Aye aye."

"A stay of execution," Gunner said to Trout.

The shore operators at Pulonga were more alert than Zenko had expected. The sonar officer had tracked a Typhoon's approach for ten minutes. Lieutenant Tarinski had repaired the mine control panel, but the anchored mines were so old no one at Pulonga expected them to work. Tarinski believed his best chance of sinking a ship in the narrows lay with the mortarmen. Extra shells had been hauled from the arsenal, and the brittle gunmetal carefully heated with electric heaters. Connected to the gunners by radio, the sonarmen in the quonset hut were prepared to act as forward mortar observers.

Tarinski called Gremikha.

At Gremikha Deminov was frantically making plans to raise *First of May*.

"Admiral, Lieutenant Tarinski is on the line again."

Deminov took the phone. "What is it now, Lieutenant?" he demanded.

"A Typhoon is approaching the strait at speed from the south, sir."

"A Typhoon? You're sure?"

"Yes, sir. Running on only one engine."

Deminov was stunned. Malakov would never leave his station without first sending a radio message. It had to be *Taifun*, and Zenko would not attempt to run the strait again unless *Sovyetskii Soyuz* was sunk. Deminov silently cursed his son-in-law. What the hell had happened? It didn't matter. Zenko had to be destroyed. "How's the weather in the strait?" he asked Tarinski, struggling to control his fury.

"Still bad, sir. The helicopters are grounded. The fixed-wing magnetic anomaly detection plane is in the air, but it's getting erratic readings, probably from the wreck of *Minsk*."

"Lieutenant, I order you to activate the minefield. Use any means at your disposal, but you must kill *Taifun*. Do I make myself clear?"

"Yes, sir, perfectly clear," Tarinski replied, understanding for the first time that his target was in fact Stefan Zenko.

"Keep me informed," Deminov ordered and slammed down the phone. "Signal *Sovyetskii Soyuz* to surface and make radio contact at once," he shouted, knowing his order would be transmitted in vain.

"Reading a second target, Lieutenant," said the sonar officer at Pulonga. "It's at least thirty kilometers aft of the lead target and fading in and out."

"Who the hell is that?" Tarinski asked, and answered his own question. "It must be a trailing decoy. That's the kind of nasty trick Zenko would use."

"The lead target has split in two," the sonar officer reported. "One target is heading directly into the minefield."

"That's another decoy," Tarinski said. "Zenko knows where the mines are. Hell, he laid half of them."

"Reading more targets now, Lieutenant."

Pulonga's sonar screens came alive with moving blips. The twenty-four-year-old lieutenant had seen targeted blips on simulators in hundreds of training sessions, but one of the electronic spots on the screens represented a real sub, and not just any sub. *Taifun* was in the strait. *Taifun!* He didn't know why, but he had been ordered to sink the most famous sub in the Northern Fleet. Instantly, Tarinski became aware of his role. A nameless boy from Moscow, he had suddenly been thrust onto the center stage of history. His heart pounded like a piston. He was ready to fire live rounds at a submarine full of live men, Russians, just like him. He was going to sink *Taifun* and kill Stefan Zenko. Promotions and honors danced in his eyes.

One of the blips on the screen approached the southernmost mines. At twenty knots Zenko's first decoy ran between two mines, activated magnetic triggers and exploded both simultaneously. In the middle of the strait two geysers erupted through the frozen surface. Chunks of ice the size of automobiles flew into the air and crashed back onto the canopy.

The explosions bedazzled the sonarmen in the quonset hut. The mines actually worked! Tarinski let out a jubilant cry and the men cheered. "The decoys will destroy themselves on the mines," Tarinski shouted through his radio to the mortarmen. "The one remaining will be your target!"

In the midst of this impromptu celebration, Tarinski returned his attention to the sonar screens. For a moment he stared in disbelief. Every screen was blank. "Holy Mother of God," he said. "We've blown ourselves up!"

At the bottom of the strait the sonar system's vital hydrophones lay wrecked by concussions from the mines. Pulonga had gone deaf. Tarinski put his head in his hands and wept.

"Fire decoys three and four," Zenko ordered.

More decoys, more exploding mines, and then the guns. Without sonar guidance, the mortarmen were laying down a blind pattern of fire along the shipping lanes over the deepest channel, and the shells were punching harmless holes in the ice. *Taifun* was passing through the narrows unheard and unseen.

Electronic blips raked across *Taifun*'s sonar screens as shells exploded north of the ship. Zenko guessed what had happened. "The mines destroyed the sonars," he said. "They can't hear us."

The danger had not ended. Persistent and methodical, the mortar shells marched south, blowing dozens of holes in the ice. Seven minutes after the barrage started, a random shell exploded directly over *Taifun*. The huge ship shuddered. Then a second shell hit the ice above the starboard rocket compartment.

"Outer hull ruptured, Captain," said the diving officer with remarkable calm. "Both pressure hulls intact. We've lost one trim tank."

"Are the rocket compartments breached?"

"No, sir. Intact."

"Run system checks on all rockets."

"Aye aye."

"Get ready to pay up, Sorokin, you Murmansk whoremonger. *Taifun* can take twenty ruptures of the outer hull and still fight."

"Comrade Captain," Sorokin said, "we have only one propulsion plant, our portside sonars are broken, and our ship is holed. If you get us out of this alive, I'll buy you a night in the best whorehouse in Murmansk."

A MAD plane circled over the strait trailing a magnetic anomaly detector. Mortar shells, mines and the hulk of *Minsk* lying on the bottom confused the detection equipment. As *Taifun* moved north, the plane flew south and the sub escaped.

When *Taifun* passed Cape Voronov, the water deepened and Zenko descended below the range of MAD detectors. He had run the strait again. With her forward sonars damaged *Taifun* was crippled but seaworthy, an American boat was in the water stinking up the equation, and as far as Zenko knew, the entire Northern Fleet was waiting in the Barents Sea. Six to one, hell, thirty to one would have been more like it. "Now we go quiet. Reduce speed to eight knots," he ordered. "Pay up, Sorokin."

Tarinski steeled himself to make another call to Deminov. "Bad news, Admiral. The mines destroyed the sonars and I don't know if *Taifun* got through. She may have reversed course. We have a reading over the wreck of *Minsk* and nothing else."

Deminov hung up the phone. The impossible had happened. The defenses of the Gorlo Strait had failed twice and Zenko was still on the loose and capable of wreaking immense havoc. According to the original schedule for White Star, the Northern Fleet would put to sea within the hour. Now, he had to call Leningrad and tell Valotin they had to postpone phase two for another twenty-four hours.

Deminov listened to clicks on the scrambled, secure phone line as the call went through. Valotin had ordered White Star as a means of crushing the republican groundswell once and for all, but Deminov doubted that he had the courage to take the last step and overthrow the government. The obese Admiral of the Fleet had balls of jelly.

After several minutes Valotin came on the line. "I hope you're going to report that Zenko is sunk and that you're ready to deploy the fleet, Ivan," he said.

"I'm afraid not, Admiral," Deminov replied. "I regret to inform you that *Sovyetskii Soyuz* is probably sunk. I'm waiting for confirmation, but I have no doubt that Zenko defeated Malakov. A few minutes ago *Taifun* attempted to return to the Barents through the strait and I fear he has succeeded."

"You don't know for sure?"

"No, sir. The sonars in the strait were destroyed."

"What else can possibly go wrong?" Valotin asked angrily. "I'm tempted to call off the operation, Ivan, and have you shot for incompetence."

"Admiral," Deminov said, "there's no need to panic. I can put to sea in *Lenin* in a few hours, and command her myself. Once I'm on station, we can deploy the ships from Polyarnyy and Murmansk. With the fleet at sea, the government will have no choice but to order a full-scale military crackdown on the republicans."

"What about Zenko?"

"I'll send the Grey Ghost Squadron after him."

"I'll give you twenty-four hours," Valotin said. "If Zenko is not destroyed by then, we cancel the operation and send the entire fleet on a search-and-destroy mission."

"I'll get Zenko myself, Admiral," Deminov said and hung up the phone. He had nothing but contempt for Valotin. Once *Lenin* was safely under the ice and her rockets aimed at Moscow, Valotin and every other nerveless bastard on the Defense Council would start taking orders from him.

Reconstructing the algorithms for the weapons codes for *Lenin* was proceeding gradually, and loading and programming rockets in her silos would require at least half a day. Codes or no codes, *Lenin* couldn't sail until the partially sunken *First of May* was moved. When two powerful tugs failed to dislodge the immense hull, Deminov had ordered a team of shipwrights to pump water from the flooded compartment and raise the ship as quickly as possible.

The dim arctic sun had set behind the Kola Peninsula. When

Deminov finished his call to Leningrad, he looked out the big window in Zenko's office and saw the submerged stern of *First of May* still obstructing the channel. The tension finally boiled over and he rushed onto the quay spouting a torrent of violent curses.

Anxious aides explained that efforts to pump water from the flooded engine compartment had stalled when radioactive primary coolant was discovered leaking from ruptured heat exchangers. Deminov scorned their excuses. "I'll pump out the damned ship myself," he announced.

A tug was lashed alongside the partially sunken ship, and a dozen men in anticontaminant clothing clustered under armed guard at the stern. In a black rage Deminov crossed in a launch and climbed aboard the tug. He struggled into "anti-c's," glowering at the frightened men. He pulled on cloth overalls, rubber boots, plastic baggies, then another pair of rubber boots, a pair of cloth gloves, two pair of rubber gloves, a heavy plastic rainsuit, a ski mask and goggles.

Properly attired to enter radioactive space, he stood before the workmen and railed at them. "This ship was sunk by mutineers. The penalty for mutiny is death. By refusing to perform your assigned duty, you become parties to this despicable crime. *First of May* must be raised. I'm going into the engineering compartment myself to position the hoses. Follow me or suffer the penalty."

Deminov hoisted himself onto the tilted deck of the ship, grabbed a length of thick hose and dragged it toward the forward hatch. The guards cocked their assault rifles. Cursing and groaning, the shipwrights followed Deminov into the sub.

A Geiger counter lay buzzing on the deck, dropped by a panicked worker near the hatch to the flooded compartment. Deminov kicked it, smashing the device against a bulkhead, and dragged the hose through knee-deep water. He remained in the compartment no more than three minutes, long enough to position the first hose. Ten minutes later contaminated water flowed from *First of May*, polluting Zenko's Cave, but the sunken stern began to rise.

Deminov returned to the tub, stripped off his contaminated clothing and motored to the quay. Farther down the pier a crane was lowering a bright yellow Type 65 through the angled weapons hatch of *Lenin*. Deminov boarded the sub named for the founder of the Soviet state and called the officers together.

Culled from the Squadron Seven at Murmansk where Deminov saw them every day, the ten men assembled in the wardroom had been hand-picked for political reliability and previous service on Typhoons. Deminov's gesture of bravado on *First of May* was not lost on these experienced submariners.

"Gentlemen," he said, "we're going to sea on a war footing, and *Lenin* will be the flagship of the Northern Fleet."

32   MAD

"I'm tired of getting shot at, Skipper," Morrison said to Gunner as the captain entered the sonar room.

"No foolin'," Gunner agreed. "Where's *Taifun?*"

"Dunno. For all I know she ran into a mine. It sounds like World War Three up ahead, but I didn't hear a hull break up. I think they missed." Morrison pushed his Red Navy cap low over his brow. "I can't say that makes me happy. I'm not real fond of guys who shoot torpedoes at me."

"That was a warning shot," Gunner said. "He wanted us off his tail, and he got what he wanted."

"Are we going to nail this bastard, Skipper?"

"I'm surprised to hear that from you, Morrison."

"They're shooting at us, sir. Makes me want to shoot back."

"We're not about to get involved in a Russian civil war, Chief."

Gunner leaned against the bulkhead, smoking and watching the sonarmen. Morrison glowered under his cap and chewed an unlit cigar. Data filled the screens. Under normal conditions the sonar room epitomized modern weaponry as high-tech electronic gamesmanship—until the shooting started. Now, the room stank of fear and sweat, like bunkers at Khe San.

Gunner stepped from the sonar room to the passageway. Alone, the calm he displayed in front of his men vanished. Feeling as if he was going to vomit, he clutched his stomach and bile retreated from his throat. If he remained in the White Sea, he'd be trapped. Angry mines waited in the Gorlo Strait. He had never felt so isolated.

He couldn't send a message without revealing his location, but maybe he could receive one. He stepped back into the sonar room. "Make a quick flash with the ice scanner and find a lead of open water," he said to Morrison.

"Mail call?"

"You got it, Chief."

Twenty-six thousand miles above Iceland a U.S. Navy communications satellite in geostationary orbit broadcast continuous messages to ships in the Atlantic and Arctic oceans. Coded by ship, the cycle of densely compressed, encrypted messages repeated every eight minutes.

Within an hour Morrison found a narrow patch of open water. Gunner positioned *Reno* directly under the lead between two sheets of ice.

"Take her up, Gus."

Reno rose until the top of her sail was three feet below the surface.

"Raise ECM mast."

A long thin antenna slithered up from the sub, through the water and into the air. In the radio room the operators watched instruments for signs of electronic activity in the atmosphere.

"No radar, Captain. It's clean."

"Very well. Run up the radio mast."

"Mast up, aye."

"Scan Soviet frequencies."

"I'm getting scrambled voice traffic on Air Gremikha frequencies."

"Helicopters or MAD planes," Gunner said. "Switch to Nav-Com One."

The tip of the mast rotated and tilted toward the Navy satellite. For eight tense minutes *Reno* remained exposed while computers sorted through the messages searching for *Reno*'s code.

"Bingo," said the senior crypto warrant officer. "Somebody wants to talk to us."

A printer chattered briefly and the warrant officer tore off the printout of forty five-digit number groups.

"Run it through the decoder," Gunner said.

While the decoding machine translated the number groups into English, Gunner ordered the masts retracted into the sail. _Reno_ dropped back under the ice.

Gunner read the message as it scrolled from the machine.

```
FROM COMSUBLANT ATTN USS RENO:
CONGRATULATIONS CHIEF TORPEDOMAN
WILLIAM GARRETT. WILLIAM GARRETT
JUNIOR BORN 12 APRIL EIGHT POUNDS
SEVEN OUNCES. END MESSAGE.
```

He had exposed _Reno_ for nothing. Shaking his head in disgust, Gunner walked into the control room. Trout looked at him expectantly. "The Navy can't help us," Gunner said "They don't know shit."

"What's the message?"

"Chief Garrett is a new father."

"That's it?"

"We're on our own, Gus. We have to go through the strait. It's time to reach into the bag of dirty tricks."

"We can lay low, let things settle down a little," Trout said quietly. "Then slip through."

"Nothing is going to settle down," Gunner said. "As far as I'm concerned, the Russians are at war and _Reno_ is the only intelligence source we have."

"The damned strait is mined."

"It'll still be mined a month from now. What in God's name is happening on this boat? Morrison the pacifist wants me to blow Zenko out of the water. And you, old cold warrior, want to back off. This is what they pay us to do, Gus."

"The Navy doesn't pay us to lose a billion-dollar sub."

"What the hell," Gunner said with a grin. "They have eighty more."

Returning to the radio room, Gunner unlocked a cabinet and took out a standard Red Navy submarine distress buoy, a silver cylinder six feet in length and eight inches in diameter. Every Soviet sub carried a pair of distress buoys, which the Red Navy had to use all too frequently. Gunner and an electrician spent five minutes rigging a timing mechanism to trigger the buoy's beeper in three hours. With the aid of an electronic black box in the crypto computer, they programmed the buoy with *Taifun*'s coded signal. Gunner carried the buoy into the sail, placed it in the buoy chamber and set it free. The buoy floated to the surface in the lead of open water and automatically extended a six-foot antenna.

"All ahead on full propulsors," Gunner ordered. "Make our course zero six zero. Attention all hands. Rig for silent running. Gentlemen, we're going to cross a Soviet minefield. You're going to earn your hazardous duty pay."

Reno's sonars had tracked *Taifun* into the strait and recorded her path on tape. Using the electronic record of *Taifun*'s passage, Gunner began to follow Zenko's route into the narrows opposite Pulonga.

Ashore, Lieutenant Tarinski sulked over his tea. His sonars were dead and *Taifun* had escaped. Suddenly an alarm sounded on one of the radio consoles.

"Submarine distress signal, Lieutenant."

"You sure? What frequency?"

"Let me look it up in the book. Here it is. *Taifun*."

"Fuck me! We can still get him! Check the code. Hurry up."

"The code matches, sir."

"Where? Where is he?" Tarinski shouted, his excitement mounting.

"South, sir. He must have given up trying to go through the minefield and reversed course."

Tarinski picked up the phone to Gremikha and reported the distress signal to Deminov.

"It's a red herring, Lieutenant," Deminov said impatiently. "Even if Zenko were sitting on the bottom, he wouldn't invite attack with a distress signal."

"Sir," Tarinski pleaded, "I still think the MAD plane should check it out."

"No. Have the plane work north and east of the narrows. If Zenko is on the bottom, let him rot."

Reno crept through the narrows less than five miles from the quonset hut at Pulonga. When the sub reached the point where Morrison had lost *Taifun's* track, Gunner ordered, "Activate fathometers."

This was the most dangerous moment. Fathometers sent noise pulses into the water, which bounced off the bottom. Timing the echoes allowed computers to determine the shape of the bottom and clearance under the keel. Fathometers could detect mines and bottom-anchored sonars, but Soviet sonars would hear the fathometer's acoustic emissions.

"Fathometers on."

A three-dimensional image of the bottom appeared. One hundred yards ahead a bulbous, artificial object resolved into a cylinder with three legs.

"Good lord," said Trout. "We're almost on top of a hydrophone."

"It's lying on its side!" Gunner exclaimed. "It's deaf."

The guns remained silent. The fathometers discovered three deep pits in the bottom where mines had exploded, but no live mines.

"Control to maneuvering," Gunner ordered. "Secure propulsors. Engage main shaft. Prepare to increase speed."

Overhead the MAD plane banked through a turn and was heading north when the needles on the magnetic anomaly detector jumped completely across the dial.

"Getting a reading here, Captain," the operator said to the pilot.

"Jesus Christ," the pilot said. "We've got one sub on the bottom that isn't supposed to be there, and the same sub right underneath us in the strait, and she isn't supposed to be there either. It's the twice vanished, twice reappeared mystery sub in two places at once. I'll come around again."

"Get on the radio to Pulonga, Captain."

"I'm going to check first."

Five minutes later the pilot was satisfied that a sub was in the strait. When he informed Tarinski, the lieutenant actually cheered.

The first mortar shell landed three hundred yards off *Reno*'s starboard bow and smashed a harmless hole in the ice. The blast clanged through the hull. Men cursed and prayed. Ten more shells pounded the ice around the boat.

"Control to torpedo room. Load two decoys. Set them to run on course zero six zero."

"Decoys, aye. Course zero six zero, aye."

"Ice scanners and fathometers on full power."

"Full power on scanners and fathometers, aye."

"Torpedo room to control. Decoy ready."

"Fire decoy number one."

The decoy sped from the tube and ran directly ahead of the sub on *Reno*'s course.

"Control to sonar. Watch the decoy. If it doesn't hit a mine, we'll follow in its wake. Control to maneuvering, make our speed two-thirds."

A shell exploded directly over the engineering compartment and shoved a piece of ice against the hull with a resounding bang. The hard steel neither gave nor flexed and *Reno* leaped through the water like a thoroughbred. The next round of shells fell aft.

Thirty seconds later the decoy hit a mine and exploded. *Reno* bucked once. Her bow pitched up and struck the bottom of the ice. Sonar screens erupted like pinball machines.

"Fire decoy number two, same course," Gunner shouted.

"Decoy away."

"Gus! Hull integrity!"

Terrified, Trout scanned the diving panel. Every light remained green.

"No leaks, Skipper."

"Goddamn, they build 'em right at Electric Boat! Sonar, can you pick up the decoy?"

"Definitely, Skipper. Decoy running true."

A few moments later, *Reno* passed out of range and the mortars stopped firing. After thirty minutes *Reno*'s second decoy ran out of propellant and sank. Gunner was convinced he had passed beyond the minefield. The water deepened and *Reno* dropped to eighty feet below the ice.

"Control to maneuvering. Reduce speed. All ahead slow."

The MAD plane had *Reno* on her screens but carried no munitions capable of penetrating ice. The closest helicopters were an hour away, but before they could arrive the plane would be forced to return to Gremikha for fuel. The MAD operator watched his screens helplessly as *Reno* steamed north. He radioed Pulonga with the bad news. The mystery sub had run the strait. Tarinski groaned in dismay, once again cursing his bad luck.

On *Reno* Gunner felt no exhilaration. He had run the strait twice, but had succeeded only because of the failure of Soviet technology. Zenko was another matter. *Taifun* was somewhere ahead, hiding under the ice. As far as Gunner knew, the Russian captain was waiting to unleash a barrage of torpedoes. Gunner's stomach was a knot of cramps. He surrendered the conn to Trout, went into his cabin and puked. Knowing he had accomplished the impossible didn't make him feel better.

33 Fishermen

The rain and sleet were borne on a warm Gulf Stream wind that brought a thaw to the marginal ice zone off the Kola coast. Inshore, ice floes careened precariously through open water, but a few hardy fishermen braved the dangers as they sought the spring's first cod.

Midway between Pulonga and Gremikha an old man in an old boat cheerfully cursed the rain and ice as he dropped his nets over the side. His annual spring argument with his wife played in his head like an old record. "You're foolish to go out among so many floes," she had grumbled. Stoutly, he had replied, "I've fished these waters for sixty years. To hell with the ice." "Well, you still don't know how to swim," she had whined. "Don't need to. If I land in the water, the sea will suck the life from my body in three minutes. I'll die no matter how strong I can paddle." The ritual conversation ran on and on in his mind when suddenly something big jerked the net and almost pulled him overboard. Within seconds the carefully coiled net had been drawn into the water and the boat was being dragged stern-first at four knots.

The fisherman knew his home waters. Only one creature powerful enough to pull his boat swam off the Kola coast. Cursing, but no longer cheerfully, he cut loose the net. The boat rocked in its wake and the net disappeared under the frothy surface. "Damned Navy!" the old man yelled. "That was a damned good net. Why don't you stay out of the damned fishing grounds? I don't fish over in Gremikha where you keep your damned submarines!"

Angry, he flipped on his ship-to-shore radio, tuned the transmitter to the Coast Guard emergency channel and shouted into the rusty microphone. "This is XBR9T, *Pulonga Starfish*, XBR9T, calling the damned Gremikha Naval Station, over."

No response. The fisherman had complained to the Navy on three previous occasions about lost nets and for his trouble had received radio static, polite denials, and no recompense. He tried again, unkeyed his mike and heard, "This is Gre . . . kha Na . . . Station. I am not rea . . . you Sta . . . sh XB . . . T, over."

Damned static. "You're breaking up, Gremikha. One of your damned subs just destroyed my net!"

"XBR9T, I can't . . ."

The hell with it, thought the old man. Jamming the mike in its cradle, he turned off the radio, fired up his engine, opened a bottle of vodka and headed home.

At Gremikha an operator in the secure communications center noted in his logbook an incomplete signal from a fisherman. The operator had been stationed at Gremikha for three years and had developed a tolerant attitude toward the locals. When they complained about subs dragging their nets, he listened politely and ignored their protests. He knew XBR9T, a crotchety old drunk with an uncanny ability to catch more submarines than codfish. This time he had snagged a big one, *Taifun*, the only sub that could possibly be in those waters. Zenko was there, right on Gremikha's doorstep.

His new supervisor, a GRU major from Polyarnyy, came over and asked, "What was that?"

The operator glanced at the pistol on the GRU man's belt and his mind produced a rush of images. Zenko gone, Riziov dead, *First of May* sabotaged, spetsnaz troops overrunning Gremikha and turning a pleasant duty station into a concentration camp. Black-booted GRU thugs had taken over the communications center and issued a rash of new regulations. No monitoring civilian radio or television broadcasts. No private communications. No messages indicating conditions were other than normal.

Normal, hell, thought the operator, these people are trying to kill Admiral Zenko, the only decent officer I ever met. I don't know why and I don't care, but I'll be damned if I'll help them. "It's springtime," he explained patiently to the GRU man. "The ice is breaking up and the first fishermen are going out. They call all the time. No matter what happens, they blame us."

"What'd he say?"

"I couldn't understand him. They have old radios, pieces of junk. Who knows?"

"Call him back. Maybe he saw something."

The operator turned the dial to the Coast Guard channel. "This is Naval Station Gremikha calling XBR9T, over."

With his radio off and a bottle of vodka open, the old fishermen was busily concocting a story of a monstrous sturgeon that had stolen his net. He never heard his call sign.

The GRU man ordered, "Keep trying."

No one on *Taifun* felt the tug of a fisherman's net. Barely three miles offshore, with her sail a scant twenty feet under open water, the sub crept over the bottom sixteen miles from Gremikha. Zenko felt like a locksmith picking a lock of his own manufacture. Gremikha's defenses were designed to interdict a submarine attacking from hundreds of miles at sea, not a sub sneaking in close to shore. "All stop," he ordered.

The props stopped turning and *Taifun* drifted, buffeted by the current.

"Command to sonar. Any contact with the American?"

"Screens clear, Captain, but the forward sonars have quit."

"Do you think he made it through, Sasha?"

"We did," Kugarin answered with a shrug. "He's a bold one. I wouldn't bet against him."

"Command to radio. Report on VLF traffic," Zenko ordered.

"Not a peep, Captain."

"So," Zenko said. "The flotilla still seems to be underground at Gremikha. Radio Officer, raise the electronic countermeasures mast."

The customary acknowledgment of the order was not forthcoming.

Zenko picked up his microphone, prepared to repeat the order in emphatic terms, then hesitated. At the diving panel Kugarin had gone white with fear. If a helicopter's radar detected the mast above the surface, _Taifun_ would become an easy, exposed target. Zenko looked around. Every man in the command center was struck dumb with terror, save Petya Bulgakov, who didn't know better. The boy leaned on the navigation table and smiled at his captain.

Zenko switched on the ship's intercom. "Men of _Taifun_," he said, "the moment we sailed from Gremikha we put our lives at risk. I am afraid, Captain Kugarin is afraid, all of us are afraid. I'm not so sure about Quartermaster Sorokin, but I've pissed in my pants twice already."

No one in the command center laughed except Little Petya.

"I'm going to raise a radio mast and listen to signals from Gremikha," Zenko continued. "I remind you that I was the author of Gremikha's defenses. I know the location of the sonars and the station's radio and radar frequencies. In theory it's impossible for a submarine to come as close inshore as we are right now. They won't be looking for us here. If by chance a sharp radar operator detects a mast, he'll think we're a fishing boat. Now, Radio Officer, raise the ECM mast, if you please."

The mast went up. In the radio room the radio officer immediately recorded Gremikha's normal shore-based radar, which Zenko knew would not detect the mast. Danger lurked in aircraft, but the mast detected no airborne radars.

"Raise radio mast."

A radio antenna poked out of the water and extended into the air. In the radio room the receivers quickly sorted out scrambled voice communications crowding six frequencies, identified by the cryptographic computers as belonging to Air Gremikha. With standard Red Navy voice decoders, electronics technicians unscrambled chatter between helicopter pilots and Gremikha. The weather had cleared and helicopters were searching the open sea north and west, the nearest a hundred miles away.

"Lower mast."

"Mast coming down, Captain."

"Attention all divisions," Zenko said. "We'll be in position to attack in four hours. I repeat, I will not attack Gremikha with atomics. Antiship rockets with conventional high-explosive warheads can destroy the flotilla. Your families will be safe. Any man who still has doubts as to our mission should speak now."

Kugarin, torn between fear for his family in Gremikha and his will to exterminate Ivan Deminov, stepped to the middle of the command center. In the strongest voice he could summon, he cried, "Kiss the sky good-bye!"

Sorokin rose from his chair and stood next to Kugarin. Petya Bulgakov did the same, followed by every man in the command center. In unison they sang out Zenko's battle cry.

Tears streaked Zenko's cheeks. He took a deep breath and picked up his microphone. "Command to torpedo room, prepare antiship rockets in tubes four, five and six. Begin preliminary checks. Prepare for submerged launch."

"Prepare antiship rockets for submerged launch, aye."

"Sorokin, plot a course to take us five kilometers off Cape Svyatoy Nos. From there we have a clean shot point-blank at the sea gates. The first rocket will destroy the doors, and the following shots will hit the submarine quays without damaging the buildings above the cliffs, or the people in them. We'll take the close-in defenses by surprise and fire three rockets into the cave. Then, gentlemen, we're going right into the harbor and reclaim Gremikha ourselves. All ahead slow."

"Ahead all slow, aye."

Taifun moved north, paralleling the shore. Zenko ran a simulated launch drill, and each member of the crew played his role to perfection.

At Gremikha the sunken *First of May* had been raised and moved. With spetsnaz guards patrolling the quays, workmen turned their attention to *Lenin*.

Deminov stood on *Lenin*'s bridge watching rocket technicians lock and seal the last rocket silo. He could feel a clock ticking like a time bomb in his head. The buoy rigged with *Taifun*'s call sign had proved indeed to be a red herring. Apparently, Zenko had failed to run the strait on his first attempt, reversed course, set the buoy as a diversion and negotiated the Gorlo on his second try. Deminov had no choice but to assume *Taifun* had reached the Barents.

Zenko. Deminov realized now that he had discounted Zenko's will to resist. Resistance was not part of the Soviet formula. For seventy years the communist regime had crushed resistance with violence and intimidation, a tradition Deminov heartily wished to continue. By now White Star should have arrived at Phase Three. The atomic threat on Tbilisi would have toppled the government and the Northern Fleet would be deployed in battle array, prepared to crush the republicans. Instead, Deminov faced disaster. His only hope was to get *Lenin* to sea before Valotin canceled the entire operation.

To find Zenko and mollify Valotin, he had finally cut loose three squadrons of helicopters and diverted the MAD plane north into the Barents Sea. So far, the Defense Council assumed the aircraft movements were part of White Star. Once *Lenin* was underway, he would order the fleet to sea with no need to maintain pretenses any longer.

Deminov descended from the bridge and anxiously paced the command center. The immense power of the ship's weapons and the historical implications of his mission gradually restored his confidence. After so many years ashore, it felt good to be back in command of a strategic rocket sub. He ran his eyes over the plush appointments of the command center. Like *Sovyetskii Soyuz*, the interior of *Lenin* was decorated in red: upholstery, carpets and paint, all red.

From one of the consoles the chief engineering officer was sending final orders to the reactor control rooms.

"Power up to critical on the portside reactor."

"Powering up on the portside, aye."

"Power up to critical on the starboardside reactor."

"Starboard reactor division acknowledges power up."

"How soon can we be underway?" Deminov asked.

"Five minutes, Captain. You can open the doors."

Deminov called Ludinov in the communications center. "Open the doors and disconnect shore power," he ordered.

"Admiral," Ludinov said, "I respectfully request permission to sail with you."

"I need you ashore," Deminov replied curtly. "You're the only officer I can trust to maintain strict security. Send the orders to the fleet the instant we submerge."

"With pleasure, Admiral. We'll drink to your success when you return. Good luck!"

Ludinov gave the order to open the sea gates and stepped to the window to watch the massive doors of Zenko's Cave slide apart. Outside, the weather was clearing. Sailors scrambled over the deck of *Lenin* casting off lines. A red pennant hung from her stern.

Water churned around the props and *Lenin* moved away from the quay.

34 Rockets

At a slow eight knots *Reno* steamed north toward the Barents Sea thirty miles east of Gremikha. Gunner proceeded cautiously, staying under the ice and well clear of shore. In less than a minute *Reno* would pass from Soviet internal waters into the high seas. Like a privateer with a letter of marque, Gunner had invaded the territory of a sovereign nation, stolen military secrets and escaped. Despite technology, governments and navies hadn't changed much since the days of brigands and pirates.

Standing at the navigator's station, Trout announced, "Ten seconds to international boundary. Counting down, three, two, one. Mark, latitude sixty-eight degrees twenty minutes north, longitude forty-one degrees ten minutes east. We're over the line. We're legal."

"Hip, hip, hooray," Gunner said dryly. "That won't matter to the Russians if they find us here."

A change had taken place on board *Reno*. The crew had the grim look of men at war. When shells are exploding overhead, no one cares who's right or wrong, only who lives or dies. A submarine crammed with sophisticated technology becomes a lethal rock in the hand of savages.

During the harrowing passage through the straight, *Reno* had survived a pounding more severe than any inflicted on an American sub since World War II. Gunner saw both pride and anger on the faces in the control room. If he could channel that energy into disciplined, concerted action, they might survive, but he wondered how much farther he could push the crew. Cold War hatred of the Russians ran deep. His crew represented the third generation of cold warriors, and the Red Navy was shooting at them. Instinctively, they wanted to shoot back.

Asking himself endless questions, Gunner played out battle scenarios in his head. Prudence dictated he assume the Northern Fleet had sortied in force. If the Soviets stumbled across *Reno*, they would shoot first and never ask questions.

Gunner considered his options. One was to sail northeast away from the Soviet naval bases on the Kola Peninsula before turning west and making a wide sweeping turn toward the NATO-controlled waters of the Norwegian Sea. From there he could communicate safely, make an intelligence report and await further orders. Such a broad maneuver would require twenty-four hours, perhaps more, during which time *Reno* would make noise and perhaps attract unwanted attention.

No. His mission was to collect intelligence on Soviet war-making capabilities and the bastards were making war, albeit civil war. Was one side threatening to start World War III and the other trying to prevent the holocaust? Stefan Zenko and his bloody ship had the answers, but *Taifun* had vanished. Was he sunk? Lying on the bottom unable to surface? The more Gunner tried to crawl inside Zenko's head, the less he understood the Russian's actions or his motives. Why had Zenko sunk *Gorky* and attacked the other Typhoon? Had the boomer truly intended to launch? Against what target? Zenko had destroyed *Gorky* with consummate ruthlessness. Only a man possessed by ferocious anger would slaughter his own countrymen. What made Zenko so angry and so determined? And yet he had fired four useless conventional torpedoes at the second Typhoon when only a nuke would have done the job. Then he had forced his way a second time through the Gorlo Strait when, with *Taifun*'s armament, he could have hit almost any target in the world from the White Sea. Why? Was he returning home to Gremikha?

Less than thirty miles from *Reno*'s position, Gremikha was the key.

"Steer hard left," Gunner ordered the helmsman. "Make our course two eight zero. Maneuvering, reduce speed to four knots. Prepare to stop."

As *Reno* turned, the sensitive sonar array in the bow swung around until it aimed at Gremikha. In the sonar room Morrison watched a slow-moving blip slide across his screen. "Sonar to control. We have contact. I hear props on the surface inshore. A Typhoon is coming out."

"Coming out?" Gunner exclaimed. "Jesus Christ, which side is *this* guy on? Morrison, can you give me an ID?"

"No, Skipper, but I register dual props. It's a Typhoon for sure."

"All stop," Gunner ordered. He didn't have to ask for quiet in the boat. No one made a sound.

"Is this Zenko?" Trout asked quietly. "Has he come back to Gremikha to rearm?"

"I don't think so," Gunner answered. "He couldn't have repaired his damaged propulsion plant so quickly. This is a different ship, and we'll follow her back into the White Sea if we have to. The Typhoon on our screens is the one that counts, whoever's in the driver's seat."

Lenin emerged from Zenko's Cave like a nuclear behemoth. From the bridge high atop the sail, Deminov piloted the sub across the harbor. Astern, the steel doors to the cavern gaped open. Ahead, the massive deck over the rocket compartments was steady in the choppy sea. Cape Svyatov Nos stretched to his right, and near the point a steam plume from a power plant rose into a rapidly clearing sky. Deminov tasted the spray splashing up from the deck and took off his cap to let his hair blow in the breeze. The lookouts cut sharp profiles in the brisk arctic air. Overhead a radar antenna whirled, and above the mast the red star and hammer and sickle of the Soviet naval ensign flapped in the wind.

"Radio to bridge," said the voice of the radio officer in Deminov's headset. "The helicopter escort is in the air."

"Thank you, radio. Order the helos to establish a standard ASW perimeter."

Deminov and the lookouts scanned the sky as four helos appeared over the horizon. Dedicated sub killers, each machine carried dipping sonars and two Type 533 torpedoes slung under the airframes.

Outside the harbor, Deminov ordered the lookouts below, took a last look at the horizon, descended into the sail, sealed the hatch and gave the order to dive. Noisy vents opened, seawater poured into the forward ballast tanks, and *Lenin*'s bow plunged beneath the surface.

Four miles away, between *Lenin* and *Reno*, *Taifun* lay on the bottom below two hundred feet of water. Three potent antiship rockets armed with high-explosive warheads were loaded in her starboard torpedo tubes. Prelaunch procedures were completed, muzzle doors opened and tubes flooded for subsurface launch. All that remained was to send up a radio buoy to sample the electronic environment.

"Release the buoy," Zenko ordered.

The buoy took a minute to reach the surface. Expecting the next voice he heard to be the radio officer, Zenko was surprised by the excited voice of the sonar officer. "Captain, I hear a sub in the water. She's submerging!"

Taifun's damaged sonars had failed to detect *Lenin* steaming on the surface. When she began to submerge, the flooding of her main ballast tanks and cavitating props created enough noise to register on *Taifun*'s stern array.

"Bloody hell," Zenko swore. "I should have been prepared for this. Sonar, give me a range and bearing."

"Indistinct, Captain. Range approximately four miles, bearing approximately ten degrees relative. She's running across our bows."

"Command to torpedo room," Zenko ordered, "load tubes one, two and three with Type 65s."

Before the order could be acknowledged, Zenko heard another voice. "Radio to command. Buoy is on the surface. We have heavy jamming on most frequencies. Air Gremikha channel is open and clear. We have helicopters, Captain. Close range."

"Diving Officer, take us up to launch depth."

"Launch depth, aye."

"Command to weapons. Arm rockets."

"Arming rockets, aye."

"Sonar to command. She's almost completely submerged."

"Do you have ID?"

"Yes sir. *Lenin*."

Taifun lifted off the bottom and began to rise.

Submerging, *Lenin* generated enough noise to deafen her sonars, giving Deminov no warning of *Taifun*'s presence now four miles away. On *Reno*, however, the sounds of two subs, one rising, the other submerging, were clearly audible in Morrison's headphones. The chief sonarman shook his head in disbelief. Where in hell did the second sub come from?

"Sonar to control. We have a second contact."

"I have him on the repeater, Chief," Gunner replied. "I see him. It's Zenko. He must've been hiding on the bottom, the crafty old whale."

"I don't know, Skipper. I sure didn't hear him."

"It's not your fault, Chief. He's probably been there for hours."

Taifun stopped rising thirty feet below the surface. *Lenin* was moving almost at right angles across her bow.

"Type 65s will never get through her defensive systems," Kugarin protested.

"I know," Zenko answered.

"Are you going to . . ."

"No atomics!" Zenko shouted. "The torpedoes might catch her by surprise, but if I have to, I'll ram her. Fire torpedoes!"

Three Type 65s burst from *Taifun*'s starboard tubes and raced toward *Lenin*.

With ballast tanks flooded and her deck underwater, *Lenin* stopped generating so much noise. Her sonar operators expected to hear local marine life, not the high-pitched whine of torpedo motors bearing down on their ship at expressway speed.

A frightened voice screamed into Deminov's ear. "Sonar to

command. Three torpedoes Type 65 in the water off the starboard beam. Range six thousand meters. Three minutes to impact."

Deminov paled. It was Zenko and if his torpedoes carried atomic warheads, no escape was possible. If not, he was prepared. He reacted instantly.

"Fire three infrared decoys."

Tubes discharged three projectiles loaded with magnesium shards. A thousand meters from the ship, fuses ignited and the decoys immediately became heat sources, attracting the infrared guidance systems of two torpedoes, which zeroed in and exploded harmlessly. Overpressure from the explosions in the water rocked *Lenin* and, seconds later, *Taifun*. The third torpedo became confused. Automated circuitry cut power to the electric motor and switched guidance to active sonar. The system detected *Lenin,* now building speed only two hundred yards away, but the onboard computer determined the target was *Taifun* and the torpedo refused to attack its own ship. It circled once more, cut power, disarmed the warhead and sank.

Deminov smirked to himself. Zenko had remarkable talent, indeed. No one else could have come so close to Gremikha without being detected, but despite his formidable prowess, he lacked the nerve to finish the job with plutonium. Deminov knew his conventional torpedoes would have no better luck against *Taifun,* and an atomic warhead would destroy *Lenin* as well as the target. The helicopters would finish off Zenko. "Flank speed!" he ordered.

Undamaged, *Lenin* struck for deep water.

The torpedo explosions thundered through *Reno*'s sonars and flared on the screens.

"He missed!" an astonished Gunner shouted. "At four miles he missed."

"Wish we had a few of those hot decoys," Trout said.

"No shit. At least they still don't know we're here."

Aboard *Taifun* Zenko solemnly gave Kugarin the order. "Sasha, unlock launch keys."

Sitting at the launch console, Kugarin punched in the code and three small blue panels slid back.

"Launch keys unlocked."

"We have to do it," Zenko said. "We can't allow three Typhoons to remain in the hands of these maniacs."

"I know," Kugarin said.

"Fire rocket number one."

Kugarin pressed the button. Compressed air pushed the first antiship rocket from the tube, to the surface and into the air. Wings and rudders popped into place, the motor ignited, and the thin, cigar-shaped ship-killing rocket sped toward the open doors of Zenko's Cave.

"Fire rocket number two."

When the second emerged from the sea, the first had reached a speed of three hundred miles per hour and was still accelerating.

"Fire rocket number three," Zenko said, turning away from the launch panel with a heavy heart. His dream was dying.

Less than ten seconds from the first impact, a radar operator in the secure communications center screamed, "Incoming."

Hearing the commotion in the radio room, Colonel Ludinov picked up the phone to ask if _Taifun_ had been detected. He glanced out the window at the cavern. An overhead crane was hoisting a section of _Rodina_. Men swarmed over the quays, sailors in jumpers, spetsnaz in black fatigues, workmen in yellow slickers. Ludinov noticed a sailor far down the quay. As the boy turned from the tea-wagon, hot cup in hand, he dropped his drink and pointed toward the gaping portals.

No more than a dozen men saw the rocket fly through the doors at four hundred miles per hour. Astonished, Ludinov watched it flash past, and before he could react the rocket slammed into the rear wall and exploded into a fireball. The blast rolled through the cavern and smashed into _Rodina_, knocking the huge ship off her dry-dock stays and cracking both pressure hulls. Three seconds later the second rocket hit the concussion wave from the first, exploding the warhead directly opposite the plate-glass wall of the secure communications center. Ludinov had time to marvel at the fantastic violence and accuracy of the rockets before flying glass sliced him into bloody ribbons.

The third rocket sank *Great Patriotic War* and *First of May*. A fireball engulfed the cavern, turning Zenko's Cave into a furnace.

Three miles north of the harbor, the helicopter crews saw *Lenin* submerge. Then, with stunning quickness, underwater infrared flares and torpedo detonations turned the choppy grey surface into a caldron of showers and light. A moment later a rocket burst from the water and skimmed over the surface toward Zenko's Cave, followed by two more.

The lead pilot kept a cool head and made the only assumption possible. "*Taifun* is right in front of us," he said. "Arm torpedoes."

"Torpedoes armed."

"This is Whitewolf One to all units. We have a live one. Arm torpedoes. We're going in."

His location revealed, Zenko understood the threat from the sky. The instant the third rocket spurted from the tube, he ordered, "Emergency dive! Flank speed. We have to get under the ice."

Taifun dropped to 150 feet and began to move forward.

"Load decoys in all tubes."

The automatic loaders filled six torpedo tubes with decoys.

"Sonar to command. One, two, three, four torpedoes in the water!"

"Helos!" Zenko shouted. "Fire decoys one through four in full array and reload!"

The decoys sped away from *Taifun*, turned to the four points of the compass and ignited into magnesium fireballs. Two of the four onrushing torpedoes veered into decoys and exploded. The third went awry, ran under the ship and headed south toward shore. The four slammed into *Taifun* and exploded outside the starboard rocket compartment.

The blast destroyed a twenty-foot circle of outer skin. With a resounding ring the pressure hull bulged inward and flexed back into place, leaving a three foot crack in the thick steel. Water spurted into the compartment as though driven by a satanic pump. A junior engineering officer was caught in the stream, smashed against a bulkhead and knocked unconscious. A klaxon screamed. Within seconds an impromptu damage control team attempted to stanch the flow but the men were pushed back. Water flowed over the deck and swirled around the rocket silos.

Running at only ten knots, *Taifun* limped toward the cover of ice. The bow sonars were completely dead and now the starboard array failed to respond. The portside and stern arrays could not detect *Lenin*. Zenko expected a second volley from the helicopters.

This time the torpedoes came from dead ahead. Four fish splashed into the sea. One suffered motor ignition failure and sank. Zenko fired four more decoys. Two worked but one failed and *Taifun* took another hit in the same rocket compartment.

The second explosion blew a six-foot hole in the pressure hull, killing three men outright and starting a fire. The lights flickered and died, but blue electrical flames illuminated sailors struggling against the rising water. The sea gushed into the compartment, overflowed the hatches and spilled into the command compartment. Acrid black smoke poisoned the air.

In the command center Zenko remained calm, but he knew *Taifun* was doomed. Water, smoke and injured men poured into the command center. A horribly burned engineering mishman fell and died at Zenko's feet.

"Grab a first-aid kit and help these men!" Kugarin shouted at Petya Bulgakov, who stood immobilized by fright.

"How many men are still in the starboard rocket compartment?" Zenko asked Sorokin.

"I don't know, Captain."

"Seal the hatches," Zenko ordered.

"Aye aye."

Sorokin punched buttons on the diving console, and the hydraulic locks functioned properly. The hatches between the command and starboard rocket compartments closed, sealed and locked. Three men still inside the rocket compartment watched in terror as the water rose to chest level. Smoke filled the space above the rising water and they died of suffocation before they could drown.

Although he had never expected to test his design, Zenko had engineered the ship to survive with one compartment flooded. Nevertheless, she was growing heavy and unmaneuverable. He had failed. Brave men who believed in him were dying. *Lenin* had escaped. Zenko guessed Deminov was at the helm, and he had no doubt that he would launch rockets against the Motherland.

"Sasha," he said quietly to Kugarin. "Perhaps a message for the Defense Council. Tell them exactly what has happened. If we can get under the ice and away from these damned helicopters, we'll send it."

"Yes, sir."

More red lights suddenly began flashing on the diving console.

"Captain," Sorokin said. "The fire is spreading through the electrical junction boxes into the portside rocket compartment."

"My God," Zenko exclaimed. "The rocket fuel!"

35
The Ice

Zenko's Cave lay in ruins. Fires burned in elevator shafts and chemical explosions rocked the smoldering devastation. At least eight hundred men were dead. Sirens screamed atop every building. Ambulances and fire trucks scrambled dizzily toward the elevators.

Aboveground the naval station was undamaged. In the airfield's control tower, GRU air controllers in contact with the helicopters heard the explosions and found themselves cut off from the secure communications center. Phone lines were dead. A moment later an excited helicopter pilot described rockets popping out of the sea and incinerating Zenko's Cave. "It was *Taifun*," he said. "We launched all our torpedoes against her."

"Is she sunk?" asked the tower's commanding lieutenant.

"She took at least two hits, but I don't think she's sunk," came the reply. "She's heading for the ice and we need to reload."

"Return to base," the lieutenant ordered. A moment later a secure telephone line from the Admiralty rang.

"Air Gremikha," the lieutenant answered.

"We can't reach your secure communications center," said the voice of a duty officer in Leningrad. "What the hell is going on down there? Where's Colonel Ludinov?"

"Colonel Ludinov is probably dead," the lieutenant shouted over the phone. "Everyone in Zenko's Cave is probably dead and we're under attack."

273

. . .

On *Reno*, the ferocious underwater battle played out on sonar screens like a fantasy video game. Dazzled, repelled, frightened, fascinated and aroused, Gunner and his crew listened to violent noises and watched exploding computer-generated blips representing rockets, torpedoes and two 560-foot-long submarines. So far, no one had exploded a nuke, but Gunner felt in his bones that one side or the other was about to step over the line.

Still within sonar range, *Lenin* drove north at a noisy thirty knots, increasing her distance from *Reno*. Gunner was tempted to give chase, but, much closer, *Taifun* was steaming east on a course that would bring her within five miles of the American sub.

"Sonar to control," Morrison said. "I think *Taifun* took a hit. She's no longer accelerating. Speed ten knots. Depth thirty feet. She's approaching the marginal ice zone."

Gunner tried to interpret this information rationally. Like a hunted whale, Zenko was seeking refuge under the ice. Crippled but still potent, *Taifun* was coming straight at him.

"Sonar to control. *Taifun*'s prop has stopped. She's slowing. Range seven miles."

"All ahead slow on propulsors," Gunner ordered. "Mr. Trout, prepare a firing solution. Mr. Sharpe, load Mark 48s in tubes one and two."

Taifun had reached the shelter of the ice, but the fires were spreading out of control.

"Emergency surface," Zenko commanded. "We can't go any farther."

"Blowing stern ballast tanks," Sorokin said. "Forward tanks not responding."

Taifun's stern slowly began to rise and the deck tilted. The rudder smashed into the ice canopy and crumpled. The top of the sail hit the bottom of the ice, bounced, rose again but failed to penetrate the pack.

"Sorokin, blow all tanks. We must have more buoyancy."

"Aye aye."

"Sasha, ready the ice cannon. We'll blow a hole in the ice."

Kugarin slammed his fist against buttons on his console to no avail. "Ice cannon fails to respond."

"Get into the sail and crank it by hand!"

Kugarin grabbed Petya Bulgakov and pulled him up the ladder into the sail. Together, they struggled with the heavy manual controls.

The fire in the portside rocket compartment raged out of control. A dozen officers from engineering rushed forward to fight the blaze. In white asbestos suits and oxygen tanks they battled the flames but the compartment had become an inferno.

"Evacuate the compartment," Zenko ordered. "Bleed the air and pump in nitrogen."

Frantically pushing buttons at the diving console, Sorokin reported, "System failure, Captain. It doesn't respond."

"Holy Mother of God," Zenko cried. "I have to get the men out of there. Get me an asbestos suit."

"Not you, Captain," Sorokin shouted. "I'll go."

For Zenko time crept forward in slow motion. Six inches of water sloshed over the carpeted deck of the command center. Sorokin plunged through the water, pulled open a cabinet and grabbed an asbestos coverall. Before he could strap on an oxygen tank, a series of massive explosions rocked the ship.

Flames reached the rocket fuel. With a tremendous explosion, the first rocket booster detonated in its silo. The unarmed warheads failed to ignite, but the expanding gases of the explosion destroyed the forward half of _Taifun_ and blew a hundred-foot-long hole in the ice.

A sheet of flame flashed through the command center, instantly killing five men. Protected by his asbestos suit, Sorokin jumped in front of Zenko, shielding the captain from the searing blaze. Smothered by the quartermaster, Zenko fell heavily, struck his shin on a cabinet and felt a stabbing pain in his leg.

All around them electronic components fizzed and burst apart. The deck tilted wildly. With the sodden bow blown to bits, the top of the sail bobbed through the hole in the ice created by the exploding rocket fuel. Sorokin dragged Zenko up the ladder.

"Open the hatch!" he screamed at the men above. "We only have a few seconds."

Expecting a rush of freezing water, Bulgakov popped open the hatch. Fresh air flowed into the sub. Bulgakov pulled himself up and jumped out onto the ice. As the ship began to sink, Kugarin followed. Sorokin could hear men screaming behind him. He shoved Zenko, conscious but moaning, through the hatch and scrambled after him. As they landed on the ice, *Taifun* slipped beneath the surface and disappeared.

"Get away from the hole!" Sorokin shouted, but Zenko slipped and fell into the icy water. Lying on his belly, Sorokin plunged a thick arm after him and dragged his captain onto the ice.

They lifted Zenko and carried him twenty yards away from the rupture in the canopy. Beneath them more explosions fractured the ice. Sorokin scanned the horizon for helos. The temperature was barely above freezing. Zenko's body temperature began to drop. He could survive an hour but no longer.

Kugarin bent over Zenko. "Stefan," he asked, "can you hear me?"

Almost imperceptibly, Zenko nodded and tried to speak. Kugarin put his ear to his friend's mouth. "Tell Margarita," Zenko whispered.

Shivering, half-mad with fear, Bulgakov stomped his feet and waved his arms. "I'm cold," he stuttered.

"Shut up, Little Petya," Sorokin snapped. "At least you're alive."

"Sweet Jesus, she's gone," Morrison said. Underwater explosions continued to light up *Reno's* sonar screens.

"Engage the main shaft," Gunner ordered. "All ahead one-third."

Lenin remained on the screens twenty-five miles distant, moving at reduced speed. "Are we going after the live boomer?" Trout asked.

"Not yet," Gunner said. "We're going to look for survivors."

"Holy shit, Jack. We don't know what's up there."

"If anyone escaped from that ship, maybe we can find out what the hell is going on. Control to sonar, activate ice scanners."

"Ice scanners, aye."

Morrison turned on the up searching sonars and said, "There's a big hole in the ice directly over where she sank, Skipper."

"We'll go around it," Gunner said. "I'm not driving over a volatile hulk. All hands prepare to surface. Gus, get an ice party ready. Break out ice goggles." He paused a moment, then added, "And sidearms."

The Russians heard the booming peal of splintering ice. A quarter-mile away a crack ripped across a long hummock and a black monolith rose through the ice like a messenger from the deep.

Sorokin recognized it first. "It's an American!" he shouted.

"God have mercy," Kugarin said. "It must be the one we shot at."

As they watched, huddled together on the ice, masts extended from the top of *Reno*'s sail.

"Radar to control. Reading emissions from Gremikha but no aircraft."

Trout and four sailors in ice gear stood under the hatch in the sail. "Open the hatch," Gunner ordered.

Trout spun the wheel, pushed open the hatch and climbed to the top of the sail. Half-blinded by the sun, he blinked and fumbled with a pair of ice goggles. As the rest of the party assembled around him, Trout put on the goggles and saw four figures in the near distance.

"Bridge to control," he said. "We have survivors on the ice."

"Get them into the boat," Gunner replied. "I'm submerging in ten minutes."

Led by Trout, the Americans jumped onto the ice and ran. Sorokin and Kugarin stood up, not sure if they were going to embrace or fight the men running toward them.

Out of breath, the Americans stopped ten feet away from the Russians. "Anyone speak English?" Trout shouted.

"I am spikin some little Anglitch," Kugarin answered. "Identical yourself, plis."

Trout saluted. "Lieutenant Commander Augustus Trout, USS *Reno*. And you, sir?"

"Capitin First Rang Kugarin, Sovyet ship *Taifun*, and this man Admiril Stefan Zenko."

"Zenko!"

"Yes, hurt. Broked leg, I tink. Exposure to cold."

Trout spoke into his headset, "Skipper, we need a stretcher. Zenko himself is here with a broken leg, and three men who appear unhurt."

"Zenko? You sure?"

"I think so. It looks like him."

"Can you talk to them?" Gunner asked.

"One speaks English."

"Get them into the boat. I'll have the corpsman standing by."

Two men with a stretcher ran from the sub across the ice.

"Radar reports a helicopter approaching, range twenty miles," Gunner said urgently over the radio. "Get those men in here quick."

"Aye aye, Skipper. Ice party out." Trout turned to the Russians. "We'll take you aboard," he said to Kugarin, pointing at *Reno*.

Kugarin spoke rapidly in Russian to Sorokin, then said to Trout, "We must be communicate with Admirilty. We have message most urgency."

"That's up to the captain," Trout replied.

"You are not capitin?"

"No."

Petya Bulgakov spoke up. "I also spiklu English. This men have afraid to ride on American submarine. But not I, Petya Bulgakov."

"Your captain will die on the ice if you stay here," Trout said. "We can help him, but we don't have time to argue."

The Russians conferred. After a moment Kugarin said, "We will come."

Sorokin and two Americans strapped Zenko onto the stretcher and the group dashed back to the sub. In the control room Gunner and the corpsman helped lower Zenko through the hatch. Three more half-frozen, wide-eyed Russians followed, two in black uniforms and one in a white asbestos jumpsuit. Trout, the last man in, sealed the hatch.

"Take her down!" Gunner shouted. "Fifty feet. Where's that helicopter?"

"Three miles."

Commands whistled across the control room and *Reno* promptly dropped below the surface.

"Did you see the chopper?" Gunner asked Trout.

"No."

"Good. All ahead on full propulsors."

The instant Zenko was lowered to the deck, the corpsman injected a cassette of morphine into his arm. "We have to warm him up," he said. "He's going into shock."

"Get him to sick bay," Gunner ordered. "And hot coffee for the others."

Two sailors picked up Zenko's stretcher and carried him aft. Gunner faced the three remaining men, saluted and said in Russian, "I am Commander Jack Gunner, commanding USS *Reno*. Welcome aboard, gentlemen."

The Russians returned the salute. Kugarin stepped forward and identified himself and his comrades. "You speak Russian?" he asked.

"I try," Gunner answered.

"I have a most urgent message for the Admiralty of the Soviet Union. I must use your radio."

"What is your message, Captain Kugarin?"

"I'm afraid it is most secret."

"I'm sure it is, but before I consider sending a message to your Admiralty from my ship, I must know what the message says."

Kugarin saw that the American captain would tolerate no argument. "I must speak with Captain Zenko," he said.

"Certainly, if he's able," Gunner said. "Gus, do we have the other sub on sonar?"

"No. She's gone quiet."

"Head toward her last position, and keep it quiet."

"Aye aye."

Reno moved away from the hole in the ice. Amazed, the Russians and the control room crew stared at one another. Lieutenant Sharpe opened a box of Marlboros and offered them cigarettes. Petya Bulgakov greedily took one and turned it over in his hands. "Marlboro," he said, reading the imprint. "Marlboro man. America. Too wonderful."

Sorokin's eyes were everywhere, absorbing a fantastic onslaught of technology. The control room was more cluttered than he would have imagined, and he couldn't read the dials and gauges, but a sub was a sub, jammed with pipes, cables, periscopes, control panels and video screens.

"Mr. Sharpe," Gunner said. "Escort these men to the wardroom and make them comfortable and get them some dry clothes."

"Aye aye, Skipper."

"Captain Kugarin, come with me."

They went to sick bay where Zenko lay on a clean white sheet covered with heavy blankets. The corpsman had cut away his singed uniform and set his leg in splints. "It's a simple fracture," the corpsman told Gunner. "Painful but not too bad. The morphine will take care of that."

"Is he going into shock?"

"Yes, but it's not serious. We got to him in time. His temperature is coming back up."

Zenko looked up at Gunner and tried to salute but could barely lift his arm. Gunner snapped to attention and respectfully saluted the Russian admiral. "Welcome aboard, Admiral Zenko," he said in Russian.

"Thank you," Zenko said in a weak voice. "Thank you for saving my men."

"Your political officer wants to send a message to the Admiralty in Leningrad," Gunner said.

"Forget it, Sasha," Zenko said with great effort. "By the time those fools make up their minds, it'll be too late. Our only hope is these Americans. Captain," he said to Gunner, his voice charged with urgency, "you must sink *Lenin*. Get close and use wire-guided torpedoes."

Gunner looked from Zenko to Kugarin then back to Zenko. He was a plump little man, and he was hurt and going into shock, but his eyes projected strength and honesty. Even so, his request was impossible. Sink a Soviet ship? Jesus Christ. In his worst nightmares he had never even considered such a situation. "I need to know why," he said. "I can't attack a Soviet warship without overwhelming cause."

Zenko tried to answer but lapsed into unconsciousness. The corpsman put a stethoscope to his chest. "He'll be out for a while, Skipper."

36 Rules of Engagement

At Gremikha a regiment of regular naval infantry flew in from Leningrad. Deprived of direction and command, Ludinov's spetsnaz troops surrendered without a fight. When the naval station was secure, Admiral of the Fleet V. J. Valotin arrived from the Admiralty. Touring the wreckage in Zenko's Cave, he tried to disguise his shock with a brusque and businesslike manner, but the devastation of the Navy's arctic bastion meant the end of his career and perhaps his life.

The corpulent commander in chief owed his appointment to politics, not military skill, and he had dedicated his career to preserving the status quo, collecting mistresses and kissing Kremlin asses. He had no taste for combat or prolonged civil war. To him, preservation of the Union meant preservation of his position with all its rights and privileges. White Star had been a wild gamble that failed. Heads would roll, his among them unless he could distance himself from the fiasco.

Valotin spoke with the helicopter pilots, called Pulonga and listened at length to Lieutenant Tarinski, then contacted the icebreaker *Arktika* and her convoy of ships stranded in the White Sea. The pieces of a confusing puzzle came together. Four subs were sunk, *Minsk*, *Gorky*, *Sovyetskii Soyuz* and *Taifun*, another three destroyed at Gremikha. More than thirteen hundred men had been killed. Of the original flotilla of six Typhoons, only *Lenin* survived.

A plausible reconstruction of events emerged. Zenko had turned rogue, entered the White Sea, sunk _Gorky_ and _Sovyetskii Soyuz_, returned through the Gorlo Strait and attacked Gremikha. The most expedient course was to blame Stefan Zenko, who was conveniently dead and unable to defend himself. Valotin decided to make a hero of Deminov, who had courageously escaped in _Lenin_, perserving one ship of the flotilla.

The commander in chief's first act was to order the ships waiting at Polyarnyy and Murmansk to stand down. White Star was canceled.

Lenin hovered in silence under the ice fifty-seven miles from Gremikha, 875 miles due north of Moscow. With _Taifun_ sunk by helicopters, Zenko no longer posed a threat, but Deminov felt as alone as a man adrift in space.

By now the fleet should have sortied in force, but _Lenin's_ sonars detected no subs or surface ships deploying from Murmansk and Polyarnyy. VLF and ELF radio frequencies were silent. Where was the fleet? Where was Valotin?

So be it, thought Deminov. I don't need Valotin. I don't need the fleet. _Lenin_ is a fleet unto herself.

All Typhoons were equipped with priority radio channels for instant communication with the Kremlin. A Typhoon commander could reach the president wherever he was within three minutes. The system was designed to confirm a launch order in case of international atomic conflict, but the circuitry worked equally well in reverse.

Deminov resolved to extend a radio mast and transmit a brief message to the president, giving him one hour to resign or suffer the consequences. If the president failed to respond, _Lenin_ would launch an SS-N-20 with eight warheads at Moscow.

Two political officers worked _Lenin's_ hand-picked crew, assuring the men their mission had the sanction of the Party, the Political Administration of the Armed Forces, the Ministry of Defense and the Northern Fleet. The fiercely pro-Union officers and mishmani accepted their fabrications without challenge. Soldiers of communism, defenders of the Soviet Union, heirs to the legacy of the Revolution, they would do their duty.

"Men of _Lenin_," Deminov ordered, "initiate prelaunch drill."

The crew smoothly galvanized into action, checking circuits and inspecting hydraulic systems. Using the hard-earned algorithms, computers in launch control matched programs with those aboard the rockets, checking guidance systems, fuel feeds, motors and reentry vehicles. All systems checked out perfectly.

Deminov picked up the intercom microphone. "Command to radio, prepare to open the emergency satellite frequency direct to the office of the president in the Kremlin."

Lenin had disappeared from *Reno*'s sonar screens. On maximum propulsor power the American sub crept toward the Soviet's last known position.

The novelty of having Russian sailors aboard distracted the crew. Suddenly, with names and faces, the enemy became human. While Zenko rested, Bulgakov and Sorokin were treated to hot showers, warm clothes and a cold lunch in the enlisted mess. Sailors crowded around watching the Russians pick at ham sandwiches and cole slaw.

Morrison couldn't take his eyes off Sorokin. "Look at this guy's tattoos," he said. "Jesus. He's a work of art."

"Look at them muscles under them tattoos," Chief Torpedoman Garrett said in awe. "Bet he can whip your ass."

"C'mon, don't start that shit," Morrison protested.

"Five dollars on the Russkie," said Garrett. "He looks like a mean mother."

Sorokin listened attentively to the unintelligible babble, then turned to Bulgakov. "What are these guys saying, Little Petya?"

"I don't know. It's all slang, but they keep pointing at your arms."

"I can see that."

Morrison produced his black Red Navy cap and put it on. Sorokin started to laugh. Garrett whipped off his billed cap and offered it to Sorokin, who perched it on his head. A sailor's white hat found its way to Bulgakov's crown. Morrison removed his glasses, rolled up his sleeves and rested his elbow on the table in the classic pose of an arm wrestler. With quiet in the boat, the crew applauded silently. Money appeared, bets were made and covered. Sorokin grinned, reached into the pockets of his fresh U.S. Navy dungarees, pulled out a huge wad of rubles and smacked it on the table. "Tell these sailormen I'm happy to take their money," he said to Bulgakov.

He flexed his wrist, pumped his biceps, and wrapped his fingers around Morrison's.

"Ready?"

"Da!"

In the wardroom Gunner and Trout listened spellbound to Kugarin's tale of Deminov's plot. As Gunner translated, Trout's skepticism grew with each revelation. When the Russian finished, he shook his head in disbelief. Unable to contain his contempt for Kugarin's post as zampolit, he said, "This . . . _political_ officer wants us to sink the last Typhoon, Jack. How do we know Zenko isn't the one who went off his nut, sinking his own ships?"

"Why would he do that?" Gunner asked.

"Somebody in this affair is completely irrational," Trout said. "Maybe Zenko's a reborn peacenik. Maybe he thinks he can end the Cold War by himself. Maybe he wants to blame the whole thing on us. They tracked us into the White Sea and knew we were there. It's a perfect setup."

"This isn't the Cold War, Gus. It's a Soviet civil war."

"If the good guys win, a Soviet civil war is the last act of the Cold War," Trout replied heatedly. "Why should we believe a political officer when he represents the Party, the Political Administration of the Red Navy, the whole goddamned communist apparatus?"

Kugarin understood the gist of this exchange. "Capitin," he said in English, "this man Deminov will launch ballistical rockettes. Every rockette have eight atomical bombs. What can I say make you believe?"

Gunner jutted his face close to Kugarin. "Even if you're telling the truth," he asked, "why should we get involved in your civil war?"

Kugarin smiled. "America was in first one," he answered. "America put soldiers at Arkangel'sk in 1921."

"I don't need a history lesson," Gunner snapped. "I'm not authorized to act on behalf of the United States in a matter like this. I have rules of engagement and doctrines I'm obliged to follow. I'm sure you can understand that. If I sink a Soviet ship, Captain Kugarin, that's an act of war."

"You already commit act of war, Capitin Gunner. You invade White Sea."

"Don't give me that crap. I was torpedoed, mined and bombarded by mortar fire without returning a single shot. I spied, but I didn't kill anybody. That was nothing but a Cold War game, and the secrets I stole are useless unless the United States and the Soviet Union go to war. Nobody wants that."

"Is not legal question, Capitin," Kugarin said. "Is moral question, I tink. If Deminov shoot rockettes, millions piples die. Piples made dead atomical firestorms radiation." In his emotional state Kugarin lost his English and finished in muttered Russian.

Gunner saw blue lights, more blue lights, endless blue lights. Throughout the voyage he had been tortured by not knowing what the Russians were doing. Now he knew a good deal and felt worse than before. "Is moral question," the skinny Russian political officer had said. No shit.

"Imagine situation revers-ed," Kugarin pleaded, regaining his English. "Imagine American capitin crazy in Trident submarine and you in Sovyet submarine. What you say to Sovyet capitin?"

"This is not a hypothetical situation," Gunner said with a tinge of exasperation. "This is here and now. I can't sink a ship because of what her captain might do. If your story is true, and if your Operation White Star is on schedule, more than eighty ships are deploying into the Barents right now. Sinking one will have little effect if the Northern Fleet backs Admiral Deminov."

Kugarin switched to Russian. "The ship commanders in Polyarnyy and Murmansk don't know Deminov's true intention," he said. "They've been told they're fighting a rebellion, not that they are the rebels. Deminov is supremely clever, manipulative and very forceful. His plan to use *Sovyetskii Soyuz* as the weapons platform for a coup d'état would have succeeded if Zenko hadn't attacked the ship. We believe her captain actually fired a rocket, but by the grace of God the rocket destroyed itself and *Sovyetskii Soyuz*. Deminov will surely launch. If you contact the Defense Council, they may call off the fleet and attack _Lenin_.

"Or attack _Reno_," Gunner said.

"Yes, I suppose that's possible, but unlikely. The Soviet Union has no more desire for war than you, Captain."

Gunner pulled Trout aside. "What do you think, Gus?"

"I don't trust this guy," Trout said. "Suppose the worst. Suppose the Russian boomer blows off a few nukes. So what? What's it to us?"

"I think nukes are a bad idea for anyone," Gunner said. "Then the guys on the other side of this civil war blow off a few more. They have thirty thousand fucking warheads."

"That could happen whether we sink this boat or not," Trout said. "We still don't know what's going on anywhere else."

Pain shot through Gunner's belly. A moral question. If he sank _Lenin_, would he prevent a war or start one? If he backed away from confrontation, would millions die as the Russian claimed? He could assign blame for his dilemma in many ways, to the Cold War, nuclear insanity, war machines, military-industrial complexes, his own lifelong desire to captain a nuclear sub, but the decision and responsibility were his.

"I'm inclined to go with the standard rules of engagement," he said finally to Trout. "If I'm onto a boomer and she's in launch mode, I shoot."

"No one can argue with that," Trout said. "I'll go for it."

"Captain Kugarin," Gunner said, "I'll take everything you've said into consideration. Gus, escort the captain to my cabin and bring the two sailors here."

When Trout entered the chiefs' mess, Sorokin was stripped to the waist and taking on his sixth challenger, Billie Stewart. "Sorry to break up the party," the XO said, "but the skipper wants these guys. The rest of you return to stations. We're still at general quarters."

A few minutes later Bulgakov and Sorokin entered the wardroom and sat down opposite Gunner. "What's your name, son?" the captain asked Bulgakov.

Petya told Gunner who he was, where he came from, his age and how long he'd been in the Navy. Gunner quickly realized

Bulgakov could tell him nothing useful and turned his attention to Sorokin. The quartermaster had the air of an old salt, mouth shut, eyes everywhere.

Gunner offered him a Lucky and they both lit up. "How long have you been in the service, Mishman?" he asked in his bookish Russian.

"Ten years."

"The entire time on Typhoons?"

Sorokin nodded and puffed the sweet American tobacco.

"I imagine you feel pretty strange right now," Gunner said, trying to draw out the Russian sailor.

Sorokin looked Gunner in the eye. "Listen, American Captain," he said, "I had my ship blown out from under me today, something I never believed could happen, but I'm warm and alive. For that I say thank you."

"Yes," Gunner said, "but a hundred fifty of your shipmates are dead and I'm trying to understand why."

"Politics, Captain, politics and bullshit."

"That's what we hear from the zampolit."

Sorokin nodded toward Trout and asked, "Is the black guy your political officer?"

"We don't have zampolits in the U.S. Navy. Mr. Trout is my assistant commander."

"What do you want from me?"

"Why is Zenko destroying his own squadron?"

"Ask him."

"I can't. He's unconscious. I want your opinion."

"I don't have an opinion, Captain. All I know is what they tell me. They say Deminov wants to preserve the Union and is willing to start a war to hold the country together. I don't care. I follow orders. If Zenko told me to sail the ship to Moscow, I'd damned well do it. If he ordered the crew to launch twenty rockets at New York, I'd beat the living shit out of any man who refused to obey orders."

Gunner turned to Trout. "We have a real pro here," he said, "a blue-water sailor. He won't tell us diddly unless Zenko orders him to do it."

"Are you going to ask him anyway?"

Gunner nodded. "Mishman, I want you to help me track *Lenin*."

Sorokin snuffed out his cigarette and folded his arms. "Go to the devil," he said flatly.

The phone beeped. Trout answered and listened for a moment. "Zenko is awake and wants to talk to you, Skipper," he said.

Zenko had managed to sit up and was holding a Styrofoam cup of tea. "This tea is weak," he said when Gunner entered the tiny room. "You Americans are not perfect after all."

A grin broke across Gunner's face. "We don't drink much tea. We drink coffee and it's worse."

Gunner summoned the corpsman. "How's his leg?"

"I've seen worse. He'll be all right."

"Okay, get lost."

When they were alone, Gunner and Zenko watched each other in silence for a minute, each taking the other's measure. Finally Zenko asked, "Are you the man who's been following me?"

"I am."

"Well, Captain, you're one hell of a sub driver. We never believed a NATO sub could enter the White Sea, let alone escape. Congratulations."

"In the last twenty-four hours I've seen quite a few things I never thought possible," Gunner said. "Your zampolit tells me Admiral Ivan Deminov is in command of *Lenin*, and he intends to attack the USSR."

"That's correct," Zenko said. "We seem to be having a nasty little dispute, I'm afraid, but it's true."

"What's his target?"

"Tbilisi, I presume."

"The capital of Georgia? Why?"

"A warning shot, to show he's serious."

"Is this strictly a naval affair," Gunner asked, "or part of a general civil war?"

"You don't know?"

"I'm asking."

"Deminov is attempting a coup," Zenko said. "Others may be involved, possibly Admiral of the Fleet Valotin, but I don't know the situation ashore. I'd be surprised if there's fighting anywhere else. Nevertheless, if Deminov succeeds in forcing the president to step aside, a military dictatorship will take power and order a mobilization. Then we'll have killing in the streets."

"And you oppose him," Gunner said.

"I don't know what Sasha Kugarin told you, but my personal views are simple," Zenko said. "I'm not concerned with civil war or anything else beyond my control. I wish only to prevent Deminov from using the atomic weapons in my flotilla against our country. In fact, I agree with some of his goals, but not his means. That is why I pursued *Sovyetskii Soyuz.* Malakov would have launched, but I think he was stopped by his crew, although I'll never know for sure. Deminov will launch unless he's sunk."

"I can sink him only if he goes into launch mode," Gunner said. "I was prepared to sink *Sovyetskii Soyuz.*"

Zenko nodded and sipped his tea. "I understand your difficulty," he said. "Have your sonar operators detected *Lenin?*"

"Not yet."

"I'm certain Deminov hasn't detected you, either. Your ship is extraordinarily quiet."

"You detected me."

"Only because you decided to chase me. When you go fast in shallow water, you make noise."

Zenko winced in pain. "Do you want more morphine?" Gunner asked.

Zenko shook his head. "It makes me nauseous." With great difficulty he sat up and pulled himself to the edge of the bed. "Captain," he said, "tell your sonarmen to listen on the higher audible frequencies. If *Lenin* is hovering near the surface under the ice, you might hear the mechanism that allows the ship to maintain station. You understand? Tiny station-keeping propellers cavitate and the sound reverberates off the ice."

Gunner picked up a phone and relayed Zenko's idea to Morrison.

"High frequencies, Skipper?"

"Try it, Chief."

"Running through the higher bands now. Nothing. Nada, Skipper."

"Keep looking," Gunner said and hung up.

"What's my status?" Zenko asked. "Am I a prisoner?"

"Let's call you a guest. You and your men are shipwreck survivors. I obeyed the law of the sea and rescued you."

"I can help you best from your command center," Zenko offered, "but I would compromise your security."

"What's *Lenin*'s maximum sonar range?"

Zenko answered without hesitation. Gunner fired a string of technical questions, stretching his Russian to the limit. After a few minutes he knew that to sink *Lenin* with torpedoes without using a nuclear warhead, he had to get within a mile, close enough to prevent her defensive systems from reacting to and detonating the torpedoes with decoys.

"Between us, we can destroy him," Zenko said, "but how do we find him?"

37 _Lenin_

Aboard _Lenin_, Deminov put the finishing touches on the text of his ultimatum to the president of the Soviet Union and went into the radio room to test the circuits of the priority scrambled voice channel. While he was in the radio room, an operator announced, "Receiving VLF message, Captain."

"From where?"

"Polyarnyy."

Deminov decoded the scrambled letter groups and read:

```
TO HERO OF THE SOVIET NAVY ADMIRAL
I. I. DEMINOV, COMMANDING SOVIET
SHIP LENIN STRATEGIC ROCKET
SUBMARINE FLOTILLA SIX FROM ADMIRAL
OF THE FLEET V. J. VALOTIN. THE
REBEL STEFAN ZENKO HAS BEEN
DESTROYED. TAIFUN IS SUNK. PROCEED
AT ONCE TO POLYARNYY. A SILVER STAR
IS YOURS.
```

In the confines of the tiny, soundproofed decoding room Deminov enjoyed a long, hearty laugh. He had no interest in medals. Returning to a hero's welcome at Polyarnyy would mean acquiescence to the system he was sworn to overthrow. His purpose was preservation of the Union and Soviet communism, not the collection of medals that would serve no purpose if the Union ceased to exist.

On *Reno*, both Sorokin and Trout spoke the language of nautical charts, and together they leaned over he navigation table. Zenko occupied Gunner's chair, broken leg awkwardly extended in splints, Kugarin by his side doing his best to translate the buzz of orders and actions of the crew.

Reno had reached *Lenin*'s last known position and was steaming north on propulsors at four knots, remaining quiet and listening. In sonar, Morrison searched a broad band of frequencies for telltale signs of a sub, a cavitating prop, a hole in the background noise, the high-frequency whir of *Lenin*'s station-keeping system. The sonars detected nothing but ice noises above and crackling shrimp below.

"How did you build your subs so damned hard to find?" Gunner teased Zenko.

Zenko grinned, flashing gold teeth. "We copied yours," he said. "I've seen design specifications for every U.S. Navy sub since *Skipjack*. Don't ask me how the GRU got them, but I've seen them."

Gunner shook his head at a host of blank sonar screens. Neither *Lenin* nor the expected sortie en masse of the Northern Fleet appeared.

Zenko wondered if he would ever see Margarita again. He felt dejected. Deminov had escaped into the vastness of the Barents Sea. His ships were gone, his career over, his life in ruins. If *Reno* survived, he had no choice but to go with her to America. Russia shrieked inside his head—more Deminovs waited in the heartland, madmen with tanks and regiments and tactical atomic weapons by the thousands. Overcome by survivor's guilt and remorse, he quietly wept. "We failed, Sasha," he mumbled. "We can't search a thousand square miles of ocean in time. With Malakov we had luck on our side, but our luck has run out."

"We haven't completely failed, old friend," Kugarin said. "We're alive and can tell the world what happened."

"Perhaps," Zenko said. "Americans may believe us, but will the Russian people?"

In the radio room an incoming message set the teletype chattering.

"Radio to control. Receiving Soviet VLF."

A minute later a radioman showed Gunner and Zenko a transcription of the coded message printed in scrambled Russian. "It's probably a message to *Lenin*," Zenko said, "but I can't decode it. My guess it it's an order to surface and make radio contact. Or an order to launch."

"From whom?" Gunner asked.

"The Admiralty, or whoever got to Gremikha first," Zenko answered.

"If *Lenin* surfaces and sends a radio message," Gunner said, "we'll know where she is."

"Yes," Zenko agreed.

"All stop," Gunner ordered at once. "One-third speed astern. Control to sonar, activate ice scanner."

"Ice scanner, aye. Reading thin ice, Captain."

"All hands prepare for emergency surface. Lieutenant Sharpe, arm Tomahawk Seven, antiship configuration, nuclear warhead."

Sharpe hesitated a moment, then said, "Aye aye, Tomahawk Seven."

Gunner found Zenko and Kugarin staring at him. "Atomic rockette?" Kugarin asked in English.

A hard glint in his eyes, Gunner nodded. "Do you want him destroyed?" he asked in Russian.

"Yes," Zenko answered, "but if you hit the rocket compartments with a conventional warhead, you'll explode the rocket fuel and sink the ship."

"I'd prefer not to shoot at all," Gunner said, "but if I must, I don't want to miss."

"If you have a target, you won't miss, Captain."

"Our weapons are not infallible, Admiral. We can easily miss with a conventional warhead. You must understand, I don't want to fire a nuke, but I have no choice."

"He's right, Stefan," Kugarin said. "Accept it."

"Lieutenant Sharpe," Gunner repeated, "arm Tomahawk Seven."

Spinning in reverse, *Reno*'s prop brought the ship to a halt within a quarter-mile.

"Sonar to command. Still reading thin ice. Eighteen inches."

"Surface. Blow all ballast tanks."

With a sharp crack the top of *Reno*'s sail split the ice and the upper portion of the hull rose above the surface.

"Control to radio," Gunner ordered, "raise the ECM mast."

"This is radio. Mast going up. Reading no emissions, Skipper."

"Try all Soviet VHF and UHF frequencies."

"All frequencies clear, Skipper."

"Run up radar mast."

"Radar going up."

"Sweep at low power."

Forty-two miles northwest aboard *Lenin*, Deminov also gave an order to surface.

The sail smashed against the underside of the ice and punched through.

"Bridge party, open the hatch and report."

Three sailors climbed onto the top of the sail and saw nothing but ice. The deck over the rocket compartment was free of ice chunks.

"Raise ECM mast," Deminov ordered.

The bridge party watched the revolving mast rise above them.

"Radar to command," an astonished radar operator suddenly announced. "I'm reading American radar, Captain. I repeat, reading U.S. Navy frequency, range seventy kilometers. Shipborne. Coming from the surface."

The mystery sub from Pulonga. Deminov shrugged. An American sub would observe at close range what American satellites would see from the sky, the launch of a single rocket with a southern trajectory.

Deminov ordered, "Lock on Navy communication satellite seventeen, secure voice frequency nine."

"Locked on."

"Open the circuit."

"Opening the circuit." A red light blinked on the radio console.

From the command center, in full hearing of his officers, Deminov said, "This is Soviet ship *Lenin* calling Bedrock Code One."

"This is Bedrock. Go ahead, *Lenin*," answered the voice of a senior duty officer deep within the Kremlin.

No one had alerted the radio staff in the war room of the Strategic Rocket Forces in Moscow to expect a signal from a sub. The chain of command from Valotin in Gremikha through Polyarnyy to the Admiralty in Leningrad and on to Moscow was not designed for quick response.

"We have a Firestorm, repeat Firestorm," Deminov said. "Put me through to Central."

The code words rattled inside the duty officer's skull. Bedrock, Firestorm, Central. An atomic emergency on an atomic sub and the captain wanted to talk to the president. Jesus Christ.

"*Lenin*, this is Bedrock, wait one. I'm putting you through."

On *Reno*, the radio officer said, "Radio to control, reading scrambled Soviet voice communication on SovNav bird seventeen channel nine."

When Zenko heard the translation of these numbers, he exclaimed, "That's the strategic submarine channel to the president of the Union."

"Control to radio. Jam the frequency," Gunner ordered.

"Check, Skipper. With pleasure."

"Try to raise him on a voice channel," Zenko said. "Let me talk to him."

"Give the frequency to the communications officer."

On *Lenin*, Deminov waited for what seemed like endless seconds for his call to be forwarded to the president of the Soviet Union. The man could be asleep or drunk or otherwise indisposed. Abruptly, the clear line turned to static.

"Radio to command. The frequency is jammed."

"Open a second channel. Double-quick."

"Receiving clear voice communication on an open VHF channel, Captain," the radio officer reported.

"What? Who from?"

"From the American sub."

"Ignore him."

"He identifies himself as Admiral Zenko."

Deminov hesitated, a chill contracting his body. Then he ordered, "Patch him through." A moment later he heard Zenko's voice.

"Ivan?"

"So you're alive, Stefan."

"You can't succeed, Ivan. Your coup has failed."

"That's absurd," Deminov said. "I've just begun."

"Your radio channels are jammed. Surrender. Walk off the ship and onto the ice."

"Shut down the voice frequency," Deminov ordered. "Open the hatch to silo three."

Aboard _Reno_, Gunner heard, "Radio to control. Soviet ship has activated telemetry systems. He's preparing to launch."

On _Lenin_, the Grey Ghosts performed with professional efficiency. A political officer in the command compartment turned his launch key and Deminov turned the forward key in the rocket compartment himself. Deminov entered the launch code into fire control and the panel drew back revealing the blue launch button.

Gunner's mind was one bright blue light. A sub forty-two miles away was going to fire a ballistic missile in less than five minutes, and there was only one way to stop her.

"Fire Tomahawk Seven."

Trout jammed his thumb into a button and announced, "Missile away!"

The slim Tomahawk cruise missile popped out of the hatch, flipped out wings and rudder and roared over the ice toward _Lenin_ at six hundred miles per hour. The missile's television guidance system scanned the horizon for the outline of a Typhoon surfaced through the ice.

. . .

"Incoming!" shouted *Lenin*'s radar officer.

"Activate radar jammers."

"It's a cruise missile! No radar."

Deminov punched the blue launch button. Compressed air began to lift the heavy SS-N-20 from the silo. The tail cleared the deck and the rocket motor ignited.

Reno's radar officer announced, "He's launched. Tomahawk impact . . . now!"

The cruise missile struck *Lenin* amidships, penetrating the command center. Deminov heard the impact and saw the pressure hull bulge inward. Too late, Zenko, he thought. Rocket away.

Powerful triggers compressed four pounds of plutonium into a critical mass and the nuclear warhead detonated. *Lenin* exploded like a star. The blast flashed into the sky and smashed into the accelerating SS-N-20, instantly vaporizing the forty-ton missile.

A quarter-mile hole gaped in the ice. Hot steam boiled on the surface of the irradiated Barents Sea and rose in a radioactive plume into the atmosphere. Sweeping across the ice at the speed of sound, the blast rolled over *Reno* forty seconds after the explosion, rocking the sub like a phantom gust of wind.

"Control to radar, Report," Gunner said quietly.

"Missile destroyed, Captain. The sub has vanished."

Gunner lit a cigarette. "Mr. Trout," he said, "send a message to Norfolk. 'Soviet ship *Lenin* destroyed in the act of launching a ballistic missile.' Then take her down."

"You were right," Zenko said. "Thank you."

Reno dropped under the ice. Sweat dripping from his face, Gunner stared at the Russians. Zenko struggled to his feet, his broken leg painful and cumbersome, and saluted Gunner. "Kiss the sky good-bye," he said.

38
Flash

In a single brief radio burst *Reno* transmitted a report to the commander of the Atlantic Submarine Force in Norfolk, Virginia. By the time the message detailing *Reno's* voyage into the White Sea and the destruction of *Lenin* was in the commander's hands, reports of a nuclear detonation in the Barents Sea had flashed from satellites around the world. Analysis of the satellite images clearly revealed the SS-N-20 launch.

Within ten minutes the president of the United States was speaking with the president of the Soviet Union. Neither was sure what had happened, but both understood that a terrible disaster had been averted.

Prevailing winds blew radioactive fallout over the ice, directly at Gremikha. At the naval station, radars and radio receivers had recorded the entire incident. Admiral Valotin had listened to the conversation between Zenko and Deminov, saw the rocket launch on radar and saw the flash of an atomic explosion from far over the northern horizon.

Valotin called for his plane to be readied. He rode in silence across the base to the airfield and ordered the pilot to fly to Moscow. Somewhere over the Kandalakshshkiy Gulf, lying on the bed in his luxuriously appointed private cabin, Admiral of the Fleet V. J. Valotin shot himself in the right temple.

• • •

Reno steamed north one hundred miles, turned west and entered the Norwegian Sea. Five hundred miles off the Norwegian coast Gunner raised a radio mast, filed a routine position report and announced his estimated arrival time at Norfolk.

The service was short. Zenko delivered a brief eulogy for the lost men of *Taifun*, translated by Gunner. "Take unto your bosom, O Lord, our shipmates and friends. Amen."

"Amen," the crew repeated.

"Chief Morrison has an announcement," Gunner said.

The chief of the boat stood facing the crew and tilted his head toward the Russians. "The Noble Order of Bluenoses is called to order."

"Hear hear," the crew shouted, rowdy and loud.

Morrison took a tube of paint from his pocket, daubed his fingertips and solemnly applied a blue stripe to each Russian nose. "We are all Sons of Neptune," he intoned. "Children of the icy deep."

"Hear hear," chanted the order, stripping off their shirts.

"Get the ice bucket," Morrison bawled. "These guys don't get off easy just because they're Russkies!" He thrust his face two inches from Zenko's blue nose. "What are you, cherry?" he wailed.

Zenko stared cross-eyed at his nose. He couldn't understand the words, but he understood the ritual. The American mishman wanted to know if he was worthy, an able arctic sailor. Zenko had lived above the Arctic Circle all his life. If he had to prove himself all over again, he would. He looked at Morrison and said, "I can see through the ice."